LIONS *of the*
DESERT

LIONS *of the* DESERT

Linda Chaikin

ALABASTER BOOKS

This is a work of fiction. The characters, incidents, and dialogues are products of the author's imagination and are not to be construed as real. Any resemblance to actual events or persons, living or dead, is entirely coincidental.

LIONS OF THE DESERT
published by Alabaster Books
a division of Multnomah Publishers, Inc.
© 1997 by Linda Chaikin

International Standard Book Number: 1-57673-114-6

Cover illustration by Paul Bachem
Cover design by Brenda McGee

Printed in the United States of America

Scripture quotations are from:
The New King James Version (NKJV) © 1984 by Thomas Nelson, Inc.

The King James Version (KJV)

For information:
Multnomah Publishers, Inc.• PO Box 1720• Sisters, OR 97759

Library of Congress Cataloging-in-Publication Data
Chaikin, L.L., 1943-
    Lions of the desert/by Linda Chaikin
        p.cm.   ISBN 1-57673-114-6 (alk. paper)   I. Title
    PS3553.H2427L5   1997
    813'.54--dc21   97-27848
                                                                        CIP

97 98 99 00 01 02 03 04 — 10 9 8 7 6 5 4 3 2 1

AUTHOR'S NOTE

The tomb of Pharaoh Tutankhamen (1336-1327 BC), "King Tut" as we know him, was actually excavated after the Great War in 1922 by a team of archaeologists led by Howard Carter. In my research, however, I ran across a bit of speculation that stirred my imagination. I read how an earlier archaeologist may have come within feet of the discovery and didn't realize it! I made use of this in *Lions of the Desert* and will carry it through in *Valiant Hearts,* the last book in the trilogy.

THE BLAINE HOUSE

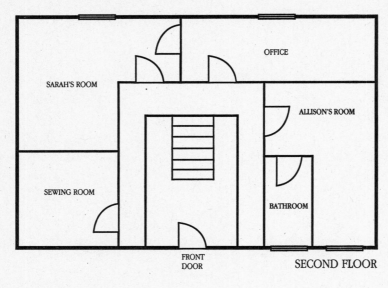

SARAH'S ROOM

OFFICE

ALLISON'S ROOM

SEWING ROOM

BATHROOM

FRONT DOOR

SECOND FLOOR

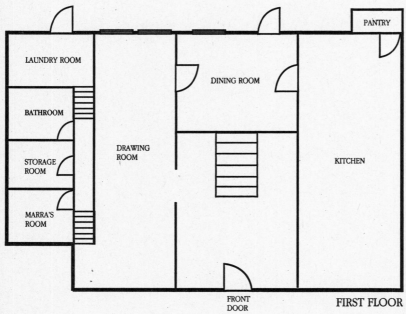

LAUNDRY ROOM

PANTRY

BATHROOM

DINING ROOM

STORAGE ROOM

DRAWING ROOM

KITCHEN

MARRA'S ROOM

FRONT DOOR

FIRST FLOOR

LIONS *of the* DESERT

PART ONE

ONE

The eternal God is your refuge.
DEUTERONOMY 33:27

August, 1915
Arabian Desert, near Baghdad

SLOWLY, SURELY—LIKE AN OMINOUS FLIGHT of locusts that advanced with destructive certainty—the noise, distant at first, grew louder.

Kurdish peasants, who were taking advantage of a pause in the German bombardment to scrabble for water and bread, heard the muffled sound above the distant boom of British artillery. An old Kurdish woman, whose head was swathed in a tattered black head scarf, heard the droning sound first. She stopped in the dusty field, listening. Resting a water jug on her shoulder, her back stooped with age, she cocked her head like an alert hen aware of danger to her chicks. Her small, tired eyes looked out from a wrinkled face burnt brown from the hot sun of the summer fields and cast an upward glance toward the evening sky, which was taking on a purplish black hue of destruction. One of her gnarled hands came up to count her blue worry beads before she struggled to hasten across the field already pot marked by bombs dropped from German Zeppelins.

Within the nearby military compound close to Basra, several British soldiers came rushing from their tents, shouting orders and running for cover.

Nurse Allison Wescott had just departed the makeshift military hospital and was walking toward the smaller kitchen hut used by

11

medical staff. This would be her first meal since the bleak cup of muddy-tasting coffee earlier that morning. It was now twilight. She had heard the sound of the Zeppelin many times in the past six months while serving with the Royal British Nursing Unit from Cairo, and she continued on her way as though unaware of the approaching aircraft.

The distant buzzing of the Zeppelin's engine grew louder. Within moments, the airship was confronted by British artillery from the thirteen thousand soldiers recently sent from India to stop the German advance into Arabia. Machine-gun fire battered the oncoming night, while a smoking darkness settled against the horizon like the pall of death.

Allison was numb to it all. *If only the Lord would make it rain*, she thought. The rain would ease the hordes of pestering flies.

And the heat. It, too, was unbearable. As was the thick brown dust that lifted in little vapors beneath her high-buttoned leather boots as she walked away from the large hospital tent—one of several set up behind the front lines. A slight breeze nudged Allison, but it brought little relief, filled as it was with the sickening odor of death and decay...an odor that seemed to fill the world around her.

The Zeppelin had gotten past the artillery. Allison could see the strange craft now in the sky above Basra, approaching like a great vulture. At the same time, an open-topped British military vehicle came tearing around the corner of the hospital tents, probably heading for the command post. Machine-gun fire erupted again, but this time it was close.

"Take cover!" a British soldier yelled at Allison as he and another man tumbled out and scrambled beneath the vehicle.

"Get down!" another soldier shouted as he ran toward her. Allison looked around frantically. The nearest cover she could see was a large hospital tent packed with the wounded and dying. Atop the tent, whipping in the wind, was a flag with a bold red cross. Allison knew the canvas would be precious little shelter, but that wasn't what kept her from running toward it. She turned back to the soldier in outrage.

"They can't bomb a field hospital!"

He didn't respond. The Zeppelin was overhead, and the buzzing grew louder and uglier. Allison watched as though frozen in disbelief as the German bombardier leaned out of the open aircraft and hand dropped bombs onto military and medical targets. Paralyzing fear burned hot in her throat as she watched one bomb fall toward the bakery near her. Suddenly a deafening explosion split the twilight. Time seemed to slow as, in the same instant, debris flew in all directions, the tent was engulfed in a billowing black haze, and the soldier still running toward Allison was blown to pieces. A cry of sheer horror was caught in her throat as the force of the explosion hit Allison and flung her backward. She landed hard and lay there, stunned, unable to move or think.

A wooden building exploded, adding new debris to the streets. The ground convulsed as though sickened by the obscene display. A cloud of smoke spread like ink; leaping flames rampaged high against the darkening sky as though trying to reach heaven in a diabolic rage.

The attack continued for several minutes. Vaguely Allison grew aware of a sound…something familiar…she closed her eyes in despair. The siren. Its too-late warning was blaring, cutting through the now-distant bomb explosions.

Allison lay there, her face turned toward the vast sky, the hot dust burning into her back. An unnatural absence of human voices held the night. Instead, the air was filled with the sound of running feet, the sizzle of burning wood, the acrid stench of fiery destruction, of smoke.

*God...God...*Allison's mind cried over and over, though she wasn't sure what she was pleading for. Release. Relief. From the horrors around her—and those within. Would she ever forget the image of that poor soldier's last moments...?

"Miss...Miss, are you all right?"

Allison blinked, suddenly aware ash was sprinkling her face. She felt an arm encircle her and gently lift her to a sitting position. She stared, forcing herself to focus. A medic studied her, worry in his brown eyes. She moistened her dry lips and forced words past her numb tongue. "I'm...fine."

He looked at her doubtfully, and she reached out to push her hair back from her face. "Please," she said, her voice firmer now. "I'm all right. There are others who need you."

He glanced behind him, his face grim, then nodded. "OK, miss, if you say so. But you'd better sit here for a while until you get a bit steadier. Then—" he looked around them again—"then you'd best head for your tent. This is no place for a woman right now."

It's no place for anyone, she thought sadly as the medic stood and moved away. Feeling suddenly bereft, quick tears burned at her eyes, but she held them back. Tears wouldn't help anyone.

She squeezed her eyes shut, willing the sights around her to go away. In their place, images flooded her mind. Rather than the Basra sky above her, she saw a night sky of a year ago. She'd been standing with Major Bret Holden. She could almost feel the warm wind that had embraced them as it whipped sand and dust around them. She could see as though it were before her now, the ruins of the Charchemish archaeological digs near the newly constructed Berlin Baghdad Railway. She felt the determined yet tender grip of Bret's hands on her forearms, and then she felt that grip loosen. His riveting blue eyes seemed suddenly lost in the void that settled between them, leaving an emptiness that still remained. His words echoed in

14

her ears again, as they had that night so very long ago: "I'll find you again, Allison."

Allison wanted to close her eyes—and her mind—against the memory, but she couldn't. The remembrance was as relentless as the Zeppelin had been mere moments before. "Oh, Bret," she whispered brokenly, grieving again the end of that memorable summer of 1914. Grieving, too, the end of the budding love that had sprouted between them, fresh with promise...a promise that had withered and turned brown, stained with blood before it had found a chance to grow.

Yet it was not the cry of death she heard in her heart. Instead, over and over, she heard Bret's words: "I'll find you again.... When you get to Cairo, return to the *Mercy*. You belong there, you know, in pristine white with a red cross on your breast and dignity and nobility in your eyes. You belong to something far more wonderful than this kind of life."

Pristine white...

How long had it been since she'd been around anything pristine? Anything clean or pure? The answer rang out in her mind: forever. And Allison feared nothing would ever be clean and white again. Everything around her, even her gray ankle-length dress was splattered with dust and sweat. The very earth itself was stained—yet only a blood-stained cross offered hope and true cleansing.

"Jesus! Lord—!" The tears dribbled down her cheeks and ran hot.

What the world had begun to call the Great War, the war to end all wars, had rampaged across Europe and had arrived here in Arabia. Allison had heard the reports of what was happening across the Mediterranean—British and French troops died by the thousands on the rugged mountainous slopes as they fought to regain Constantinople from the Turks, an objective that grew more hopeless as the casualty lists grew longer.

Suddenly the Arabian wind blew strong about Allison, kicking up sand in front of her. In her mind the winds became a voice that called for valor and sacrifice, and she heard Bret saying: "David tells of a Jewish tradition. Upon rising each morning, however dark the day, however hopeless it may seem, they say: 'Rise up like a lion, for the service of the Lord!'"

The day he'd said that to her their gazes had held, and he'd gently cupped her face between his hands. Then, as the wind blew her hair, he kissed her tenderly. "I'll find you again, Allison."

Find you again, the words echoed as the sound of distant machine-gun fire ripped through the night.

That night seemed so long ago. She had looked eastward in the black sky to see a star winking its promise, but now...now, tonight, like so many other hundreds of nights that had come and gone, there was no silvery star of hope breaking through the war clouds. There was only gloom.

Where was Bret now? alive? dead? It had been so long since she'd heard from him, she couldn't help but wonder...had he decided he didn't love her after all? The thought cut through her heart like a piece of shrapnel. Bret hadn't told her he loved her before he left for England. Perhaps what drew them together had been mere infatuation bred of danger, sacrifice, and the threat of death. Yes, he'd said he would find her again, but he hadn't. Perhaps it was because he had already forgotten her.

"Allison!"

At the sound of her name, Allison blinked and looked around her, startled by the blaze of hope that raged through her. But the weary, smoke-smudged face that looked down at her was not Bret's. It belonged, instead, to her comrade-in-medical-arms, Emily, a plucky little nurse from Australia. Though in her early twenties, Emily had proven herself capable, efficient, and courageous many

16

times over since she had come to the compound. She knelt beside Allison, checking her over to see how badly she was hurt.

"Blimey, you're all right, mate," came the chirpy tone. Before Allison could respond, Emily lifted her as if she were a child. Allison came to her feet and stood there swaying. For a moment it looked as if they would both go down. Allison wanted to protest, but she found she couldn't speak. The wind washed her face as her head fell back across Emily's arm.

Emily struggled forward, half carrying Allison through the mud, breathing in ragged gasps. Suddenly she halted and called out, a glad tone to her voice: "Ho, there! Cap'n Findlay! Lend a hand, sir, won't you? It's Allison!"

Captain Wade Findlay, head medical orderly in the nursing unit sent up from Cairo, gently laid Allison on a bunk in a large tent near the back of the main hospital. Wade held his anxiety in check, fully aware of Nurse Emily Howard's sparrowlike eyes. Sometimes he felt as if he were a patient under scrutiny, rather than chief intern. In this case, though, it was his heart, not his actions, that fell under the telescopic gaze. The cheery Australian nurse had already smiled too sympathetically at him at breakfast.

On several occasions he'd felt the need to safeguard his feelings from the bright gazes of the nurses, not that they were overt in their curiosity. Emily, Marra, and Flora were the essence of propriety. But somehow, despite his best efforts to the contrary, they had all discovered his secret: he was in love with Nurse Allison Wescott.

The nurses had picked up, apparently, that Allison didn't return Wade's feelings—hence their sympathetic glances and encouraging smiles. But what they didn't know was why she was so unresponsive. Wade, on the other hand, was far too aware of the reason:

Allison was brooding over the handsome—and absent—British Intelligence officer, Major Bret Holden.

Allison's past with the delinquent Major Holden was supposed to be a secret to everyone, even to him. She had yet to speak of it, either to him or, from what he'd gathered, to the nurses she served with in the unit. But her feelings had been all too clear in her eyes and her smile…and in the change between them. Not that she spurned him. Not at all. She was just…different. Distracted. Distant. Still, Wade patiently waited, thus far in vain, to know just where he stood with Allison. Their relationship was fairly long-standing, having begun several years earlier while they were at Oswald Chambers's Bible Training College in London. And for all that, Major Bret Holden seemed to have come between them while she was in Charchemish…well, Holden wasn't here now, was he?

"Is it a concussion?" asked Emily.

Wade shook his head. "In shock, more likely. She'll do well enough considering the Tommy was blown to bits." He kept his tone professional—an effective cover, he hoped, as he bent over the bunk and checked Allison's eyes. They were as warm and clear as his recollection of the Mediterranean, except they weren't blue but sea-green, an unusual gift from her Creator. Most people had ordinary eyes, like Nurse Emily's nondescript brown ones. Allison's were the exception. As was her face, which bore a noble tenderness. *Like the pureness of fresh snow,* he thought—not that he'd ever see snow out here in the Arabian desert.

He inspected Allison's face carefully. It was streaked with dust, and there was a cut above her brow from flying debris. He'd learned early on that any scratch must be dealt with at once. He'd seen soldiers die within hours of an injury. As though the death wasn't enough to bear, the resulting flies were horrendous!

Emily handed Wade a bottle from his bag, and he cleaned the

wound. Even in her unconscious state, Allison winced as he daubed the injury clean. A moment later, he cleared his throat and adjusted his small round spectacles on his face, but they remained steamed up, and he swept them off and dried them on a cloth. He turned his head and gave Emily what he hoped was a professional stare, defying scrutiny. He need not have worried. She was distracted by the sound of the wounded who were being brought into the front of the hospital. At that sound—and at the stern orders of Doc Murphy shouting to the other orderlies—Wade and Emily both turned and ran to their duties.

Wade rushed inside the hospital tent with Emily swiftly behind, and as they entered the hot, cramped structure so full of wounded soldiers that they had to step over the men, Doc Murphy bellowed: "Findlay! I could have you court-martialed for this! Where have you been? Don't you know men are dying?"

"Yes sir! Nurse Wescott was inj—"

"The Tommies come first! Understood? They always come first!"

Steeling his emotions against the rebuke, Wade felt his face grow warm and clamped his jaw. He swiftly took position on the other side of the brittle-eyed military doctor while stretcher bearers fresh from the field were hauling in more wounded. One of the wounded was a sepoy, an East Indian national hired by the British army, from the regiment in India. When Wade had first arrived, he'd been surprised to see so many of the sepoys until he realized the troops serving in this region had been sent from the British-led army in India.

The older square-faced Doc Murphy jerked back the cover to check whether or not the man could be treated. Wade's jaw tightened at the sight of horrific gaping wounds. He glanced at Emily to see how she was taking it. She didn't flinch. Wade had to admire the girl. He wanted to jerk his head away with horror, but he knew if he did, it would be the end of his service here. Doc was looking for any excuse to send him back to Egypt. He'd made it more than clear that he didn't approve of an intern who had abandoned several years of study toward a doctor's degree to study the Bible with Oswald Chambers.

"If you want to be a doctor, then it demands all of you," he had lectured, his ruddy face mottled by the heat when he'd first discovered Wade's choice. "If you prefer to preach, then join the YMCA at Zeitoun!"

Wade didn't have the words to explain that he wanted to heal both spiritually and physically, nor did he think Murphy would understand. Not that the man couldn't, he just didn't want to.

As Wade stared at the sepoy, he was unprepared for the sudden nausea that threatened to overwhelm him. *God of mercy, help me. Don't let me disgrace myself even further!*

Long hours later, Wade at last took a break outdoors, hoping against hope he could find a mug of coffee. He'd uttered a heartfelt sigh when he finally turned his duties over to the tall British girl named Flora and was able at last to step outside into the night. The dry wind was blowing in gusts, and everywhere there was dust and sand. He felt the grit between his teeth, in his hair, in his ears. His spectacles, fortunately, gave more protection to his eyes than most received, but he could feel that his eyes were red rimmed and sore all the same.

Ahead, several soldiers were on guard. Wade stood beneath the tent awning, listening to the canvas snapping. He walked over to a small sheltered campfire beside one of the newly constructed cook tents, where a huge blackened coffeepot sat full and steaming. As he glanced about for a tin mug, he saw why the pot remained full; there weren't any mugs.

He was startled when a soldier said, "Allow me, sir."

Wade couldn't see him well in the dim lantern light, but the soldier seemed to be about his own height but with a strong build. The wind tugged at the man's tan Australian desert hat with its wide stiff brim. He produced a tin from his backpack, poured the coffee, then handed it to Wade with a shadowed grin.

"Here you go, Doc."

The voice jarred his memory, and Wade gave the soldier closer attention. He had a shock of brown hair and a grin that could melt an iceberg. Wade's eyes widened in surprise.

"I don't believe it! David—David Goldstein. I thought you were being held by the Turks in Jerusalem! You mean I've been praying for you for no reason?" And Wade laughed, utterly delighted. The two men slapped a pleased greeting to each other on the shoulders.

"Do you need a desperate reason to pray for me?" David flashed a smile, pushing back his hat, and in the glowing light from the campfire, his brown eyes shone with laughter.

Wade, too, laughed, until he noticed a scar across David's left cheek. It hadn't been there when they met in London at Chambers's school.

David noticed Wade's reaction. "Just a memento from my friends in Jerusalem," he said with a cheeky grin.

"Well, thank God they didn't carve you up too badly. You're free, anyway. This is great news. Does Allison know?"

"Not yet. I've been looking for her."

Wade noted the armband identifying David as a corporal in the new medical rescue unit sent up from Cairo. "Looks like you belong to the new Camel Corps. Wasn't it started by some clever fellow in Cairo Intelligence named Holden?"

David turned his shoulder toward him, showing his armband fully. "I'm a full-fledged ambulance man now, hauling the wounded back from the front." The so-called "ambulance" consisted of two camels with a stretcher slung in between. "It pays to have political connections, old man. And what of you? Say! Weren't you supposed to serve as a chaplain at Zeitoun? You didn't come here as a medical intern because of Allison?"

Wade laughed, hoping he didn't sound as uncomfortable as he felt. "Maybe she came because of me. So how did you know she was here?"

"I told you," he said good-naturedly. "I may be a corporal, but I've friends you wouldn't believe. All in powerful places—Cairo Intelligence, British India, even a German Baroness draped with diamonds now deigns to call me a friend in arms. Anyway, Allison and I have been through a few things. We keep in touch." He flashed another smile.

Wade wasn't worried about Allison falling in love with David since she'd already told him she looked on the young Jewish Zionist as a brother, but it wasn't as clear what David felt toward her. Allison, it appeared, could have any man she wanted, except one; an elusive British agent.

"Her father's returning from Bombay to Cairo," said David. "She won't be here long now. He'll want her out of here. Can you blame him?"

Wade knew about her father, Sir Marshall Wescott. He was to have arrived in Egypt last December, but with Turkey declaring war on England in November of 1914, his plans had been altered for a time by the viceroy of India. Instead, plans were drawn up to land British and Indian troops at Qurna to safeguard the Anglo-Persian oil pipeline at the Abadan oil fields.

When Wade had first learned that Allison had joined the British Corps of Nurses, he expected her influential family to make certain she was stationed in a safe zone—most likely Alexandria. Then he found out that her father didn't even know she was in Arabia. Wade then approached his commanding officer with a request that Allison be transferred back to Egypt, but the stone-faced Major General Crawford had shown little cooperation.

"Did Nurse Wescott send you?" he'd asked over his pipe.

"No, sir." Wade flushed under the officer's bored gaze.

"Then I suggest you allow Nurse Wescott to speak for herself. Nurses are needed here, regardless of their pedigree. She happens to be a good one. Wholly dedicated."

"Yes, sir, but this nurse is the daughter of a friend of Secretary of War Kitchener."

"I know that. And Sir Marshall will be as proud as aces of her when he finds out about his daughter's bravery." He had then changed the subject by calling for his staff officer.

Remembering, Wade tossed the dregs of his coffee into the sand. As well as David knew Allison, he most likely could tell Wade something about a certain intelligence officer that Allison had met in Egypt. But Wade found he couldn't bring himself to ask outright. Prying behind Allison's back made it appear as though he didn't trust her. Besides, if she wanted to tell him about the officer, she would. The fact that she hadn't done so disturbed him even more, since it might mean she cared deeply.

The one man Allison had spoken much of was Neal Bristow, but he was her cousin and a civilian. Neal was somewhere in London on government business with Secretary of War Kitchener. With the worsening of the war and a thousand Brits dying every day on the various fronts with Germany and Turkey, Kitchener had called on the enlistment of all able-bodied men up to forty years of age. From what Allison had told him, Neal had worked first with the British Museum here in the Arabian desert near Jerablus and Baghdad. She told him that Neal had gone to England to meet with the British

Museum curator over safeguarding the Carchemish digs. Later, Neal had written of a post as an aide to Kitchener. With the increased U-boat torpedoing of civilian ships, she had a right to be concerned about any plans her cousin may have in returning to Egypt.

Wade saw that David was watching him.

"I'd like to see Allison tonight. Can it be arranged?"

Wade shrugged. He had no right to be possessive of her. "She's off duty, thanks to an injury from that Zeppelin that came over."

"You're sure she's all right?" came the low urgent voice.

"A bit of shock, mild concussion, a few bruises. Could have been worse. The Lord has plans for her." He returned David's tin mug. "It blew up a soldier right in front of her. Wasn't enough of the poor wretch to scrape into a wheelbarrow and send home." He looked away, troubled. "The situation can always be worse, but I'm beginning to wonder how."

David's voice was calm and ominously quiet as he looked off toward the Mediterranean. "The Huns have nothing on the Turks when it comes to making things worse."

Wade didn't pursue the comment; he was sick of butchery and he could do without one more tale tonight. In the months he'd been here, he'd seen too many good men hauled into the hospital limbless, blind, horribly scarred—and worse.

"When can I see Allison?" persisted David. "I'm off duty for only a few hours more. Do you think—? Can I bring her a cup of hot tea?"

Wade watched the wind whipping the tents before he turned. "She may not be up to it, but if she is, I don't see why I should restrict it. Go on, bring her that cup of tea. You'll find the kitchen out back." He turned and gestured. "That is, if it's still standing and the Zeppelin didn't bomb it to smithereens. Hey, Emily!" he called suddenly, gesturing. "Escort the corporal to Nurse Wescott, will

24

you?" As Emily walked across the sand toward them, Wade looked at David who was gathering up his pack. "I'd better get back to the hospital. Captain Murphy will need a break by now. We've fifteen new patients to keep alive tonight."

David left with Emily, and Wade went back inside the hospital tent. He hadn't been there more than twenty minutes when he heard the news. The major general would be receiving an important British military and civilian delegation from India, perhaps in the next few days if the ship could sneak past a Turkish destroyer in the Persian Gulf. Wade thought he knew what brought the top brass to Basra to confer with the military officers here. He scanned the hundreds of wounded and fought back the sense of despair that wrestled to take possession of his heart. When it came to saving men's lives, his heart was fully involved—but he cared little about fighting battles, and he knew even less about military tactics. Even so, it was plain to even him that the British couldn't continue to hold back the Turks once they determined to land near Baghdad.

If new British troops didn't arrive soon, those unfortunate enough to be around—including Allison, Emily, and the other nurses—would be overrun.

Two

Underneath are the everlasting arms.
DEUTERONOMY 33:27

THE MESS HALL CONSISTED OF some wooden picnic tables and benches set up in rows beneath a large overhanging roof made of weather-faded canvas. The canvas sides of the enclosure were rolled up, but when the wind blew, they could be let down for some protection. Despite the effort, the food was always gritty.

The white moon shone in the black sky and the wind sang along the roofing as Allison sat across the table from David, holding her cup of tea and smiling as he exaggerated his escape from Jerusalem.

"So there I was, tied with a rope under my arms while these Arabs—followers of Mohammed!—" he looked toward the roof as if for mercy—"lowered me down into a dark cavern of some well near El-Arish." He leaned toward her, eyes narrowing, glinting brown. "'Trust us!' they hissed to me over the rim. Imagine! Trust them? 'The Turks are coming. We'll be back when it's safe to pull you out.'"

He smirked. "Let me tell you; flashes of Joseph were quickly resurrected from old stories at synagogue school. Here I was, David Samuel Goldstein, left to the mercy of Arabs—son's of Ishmael. I knew I was ready to be sold to the Turks! It gave me a good sweat!" He looked at her and winked.

Allison laughed quietly. She could now because there was no reason to be afraid for the outcome. But how well she remembered that night, the last time she saw him. They were in Jerusalem, the

Turkish general had evicted all Jewish leaders from Palestine, and David had been arrested. It had been terrifying, and she had hated running when she knew David was in such danger…but he would have it no other way. She didn't know how much of his wild story was meant to entertain her and how much was actually true; she was just grateful he was safe. She touched the small bandage above her brow. Her head ached and she felt weak after her own ordeal earlier that evening at twilight, but otherwise she was feeling in a better mood in the company of David. During the long arduous year since she'd last seen him, she'd heard nothing of his condition. Not even cousin Neal had been able to learn anything from Rose Lyman, his British contact in Jerusalem. Allison wouldn't admit it to David now, but while she had continued to pray for his release, she'd given up hope he was even alive.

Now, here he was, a corporal in the Camel Brigade!

She could see he was trying to amuse her. She imagined how weary and solemn she must appear after six dismal months here in Arabia, or Mesopotamia as some called it. She had served with Dr. Murphy in the field hospital from the day the Sixth Division from British India arrived at Abadan to secure the flow of oil from the Anglo-Persian pipeline.

David sobered and spoke quietly: "You've lost weight."

She smiled. She had, though she'd never needed to diet. Her uniform was getting looser with the weeks of heat, but that was hardly a surprise when temperatures in the afternoons sometimes climbed to well over 110 degrees.

"Beth would envy me," she said lightly and sipped her unsweetened tea. "If I miss anything, it's sugar. Sugar is a rare treat and cream is a delicacy no one mentions. Even if we could find a milk cow," she joked, "the cream would curdle overnight."

David did not smile. He looked anything but in a joking mood

28

now. He folded his strong tanned hands on the table and interlaced his fingers, watching her with an intensity that stirred unwanted memories of another.

"Be serious," he said in a brotherly tone. "I knew from the time I met you at BTC you were the martyr sort."

"David!" she began indignantly, though smiling ruefully. "What I'm doing is important and needed."

"Sure it is, and it's also dangerous. Let me tell you, to have such a mindset is asking for trouble when the world is at war. There are always those in authority who will take advantage of your dedication to God and country."

"I expect them to," she returned. "It's a time for patriotism, for sacrifice. Never mind me, look at these soldiers! Do you know how many would die if the medical support team wasn't here?"

"Yes, I know, but men should do this work, like Wade and Doc Murphy and me." He turned his muscled arm toward her, smiling as he patted the insignia of two camels with a long stretcher in between them on which were four wounded men.

She smiled softly. "I'm proud of you, David. But I can't retire to the safety of Port Said. I'm needed, too. We all are. We're a team and we need to pull together to save as many lives as possible."

She wouldn't admit, however, that unlike Emily and Marra who seemed to have their emotions all neatly packed away in a kitbag for tomorrow, she'd been accused by Doc Murphy of becoming too emotionally involved with the soldiers. Well, how could she not? She heard them talking, laughing, moaning, dying. When she first arrived, the shock was dreadful. How many times had she cried in her bunk at night when no one but the Lord heard, remembering each soldier who died bravely while she attended his gaping wounds. Soldiers were buried in the sand with hundreds of little white crosses sticking up as far as the eye could see—not Christian soldiers only, but sepoys also, who were serving their British officers loyally: Hindus, Sikhs, Moslems—thousands of them! And how many from this harvest of death were ready to enter eternity? How many knew Jesus the Savior? Only a few, she thought grimly. Yes, men were dying on all sides—England, France, Serbia, Germany, Austria, Hungary, and Turkey…all had suffered terrible losses.

"Allison?"

She felt David's hand close over hers with a hard squeeze. She winced and came back to the moment. Looking into his eyes she saw growing concern.

"You're too good to be here."

She gave a laugh, not only embarrassed but troubled by the look in his face. There had been a time when she'd thought she could love David, but that was before—

No! She put the brake on her emotions quickly before her thoughts traversed the familiar, hurtful path. There'd been a time when she'd thought herself in love with Wade, too. They'd even considered themselves engaged.

Maybe I'm fickle. She wanted to smile at the wry thought, but she couldn't. She knew it wasn't true. She cared about them, that was true. She cared what happened to each one. And there was something within her that wanted to comfort them. But what she felt for these men was not 'romantic.' They were friends, brothers. Of course, she'd been told often enough by her mother that friendship was the path that could lead to true abiding love. Well, if that were all there were to it, why did she feel so strongly about Bret?

I certainly don't feel friendship for Bret, she thought, and her jaw tensed. She drew her hand away from David's and tried to smile.

"Believe me, I'm not a saint, David. And if you could speak to Emily and Marra, you'd know soon enough what a trial I can be." She laughed. "They'd agree with you quickly enough to send me

packing and home to Cairo. Marra," she said dryly, "would be willing to pack for me. She doesn't like me."

When she'd first arrived, Marra was always carrying around an
old photograph in a pewter frame that was just small enough to fit
into her nursing pinafore pocket. In the months Allison had been
here, she had yet to see who was in that photograph. Allison had
been around her long enough that she could easily guess, though.

"I'm worried about you," insisted David. "You've changed since
Jerusalem."

She played with the rim of her battered mug and avoided his
eyes, hoping he wouldn't inquire about a certain mutual friend. She
shrugged. "It's the hour we live in."

"Yes, I know, and if we didn't change we'd be wooden soldiers."

She nodded somberly. "Much has happened since we were with
Neal at Rose Lyman's house. I often wonder how she and her little
boy, Benjamin, are doing."

"She's doing better than you, I think."

Allison looked at him for an explanation of that cryptic statement.

"Rose doesn't believe in rainbows."

"And I suppose I do?"

"Big bright ones that fill the entire sky with color! Rose isn't sensitive, she's developed the hide of a camel—and she can go without
the water of hope for months."

Allison laughed at him and reached over to place her hand on
his wrist. "Oh, David, I've missed you! But you mustn't think I'm
some delicate white blossom growing in a London garden. I can live
without the dew of spring," she jested. "I know quite where I am in
life. I'm under no sentimental illusions. I can taste the sweat on my
lips and sand between my teeth. I'm professional enough to walk
away from an injured soldier and let him die—even when he begs

31

me to stay, but—" she stopped, and in contradiction to everything she'd just told him, tears welled in her eyes. She wouldn't tell him that the first time she was forced to walk away from a British soldier, she'd found it necessary go outside alone to be sick. The voice of the young man pleading with her to help him continued to ring in her ears.

David grew sober as he leaned across the table. "You shouldn't be here, Allison. Why not go back to Egypt?"

She smiled. "You sound like Wade. No one seems to worry if Emily or Marra pack up and go home to tea parties."

"Forget the tea and crumpets! It's not what I mean. Anyway, I don't know Emily and Marra. And their last name isn't Wescott. They couldn't go back if they wanted to, but you can. You're the daughter of Sir Marshall Wescott, soon-to-be chief consul in Cairo."

"That's another thing," she said, shaking her head. "I won't use my father's position to surrender responsibility."

David settled back on his bench. "Do you know your parents will be back in Cairo within a month?"

"No," she said suspiciously, "and how do you know?"

"I told you, I've friends in high places," he said with a grin. "When your father learns you're here, he'll put pressure on the major general to send you back."

She felt her eyes crinkle with amusement. "Your friends in high places don't know my father the way I do. We're alike, he and I. He doesn't always agree with me, but he'll be proud of me." She lifted her empty cup in a self-deprecatory toast. "To Nurse Allison Wescott, serving bravely with the British troops near Basra!" She lowered her cup. "But if my family doesn't know I'm here...well, they will soon enough, I suppose, if Aunt Lydia is in Port Said at the house as you've said."

"She is, and most unhappy about her boat being confiscated by General Maxwell."

"Yes, I was on her boat for a while. That experience was one of the reasons I joined the British Corp of Nurses."

Allison remembered with tender longing Aunt Lydia's selfless work aboard the medical missions boat, the *Mercy*. Allison had served beside her aunt, attending the *fellahin*—the Egyptian peasant farmers who grew cotton along the Nile—until the war erupted. When the BEF, the British Expedition Force, had informed Aunt Lydia that it was too dangerous to be sailing on the Nile, the work with the fellahin at Luxor was abandoned, and they returned to Port Said. Lydia had been heartsick and a bit disgruntled, and Allison had felt it her duty to join a nursing unit in Cairo. When Wade had arrived from London and told her he had joined the force and would be moving out with Dr. Murphy to support the Sixth Division from British India, she felt it her calling to sign up for the Medical Corps. She wouldn't admit that not hearing from Bret had also prompted her decision.

Stop it! she chided herself. She knew she shouldn't judge Bret too harshly for his silence. He'd been committed to serving at the War Office in London, and everyone knew mail nowadays was excruciatingly slow. True, he could have sent her a wire, but such things did not go over well with military intelligence. All this she had told herself a hundred times. She refused to even consider other reasons for why she had not heard from the man for a year.

David studied her face. "There's top brass from Bombay coming to meet with the major general. I think there's going to be a big push toward Baghdad."

She wondered how a corporal in the Camel Brigade would know such things, but she was fairly certain that, if she asked, he'd give her another light remark about friends in high places. She remembered that David had once suggested he was involved in intelligence. She wondered if his position as a corporal in the ambulance service might not also be a front for something more covert.

But she didn't dwell on this, for the idea of another move toward a battle engaging twenty to thirty thousand soldiers on both sides filled her with sick dread. "Many of the soldiers are already down with a host of sicknesses," she protested. "Malaria, dysentery, cholera—and we've no water purification system. Do you know how bad the terrain is in this area? Each spring the Tigris and Euphrates overflow their banks and the plain becomes a marsh. Some places never dry out near the rivers. It's a breeding ground for fleas, mosquitoes, and pitiable dogs, so filthy that—"

"Hey, easy! I'm with you."

"Anyway," she said, "I don't know the top brass coming from India, and I don't expect my father to be with them, though he, Mother, and Beth are still in Bombay. They'll be returning to take up the British residency in Cairo this December, I think."

That her mother had wanted to return to England with Beth rang clearly in her memory. But matters had changed. Now, her mother wrote glowing letters of duty and honor, of the need of being at the side of her husband. The letters, first sent to Aunt Lydia who forwarded them to Allison, were meant to encourage her. Even Beth, it seemed, had fallen in love with the British social circuit in India.

I could stay in Bombay forever, her sister had written with gleeful sixteen-year-old exuberance. *There are balls every week at the British residency, and twenty British soldiers to dance with. And—I've met a long-lost cousin of ours. His name is Gilbert. He's so grand! He's much older than I, at least twenty. He's the son of a forgotten cousin of Mum's named Sir Edgar Simonds. Ever heard of him? Mum's cousin Edgar is coming to Egypt to take over the position of inspector general for the Cairo police. He's widowed, and his son Gilbert is so clever. He tells me he'll be rich one day on Egyptian treasure and wants to marry me. He dances divinely and is so worldly wise. He says he's going to teach me to be very sophisticated...Mum's worried....*

David leaned over the picnic table again. "Say, is something wrong?"

She looked at him, feeling a bit dazed. "What?"

"You were frowning."

She smiled. "Oh, was I? It's nothing, I guess. Anyway, David, as I said, I don't expect my father to be with the entourage coming from India. They'll sail straight from Bombay to Alexandria, then take the train to Cairo. My father will assure Mum that I'm perfectly safe here behind the lines in the field hospital."

"Yes, well, if the top brass from India have it their way, there may be no safety behind the lines. Not if they lead us toward forty thousand Turks at Baghdad."

There had already been several battles since she first arrived. The Brits had captured Qurna and secured the oil pipeline, then Lieutenant General Sir Arthur Barrett had dispatched a brigade to Ahwaz to fend off a Turkish attempt to cut the pipeline. Lord Hardinge, the viceroy of India, visited the troops thereafter and returned to British India with a glowing report of the military situation. He had scraped together more troops to form an incomplete infantry corps under the new general, Sir John Nixon, assigning him the mission of occupying the entire province of Basra to counter the Turkish Thirty-Seventh Reserve Division, which had since reinforced the area. It gave Allison goose bumps along her neck when she thought how precarious their situation could be if they were cut off from the mainline troops near Abadan.

David was right. They were in a dangerous situation, but the general and his staff knew what they were doing. Surely the commander wouldn't lead them farther north toward Kut-al-Amara and Baghdad unless they were sure they outnumbered the enemy army of the Turkish commander, Nur-ud-Din, and his Thirty-Seventh south of the Tigris River.

David's eyes were on his empty cup as he twirled it on the table. "I keep thinking that Captain Mustafa might still be hanging about Baghdad. He and I have a few unsettled issues."

Captain Mustafa. Allison had not thought of him in a long time. Now, however, she remembered that day on the road from Aleppo to Jerablus when Captain Mustafa and his soldiers had stopped them for questioning. She had been on her way out to the archaeological digs to try to locate her cousin Neal and tell him of his sister Leah's murder and of the murder of a British agent in disguise as German Major Karl Reuter. Allison mistakenly wore her nurse's uniform with its red cross, and Captain Mustafa had arrested them. Only the arrival of Bret, who had been impersonating a German colonel, had rescued her and—eventually—David.

She pushed the memories away. True, they were now scars rather than raw wounds, but she knew that if she probed too long, she would uncover an injury that hadn't completely healed.

With deliberate purpose, she turned her mind to David's problems. She knew what a Jewish homeland meant to him and to the others like Rose Lyman and David Ben Gurion, who'd been evicted from Jerusalem. With the war raging on all fronts, dreams of a state of "Israel" were delayed indefinitely. Even so, David had informed her that Ben Gurion was in America trying to gather support for an all-Jewish military brigade to fight in Palestine. People like Rose served as secret agents of the Allies: England, France, Serbia, and Belgium. It was just as true, however, that loyal Jews fought and were killed in the war serving in the armies of Russia, Germany, Austria-Hungary, and in the army of every other country fighting in what Winston Churchill had said was "The war to end all wars." Allison wondered. The Lord had said there would be wars and rumors of wars until the end.

She now watched David with concern, thinking of Mustafa. "War isn't supposed to be personal."

"It is with me," he admitted frankly and ran his finger along the scar. "I've worse than this, but I won't show them to you even if you are a nurse. No, I'm not a eunuch," he said bluntly, "but if I'd been there much longer, they probably would have resorted to that, also." He stood abruptly as though his seething anger couldn't be bottled up. "They've done worse things to Jews—and the Christian Armenians. Bret says there's a chance of extermination."

Allison's gaze flew to David's face. *Bret* had told him. When had he seen Bret? Did this mean Bret was not in London?

"I've said enough," he apologized. "C'mon, Allison, you look worn and tired. I'll walk you back. You're a nurse, can't you give yourself something to sleep?" He looked at his watch. "Yeow! If I don't get back, I won't need to worry about Mustafa. My good British officer will cast me into a dungeon."

She longed to question David but could not. Her emotions were in too much turmoil right now. Besides, he probably talked with Bret long ago.... She stood, and they left the mess hall, ducking under the lowered canvas awning.

It was warm and windy as they walked back to her quarters; the stars were bright in the sky above. She could almost believe the Zeppelin attack hadn't occurred, that there hadn't been casualties...but the destruction and debris and the lanterns glowing brightly in the hospital tents, all bore mute evidence to the contrary.

She breathed in the night air, feeling a bit refreshed. It was good to see David, his presence brought back the memory of happier times, and although she was weary and her head ached from the concussion, she disliked saying good night.

"So how did you get out of the well?" she asked, remembering his story earlier that evening. She pushed back a strand of hair from

37

her face and glanced at him. Except for the scar he'd indicated, there was little to prove he hadn't spent the last year basking in the sun and surf on the Mediterranean. His handsome face was tanned and full, his brown hair fell across his forehead, and his keen eyes were spirited.

He straightened his expedition-style helmet and waved a hand. "Viola," he jested, "My Ishmaelite comrades returned, after all. Imagine that." Allison smiled. She knew it was unusual for a Jew to be helped—even befriended—by an Arab. But David had proven himself an ally to Rose Lyman and her people. He grinned at her, dramatically placing a palm against his chest. "I confess I was shocked. Then I knew why. The dear sweet wild rose of the Arabian desert was with them, leading the way. Rose Lyman. She called: 'My son David, are you yet alive?' And I called up: 'Oh, king—I mean, queen—live forever!' And they pulled me out. Never was I so glad to see hot sand again. I knelt to kiss it, burrowed scorpions and all."

Allison smiled. His voice lowered. "Rose had the map. I brought it to Cairo as planned."

Allison blinked. "Map?"

"Of the desert wells, remember?"

She thought back to the little house in Jerusalem, of Neal and David telling her how Rose was secretly a British agent cooperating with the London War Office for the future good of Zionism, a Jewish homeland. In her covert work with intelligence, Rose's main contact was one man in particular: Bret Holden. Among other activities, Bret had smuggled guns to Jewish activists like David...and he'd had Rose working on a map....

"Yes, the map," she whispered. "What about it?"

"The Brits in Cairo have been waiting for it. General Maxwell has wanted the location of the German wells since Bret made contact with Rose two years ago."

The mention of Bret's name brought a tightening in her chest. "Neal was also in contact with Rose," she said. "He's gone to London to meet—Major Holden. Neal didn't explain, but I suppose he went to bring him the map." There. She hadn't come out and asked, but the question of Bret's location should be obvious enough.

David's surprise alerted her. "The top brass in Egypt already have the map! Rose passed it to me and I to—" he broke off, looking at her.

She held his gaze while a slow unpleasant realization stole over her.

David hurried on. "Anyway, if Leah were alive, she would be pleased to know her espionage work wasn't in vain. Speaking of which, I heard about your terrific work, Allison. The king ought to give you a brevet or something."

She didn't smile. The mood between them had changed. Her heart was impaled on a truth that David obviously felt he'd blundered in mentioning, and Allison had picked it up at once. He wouldn't admit it, but David had brought the map from Rose to Bret—not in England as she'd been thinking, but in Cairo. *In Cairo.* Over a year had passed since that night at the Charchemish Digs, and Major Holden had been no farther away than Cairo.

Yet he hadn't contacted her. Not even once.

Allison walked in silence. Beside her, David simply talked on until they'd reached the door to her quarters. Apparently hearing them, Marra poked out her tousled blonde head, offering no apology for interrupting.

"Not another mooning boyfriend! Aren't Wade and a half dozen other Tommies enough? Come on, soldier, move it, will you? I need my sleep. Tell her you love her somewhere else besides beneath my cot. It isn't often a nurse gets a break around here that's actually long enough to get some shut-eye. Tell her you love her when the birds get up—oh, yeah, I forgot," groaned Marra. "There aren't any robins around here, are there?"

"No," quipped David. "Only buzzards."

"David is a *friend,*" Allison said, trying to be patient with her hostile roommate. "But I am sorry we woke you, Marra." She turned to David, sad that their time together had ended. "And she's right, David. I'm tired, too. So much so I could sleep on my feet."

"Say no more, my dear," David said, sweeping a courtly bow. "I shall see you as soon as I get some hours off. Sweet dreams." He cast a grin at the still glaring Marra. "And good night to you, too, sour puss. Sweet dreams about the poor feller you left behind in the East End of London."

Marra threw something at him through the window flap. David ducked and, laughing, was gone.

Allison stood there in the night. Mosquitoes buzzed, but she hardly heard them as she sank wearily to the broken hard-backed chair in front of the tent and stared off toward the distant front line where the army was dug in. All was quiet; there was no machine-gun fire, no thundering artillery, no sound of airplanes. She knew, despite Marra's impatient words, that she'd been waiting for her to come in and go to bed so she might ask her how she was feeling, and who David was. But she needed to take a moment, to give herself time to quiet her heart and convince herself she was behaving foolishly about Bret.

So what if he hadn't contacted her? It was better this way.

But she knew it wasn't, not for her.

She swallowed, but her throat felt dry. She wanted water but was too drained to get up and dip the urn in the water barrel beside the tent.

She might as well face the brutal truth: Bret hadn't been in love with her after all, despite his suggestion when they'd parted at

Charchemish. What other conclusion could she draw from the fact that he'd been back for months yet hadn't contacted her? Nor, for that matter, had he written even once from the London War Office.

Marra came out of the tent, wearing an old, worn robe that had a hole in both elbows. A few years older than Allison and Emily, at times she reminded Allison of her cousin Leah—except Marra was taller and willowy, with blonde hair that she boldly cut short. Few women ever cut their hair in such a manner!

"Look, I'm sorry if I embarrassed you," Marra said with a shrug. "I was joking, is all. I guess sometimes I'm a little too blunt. No need to sit out here mad at me, though. I'll behave better next time Romeo calls."

"What?" Allison looked at her, confused.

Marra sank to an empty crate, folded her arms around her legs, and rested her chin on her knees. "You can have as many admirers as suits your fancy. It's none of my business. Anyway, you've behaved marvelously since you've come. Emily's always after me to leave you alone. The fact you've joined the chaplain on Sundays, helping out down there, shows you take your religion seriously enough."

Allison, exhausted and struggling to follow her words, ran a hand over her scratchy eyes. She longed for sleep. "Thanks," she murmured. "But don't apologize. There's no need. David's a friend, like I said. We go all the way back to Chambers's College in London. He's a Zionist."

Marra groaned.

Allison looked at her, trying to see her face concealed in the night shadows. "What is it?"

Marra reached around her neck and brought out a silver chain holding the emblem toward Allison. It was a star of David.

"You never told me you were Jewish."

"Should I?" Marra's tone was testy. "With you, hauling a bag of Bible papers and things around with you every place we set up camp? Don't tell me Romeo is a Christian Jew?"

"No...but I've tried to convince him." Allison laughed, reaching over to give a friendly yank to Marra's torn sleeve. "Maybe I'll work on you next."

Marra rolled her eyes toward the stars. "Oh, no, you won't. Now there's two of you to worry about—Wade's been anxious to discuss Yeshua as the Messiah, too. No, thank you." She slapped her palms on her knees and stood. "So Romeo hasn't converted yet. Well! That says something about his head being on right." She yawned. "I'm dead tired and going to bed. You coming or not?"

Allison looked toward the luminous moon, and her heart knew a pang of memory. "Yes," she said quietly. "In a moment. Good night, Marra."

Marra mumbled something and pushed her way back into the tent.

THREE

When you walk through the fire, you shall not be burned.
ISAIAH 43:2

DESPITE PRIVATIONS AND HARDSHIPS, the mood at camp was optimistic when a week later Allison walked with Wade across the compound for lunch in the officers' quarters. The day was typically hot—glaring sun bore down on the sand and rock, threatening to scorch everything in sight.

Allison, wearing her best nursing uniform, which swirled about her high-top boots, and a nursing scarf over her flame-colored hair, smiled at Wade as they walked together. "You know what I keep thinking about?" she sighed.

"An ice cream sundae?"

She laughed. "No, a green salad…with ripe, sweet tomatoes from Mum's garden, cucumbers, radishes, and crisp lettuce smothered with dressing—"

Wade groaned. "Keep that up and the Turks won't need to brainwash us into surrendering. How 'bout some Crawford's stew instead?"

She grimaced. Crawford's stew, named after their unpopular commander, was what the soldiers were calling the terrible rations. Lack of proper rations was beginning to grow serious. A month ago the encampment ran out of fresh vegetables, and supplies were painfully slow in arriving on the few flat-bottomed boats that could make it safely down the Tigris.

Wade was serious now. "Medical supplies are running low. With a battle in the wind, I wonder about the Tommies. Did you hear about Lieutenant General Bentley?" He looked at her. "He's fallen ill—of what I'm not told—but he's going to be replaced by Major General Townsend from the India forces."

Wade stopped in the middle of the compound some hundred feet from the mess hall. Soldiers were milling about, recuperating from injuries of all sorts. Some of the men waved or called to Allison as they hobbled by. She had grown accustomed to becoming the secret sweetheart of lonely young men far from home and took their attentions for what they were, an outlet that meant little. Of course, there had been occasions when she needed to be firm with several who had been too energetic in falling in love with their nurse. Allison regretted that. It was hard for her to be firm because she felt so sorry for them, knowing so many would never go home. She wasn't sure which was worse, not going home at all or going home blind, crippled, or mentally deficient. More than ever lately she longed for true spiritual work to be done among the thousands of soldiers coming to Arabia and Egypt from England, Australia, and New Zealand. She hadn't said anything to Wade, but she'd been nearly as disappointed as he when the chaplain's position, which he had expected to receive on arrival from London, had been phased out.

Wade had accepted the closed door as coming from the Lord. "Medicine was what I'd trained for before I ever went to BTC," he told her when he arrived in Cairo. "At least I'll be able to help the chaplain coming out from India. There'll be days when he can't preach," he told her optimistically, "and I'll be able to fill in for him."

So far the opportunity hadn't arrived, and Wade spent his free time—what little there was of it—trying to make the small YMCA-style recreational tent spiritually conducive to meeting the needs of the Christian soldiers. But more often than not, he was bandaging the wounded, dispensing medicine, and aiding Doc Murphy in surgery.

"He's got a temper like a disgruntled camel," Wade told Allison now, watching the big bearded man stride toward the mess hall, his chin jutted forward.

Allison smiled. It was true, she knew. As was the fact that Doc Murphy was dedicated to the men.

"I dropped one of the surgical instruments, and I actually thought he was going to hit me," said Wade.

"Try to be patient," Allison soothed him. "Think how he must feel—he's a good deal older than we are, and this heat and the long, endless hours are debilitating. He's under so much pressure, as we all are, but he's the only full-fledged physician. We can only do so much. I don't know what would happen if Doc Murphy got sick."

"Let's not talk about it. Maybe it won't happen." Wade's light blue eyes flickered in the sunlight. "You know what he said when I questioned him about running out of morphine this morning?"

"I don't think I want to know."

Wade laughed at her rueful statement, and they walked on slowly. The thought of tasteless salty stew did nothing for their hunger except to make them long even more for the meals of home.

"All right," she said. "What did Doc say about the morphine running out?"

"He said: 'Then we'll need to send you to the Turk commander, Nur-ud-Din, to borrow some, won't we?'"

Allison winced. "Sarcastic, indeed. Did he really say that to you?"

"He did, and the way he looked at me I think he meant it." Wade laughed. "Now I know why the Lord put me here to work with Doc. 'Count it all joy when ye fall into various trials and testings, knowing that the trial of your faith worketh patience,'" he quoted from the epistle of James.

Allison turned to smile at Wade's positive outlook when the squawking sound of motorcar horns and the revving of engines stopped her. She and Wade halted and looked ahead. A motor bicycle with a snapping flag led a delegation of four open-top military vehicles across the sandy flat.

"Looks like the entourage has arrived from British India," said Wade.

Allison thought of her father, Sir Marshall Wescott. There was little chance he would be in that delegation, but even so, her heart knew a moment of hopeful anticipation.

"I heard them talking about it this morning at the hospital," said Wade. "It's Major General Townsend to replace Bentley. From what I've overheard, both Townsend and the general are self-serving and incompetent."

The Sixth Division had advanced far from its original operation of securing the oil pipeline at Qurna. Here, near Basra, they were some 320 miles inland from their original goal; with Amara, Kut, and Baghdad ahead.

The military vehicles came to a halt, and a small colony of high-ranking officers, each one smartly uniformed, stepped out onto the sand. Allison noted the polished knee-high boots, duckbill hats, gold braid, sabers, revolvers—

Then her gaze locked with that of an officer who lingered beside the vehicle a moment longer than the others. He pushed his hat back from his thick dark hair and stared in her direction, steely blue eyes watching without expression. A warm, almost sickening weakness took her breath away.

"Allison! You've gone so pale! The sun getting to you?" came Wade's concerned voice. "We better get inside."

She was aware of his hand on her elbow as he bent to squint at her. She ripped her gaze from Major Bret Holden's to look at Wade, her eyes seeking support. She took solace in his placid, light blue eyes, as though they brought her spiritual refreshment. She smiled.

"It's just the thought of Crawford's stew," she told him lightly, hoping to sidetrack him from suspecting what—or who—had really gotten to her. "Suddenly I don't feel up to facing it, let alone eating it. I think I'll go back to the tent. I'll get an hour's nap while I've the opportunity."

Wade looked completely confused. "Oh. Well. Of course, if you're tired, but you shouldn't miss your meals you know. You need them."

She couldn't help but smile. It was so like Wade to say something like that. He could be so naive, so gentle—so unlike Bret, who most likely would have made some cool, sophisticated response.

"I know, Wade. Thank you. But right now I'm feeling quite tired," she insisted. "You go on ahead. You don't mind eating alone?"

"Alone?" he laughed. "With fifty officers of assorted ranks, no, I don't mind being alone—" his smile turned into a frown, "but—"

"Emily will be there," she interrupted. "She was asking the other night about some Christian papers to read. It's a good opportunity. We shouldn't let it slip by."

"Yes, maybe the Lord is answering our prayers. I'm to give a small devotional before lunch." He grinned. "We'll need it before the stew is served." He shook his head, then glanced around. Allison saw his gaze come to rest on Bret where he stood by the motorcar, watching them. Her heart raced for a moment, then stilled. Wade wouldn't know it was Bret. They'd never met. He looked at her again. "Maybe I can bring you something later?"

She was anxious to escape. "No, thank you. I'll see you later at the hospital." She turned to walk away, glancing as she did so at Major Holden. While there was no way to tell at this distance, she had the odd impression that he was not surprised to see her here.

He always has the advantage, she thought, rankled. She schooled her expression to that of a stranger, not allowing the faintest crack to show in her poised demeanor, and walked past the parked vehicles with cool dignity.

Bret couldn't have spoken had he wanted, for there was some forty feet between them, but she was afraid he might call out to her. Thankfully, he did not, nor did she behave as if she saw him, though he must have wondered.

He doesn't want to see me again, either, she thought, realizing but not caring that the thought was a bit irrational. *Good.* She reached up and adjusted her scarf. *It will definitely remain that way.* She must never let him think she'd been languishing away this past year waiting for a letter, a mere crumb from his table. She would show no anxiety, offer no pleading. As much as her heart cried out to do so, she would not demand of him, "What happened? Where have you been? Why didn't you write me like you promised? I thought you—" the thought-words choked in her throat—*"I thought you loved me."*

Suddenly she heard bootsteps on the sand behind her. His voice came then, resonant, too calm....

"Allison?"

She must not stop now. She couldn't bear it. She blinked hard and kept walking. She mustn't run. He must not know how deeply she felt. She'd make a fool of herself if she ran. Everyone would know, including Wade. . . .

As her pace quickened, Bret didn't call again, and she became aware that his steps no longer pursued her. Was she disappointed? She told herself she wasn't. She needed this time to be alone, to adjust to the fact that he was here. But how long would he be here? She felt panic. *Please, not for long.*

The hot sun reached down to steal away her strength. Heat

waves spiraled up from the sand, and not a breath of wind stirred. *I won't faint. I won't.*

When she reached her tent quarters, she was so exhausted, physically and emotionally, that she nearly stumbled inside. She was relieved to see that Emily had already left for the mess hall, and that Marra was still on duty until three that afternoon. She had time to be alone, to think...to recover.

So David had been right.

She poured water from a canteen into a small bowl and wet a washcloth. Bret had been back in Egypt and Palestine for months. And he must have gone to India on military matters, accompanying Major General Townsend here to Arabia to serve with General Nixon. As though drained from the heat, she laid the wet cloth to her face, then to the back of her neck. She glanced toward the tent doorway, half expecting to hear his bootsteps. Except for the stark hissing cry of a desert bird in the sparse shade of a tree, only silence greeted her.

He wouldn't come after me, she thought, beginning to calm. He was much to cool and casual for that. If he hadn't wanted to write and contact her before, he surely wouldn't feel pressed to come and offer some ineffective excuse. He would give their relationship that much respect. There would be no pleading between them, no lack of dignity. He already knew that she wasn't the type to run after him if she thought he didn't want her attentions. He would also know that she had accepted his year of silence as an intentional closed door between them.

Still...it insulted everything that might have been between them when he had simply disappeared without offering even a polite explanation. At least he could have said, "I've thought over what I thought we felt at Charchemish, and I was wrong. I'm sorry. Good-bye."

And she would have let him go.

She looked at her image in the mirror, searching her eyes as a stranger would. Who was this girl that stared back? Did she know her as well as she believed? *Would* she have let him go?

She pressed her lips together firmly. Yes, and he knew it as well. Could that have been one of the reasons he hadn't bothered to be gentle in saying good-bye? He thought her too aloof?

No. I'm only looking for an excuse because I don't want to lose him. If I think he had a good reason—then I'd forgive his too-long silence.

She didn't throw the washcloth down in frustration, though she was sorely tempted. Instead, she laid it down gently and looked down at her fingers. They trembled. A sign that all was not right in her heart. It bled.

She loved him.

She gave a little cry of rage and, grabbing the washbowl, hurled it out the tent.

A saint, was she? So David and Wade both thought. Oh, how wrong they were! Only God knew her true condition. She turned away, her hands gripping the table, and allowed the hot tears to run down her face. Thank God no one was here! No one saw her! *I want to be alone! I want everyone to just go away and leave me alone!*

She half stumbled to her cot and threw herself down, burying her face under one arm, while her fingers clawed the thin coverlet. "I hate him," she mumbled into the material, doubling her fist and pounding the bed with total frustration.

CHAPTER

FOUR

A bruised reed He will not break.
ISAIAH 42:3

"ALL RIGHT, I CONFESS, OK? I did know he returned to Egypt months ago."

Allison glared at David, unwilling to accept his apology. "And you didn't tell me. So why tell me now, when it doesn't matter to me what the major does?"

He cocked his head, and his expression told her he didn't believe her. "When we talked last week in the mess hall, I thought you knew he was in Cairo. Then I could see you didn't. I thought I'd best keep quiet about it. This matter is between you and the colonel."

Colonel. She thought back to his masquerade as the German Colonel Holman. "So he's a colonel again."

He shrugged. "For real this time. Some guys are dedicated. He deserved the promotion."

Just then, Marra walked by and paused. She looked pointedly at David's corporal stripe. "You're not including yourself in the celebrated round of dedicated military are you, Romeo?"

David's brown eyes squinted at her. "Say, sweetheart, who asked your nosy opinion?"

Marra wrinkled her nose and smiled too sweetly, then walked over to give one of the soldiers his medication.

David was still glowering after Marra when Allison dried her hands on the sterilized towel. She glanced back at her patient stretched out on the cot and raised her watch. She told herself she was settled in her decision.

"You can tell the colonel I'm too busy to get away."

She untied her apron, dropped it on the bench, and walked to the back of the hospital tent.

David sighed and followed. "Give it a chance, Allison."

"No, thank you."

"Just a late night chat at the recreation tent when you get off duty? What's a chat?"

She looked at him accusingly, her voice in a low whisper so Doc Murphy wouldn't hear. He was in the next partition and David wasn't supposed to be here. "You're a fine one to try to talk me into this! There was a time when you didn't want me to see him, or anyone else, including Wade!"

He shoved his hands into his pockets and sulked. "I've wised up is all. I don't stand a chance, and we both know it. You know if I thought I did—"

He stopped abruptly, and her conscience was smitten. She shouldn't have spoken to him like that. She'd been unfair. She didn't want David to care about her in that way, because he was right. "David, I'm sorry—"

He halted her. "Don't be," he said too casually. "I understand. We're friends, good ones. Think nothing of it."

The cynicism in his voice heightened her despair. For a selfish moment she wished they *were* more than friends. That would have protected her from dealing with the pain she felt.

David continued, more sincerely now. "The colonel's a friend of mine, too. He's a great guy, Allison. One in a million."

She knew that, but she was wishing she didn't.

"Look, I've an idea. I'll come with you. We'll have tea, he can say what he wants, and then I'll bring you back here."

"It's no good."

"Yeah, you're right. He wouldn't go for it." He grew silent, fingering the note Bret had given him to deliver to her.

The thought of the note stirred her anger again. The colonel wanted to see her. Alone. Nothing else, just that. He wanted to speak with her at the recreation tent. It was like him. Brief, demanding, yet giving little of himself in return. He had even sent David instead of coming himself. Well, she was disinclined to accommodate the dear colonel!

But was she being fair? Was Bret really so ruthless, so cynical? Maybe she was being proud and stubborn, simply to show him she could live without him. This way she could prove he didn't own her. She could say, "You haven't hurt me. You can't, you see, because I just don't care."

What a pity it wasn't true.

She stood as if in a trance, listening to the distant rumble of artillery, remembering another time, another place, when she'd realized just how deeply she did care.

"Allison?" said David quietly.

She turned her head to look at him, and she didn't bother to hide what she knew was reflected in her eyes: frustration, fear, pain that throbbed in her soul.

David lapsed into silence, leaning against the table, his gaze moving over the fifty or more men on the cots, some of whom were in too much pain to know they were even there.

"What a blighty mess," he ground out.

Allison blinked hard and blew her nose.

"I've heard we're moving to the front soon. It'd be a tragedy if either of you let pride ruin what you have. That kind of bond isn't easy to come by, but it's far too easy to lose."

Her eyes faltered, fixing on the watch. Time.

"There's more to Bret than that uniform he wears, and you know it. He's risked his life for his friends when he wasn't supposed to. He's done it for Rose, for me, and Neal. And for you, if I recall. He's one great guy."

She was trying to muzzle the nagging voices that contradicted her decision. She turned away, fighting exasperation with herself. "Will you stop sounding his trumpet? I don't need you to tell me that. I want to forget!"

"All right then, so be it. I've run out of words."

A growling voice interrupted: "I hope so. Look, corporal, stop hanging around here, will you? Go water your camels," said Doc Murphy, his hair awry and a scowl on his worn face. "Don't you ever have duty? I'll need to talk to your commanding officer about this. Now get moving!"

David saluted. "Yes, sir!" he barked and hurried away.

Allison looked after him, and Doc Murphy popped a stomach pill for his ulcers, eyeing her narrowly. Then when she flushed, he strode away.

"Marra!"

"Coming, Doc!" Marra snatched fresh bandages from the table and hurried after him.

FIVE

Be still, and know that I am God.
PSALM 46:10

I DON'T LOVE HER, Colonel Bret Holden informed himself again, as he had done countless times during the past year. His silence, if not intended to portray him as inconsiderate and ruthless, had been deliberate and meant to convey his well-thought-out decision to break off any further relationship with Allison Wescott before it had the opportunity to progress.

No, he wasn't going to get involved again. He would stick to his decision. It was right; it made sense. So the feelings that had resurfaced when he accidentally ran into her that afternoon had startled him with their intensity. It was only the shock of seeing her here, in this miserable location. At least, that's what he'd been telling himself since that brief encounter. Whatever emotions stirred to life again were a desert mirage. They couldn't be trusted. They were the kind of strong but fatal attraction two people felt for each other in time of war, when the crises of life and death turned the best minds into putty and otherwise honorable hearts into foolishness.

He'd behaved unwisely in the past. He never should have promised he would find her again, for in that promise was the certain hint that he must have her, that he couldn't live without her.

And can you?

He quelled the impertinent question with an angry snort. He had to put the lid on this situation now. Once and for all time! If one wasn't careful, those untrustworthy feelings could erupt like a volcano—and leave as much ruin in their path as any searing lava flow.

I don't love her, his mind recited coolly. He wouldn't permit himself to love any woman. The war would drag on for years, he was sure of it. The common citizens expected it to be all over by Christmas, but he knew better. Christmas would come and go, followed by spring, and the destruction and misery would go on.

His eyes narrowed. He was determined to squelch any feelings, to keep them from stirring to life again, as coolly and methodically as he had recently stared down the German officer in France who had held him prisoner, holding a Luger aimed at his heart. The Luger, which now rested in his shoulder holster, was evidence of who had won that encounter.

His bootsteps sounded on the hollow wooden floor as he walked over to one of the many empty benches and tables at the back of the tent. In the shadows, he stood moodily, looking out across the dark compound toward the hospital tent and medical quarters.

So if you're so detached, why are you here still waiting when she hasn't shown up?

He ignored the question. He knew the ways of women well enough. His silence this past year had hurt her, and she was now in a position to punish him for that silence. He deserved it, he supposed. Still, his reasons had been logical, and not all of them were for his own preservation, but for hers. He'd told her on that train from Damascus that she was too noble for him. It was true. So why didn't he take the door she was leaving open for him now and make his casual departure? It would make sense. By walking away again, he could show her she couldn't punish him. She could only do that if he cared deeply.

And, of course, he didn't. He wouldn't permit it.

Nor, it seemed, would he permit himself to leave the tent. He removed his duckbilled officer's cap and dropped it on the table, frowning at it.

Lanterns glowed and voices filtered through the night sounds. The fingers of wind tugged at the front lapel of his jacket, which regulations deemed he must wear despite the sweltering heat. Of course, the jacket also concealed his shoulder holster.

He looked at the tin mug of tea he held. Whatever was inside tasted like lukewarm water. He looked toward the field hospital, brooding. What would he say to her? How would he explain? He hadn't intended to, until the misfortune of seeing her today. *Misfortune*—? Did he mean that?

"'Yes!" he muttered fiercely. "Misfortune!" What else could it be? It had stirred to life emotions better left dead, or at least numb. He didn't want to care and he wouldn't, no matter how strong the emotional bond that seemed to grip them that night at Carchemish. A bond that had been short lived, by his own choice. War was no time for love, no time to become involved in an affair of hearts. He'd almost been killed in France. He would be in equal—or worse— danger again. The more he allowed her to care for him, the more selfish he became, and the more danger *she* was in; because if he did think her noble, he wouldn't leave her alone. What if one day she was a widow…no, worse: a married woman facing a man without arms or limbs. Then what?

Yes, he had held and kissed her, and for a month after his return to London, he couldn't get her out of his mind. But he had emerged unscathed from all that dangerous sentiment in the past year, and he meant to keep it that way.

Then why are you still here? the question repeated. *Why don't you simply make your plans to leave and return to Cairo?*

Irritably, he waited, growing more moody by the moment.

It was suffocating inside the recreational tent, even though the fly netting was rolled up on all four sides and the hot wind blew through, sometimes in gusts strong enough to send sand scattering across the flooring. Off-duty soldiers sitting on canvas chairs grouped around tables were playing cards or shooting dice. A few men played harmonicas, and the melancholy music moaned on the dry wind that sent the canvas roofing flapping monotonously. Despite Bret's usual efforts to repress his feelings, the atmosphere of loss and death, and the memories of a less demanding time, were driving at him, leaving cracks in his emotional armor. If he surrendered to them and allowed himself to remember too many things best forgotten…

He clenched his jaw. He wouldn't allow himself to remember, to become an emotional slave. Emotions meant weakness. Weakness meant you—or the people you cared about—got hurt.

He tasted the weak tea and narrowed his eyes, glancing at his watch again. It was ten-thirty; Allison had gotten off duty at ten. So she'd refused him. He flipped the brew onto the sand and beckoned for the soldier on duty, who left the harmonica players and hurried up.

"Yes, Colonel?"

Bret handed him the tin mug. Affecting thoughtfulness he tapped his chin. "I'm remembering my dear old mammy."

"Yes, sir."

"She used to make the best tea in Cornwall."

"Sir?" the corporal questioned uneasily, eyeing him as though wondering if he were all right.

Bret's eyes narrowed. "You, however, have accomplished the exact opposite! This brew is disgusting. You look like a brilliant fellow. Next time you make tea, Corporal, don't just simmer the water, but bring it to a boil before adding the leaves. Is that understood?"

"Yes, sir!"

"Good." He looked toward the field hospital. "The nurses over there—do they come here often?"

"You mean the women, sir?"

Bret felt his mouth twitch. "Yes, Corporal. Women."

The soldier grinned. "Sometimes, sir."

"There's one in particular I'm curious about."

"We're all curious, sir, but it don't do us no good."

"Her name is Allison Wescott."

"Yes, sir! That's the one, with the shiny red hair."

Bret raked the younger man with a cool glance. "And don't forget the green eyes."

"Oh, no, sir, I wouldn't, I couldn't—"

"I didn't think so."

"She comes now and then, not often though. A real lady that one, and saintly, too. When she does come, it's only for an hour or so, and then it's with a religious fella. He wears specs and has red hair, too, but its sort of a muddy-looking brown."

"You're very observant, Corporal. Do you know the name of the soldier she comes here with?"

"No, but—" he turned to one of the harmonica players— "Hey Tommy, what's that fella's name who helps the chaplain?"

The tall, lanky soldier with freckles and homesick eyes lowered his beat-up harmonica. "Wade Findlay."

So…Allison and Wade were together again. Bret had been unaware that either of them were here with the field hospital. He'd been so taken up with his duties that he had let personal inquiries slip. Wade's presence here cast a new light on matters, including, perhaps, the reason why Allison had chosen not to meet him tonight. The man she'd been walking with when he saw her, was that Wade?

"Wade led in devotions before supper tonight," said the Brit with the harmonica, and, in tribute, he began a moving rendition of "Amazing Grace" that brought a tense silence to the rec room, save for one deep voice that sang along.

"Thro' many dangers, toils, and snares, I have already come;
"Tis grace hath bro't me safe thus far, And grace will lead me home."

Bret flexed his jaw. He remembered Allison's glowing reports of Oswald Chambers's Bible Training College—and of the honorable Wade Findlay, whom she'd known there…the man she'd considered her fiancé when Bret had first met her. Though she seemed to have all but forgotten Findlay during their time together, in a setting like this, with death all around, their bond of shared Christian faith may have brought their hearts together.

And his silence over the last year most likely had helped that bond along.

Bret contemplated his own faith in the Lord as the harmonica music and the words of the hymn walked gently through his soul. He was certain of Jesus Christ, certain that he was Lord and Savior, certain that he had believed in Christ since a young boy. Certain, too, of the decision to trust Jesus that he'd made in his grandmother's attic in London. There'd been an old painting of the Crucifixion on the wall, all-but-forgotten since it had been brought up to hide away in the attic by some fashion-conscious mistress of the big house who had replaced it with a boring painting of a bowl of pink roses. Bret, who had no parents, had been raised in Charles H. Spurgeon's school for boys until a woman in her sixties, whom he called his grandmother, had brought him to live with her. Between the painting and his "granny"—who had the real name of Mattie—he'd put his trust in the One who had willingly died on a cross, shedding his blood to redeem sinners.

Bret smiled, remembering how thrilled his granny had been with his decision—and how she'd brought the painting downstairs and hung it in the entrance hall.

"He ought to have first place in any home," she had said.

Footsteps outside on the sand caused him to turn. If he anticipated limpid green eyes and flame-colored tresses blowing in the Arabian wind, he showed nothing—not even a keen disappointment—when his broad-shouldered and stocky bulldog assistant from Cairo, Captain Mel Colby, entered. As usual, Colby looked grumpy and bleary eyed from the blowing dust and sand. He stood at attention in his too-tight uniform.

Bret tried not to smile. Colby looked miserable. The common soldier had many problems, and one of them was his uniform. It was made of heavy woolen material, usually ill-fitting and anything but wind or water repellent. The spiral leggings, or "puttees" as they were called, consisted of a long strip of woolen fabric wound around the legs from the ankles up and fastened with a tape tucked at the top. It took time to put them on, and they frequently came unwrapped at the worst possible moment.

Bret, as an officer, fared better since he could spend his own money to have his uniforms made. They were stylish, made of the best materials, topped off with the popular leather Sam Brown belt and with comfortable leather boots to wear instead of the wraparound woolen puttees.

There were decided advantages to being an officer.

"I thought I gave you leave to get some shut-eye."

Colby swallowed, his Adam's apple bobbing above his tight collar. "I had my blasted puttees off, sir, when the bell rang. Major General Crawford's asking to see you at once."

Bret picked up his hat and set it smartly on his head. "I suppose he has insomnia again. At least something has worked in our favor;

he must have my report. Maybe he has a wire from General Paxton to pull back to Abadan."

"Crawford's chief of staff says Paxton's not here. He's meeting with the British viceroy in India. One thing's for sure, Crawford's got his map out. He's anxious to carve up the Turks at Baghdad."

"I was afraid of that."

"I've got the motorcycle outside, sir."

Crawford had served in British India and had been requested by General Paxton to take over for the ailing lieutenant general. Bret was concerned that Crawford might live up to his reputation of authorizing too many risks with the Sixth Division.

From what Bret had heard through Major General Crawford's personal friends and enemies, he was out to make a name for the Sixth Division. In Bret's judgment, the general's determination, though honorable, bordered on recklessness with his troops. Perhaps that was the real reason he'd decided to stay to speak to Allison. She was serving in the worst possible field hospital—the one place where there would be the most danger, except for the front trench lines in France or Antwerp! That she was here frustrated him. Her dedication earned both his respect and a temper he couldn't explain.

Bret had come to the camp with information from the intelligence office in Cairo on the recent buildup of Turkish troops in the region. He hoped to avert a new forward thrust to capture Baghdad. Bret had a dozen reasons why he believed such an advance would lead to a defeat rather than victory. The information from intelligence backed him up. But would Crawford pay heed? The general wanted that victory badly enough to drool over it. Now, the fact he was calling for Bret aroused his doubts. He wouldn't have had time yet to study that information.

Bret followed Colby to the waiting motorcycle. Attached to the vehicle was a sidecar mounted with a Hotchkiss machine gun. The sidecar, unlike most other units, had two wheels of its own that also acted as a gun carriage when the sidecar was separated from the motorcycle. Bret got into the sidecar while Colby rubbed his eyes and shook his head clear, then started up the cycle. They rode out across the sandy compound toward Crawford's command post.

Bret gave a last glance toward the hospital. David hadn't told him Wade Findlay was stationed here. His tanned fingers drummed the sidecar door as he settled back, propping his black polished boots on the gun rigging.

Forget Findlay, he thought. *Forget Allison. Forget them all.*

With a supreme effort, he forced his attention on the reason that had brought him here.

In 1914, the British Royal Navy had nearly completed converting its capital ships to use oil rather than coal. When war broke last August, the fleet facing German destroyers and U-boats was dependent on oil, which came primarily from the refinery on Abadan Island at the head of the Persian Gulf. Knowing this, in October, prior to Turkey's entry into the war, the British colonial government in India had wisely dispatched its Sixth Poonah Division for the purpose of protecting the refinery at Abadan, some four hundred miles down the Tigris River from Baghdad. Four days after England declared war on Turkey, the Sixth Division landed at Fao. The Turkish response had been slow; by the time troops had been sent from Basra, the British force was in control, supported by gunboats on the Shatt-al-Arab estuary. When the British attacked the trench line at Sahil, the Turks broke and ran, losing many of their number and leaving Basra undefended.

Unfortunately, from Bret's point of view, matters had progressed beyond protecting the navy's dependence on oil. The British success against the feeble Turkish resistance had falsely encouraged the commanders in India to order a farther advance inland to Qurna, at the confluence of the Tigris and Euphrates Rivers. Following light resistance, Qurna fell on December 9, 1914 a few months after Bret had arrived back from London to take up his post at Cairo Intelligence. The oil refinery at Abadan, the original objective, was now fifty miles behind the British front, and troops of the Sixth Division controlled the only route to the pipeline. The British government considered the campaign successfully concluded, but unwise political decisions in British India—and on the part of the general on the field—had reopened the tactical front. Bret's intelligence report from his secret work in Baghdad and Constantinople warned of the danger that awaited the Sixth Division.

Since his arrival yesterday, Bret had become even more convinced that the decision to press forward to capture Kut and Baghdad was a mistake that would lead to disaster.

"It's one thing to secure the oil at Abadan," he told Colby, "but quite another to take on the Turks in their backyard."

"Crawford is deluded, if you ask me, sir. He has our report. If it were Field Marshal French here, he'd be smart enough to pull back to Abadan. Or at least to Qurna."

The BEF, once stationed in Egypt, had since been withdrawn and sent to fight in France under Field Marshal Sir John D. P. French. The withdrawal of the BEF from Egypt was another matter of concern to Bret. Intelligence expected Kress von Kressenstein to attack on the Suez Canal in an attempt to take Cairo. Bret wondered if the unseasoned colonial troops from Australia and New Zealand, which had been sent to fill the gap of the trained BEF, were up to holding these more experienced troops back.

Here in Arabia, the field commander, appointed by British India which considered itself the authority on this region, had already requested more troops, especially cavalry. But the British secretary of state in India, Austin Chamberlain, had been concerned that the general was overly aggressive in his plans.

The general believed his position near Kut and Baghdad secure, but Bret knew he was in error. The earlier attack by the German Zeppelin proved that.

The secretary of state in India had wired the British viceroy that no advance beyond the present theater of operation was to be sanctioned. Bret agreed. Aside from the military futility of advancing into Arabia, any further operations could not be supported because of the impending invasion of Constantinople. That attack would draw all British troops and supplies that could be spared from Northeastern France. But the general had continued his request for more reinforcements and for permission to seize Kut. Reluctant to overrule the military men in the field, the viceroy and the political leaders in London had finally sanctioned the advance.

Bret could only hope his information, which proved the forward advance unwise and a risk not only to the soldiers but to the field hospital, would stop the general. If not...

Thoughts of Allison intruded again, intensifying the concerns that had brought him here. He had no choice. He had to get Allison back to Cairo.

The motorcycle scattered sand as it drew to a stop outside the command post where several flags snapped in a gust of wind. Bret stepped from the sidecar and returned the guard's salute, then turned to Colby. "Get some sleep. I'll be here awhile. Crawford's long winded."

A member of Crawford's staff waited, and Bret followed him into the large desert tent. It was crowded with chairs and tables, and a large map was pinned on the wall behind Crawford's desk. Other members of his staff manned stacks of papers, reference books, and more maps. There was a wireless station set up in the adjoining room to report Turkish troop movements. Messages were sent by code rather than voice. Equipment was carried in a Signal Corps trailer drawn by light truck. There was a bamboo aerial mast, and the operator of the wireless wore a heavy headset. The range was limited and not always accurate, but still it was tremendously important to military maneuvers.

Nearby a sparse man with thinning hair sat stiffly beside a table with a wobbly leg, a well-oiled typewriter before him. One of the staff had brewed coffee and offered Bret a cup.

"Arabian coffee, Colonel. Beats anything you'll find over in the mess hall."

Major General Crawford entered from another cubbyhole, wide awake and looking in a pugnacious mood. Bret knew he was in for conflict and saluted smartly. "General Crawford."

Crawford was a prototypical commander, the sort Bret had seen often in his military career. The general stood with his shoulders straight, his arms at his sides, dressed in full regalia down to the pair of dark brown leather gloves he held in one hand, as though prepared to take a jaunt on a white stallion to look over his troops. Square of face and liquid of eye, his bottlebrush mustache lined a hard, narrow mouth that formed a drooping half circle.

"Colonel," he clipped a greeting. He flipped his glove toward a chair in a command to sit.

"I'd rather stand, sir, if you don't mind."

Crawford tossed his gloves on the desk. "I've read your report. It's what I would expect from the nervous hens at Cairo Intelligence."

Bret showed none of his inner anger at this cavalier attitude. He would have liked to tell the arrogant Crawford that those involved in gathering intelligence faced death more often than the general ever had.

"I don't know the nervous hens you speak of, General. I only know the men doing their job at considerable risk from German Lugers and Turkish scimitars."

Crawford waved a hand. "Nothing personal, my boy! I've heard good things of you from the war office in London, but the conclusions in this report—" he snapped his fingers at his secretary who jumped to his feet and handed it to him— "Are a bunch of rot!" He dropped the report onto the desk beside his gloves.

Bret's gaze fixed on the papers. He'd written the report himself from firsthand knowledge. It contained anything but "rot."

A tense silence settled over the men in the command post as Bret waited.

Studying Bret, Crawford held out a hand to one of his staff, who promptly filled it with a mug of coffee.

"With all due respect, Colonel, I can only say that the information must be rejected. Our decision to move forward toward Baghdad must, and *will*, proceed."

"Do you reject it, sir, because you have reason to believe my report is unfounded?"

Crawford raised his mug and took a swallow. "No. I've no doubt that the Turkish commander Nur-ud-Din has arrived at Baghdad with reinforcements for the Thirty-Seventh. Your information is noteworthy, and you're to be commended for a duty well done."

The secretary shifted in his uncomfortable hard-backed chair, setting the table beneath his typewriter to rocking precariously.

Crawford walked over to his large map and stood with his back toward them, fingers interlocked behind him as he stared at it.

"I suggest Cairo and its ties to the London War Office permit the command in British India to control operations here in Mesopotamia. If I recall, General Maxwell has enough problems dealing with the Germans and Turks trying to overrun the Suez Canal."

Bret focused his attention on the coffee. He calmly lifted his mug and drank. The captain was right; it beat anything he might get from one of the Tommies.

Crawford turned his head and favored Bret with a glance. "I must say, Colonel, that I think you wholly overestimate the fighting capability of the Turkish army. My men can defeat them—here and here." Taking the pointer offered by his secretary, the general went on to tap out the two areas that lay between his Sixth Division and Baghdad on the Tigris River: Amara, and Kut-al-Amara.

Bret didn't argue. He drank his coffee and said calmly, "I've no doubt the soldiers of the Sixth Division from British India are of excellent fighting caliber, sir."

"But you still disagree with the decision coming from the top?"

Bret knew he spoke of General Paxton, a man brilliant in many ways but considered by some to be incompetent. "General Nur-ud-Din has thirty-five thousand rested soldiers fresh from the Constantinople region," countered Bret. "And as my report carefully points out, sir, Baghdad is newly refortified. He expects you to attack. Surprise is half the victory. He's prepared and waiting."

"I'm aware of that, as are General Paxton and the British viceroy of India. Needless to say, Colonel, we'll defeat him. I've no doubt of it."

"But you'll admit we have logistical problems with supplies and water, sir. It's all in my report—"

"I've studied your report, Colonel!"

"Yes, sir! But what's not in my report is what I've learned since my arrival here. Your field hospital is filled with soldiers, less than half are wounded from combat. The men are suffering with disease, exhaustion, dysentery—"

"We also have a report." The general gritted his teeth and turned to his secretary. "Read it!"

The secretary stood from behind his typewriter and, holding a document in shaking hands, began to read off the recent victories in rapid-fire succession. Major General Crawford sat in the chair behind his desk, removed a long-stemmed black pipe, and filled it. His staff officer struck a match and leaned toward him, holding the flame steady.

Bret stood, hands behind his back, listening to the victories, every one of which he was already well aware.

The pipe tobacco spiraled like homage incense praising Crawford's military prowess.

"On 31 May, Major General Crawford began his advance with an attack on the Turkish position north of Qurna."

Bret looked at the map. The location was circled in black.

"The extensive marshes in this region, due to the seasonal overflow of the Tigris and Euphrates, came between the British and Turks, and the Sixth Division had to pole forward in native flat-bottomed boats, many of them shielded with iron boilerplate. Once the Turkish position was breached, the enemy panicked and fled. Major General Crawford and less than one hundred soldiers then boarded five river gunboats and relentlessly pursued the beaten Turks all the way north to Amara. By the time the remainder of the Sixth division had caught up with its vanguard, Crawford had captured two thousand enemy troops and sunk three gunboats. Along with the capture of Nasiriyeh, and the seizure of Amara—"

Crawford held up his hand. "Enough, Lionel."

"Yes, sir!"

Crawford looked pointedly at Bret. "Colonel Holden gets our point."

"Your victory is hailed in Cairo, sir, and General Paxton has urged London to grant permission to seize Kut-al-Amara, but—"

"No 'buts' required, Colonel. Request already granted! Know that it was our success in routing the Turks here that has convinced London and the British viceroy in India to reinforce the Sixth Division for a further advance on Baghdad. I sit on its doorstep, a mere forty miles away."

"It's also true, sir, that the bulk of your command is twenty-four hours removed. You would be without reinforcements should you find yourself trapped and cut off."

Crawford stood impatiently, chomping on his pipe stem.

"Your work as an intelligence officer is held in high honor. However, the command in Mesopotamia does not ultimately rest with those in Cairo, but with Sir Beauchamp Duff, commander in chief of the British Indian army, who by the way, has already instructed General Paxton and me to retain control of all lower Mesopotamia, to secure the oil pipeline."

"We're well aware, sir, of a mission completed: the oil is secure. May I say, sir, I'm not the only one who believes an attack on Baghdad will prove a grave error?"

Crawford smiled patiently, but his bulldog eyes were hard. "I'll not recommend court-martial for an opinion expressed, Colonel. We'll just have to prove you wrong," he said sharply.

"As you say, sir."

"Since you're with Cairo Intelligence, Colonel Holden, it won't be necessary to see the British victory firsthand. You may return to your office to hear about it."

Again, Bret did not allow his frustration to show. "I've already made request at Cairo to remain, should it be necessary, sir. I received permission from the viceroy in India before I left Cairo."

Crawford was plainly startled by what he believed inconsistency in Bret's behavior. Bret remained expressionless as he removed the letter from under his jacket and handed it to the general.

"Let me get this straight, Colonel. You disagree with our advance into Mesopotamia to take Baghdad, yet you've already sought permission to remain?"

"Yes, General. I have my reasons."

Crawford looked at him a long moment, then read the letter. "Does this decision have anything to do with Sir Marshall's daughter? You wouldn't be the first to talk with me about her, you know."

Bret was aware of the glances shot his way by the others.

"No, sir, it has to do with the Berlin Baghdad Railway. I didn't know Sir Marshall's daughter was serving in the field hospital until I arrived this afternoon. But my staying on for a time does concern her now. I expect to oversee her transfer to Alexandria before the advance on Kut."

The other staffers glanced at Crawford, who dropped the letter on his desk. "Nurses are desperately needed. We've hundreds of sick soldiers. There will be casualties in the upcoming battles. While I understand and share your concern, the field hospitals always remain a safe distance behind the front trench line."

"I wouldn't call the field hospital here at Basra behind the lines, sir. The nurses are at risk with the main troops a day from here."

"Does she wish to return?" he asked bluntly.

"I haven't spoken to her about it yet."

"If she wishes to return to Egypt, she'll need to arrange it with Secretary of War Kitchener."

"That would take weeks, General Crawford."

"So it would, Colonel. As I said, we need every available nurse, whether she's the daughter of Sir Marshall Wescott or not. And now, neither General Paxton nor I are inclined to alter our plans to humor Cairo. The offensive to capture Kut and Baghdad will go forward. We'll be moving out within the next few days, and I give you leave, Colonel, to return to Cairo, or do your business with the Baghdad Railway. If you intend to blow it up, I wish you Godspeed." He looked at his watch, puffing on his pipe. "I have an early morning staff meeting." He casually saluted. "Good night, Colonel."

Bret knew his anger sparked in his eyes, but he found he didn't care. He saluted too sharply and, turning on his heel, was striding toward the exit when Crawford said more gently: "How goes the war on the western front, Colonel?"

Bret turned his head, restraining his anger. Was he serious?

"Maybe a thousand Brits are dying every day. The Germans are using poison gas. They're within weeks of marching into Paris. Belgium is in rubble; we're losing on the eastern front as well. Thousands of the czar's soldiers have no armaments for their artillery, no bullets for their rifles, no boots for their feet, no bread to eat. And the British secretary of war has unwisely agreed to land troops on the Dardanelles to take Constantinople—an impossible feat since the Turks hold the high ground. All in all, General Crawford, I'd say we're in a bad way."

Crawford calmly relit his pipe. "Precisely my conclusion, and that of British India. And perhaps now you'll think again of the reason why I must take Baghdad." He fixed Bret with a granite stare. "As you aptly say, we haven't had a victory since the Marne in France. A British victory is crucial to keep up morale for the citizens back home. We're going to give Baghdad to England as a Christmas present."

Their eyes held, and for the first time, Bret understood.

"You can wish us God's speed, Colonel Holden."

"I do, indeed, General. But before this is over, we'll need another Angel of Mons."

The general smiled slightly. "So you think it will take a mysterious, legendary force to intervene and save us from annihilation as it did during the British retreat at Mons?"

"I don't know, General," Bret replied. "But if it does, I only pray one will be there."

Without another comment, Bret left the tent and went to throw himself into the motorcycle sidecar. Sitting in silence, he stared off toward the glowing lanterns. Could he convince Allison to request a transfer? Remembering her dedication to what she believed and the sacrifice she'd made at Aleppo to regain the Constantinople papers, he knew convincing Allison of anything of the sort would be difficult.

And, unless he missed his guess, with Wade Findlay here, it would be nearly impossible.

SIX

Uphold my steps in Your paths.
PSALM 17:5

ALLISON STEPPED BACK INSIDE THE HOSPITAL, looking around with a heavy heart. Soldiers lay everywhere, some dying; others missing arms or hands; some with irreparable stomach wounds; some blinded; and some on the road to recovery—which meant they would be sent back to the front lines to confront German and Turkish bullets anew. Allison sat on the edge of a soldier's bunk and read his identification tag, then dipped a clean cloth into a bowl of water, wrung it out, and wiped his sweating face.

He groaned. "Mary...? M-ar—!"

"It's all right, Douglas," whispered Allison.

"Mary—" his trembling hand clutched her arm as he stared up at her, delirious. "Lov—you—Mary—"

"Yes, I know, Douglas. You must rest now." She would never get used to the tragic sight of dying young men calling out to wives and sweethearts. There'd been only one young soldier who had died in her arms with the name of Jesus on his lips. It was a memory she would never forget.

Allison looked upon the ruddy-faced country lad from Lancashire, England. She tried to comfort him, to ease his agony. "You'll soon be home again. It'll be summer, and the flowers will be blooming, and Mary will be waiting. And your little girl, too."

"Pamela—"

"Yes, Pamela. Don't worry. The Lord is the Father of the father-less, a comfort to the orphans. He's promised rest and hope when you trust in him."

"T-hat you, Mary?"

The glazed eyes stared up at her with an empty look, as though he didn't see her, but someone else. He tried to raise his head, to speak again, but a death rattle sounded in his throat. Allison watched sadly, strained with exhaustion, drenched in sweat. The room was horribly warm, and the smell of sickness filled her nostrils. Outside an explosion shook the wooden beams, and a lantern flickered and trembled before it went out. She stared down at the soldier's face, now sealed in darkness. Her head bowed. "How much more of this can I take—?"

Slow footsteps approached, and Emily stood beside the bunk. She drew the cover over the soldier's face. "I'll bring his things to Doc. He'll see the family gets them."

Allison stood. "No, it's all right, Emily, I want to do it. I want to write his wife and little girl."

Allison stared at what was now an empty body, a fragile container vacated by the soul that had lived within. Where had the real Douglas gone? She wanted to think he'd believed in Christ and was now in the glorious presence of the Lord, experiencing great joy. She would write his wife and little girl, as she had for dozens of other soldiers since she'd arrived at the field hospital. It not only gave her an opportunity to share information loved ones would hold dear about the last hours or minutes of husbands and sons, but it also gave her the chance to tell them of the One who has conquered death.

"You're going to get sick yourself, writing all those letters. Still, a word of comfort from the Bible can't hurt anyone, that's what I always say. And if anything happened to me, I'd want my mum to think I'd see her again." She looked at Allison, frowning. "But between you and me, I don't see how you can say there's a real heaven with so much evil everywhere."

"It's not what I say that matters," Allison replied wearily. "I can't see much beyond what you do, all the death and waste. It's hard to understand where God is in the face of all of this." She shook her head. "But I can't escape the fact of God's promises in the Bible, and all that God has consistently revealed there through his prophets for thousands of years."

Emily pushed her hair back from her face, and her eyes were filled with an unutterable fatigue. "I don't know about thousands of years," she said, "I only know what I see today. And it's awful."

Allison nodded. "Yes, it is. I suppose that's why I'm so glad there is a joyous eternity to spend in God's presence. Once there, we'll see him as he is, and then we'll understand and rejoice. All sorrow and tears will pass away. 'In thy presence is fullness of joy,' it says in the Psalms."

"But didn't Christ speak more about hell than heaven? All I recall are the warnings, don't do this, don't do that."

"He warned us about hell that we might avoid it. It was made to contain the devil and his angels, but all those who die rejecting Jesus will go there, too."

Emily looked skeptical. "What kind of God would do that?"

"What kind of father would punish a child for doing wrong? One who loves deeply enough to do what's hard. God is a God of holiness and justice, as well as love. The depth of his love was revealed when Jesus suffered for us. The death of God's innocent Son was necessary in his plan for our redemption—and there is no other strong enough remedy for our sin. Imagine if one of your patients refused the medication that would make him well."

Emily scowled. "You mean if he refused the prescription? Well— I suppose he'd die."

"He couldn't blame you for his condition could he?"

"No, I guess not. It'd be his free choice, but a foolish one."

"Yes, and the person who refuses God's remedy is like that. Jesus said, 'I am the Way, the Truth and the Life. No one can come to the Father except by Me.' Emily, I wish I could help you see that the Lord Jesus is wonderful. He's the One who will fill your needs for this life and for eternity. He is God."

Emily stirred uncomfortably. "I heard all that before, mate. Maybe I'll even believe it…one of these days."

"Don't put it off," urged Allison. "Today is the day. He's standing at your heart's door and gently knocking. Yesterday is forever gone; tomorrow is always an uncertain promise, and death surrounds us. Choose Jesus, Emily. Choose life."

Emily's fingers fidgeted with the red cross sewn on her uniform. "Is that why it's red? He shed his blood for our sins?"

"Yes. And now we can be cleansed within and become whiter than snow."

"Nurse? Can you bring me water?"

Emily turned and looked over at one of the recovering patients. She smiled. "I'm coming, Jeb, but I think you just want attention."

He grinned. "How'd you know, mate?"

Emily looked back at Allison. "I guess this will have to wait a bit longer, eh? Thanks for talking, though. It was interesting." She turned to leave, then looked back at Allison. "Oh—I almost forgot. One of the officers is sick with malaria and needs quinine. Can you deliver it?"

Allison collected the dead soldier's identification papers, anxious to take her break. "Yes, I'll do it on my way. Have you seen Marra?"

"She's due back now, unless David's keeping her."

"David?" asked Allison surprised, then pleased. She smiled. "I thought they didn't like each other."

Emily rolled her eyes. "Blimey me, I don't know what gets into mates sometimes…! Must be 'cause we're moving toward the front again. We all get sentimental when we hear the artillery. If I ever get out of here and back to Cairo, I'm going with Jeb to sup at the fancy Ezbekiah Gardens. Say, you and Wade should come with us. We'll double up and dance the night away under the Egyptian stars."

She left, and Allison's smile faded. Holding Douglas's papers, she walked through the crowded bunks where soldiers lay either moaning or in silence. When she reached the medical supplies, she saw the list of outpatients was clipped to the tent flap. She filled the prescription for quinine and then checked the list to find out the officer's name and learned that a military escort waited to bring her there instead.

Allison hadn't realized how exhausted she was. Recently, though, she noticed she didn't have much appetite and that it was harder to get out of her bunk at the first light of dawn. Now the wind was against her, tugging at her heavy skirts and at the nurse's scarf tied at the back of her neck. The white pinafore-style uniform covering her gray dress shone in the starlight. Her boots sank into small mounds of sand, encumbering her stride. Her head ached and there was a buzzing in her ears. *In sacrificing my ease and comfort, I sacrifice for Christ,* she encouraged her rebellious body. *If the soldiers are willing to die for their country, I can attend their wounds as he allows. Who knows whether or not one of them may live another hour to accept the Savior?*

Allison trudged along in the field behind the silent soldier, who kept pausing to look back and apologize for the rough terrain. "I'm sorry, miss, it's fairly rough here. Are you sure I can't carry that pack for you?"

She smiled. It was marvelous how the soldiers treated the nurse corps with such honor and deference. It was clear how thankful they were the nurses were here to care and share their abilities in this hour of tribulation.

"I'll make it," she said with more brightness than she felt. "But how much farther, Private?"

"Not far, miss—" he pointed—"this is the last hillock. The officer's tent is right over there."

"Perhaps you should have brought him in a truck. I may need to transfer him to the hospital."

"Yes, miss, the truck had a flat tire and the others were all in use. They're scarce out here. All our supplies are slow getting in. Hope they catch up with us before we meet the Turks near Kut."

She struggled up the mound, and he caught her hand and pulled her to the top. "Sorry, miss," he said again. "You deserve a Victoria Cross for all this."

"Hardly, I've only done my duty."

The vast black sky spread from horizon to horizon. The light from Allison's lamp cast a swaying amber glow across the upward path. Miles away she heard the ominous boom of guns. She shifted her medical pack to her other shoulder and felt the wind drying the dots of sweat that prickled her flesh.

He gestured. "Right over there."

Allison saw the lantern light glowing from inside the command tent and noticed the Ford truck. "They must have fixed the flat," she said, looking at the full tires as she walked past with the soldier in the lead.

"Yes, miss," was all he said.

Allison left her lamp on the wooden table outside as the soldier poked his head in through the fly net. "The nurse is here, sir."

Allison removed her backpack and turned to thank the soldier for his escort. "You haven't told me the officer's name."

"Colonel Holman, miss."

"Colonel—!" She spun around to stare at the tent. *Why that unspeakable cad!* She flung the fly netting aside and stepped in.

Bret lounged in a canvas chair as though he didn't have a care in the world. His booted legs were stretched out before him, his military jacket was off, his shirt was open at the neck. On the card table beside the canvas chair was a holster and a Colt .45 pistol. She noted a German Luger as well and wondered where he'd gotten it.

He stood with a brief bow and a smile. "You are indeed a ministering angel, *fraulein.*"

Allison's nails dug into her palm. *Stay calm.* She stared at him in silence.

Undaunted, Bret returned her appraisal. "Knowing your noble spirit, I knew you couldn't resist a suffering soldier who was too ill to leave his tent. Of course, if you'd met me last night as I politely requested, I wouldn't have needed to resort to such highly imaginative means to get you here."

In spite of herself, a surge of ironic humor fought its way to her heart and brought a rueful smile. She surveyed him again, as if taking his role of a sinister German colonel seriously.

"How satisfying to know you've been captured and have at last come to your just end, Colonel Holman," she mocked. "When is the execution to take place?"

Bret's smile turned cynical. "You'll want a front-row seat, of course."

"I'm sure that won't be necessary. If you do meet your dubious end, it won't be meted out by the British."

"Major General Crawford might disagree. At the moment, he'd take satisfaction in my sudden demise." He gestured to a chair. "Better sit. You look as though you might be the prisoner of war in need of kindness."

Allison wavered. Should she stay or escape with her dignity intact? She had already learned that Bret could be a master at turning things to his advantage, and as weary as she was, she was in no state to do emotional battle with him.

In the moment she hesitated, he drew out a second beat-up canvas chair and took her medical bag from her to place it on the card table. To her outrage, he opened it, rummaging inside.

"Stay out of there! It's against regulations for anyone but a nurse to be in there."

"Is it?"

She snatched her bag away, but not before he'd found what he was looking for.

"Smelling salts," she said stiffly, then gave a little laugh. "Don't tell me the daring spy feels a trifle faint? My, you are out of role, Colonel! I didn't know you carried vapors along with your German Luger."

"Very amusing," he said as he held out the salts. "Take a whiff. You're on the verge of physical exhaustion. And, I suspect, spiritual depletion as well."

She plucked the salts from his hand and replaced them where they belonged, snapping her bag shut. "Still giving orders, I see. I can quite take care of myself, thank you. I've been doing so, with the Lord's help, for months. Twelve of them, in fact." She folded her arms and looked at him.

Unperturbed by her challenge, he sat down, lifting his cup to his lips and considering her. "Heroic to the bitter end. How many times has your heart been ripped out while sending dying soldiers on their way with whatever bit of faith and courage you could give?"

She turned away from his knowing gaze and walked over to the chair. Why did this infuriating man understand her so well?

"Your assessments can be brutally frank." Her tone was weary.

"Then let me go a step further. You're going to kill yourself if you keep this up, Allison. You're not the type to block out the fact that hundreds of soldiers are dying on the blazing battlefield. Nor are you the kind who can forget their faces when you turn out the lights."

Allison whirled, defensive and intimidated all at once. She detested the way he knew her heart when even Wade merely accepted what she did as fulfilling her obligations. Of course, that was how it was supposed to be: duty and self-sacrifice with few questions asked. But, as Bret had surmised, she was not one who could live that way. And she hated that he knew that about her.

"I suppose showing Christian mercy to the dying is a waste of time, Colonel?" she accused. "I daresay you've never wasted compassion on anyone."

He appeared to consider the accusation while he watched her over the cup he held. Then he set it too quietly on the table. "Is that what you want from me? Compassion?"

The wind shook the tent, and the sudden silence between them made her fingers clench as they looked at each other. Finally she turned, her nerves frayed to the limits, and started to walk out. In a breath he was beside her, his fingers closing around her upper arm.

"I can't let you leave yet. You're going to stay and listen."

"I'm not interested in hearing you defend your tarnished honor, nor do I want to be entreated with so-called gallant apologies."

His hand dropped from her arm. "Apologies!" He gave a harsh laugh.

Stung, her eyes confronted his, seeing a flicker of amusement in those blue depths...and something else.

Bret shook his head. "Why is it women always expect men to fall all over themselves apologizing? On the contrary, I've no apology to hurl like orange blossoms at your feet. The past is the past. This is now. And my wishing to see you has nothing at all to do with the emotions of the past when last we bade our adieux."

His words thoroughly undid her. She fought back the sudden tightness in her throat; blinked away the sting at her eyes. She drew a steadying breath, and when she spoke her voice was low and angry. "You are, by far, one of the most loathsome men I've had the misfortune to meet. I'm sure you must be of some merit to the war office, or they wouldn't keep you around. But I must admit I fail to see what it could possibly be."

He stepped back, offering a slight bow. "And I must admit that seeing you again in this intense and dangerous location has stung my conscience and brought your pristine qualities to mind." He smiled slightly. "Not to mention your untainted loveliness."

His calm arrogance infuriated her. So he had no intention of explaining his year of silence, or, apparently, of admitting there'd been anything between them.

Allison looked into the handsome face before her. What she saw was an impenetrable gaze, one that declared she was not welcome to go beyond the barriers he had so clearly erected between them.

Well, so be it. She would not lose her self-respect by forcing an issue he was determined to avoid. He wanted distance between them, and far be it from her to act the betrayed, hysterical female! She had already given too much away by letting him know she thought he owed her an apology.

"So, then, we understand one another, Colonel. I can call you 'colonel,' after all," she said with benign innocence, "since David did say you'd been promoted in London?"

"Colonel will suffice," he said agreeably.

"Congratulations."

"Thank you."

"I suppose it was because you successfully delivered the

Constantinople papers to the war office in London?"

Her tone was half accusing, though why it should be she didn't know herself. She just wanted to let him know that there wasn't anything about him that drew her trust.

"The papers were safely delivered, yes. As for my new rank, it had nothing to do with our delightful little 'vacation' at the Aleppo huts. However, since it was your work in part that made that a successful enterprise, I've come to reward you," he said silkily.

Reward her? He wasn't serious, he couldn't be...she grew cautious, wondering.

"You've been promoted, as well," he said. "From this typhoid-infested hole in the desert to the overcrowded hospitals in Alexandria. And I don't want any arguments. I outrank you by far."

He could not possibly have the authority to transfer her, and yet she realized by his determined expression that he was serious about her leaving for Alexandria. Well, she wouldn't oblige him.

She sank into the canvas chair. "I can't go to Alexandria," she said flatly.

His gaze flickered with restrained irritation. "You'd turn down the refreshing warm, blue waters of the Mediterranean beaches after months in this mosquito-infested oven?"

"Be fair! You know it sounds heavenly. I wish you wouldn't even talk about it." She pulled off her nursing scarf and lifted a strand of damp hair from the back of her neck, scowling at him.

"I'm afraid we *will* talk about it, because I can have you transferred there in a few days if you'll let me."

Her gaze wavered, but she shook her head. "No. Please, I don't even care to discuss it."

He watched her carefully. "Suppose I insist? I could use whatever authority I have in Cairo Intelligence and pull it off without your consent, but time doesn't allow me to do it that way. You'll need to wire your father or Lord Kitchener."

She decided there was some of the cool and relentless Colonel Holman in Bret after all, and that when he chose to accomplish something, he pursued it with a determination not easily turned aside.

"No."

He gritted his teeth. "Why?"

She shrugged, narrowing her eyes. "You have your duties, Colonel; I have mine. And never the twain shall meet—again."

He folded his arms and took her in.

"Maybe things here aren't as bleak as you suggest," she said lamely, not believing it for a moment.

"Don't waste your energy hoping. Under Crawford's guidance, they will be."

"But he's the field commander," she argued. "He must be certain of what he's about to do. He wouldn't place so many soldiers' lives at risk unnecessarily."

"I don't want to belabor the point, but striving for power and fame are very much a part of the system of war. The generals in Germany, Turkey, France, and Britain all have pride and ambition mingled with honor and duty. Crawford wants to make a name for himself. So though defeat stares directly upon him, he prefers blinders."

She shuddered. It was unthinkable to believe the soldiers in the trenches were considered expendable to accomplish personal ambitions. Could Bret be right? Was a victory for England merely a way to satisfy Crawford's need for victory? If so, they would need her here more than ever.

"I can't transfer," she said again quietly. "It would be like running out on my friends."

"You'd rather become a prisoner to the 'gentleman Turks?' Shall I enlighten you as to their humanitarian tactics on the Christian Armenians?"

"I don't want to hear it. It has nothing to do with my decision."

He ignored her. "They drove them out of their villages, then marched them across the mountains into the barren wastelands. Women, children, babies, the old—perhaps a hundred thousand displaced villagers are trying to cross to freedom, but they don't have a chance. The Turks deny them water, food, rest. They're driven like cattle—no, a rancher has more mercy. The Turks are committing genocide because the Armenians are Christians. And do you think twenty thousand British and Indian soldiers will be treated any better? Or the Christian nurses in a field hospital?"

She touched the red cross on her uniform, and his eyes narrowed as he followed the action. "You remember Mustafa? If I hadn't come along when I did, you'd have been arrested."

She was sickened at the thought of the Armenians. "Why can't something be done to help them? Are the western governments just going to stand by and allow the slaughter to continue?"

"England and America have protested, but when the world is at war, who is listening? Thousands of soldiers are dying daily."

She shook her head, unable to fathom the horrors taking place.

He walked to her chair, placed a hand on each armrest, and leaned over her. Trapped within the circle of his arms, she was forced to meet his intense gaze as he spoke. "Crawford's decision spells disaster. Even if he can drive his men forward, beaten and exhausted, his logistical support system isn't adequate to hold Baghdad should he, by some miracle, take it. The British forces will run out of food, water, and medicine. You'll be trapped with the others. Taken as a prisoner of war. Need I tell you what will happen to you, Allison?"

She lifted a hand to her aching head. "I can't leave the others behind! The field hospital is inadequately staffed! We can barely treat all the soldiers as it is. To leave them one nurse less—"

"Precisely my point. You and the others can't handle the thousands of wounded certain to arrive from an attack on Kut."

She thought of the lack of medicine, bandages, beds—

"How many casualties from the battle of Nasiriyeh?" he asked evenly.

"You already know. At least 450," she admitted dully.

He straightened. "There are some forty thousand Turks at Baghdad. What do you think is going to happen to Crawford's beleaguered troops? Instead of hundreds, you'll be treating thousands. It can't be done. You'll go insane trying."

"Forty thousand! But what about the river fleet?" she protested, because to face the facts was too painful. "Supplies will arrive from India. And more soldiers."

"Don't count on it. Your father told me in Bombay the river fleet is already stretched too thin. The British line of communication becomes longer and more vulnerable, while the Turks have a well-fortified defense system. You'll be surrounded, cut off from the main line near Abadan. If that happens, no one will get through with relief."

She knew Bret had to be right. He always had his finger on the pulse of the situation. It seemed to come with working in intelligence. "Have you explained this to General Crawford?"

"My dear! But of course I've explained it. That's why I'm here. And like the stubborn ruddy old boy he is, he brushes the facts aside as though I have a case of the vapors!"

"But I can't leave. Even if I wanted to, it's impossible."

"Not impossible," he said smoothly. "Not when your last name is Wescott."

She looked at him defensively. "What's that supposed to mean?"

"Only one thing. You're the daughter of Sir Marshall Wescott, the new chief consul of Egypt. You can send a wire to London, to Secretary of War Kitchener. He's a friend of your father."

"And beg to be bailed out?" She couldn't believe he'd suggest such a thing!

"You've given everything you've got to the cause, Allison. It's time you thought of yourself. I want you out of here and back in Egypt."

She got to her feet. "I *have* thought of myself. I'm a nurse with a job to do. And I'm a Christian. I can't run out on these men, Bret, I'd never forgive myself." She looked away. "There's nothing more to discuss." She went to pick up her medical bag, feeling unutterably weary. "I've got to get back. I have duty at four o'clock this morning."

He came beside her, but she refused to look at him. He took hold of her arms and turned her briskly about to face him, his gaze searching. His jaw flexed. "If you won't wire Kitchener, I will."

"I'll refuse to go."

"I want you safe! And David, too. I'm transferring him to my staff in Cairo. He'll be leaving in the morning."

As much as she hated to admit it, the idea of leaving did appeal to her. But she would not give in to thoughts of safety and ease. She thought of Wade and stole a glance at Bret, then at the table where his jacket lay, the colonel stripes apparent on the sleeve.

"I've a friend," she said slowly, "whom I'd like to see transferred to work with the chaplain at Zeitoun. Do you think you could arrange it?"

The silence grew long and rife with sudden tension. She felt his fingers tighten on her arms.

"Wade Findlay?"

Allison contained her surprise. So he knew already that Wade was here. What did he think about that? But there was nothing in his voice that told her what he was thinking. She remembered the time she had been with Bret on the steamer from El-Arish sailing to Port Said, and how Bret had asked too many questions about the depth of her relationship with Wade. He'd come to the audacious conclusion that it lacked the necessary…what had he said?…ah, yes, the necessary *fire*.

Well, sometimes fire wasn't all it was made out to be.

"Yes, Wade Findlay. If it's going to be as dangerous as you say, I want him out of here, doing what he trained to do at BTC—working as a chaplain. Somehow I think you could arrange it if you wanted."

He released a frustrated breath. "Now this is curious. A woman refuses to protect herself from the oncoming battle, but she will intercede for a soldier whose job it is to stand and fight."

She tried to pull free, but he held her tight. "Fighting isn't Wade's job! You know that. He's here with the medical corps for one reason alone: Cairo made a mistake in placing him."

There was little sympathy in Bret's tone now. "Muddling through is typical of the military," he said wryly. "So you want your Wade safely tucked in bed at Cairo?"

She fixed him with a glare. "You're impossible! Didn't you just transfer David? You don't think it's a flaw in *his* masculinity or patriotism, so why suggest such a thing because I want Wade transferred?"

"It's different with David. He's already proven himself, and he was recently released from a Turkish dungeon."

"A man can prove his courage by serving the Lord just as well as by carrying pistols and boasting colonel's stripes!"

Outwardly, Bret seemed unruffled by this shot. But she saw the flicker of anger in his ice-blue eyes and knew she had made a mistake.

"You're right," he acquiesced, inclining his head slightly. "Many have. And since Wade is sure to want to do so here, who am I to interfere in his work?"

"Are you saying you'll go off safely to Cairo and leave him here?" she demanded, incredulous.

"I'm not going to Cairo. Not yet. As for Wade, he's out of my jurisdiction."

"You're refusing because you don't like him—"

"I haven't even met the man. Look, Allison, the truth is, I can't transfer him."

"I don't believe you. You did it for David."

"David is different. I was in contact with him before the war in London. I think he told you that."

He had. It had something to do with espionage in Palestine. "Yet, you're also insisting I leave. Why not Wade?"

"I had to resort to every trick I could come up with to get David on my staff."

"And you have no more tricks left, is that it?"

"That's about it. If I had the authority you attribute to me," he said flatly, "I'd transfer you without your knowledge. I wouldn't be wasting time arguing with you, but Crawford insisted that you must request it."

So that was why he had arranged this meeting! He hadn't actually wanted to see her. He'd simply needed to convince her to send a wire.

But if he didn't care, why would he go to all this trouble? a small voice inside her asked. *And even more important, why isn't he returning to Cairo himself?*

She looked at Bret with growing concern, forcing herself not to grasp his arms. "If you're not returning to Cairo yet, what are you planning to do? Does it have anything to do with the Berlin Baghdad Railway?" He didn't answer, which only added to her concern.

His grip on her arms gentled. "I want you to send that wire to

London. Crawford has granted permission, but *you* must make the decision. We can leave tonight for Abadan."

Their gazes locked, and suddenly Allison felt as though she were being drawn in, surrounded, enfolded. She wanted to lean forward, to let him hold her close, protect her, tell her he still cared....

But he didn't. Hadn't his year of silence proven that? Abruptly, she broke the intensity of their gaze by turning her head and pushing away from him. "I'm staying."

She felt more than saw his anger. "Because of Wade?"

Now was an opportunity to put distance between herself and Bret. "Yes, because of Wade." She turned and looked at him. "And because it isn't in me to run from my duties and leave the fighting men of the Sixth Division without sufficient care."

"If Wade loves you he'd want to see you safely out of here, not mopping up blood and guts!"

"He knows I belong here because he cares about the soldiers! He'd die to save them!"

Bret's lip curled disdainfully. "And you asked me to transfer so selfless and sacrificial a saint to the safety of Cairo? Heaven forbid! Far be it from me to come between him and his martyrdom."

Allison whipped about and started out of the tent when Bret's hand caught her arm again, spinning her about. "You'll send that wire to London."

"Don't tell me what to do!" she stormed. "I'm staying with Wade."

"You don't love him," he ground out. "You're only trying to hurt me."

She gave a harsh laugh. "As though I were fool enough to believe I could hurt the great *Colonel* Holden! And yes—yes! I do love him!"

Her fierce words surprised even herself.

His jaw tightened. "How is it you can seem so naive and noble one moment and so bullheaded the next?"

Startled, she refused to look at him. She was not stubborn.

"What do you expect to do? Follow him out to the front trenches? You won't be content until you can hold each dying soldier in your arms is that it?"

"That's right, Colonel. That's exactly what I'm going to do. And I'm going to make certain I comfort as many young soldiers as I can with the promises of Christ. And now, sir, would you be so kind as to let go of my arm!"

For a moment he didn't move, and neither did she. The whistling wind sent the tent trembling.

"Very courageous," he said. "And very exasperating. It fits my memory of you well enough."

Memory? Was that all she was to him? Well, she had her memories, too, but she intended for them to die on the battlefield.

She looked at Bret, intending to tell him just that, but the words stilled in her throat at the near-desperate look in his eyes.

"Allison, stay and your luck will run out. You'll get blown up in the trenches along with Wade."

Tears prickled her eyes, though she tried to hold them back. "I don't believe in luck. My faith is in the God of time and history. He's called me here, and I intend to serve until he says it's enough."

"Like Esther, eh? You've come for such a time as this. How do you know he isn't speaking to you through me instead of Wade? Maybe the Lord wants you back in Cairo."

"Whether Wade's the reason I choose to stay, or whether it's because of a thousand other men like him—like you—what does it matter to the bold Colonel Bret Holden—?" She broke off. There was so much more her injured heart wanted to say. *I could have died before now, and you wouldn't have known or cared,* she wanted to throw at him, but she'd already said too much. When his hand finally released her arm, she fled into the windy, star-studded night.

Warm gusts of wind struck her face and made her eyes smart as she impatiently brushed away the tears that betrayed her. Had he seen them?

And had he believed her declaration of love for Wade? Were her words true? Yes...or at least, they could be. She could love Wade, could grow into love with him. She could learn to build a oneness with him centered in devotion to their work, to their God. Bret believed in the Lord, too, but he was still wrong for her. She could learn to suppress the feelings he evoked, yes, and the hour would come when she would be able to forget him completely. She would look back and wonder if what she felt was love at all. Maybe it was pure selfishness. Mere attraction to what he was on the outside. Wade was all the man she needed on the inside. What was it God had said to the prophet Samuel? "Man looks on the outward appearance, but God looks on the heart.... Look not on him because of his height and appearance," God told Samuel about Saul. "Because I have rejected him."

Yet God hadn't rejected Bret. He loved him. Had plans for him. Was she included in those plans? Could it be true that God was speaking to her through Bret, at least about returning home?

How was she to know? How could she decide when her feelings left her so vulnerable to pain?

She ran ahead, fighting the rising desert wind and her own exhaustion. Maybe she didn't love anyone, not herself, nor even God. Maybe she was like Peter, trusting in his own carnal strength apart from the Holy Spirit. "I'll die for you, Lord! Oh yes, You can count on me. I'll never deny you!" Yet before a fire in a cold courtyard, fearful of being identified by a little maiden, he had denied Jesus.

What am I afraid of? What would cause me to deny Christ?

"Please Lord, help me."

She hurried forward, not knowing how she would make it back to her quarters, but determined to try, to get as far away from Bret as she could. Determined, yes, she was always determined. But was her own determination enough? She could plod steadily on in her emotions, muddle through, grit her teeth, and clench her hands. She could say she could make it without Bret, but when the emptiness of the night surrounded her and she lay alone in her quarters, remembering, aching, would determination ever be enough?

She half expected him to come after her. In spite of the rubble that was left lying between them, he was an officer and would feel it his duty to see that she arrived safely back at her tent. After all, it was his clever manipulation that had brought her here.

Nevertheless, she wasn't prepared when he caught up with her. She stiffened, anticipating his hand catching hers, making her stop. It didn't happen. He merely reached out to relieve her of her satchel. They walked together in silence.

What was he thinking?

She trudged along, weary but refusing his help, and at the same time aware that he, too, was frustrated. Good. She remembered another walk they had taken in Jerusalem when leaving Rose and her boy Benjamin behind at the Mount of Olives. At that time she had also refused his help, and he had made much of it. This time, he remained silent.

After several minutes, her steps began to slow. She was simply too tired to go on. Bret paused, stepping in front of her on the path.

He stood there, a towering silhouette, wind tugging at his shirt and hair, one hand holding her bag over his shoulder. The black sky behind him seemed enormous, as though they were all alone in the universe with the wind embracing them, singing mournfully through the dried yellow grasses.

This is the end, she thought dismally. *We've got to face it. We're not meant for each other, and we must end this pull between us. It's not good; it's harming both of us.*

Bret studied her. When he spoke, his voice was surprisingly gentle. "A year ago when we said good-bye, I was wrong to promise anything, because—"

"I already told you. Spare me your gentlemanly apologies, Colonel!"

"Stop calling me that!"

"No, because that's all you are! A colonel in a uniform. You have no feelings. I don't want to hear your rationale behind what you've done."

"Don't say you don't want to hear my explanation, when you do. That's why you're angry with me, why you insist on staying with Wade, when common sense says—"

"Don't tell me what I want! Stop lecturing me about logic! Give me my bag and go away!"

He sucked in his breath. "You don't want me to go away."

"Yes, I do!" She stamped her foot in the sand. "But even if I didn't, what I want doesn't matter to you. You'd leave, even if I begged you to stay."

"Don't! Don't beg me," he ordered through gritted teeth. "You've too much honor for that."

"Don't worry, Colonel," she said her voice shaking with emotion. "God intends I should live without you, and so I shall. All you think about is duty! Duty! Well, go ahead, then. Fulfill your duty!" She pointed back toward the command post. "You speak so ignobly of General Crawford, but you're not so far removed. Instead of self-glorification, you'll sacrifice yourself at any cost because you don't want to care about anything or anyone."

"You don't know what you're talking about. You attribute every

96

decision I make to arrogance and selfishness!"

"No, not every decision. You'd die for England, but when it comes to doing something for Bret Holden, you prefer to think he's expendable. And because he is, you won't commit to anything else. You won't allow yourself to love. There's no room for me, for anyone."

"Remarkable deductive reasoning, Nurse. Remind me to come lie on your couch for counseling next time I need clarity of thought. Or maybe I should lie helpless in a trench, bloodied up. That would suit you wouldn't it? You don't want a man, you want a patient."

Her hands clenched at her sides. "As far as I care, Colonel, you can take your logic, take your insufferable masculine self-sufficiency, and—" she broke off before she said something she'd only have to apologize for later. She drew a steadying breath. "And return with David to Cairo," she finished.

He refused to budge out of her path. "You think you know what's inside of me, what's inside of these men you're willing to stay to help. But do you see them?" he breathed. "Do you really know them, Allison? What good is it if they sit in their trenches tonight writing their hearts to a girl back in England, or India—within days their bodies will be bloating in the desert sun, the feast of flies— lives wasted for nothing except the whims of generals and kings. They're sheep for slaughter, all following shepherds of death. In the end, whether they loved deeply or not won't matter, because their wives will be widows, their sweethearts will place fading photographs in a scrapbook and marry John Doe when the war is over. And do you know who John Doe is?" he asked angrily. "He's the one who was unfit, or the smart guy who stayed behind."

"Stop it!"

"There's only one difference between me and the soldier in the trench; tomorrow I, too, could be dead, but it will be by choice.

They'll die because Crawford made the stupid decision for them. And why? To fulfill his ideas of victory and honor. If I didn't care, as you so glibly say, why would I have come here to bring him information that might change the outcome? But he won't listen. He thinks he knows everything. So forgive me if I reserve my pity for the women back home, not Crawford."

With a muffled sob, she turned away from him. He muttered something low and angry, and she heard him dump her bag on the sand. Then she was pulled around and held fast, imprisoned in his arms.

She stared up at him, trembling, wanting to pull away—but she was too exhausted, too hurting to try.

"So I'm a uniform without a beating heart inside?" His eyes blazed. "I don't care about anything? Maybe you're right. But did it even once occur to you that staying away from you showed more unselfish concern for you than an eternity of pounding on your door?"

He bent toward her, and she felt his breath soft against her face as he whispered, "And during that entire year, I could never get the memory of this out of my mind...."

The sure knowledge that he was going to kiss her spurred her into action. She fought furiously, struggling for emotional survival—not only for herself, but, oddly enough, for Bret, too. She knew with sudden clarity that in this moment he was incapable of fending off the loneliness and longing that swept them both, like fire in the desert grass, when they were together. If there was to be any chance of enduring love between them, she had to stop him, to stop them both.

She turned her head, pushing against him, fighting. At first he wouldn't let her go, but as she persisted he dropped his arms and stepped back.

She turned away, rushing forward into the windy night, afraid he would reach for her again. She knew, if he did so, that she would throw her arms around him, wanting desperately to feel his lips on hers. She ran from the temptation, much like Joseph—but unlike her hero of Genesis, her heart felt ripped in two, for she desperately wanted Bret Holden.

The warm wind swirled about her, wrapping the heavy skirts about her legs, and threatening to drag her down. Now too numb to cry, to feel anything but sorrow and fear, she prayed the Lord's name again and again. No other words could heal, no other balm of Gilead could turn bitterness and sorrow to sweetness—none but the name of Jesus. The Lord knew her pain. He understood her loneliness. He knew Bret, too, and saw his struggle with cynicism, with frustration, with secret fears buried beneath a hard demeanor. Jesus saw the thousands of men on the fields of battle throughout Europe and here in Arabia, and he offered the one door of hope if they would but take it. Jesus was the gift the Father had given to cure a sin-sick world.

Here, perhaps not so very far from where she struggled beneath a starry universe, Abraham had once looked up and heard God say: "And in your seed will all nations be blessed."

That divine and holy Seed had come, born of the royal family of King David. Hope had sung not only in the choir of angels over the shepherd's fields, but in the words Jesus had spoken to those who embraced him as their spiritual deliverer: "Lo, I am with you always, even to the end of the world."

"O God," she whispered, and her heart ached with a dull throbbing. She stopped, too tired to move. When the sun would come up tomorrow, hot and burning, she would still be here, she thought, a statue, a pillar of salt, like Lot's wife.

It didn't matter. Nothing mattered any longer.

In the distance behind her she heard Bret calling an order to someone.

A few minutes later she heard a truck come rolling slowly toward her, and she closed her eyes against headlamps as they pinned her in full view.

Maybe he'll run me over, she thought, dully. *I'll die and it will be all over. I'll be with Leah.*

The truck ground to a halt, the motor churning. The door opened and footsteps approached.

"Miss?" came the quiet question. The soldier cleared his throat. "The tire's fixed. I can bring you back to the field hospital now. You must be awfully tired."

She turned to the soldier who had escorted her to the command post. His eyes were sympathetic, and she couldn't stop the thought: *Will you be one of those to die in the sands near Kut?*

She felt his gentle hand on her arm leading her to the passenger side and helping her onto the seat. Allison felt the hot upholstery beneath her hands, smelled tobacco and brandy. Then the soldier laid her bag on the floorboard, slid behind the wheel, and drove toward the hospital tent.

They bounced along, and he began to talk about his wife and children back home. She was too tired even to think. "It's harvest there now. The fields are golden." He put his hand out the open window against the air. "Feel that wind? When it begins to blow, I don't see Baghdad, I remember the grain blowing back home, the wheat so heavy the heads bow to the pale blue sky. There's not a more beautiful sight, miss, except my wife and my little girl. Annie's five now."

Allison could only look out the front windshield at the passing night.

SEVEN

I said, "Oh, that I had wings like a dove!"

TWO DAYS LATER, ALLISON SAT ON HER BUNK in the tent quarters reading the letter David had written her just before his midnight transfer.

Emily was on duty, but Marra was just outside the fly net scrubbing her gray-white nurse's pinafore in a large tin wash pan. She scowled, pursing her lips and blowing against the damp strands of blonde hair that fell across her eyes. She groaned as she straightened, holding a hand to the small of her back. "It's miserable being tall. We've more back trouble. I'd rather be short. Least your nose is to the ground." She looked up at the white-hot sky. "Even autumn doesn't cool things. Flies live all year." She looked back at her uniform. "And no bleach. I'll never get this white again." She looked over at Allison, who sat holding the letter as though her thoughts were far away in England. "I wish you'd complain sometimes, Ali, you're too good to be bunking with me and Emily." She lifted her dripping uniform and stared at it. "You know? It would make a lot more sense to have brown nurse's uniforms. I guess white gives the impression of purity. Is that letter from David?" she asked a moment later.

"Um, he's soon to be on his way to Cairo."

Again, Allison thought of Wade, and again she felt a stirring of irritation toward Bret. She still believed he could have done something more to see Wade transferred, not that her friend wanted to be moved. He didn't even know she had asked Bret to use his influence. Rather than thinking of himself, Wade grew more concerned for the plight of the soldiers and talked incessantly of their growing needs for basic commodities. "The soldier in the trench is forgotten," he commented yesterday, "when supplies are this low in the medical corps."

Marra looked at her again. "So David popped up with a transfer on the eve of moving out for dear old Baghdad." Her mouth formed a friendly smirk. She shrugged. "Oh, well, more power to him as they say. I guess he believes in fairy godmothers now. What about you? I still think you should wire London and get yourself out."

When Marra and Emily had learned how Bret tried to get her to return to Cairo, they both had urged her to listen to him. "Always make use of your ins and outs, mate," said Emily.

Allison stood, replacing David's letter in the reed hatbox she used to hold personal odds and ends.

"The Wescott name is also a military name," Allison told Marra with feigned cheerfulness. "Both my father and grandfather served their country in war. I've told you about my cousin Leah. On the brink of the biggest battle we've seen, do you think I'd leave you shorthanded? Besides, how would you and Emily get along without me?"

Marra grimaced. "Well, I'm not so valiant hearted. If the colonel could get me a transfer, I'd snap at it as fast as a trout takes a mosquito—never mind you and Emily." She slapped at a buzzing insect, then returned to her futile scrubbing.

Allison smiled, not believing a word the girl had said.

Marra looked at her hands. "Would you believe these used to be soft and supple?" She stroked the back of one hand with dripping fingers. "I even had a boyfriend, once. Used to say I could model my hands for cold cream in *Vogue* magazine."

Allison smiled, still thinking of Wade. It was possible for Bret to change his mind and have Wade transferred to Zeitoun. Even now, he might be working on the papers, she told herself. Bret might underrate his authority, but she felt certain a colonel of his qualifications could arrange something. He had influential friends in powerful positions in Egypt. Hadn't he used Baroness Helga Kruger to arrange David's release from incarceration in Jerusalem?

"So what happened to your boyfriend?" asked Allison absently, joining her outside.

"Robbie? He was killed...in Belgium. Didn't I show you his photograph?" She dried her hands and reached into her apron pocket bringing out a pewter frame with a scarred picture of a serious, dark-haired young man.

"This is him," she said, heartbreak in her voice. "Robbie was there, holding out at the Liege forts when they fought all those months against German invasion. They were doing grand, too, until the Germans brought in those heavy howitzers. He was at Namur, the last fortress barring the Meuse route into France."

Allison was now paying full attention. "I didn't know," she said softly. "About your young man, I mean. I'm sorry. I shouldn't have asked."

Marra slapped her uniform onto the washboard and scrubbed more energetically. "Most of us have someone we lost by now. You mentioned your cousin Leah." Her face softened, and she looked pretty and feminine. "Robbie and I were going to be married the month the war broke out. August 18th...Robbie was to come home, but then Germany invaded Belgium. His commanding officer shelved his leave. I still have Robbie's last letter. He told me he had a ring for me...bought it in Brussels." Her face hardened. "It either got blown up with him, or some German soldier got it. Maybe sent it home to his wife and bragged about how—" she stopped, biting her lip.

Allison wanted to say something to soften the pain, but she didn't know what. She knew the Lord could help Marra, but felt this wasn't the right time to say so. *Father, help me know when,* she prayed, wanting with all her heart to help this brave young woman. Words Wade had spoken a few days ago came back to her: "It's best just to remain quiet and hurt along with them. First they have to know you care. Chambers taught me about that deep caring. Any witnessing for our Lord without it is like clanging bells."

Allison saw Marra through new eyes. Beneath her caustic tongue lived a young woman who once sat dreaming in the summer moonlight about her white wedding dress and saved Victorian valentines in a pink box.

What about my valentines? thought Allison. *Do I still believe in pretty red hearts trimmed with lace?*

Had Bret ever sent a valentine to a girl?

She shook herself from her thoughts and gazed down at the photo again. "He's handsome," Allison said, handing the photograph back with care. "So you joined the military."

Marra stared at the picture. "Seemed a good thing to do with my nursing certificate. And there wasn't much to stay behind for, was there? Both my parents are dead and my older sister is married."

"Does your sister's husband serve on the western front?"

"No, he's a rabbi. But Sol's interested in a Jewish organization in London trying to raise an army to fight for England in Palestine."

Allison looked at her alertly, remembering how the Turks had expelled Ben Gurion from Jerusalem. "Did David ever mention his involvement in the Zionist movement?"

"No, but I'm surprised to hear of it since he made a beeline back to Cairo when the going got rough here."

Allison caught Marra's inference and wondered how much she should she say. David was anything but a coward. "David was a prisoner in Jerusalem last year. Did you see that scar on his face?"

Marra's eyes glimmered with subdued surprise. "I thought he got that in a brawl somewhere. Well—that's interesting. I didn't think he had it in him."

"He does. And I've a notion Bret—the colonel—transferred him to Cairo to work with him in...some very sensitive areas. I'm surprised David didn't tell you more about his work in Jerusalem."

"Are you being funny? He can't stand me." She shrugged. "Anyway, I'm glad he's gone." She scrubbed harder.

Later that afternoon when Allison took over her duties in the hospital, one of Marra's glib remarks—"What good's a last name if you don't make use of it in all the right places?"—was borne out.

Bret might have the authority to change some things, but so did she. He had used the same argument to try to get her to see Major General Crawford about a transfer to Alexandria, but couldn't she also make that same appeal for Wade? Perhaps she should wire Cairo and request transfers for Marra and Emily as well—maybe even for the young soldier who had been her escort to see Bret.

She sighed. If she began doing that, why not request the entire Sixth Division be transferred? After all, wasn't that what Bret had come about, to try to influence the command to pull back to Abadan? If Bret hadn't been able to convince them, certainly she could not. An order must come directly from British India and London. Unfortunately, that wasn't likely to happen.

She found Wade at the back of the hospital tent musing over the dwindling medical supplies. "Quinine supply is low," he said when she came up beside him to open a new carton of bandages.

She checked the alcohol supply. "Doc Murphy expects the supply rafts soon."

Wade was grave. "Doc learned this morning they won't be arriving. The Tigris is low, and the boats are stuck. And the mule train got ambushed by Arabs friendly with the Germans."

Allison remembered Bret's warning that the boats would not arrive. She noted the dark smudges beneath Wade's eyes. Lines of mental strain and physical exhaustion made him look older. *Before this war is over the entire world will age,* she thought bleakly.

"And when ye hear of wars and rumors of war see that ye be not troubled for all these things must come to pass but the end is not yet."

"The end is not yet," she echoed quietly.

Wade had lost weight, and his uniform hung loosely; the red cross on his armband had to be pinned in place.

He removed his spectacles and blew on them, wiping the glass clean with a towel she handed him.

"Did you ever consider trying to get a transfer to Zeitoun?" she asked too casually. "The YMCA could use help, I'm told. The Australian Lighthorse has arrived."

Both reddish brown brows shot up and his clear eyes smiled. "I already prayed about that when I arrived in Cairo." His eyes brightened. "Did you know Oswald and Biddy may come out and serve with YMCA in Egypt? If he does, maybe I can arrange a transfer to help him out."

The mention of Oswald Chambers brought a rush of hope to her heart. "It would be grand if he did. Oh, to see Biddy again, and baby Kathleen! I could use that innocent little smile now. Oh, Wade, let's see if we both can arrange a transfer now."

His smile was wistful. "It wouldn't do any good. The division's moving on a forward advance to capture Kut within forty-eight hours. Of necessity, the field hospitals will not be far behind the front line."

Forty-eight hours.

He smiled at her. "We're together. That's what we wanted and planned on in London. When they sent me here, I believed it was of the Lord. That he had brought us together, to serve together. And after the war, I hoped we'd make our plans to serve on the *Mercy* with your Aunt Lydia, traveling the Nile."

"Yes, I remember," she said wistfully, recalling her plans to voyage the Blue Nile into Ethiopia, ministering along the way. It was still a goal, but was it a God-given goal? A hundred contrary circumstances had interfered. The war of course was the primary cause for the delay. But the book of James said wars came from within, born from lusts that produced outward battles. She could see that Satan was stirring up the desires of the kings and emperors of Europe to fight and conquer other peoples to expand their own kingdoms. No one seemed satisfied with their allotment in life. Everyone wanted more—of everything.

Lord, help me by your Spirit to desire more of you. You are my portion.

Now there were other hindrances to serving the Lord as a missionary with Aunt Lydia on the *Mercy,* including her feelings for Bret. *Help me be content with the man you apparently have brought into my life,* she prayed, looking at Wade.

"Wade," she said gently, "I've noticed your failing health for the last month, even though you've done your best to hide it from everyone else, including Doc Murphy."

He looked at her for a long moment, then relief filled his face. As did exhaustion. "I thought I did well in hiding it. I suppose I did, from everyone but you." He smiled tiredly. "That's the trouble with loving a nurse."

She allowed the confession of love to slip by and stacked more bandages. Before she could say anything further, Doc Murphy strode past them, head thrust a little forward as though prepared to charge with a football under his arm. He was lost in his thoughts and didn't pay them any attention.

"Is it malaria?" she asked in a lower voice when Doc Murphy had gone.

"Yes, but I've been doing well enough. I don't want you worrying about me. You've enough burdens."

She looked over at the quinine and suspected he'd not made use of it. "The supplies are for the soldiers," he'd said more than once.

"Allison? There's something I want to tell you. I'm going to the front with Doc Murphy."

Wade's gentle words struck her hard. The front. The open trenches, open to mustard gas and exploding shells. She laid a hand on his. "You can't! Not with malaria."

"We're understaffed," he whispered. "Don't say anything. Doc Murphy needs me. There's no one else. It's going to be rough out there, Allison. Doc Murphy's seen it all before. He's served in India. He's thinking a thousand may be injured, maybe hundreds more killed. The ambulance and medical orderlies must be out there with them. We can't leave men bleeding in the trenches on the desert sands. A few hours in the heat and flies will mean the end. We've got to position ourselves out there with them."

"Can't Doc Murphy find someone else? What about Smitty? Elsdon?" she asked hopefully of the two medical interns newly arrived from India.

"We'll all be there. It will take every field medic available. If nothing else, I can run the wounded on the camel ambulance." He paused thoughtfully. "We're going to miss David."

Allison's loyalties were divided as she considered David's departure. Naturally she was pleased he was out of it, and she wished that the rest of the medical corps could all be safe too. But, like Wade, she realized they were not just one man short, they were short one of the best. David's loss certainly would be felt. Perhaps knowing this was what had prompted Marra to suggest David let them down. Allison didn't believe it for a moment and would defend David to the end, but she could understand the mild resentment experienced by members of the team who would need to fill up the shortfall in the heat of battle. Her decision to remain was now reinforced. She could not go.

Wade watched her. "I'm dreadfully worried about you, though. The other women, too. Emily told me how Colonel Holden came here to see you transferred to Alexandria." Wade continued to watch her. "I was told you'd refused the colonel unless I, too, was transferred." He laid a hand on her shoulder. "That means more to me than you know, but, Allison, I want you out of here just as much as the colonel does."

"How did you know about Colonel Holden? Did Marra tell you?"

Wade's expression changed. "Colonel Holden told me himself. He came to me before he left. I think he's right. He wanted me to tell you so, since you wouldn't listen to him. He thought you'd listen to me." He smiled. "Though why he should think so is a bit beyond me."

Allison felt her face flush. "He shouldn't have come to you. He overstepped the bounds doing so."

"I thought he made a lot of sense. If it turns out he's right about Crawford's push to take Baghdad, I want you safe in Cairo."

Allison turned her shoulder toward him and went on working with the bandages. So Bret had come to Wade.

"Well, if you're staying, then I'm not going, either. Doc needs me. You and the colonel had best understand a woman's devotion to her country in time of war. The argument you use to stay and help Doc is the same argument holding me here."

"God bless you, Allison. But Colonel Holden—"

"Please, Wade! I'd rather forget the colonel and his meddling."

He studied her for a few moments, then nodded. "Of course."

"General Crawford has taken care to see to our security," she said, trying to defuse his concerns. "The field hospital is always far enough from the front line to ensure our safety."

Wade didn't look convinced. "Out of necessity it may not be that way this time. Doc Murphy was saying Colonel Holden had a row with command post about it before he left with David."

This was the first she had heard that Bret had returned for a second meeting with Crawford. She could easily soothe herself into thinking he'd gone to confront command because of concerns for her, but she knew it was more than that. Bret was dedicated to the military, to the men who wore the uniform, and he had wanted to do what he could to save lives.

"He was sent here by Cairo with information for General Crawford," she explained. "They disagree over the political decision coming from British command in India to try to take Baghdad."

"Yes, so David told me. He rather hinted they wouldn't return to Cairo as soon as expected. I know because he asked me to pray for success and safety."

"David asked you to pray?"

"Surprised me, too. Of course I didn't show it when he asked, I didn't want to make him uncomfortable, hoping he'd feel free to ask more questions in the future."

Allison's pleasure over David's interest in Christianity died from her eyes as she pondered his words further. "Pray for success and safety for what? Did he hint at what his mission might be about?"

Wade lowered his voice. "I'm thinking the Colonel and a few others are expecting to blow up sections of the Baghdad Railway."

Cold fingers of fear enclosed her heart. If that was true, then Bret was in as much danger as soldiers on the front line.

Mustafa, the Turkish captain, popped into mind. If Bret were captured, the Turks would surely recognize him as the British agent who had masqueraded as Colonel Holman.

Pain filled her heart when she thought about Bret's ironic remark about her wish to view his demise before a firing squad.

"There's something I want to say to you before we leave tomorrow," Wade was saying. "Do you think we could get together tonight after Bible study at the tent?"

She forced herself to pay attention. "I know what you want to say," she said gently.

He took one of her hands and held it tenderly between his own, searching her eyes. "Do you? I love you, Allison."

"Yes, I know," were the simple words that came in response. The moment brought no heart-pounding reactions, no burst of joy or emotion. She studied Wade's dear face and wondered how she could tell him she loved him, too, but in a quiet, peaceful way. She loved him for his dedication to the One she, too, wished to please above all others; loved him for the fine qualities in his character, and his understanding patience toward her reticence to discuss the inevitable. Yet here it was, coming now, because war and death demanded decisions before they were too late.

Even as she considered how she loved him, she knew she cared too much to deny him all her heart should the moment come when she was free to offer it. For now, though, she was not free. The image of Bret came between them as though he were quietly yet insistently demanding she wait. It was as though Bret were bound with chains that not even he could break to satisfy her heart's cry. Was this image a mocking shadow or a harbinger?

Wade smiled gently. "I'm selfish. I like to see worry on your face for me. It tells me you still care about me."

It wasn't in her to tell him that she'd been thinking of Bret.

"I care, Wade." She could say that much and have no qualms. If their relationship was right in God's eyes, then love would grow. The moment would come when she would know with peace and anticipation that Wade was to be her heart's partner through life.

Many successful marriages had been arranged by parents and pastors in the old days. Allison continued telling herself that, for the most part, those marriages had worked out even without the bride and groom being starry-eyed about one another. Maybe being starry-eyed was a dangerous game, built on feelings that could be put out as easily as they were sparked.

What was true love? Time would tell.

All she knew right now was that she cared deeply about Wade; yet she still suffered terrible pain over Bret. She remembered how agonizing it had been to resist him when he wanted to kiss her, yet she'd done so because it had been right. She'd known, even in the midst of her emotions, that sharing such intimacies without being committed to each other would have been wrong. She'd never felt this kind of turmoil with Wade. Their relationship was quiet, a comfortable affection that, as he said, "made her worry about him" and want the best for him. Did she want the best for Bret? Yes, but somehow there was a difference.

"I was beginning to worry about Colonel Holden and you."

Wade's words brought a flush of guilt to her face, and she busied herself by rearranging the bottles of medication. "I told you about the work we did together in Aleppo. All that is in the past." She turned, "Wade, let me speak to Doc Murphy about your malaria, or to General Crawford."

He smiled his refusal. "There are few soldiers who aren't sick. I don't deserve better treatment because I'm part of the medical corps. I'll be all right."

"You've lost weight," she disagreed, noting his shallow cheeks.

"That's due more to the menu than malaria," he said with a smile, then grew serious when she frowned. "I'm doing fine. I feel confident I'm in the Lord's purpose in being here with this particular division. I've even been able to speak to a number of soldiers about their need for the Lord. There's nothing like facing death every day to convince a man to think soberly about eternity."

She had seen that the men knew Wade cared about them as friends. He was with them in the same circumstances, dealing with the heat and flies, eating the poor food. It made an impression.

"I don't have to labor here, and they know it. So far, some have shown response to Christ's love and offer of forgiveness. I feel as if several are on the verge of receiving him before we move forward toward Baghdad."

"You could serve the Lord at Zeitoun."

His tolerant eyes rested on her and he smiled. "We'll pray about it. If the Lord wants me there, then he will arrange the circumstances."

His confidence was reassuring, and she returned his smile, even though her questions remained. "We'll meet for Bible study. I better get back to my patients."

The next day settled in with a pallor that depressed everyone. Even Doc Murphy sensed it and was kinder with his staff and suggested the cooking staff do something "a little special" for the hospital patients before they moved out.

"So do we get something reminiscent of Grandma's cooking?" asked a grinning soldier when supper was brought that night.

"How's an extra bit of butter on your bread?" Marra teased.

"Blimey me, it's a bit mor'n that. Why they've made the last of the chocolate pudding," said Emily, and wheeled in a large table filled with small cups piled with wiggling pudding. "Look now and feast your eyes on that, soldier."

"Best enjoy it, too," quipped Marra. "Tomorrow night the artillery will be blasting again and rattling dishes and spoons."

Emily nudged her aside with a frown. "Here, Duckling," she said to a soldier with two bandaged hands, "let me help you with that."

Several weeks later, on a night in late September, with the fighting begun near Kut, the field hospital was packed with new wounded. Wade arrived to bring fresh supplies forward to Doc Murphy and his trench staff.

Allison hadn't seen Wade since the day the division had begun its advance. Now she stared at him. He had lost at least ten pounds, and the circles beneath his eyes were dark blue. Yet he managed a smile as he took hold of her shoulders and commended, not himself, but her for the brave work she was doing in the hospital.

Allison held both his thin hands between hers and looked into his eyes.

"Oh, Wade, Wade—"

"I love you," he choked, grasping her to him, and she heard restrained tears in his voice. He buried his face in her hair. "It is the picture of your face in my mind and heart, and the sustaining grace of our Lord, that keeps me going."

"It won't be long! Soon you'll be transferred to Zeitoun, you'll see!"

Whether or not he believed her was uncertain. He held her from him. "Just let me look at you for a moment. The goodness in your eyes feeds my hope and faith. I want to remember you looking like this. It will need to last through many dark nights."

They were able to spend a few hours in Bible study and prayer with the chaplain, and before Wade left with the medical supplies for Doc Murphy, he informed her that he'd heard that a key section

114

of the Baghdad Railway had been blown up. Those involved were safe and on their way to report to General Crawford.

Which could only mean one thing: Bret was headed for the front lines.

EIGHT

How can you say to my soul, "Flee as a bird to your mountain"?

PSALM 11:1

THE SIXTH DIVISION MOVED FORWARD with the goal of capturing Kut and Baghdad. Fighting with the Turkish army began in earnest in September, and as days of autumn passed with no relief in sight, the soldiers' suffering only intensified. The heat in the summer often climbed to near 120 degrees for ten hours a day. Besides the wounds from battle, other enemies took their toll in death. Bacteria carried by flies, fleas, and mosquitoes wrought deadly work, and unclean water spread dysentery, malaria, typhoid, and cholera among the troops.

Medical supplies were low as well, and troops and staff were exhausted. Yet despite the hundreds of wounded men being carried back from the front trenches by camel ambulance, Major General Crawford pushed forward relentlessly for the victory that would make headlines back home in England.

When Allison and the others arrived near Kut to set up the field hospital on the 24th of September, Allison heard that the Turkish army was well situated and dug in to halt the British advance.

The field hospitals were divided into smaller units and scattered behind the front fighting line in strategic locations. In the cramped and overheated nurse's quarters, Allison awoke daily to the boom of artillery. She fell sleep with the sporadic firing of machine guns and the shudder of exploding shells. As the sounds of fighting grew closer, neither Allison nor the other nurses mentioned it. They knew fear and anxiety could be as contagious as typhoid and as plaguing as the insects that buzzed maddeningly during the day and droned at night.

Allison's hours off duty became scarce as the wounded multiplied, but those times away and alone grew more important, more precious, as she stared into the haunted faces of the British and East Indian soldiers who were a harvest for death. Though she could at times share a word of salvation to the British, she found her heart deeply troubled by the young Indian men, many of whom were unable to converse in English since their British officers all spoke the native language. For these men she could do little except try to lessen their physical suffering. Often their dark brown eyes gazed up at her with such emptiness that desolation gripped her heart. Daily the ground was wet with blood; daily men died, eternally lost. The horrors began to sap her spiritual strength; the environment depleted her body.

"Lord, I can't take much more," she prayed one morning at the stacked barrels of water where she'd gone to fill endless canteens. "I'm weaker emotionally than I thought, but I can't cry on Marra's and Emily's shoulders. I can't add to their burden by asking them to carry me emotionally. Lord, strengthen me as only you can."

She hadn't heard from Wade in weeks, and she was worried. She glanced around as she filled the canteens, and her heart quickened when she saw a camel ambulance arriving from the front carrying a stretcher with several wounded soldiers. She left the water barrels and went to meet the medic, Corporal Hendricks.

"Have you seen Wade?" she asked as she helped with the men.

"He's still with Doc Murphy in the south trench. I was there yesterday, and they were all right."

Even with this good news, she was worried. She knew Wade

would collapse with fever before abandoning the soldiers at the front or leaving Doc Murphy shorthanded in a raging battle. Anxiety came to steal her peace like little rats carrying off what should have been her treasury of confidence in God's watchful care.

"The Lord has his way in the whirlwind and the storm," she quoted from the Old Testament book of Nahum. And God was there now, even when death and destruction ran unbridled.

As September drew to a dry, hot end, Allison lost weight and grew ill. She managed to keep her declining health concealed from Marra and Emily, who were too overwhelmed with their duties to notice much of anything. Emily had twice attended a prayer and Bible study with Allison, but otherwise had little comment about all they were experiencing.

Marra had not changed. She remained cynical about everything and blamed the persecution of her people on the forgetfulness of the God of Abraham. Allison opened the Bible to the Old Testament book of Isaiah and read to her from chapters 40, and 41. "Why sayest thou, O Jacob, and speakest, O Israel, my way is hid from the LORD, and my judgment is passed over from my God?…Fear not, thou worm Jacob, and ye men of Israel; I will help thee, saith the LORD, and thy redeemer, the Holy One of Israel."

Marra turned without a word and left the tent quarters. Allison grew more convinced than ever that Marra's cryptic attitude was a cover for her hurting heart. One night she awoke in the hot smothering tent to hear Marra crying out in her sleep.

"Robbie!"

The sorrow in her voice pierced Allison's heart, and she lay there, wondering if the soldiers Marra nursed with such dedication all had the tortured face of the boy who died in the Belgium forts guarding the road to France.

It wasn't long before a weakness in the Turkish position was reported to Major General Crawford. The Turkish army lay astride the Tigris River with the only bridge across five miles upstream, behind the Turkish position. Crawford took advantage of this lack of Turkish mobility by ordering two of his brigades to conduct a demonstration on the right bank to draw the Turkish reserves. When the Turk commander, Nur-ud-Din, placed his reserve Thirty-Seventh Division south of the Tigris, Crawford moved his two brigades back north of the river on the night of September 27th.

Allison could hear the artillery as the British attacked, enveloping the Turkish flank. She saw the British going by, so exhausted by the long march, the debilitating weather, and lack of water that they and their horses were too weary to pursue the Turks who had fled before them. Soon, however, Crawford's troops were reinforced from Abadan. Even so, he could muster little more than thirteen thousand men.

Within two days, Allison heard the news from the soldiers being hauled in by the field ambulance stretchers. They had taken Kut! About two-thirds of the Turks withdrew in good order up the Tigris. The lure of Baghdad, forty miles away, became irresistible.

The Sixth Division had already advanced up the Tigris for more than three hundred miles. One more battle against the oft-defeated Turks seemed a reasonable risk, even though once captured, Baghdad could not be secured.

Allison was aware of what was happening. She heard about the inadequacy of the British force, and she heard it was being concealed from military superiors in India and London. A victory was deemed needful, and the general was willing to push ahead. She knew what Bret would have thought of the decision, and that set her to wondering where he was and whether or not he knew what was happening. Wade had told her at one point that neither Bret nor David had returned to Cairo. The destruction of sections of the Baghdad Railway told her that Bret was in the area somewhere.

This much she knew, Bret wouldn't be pleased with Crawford's decision to use the victory at Kut to march on Baghdad. Nevertheless, the troops moved out the next day, the medical corps following right behind.

The hot days and long torturous nights continued.

The logistical situation was chaotic. Basra, the only port supporting the British troops, still had no wharves. Ships had to be unloaded at anchor by native boats, causing delays in port that averaged six weeks. Many critically needed items were not available.

"Including water purification," said Emily. "And still no fresh vegetables."

There were insufficient riverboats to support Crawford, who required more than two hundred tons of supplies daily. "I've heard he's only receiving about 150," said Emily.

Because of low water levels during the autumn, only six small steamers could traverse the Tigris, and these couldn't carry full loads. Lack of fodder made wagon transport impractical, but no plans were made to build a railway up to the front. Finally, the Arabs had taken to murdering guards and stealing supplies, so large numbers of combat troops had become a necessity to secure the support lines.

Despite these setbacks, Crawford launched his sick, ill-equipped men against an equal number of Turks who were strongly entrenched.

Although the British managed to penetrate the first and second lines of trenches, they lacked the strength to turn opportunity into victory. Nur-ud-Din successfully counterattacked. The day's battle cost Crawford over four thousand men.

The wounded kept arriving, and all available blankets were hurriedly laid down on the ground outside the hospital tent. Medical bags spilled open with bandages, brown vials, and nickel-plated instruments. The wounded kept coming and going; as soon as one was bandaged, there was another hollow-faced patient waiting to take his place. All around, severely wounded soldiers were laid out, inert, on stretchers.

The day after this disastrous attack, Crawford collected his wounded from the battlefield while Nur-ud-Din received reinforcements. The British began withdrawing, with the Turks in aggressive pursuit.

On that wretched and bleak afternoon of the lost battle, Allison—along with every available medic—was ministering to the injured. The sun beat down without mercy, yet nothing could be done to bring the relief of shade since no canvas roofing was large enough to form a covering over the rows of wounded. The medical corps strung fly netting at intervals, but still there were gaps between those in the shade and the soldiers forced to endure the sun. The workers spent hours rotating the men and bringing water by the barrel to try to quench their patients' fevered thirsts.

A dozen ambulances were taking the less gravely wounded men to the rear, but however many were taken away, more were brought in. The wounds Allison saw made her turn away with wonder that a man could be so mutilated and live. It twisted her heart to turn away without aiding them, but there were so many soldiers needing help that they were commanded not to waste time or medicine on seemingly hopeless cases. And yet, though she knew they were right, the cost of obeying this command was great to her raw heart.

Flies abounded, and more fruitless hours were wasted in an endeavor to alleviate the torment they caused. Allison and Emily smeared the patients' faces and throats with ill-smelling camphor salve and covered them with all the remaining bed coverings they could find in the tents.

Allison tried to fan the flies away from a patient before moving to crawl past him to the next soldier who groaned. She lifted the cloth and remained expressionless as she saw his stomach wounds. The orders were firm. All soldiers with stomach wounds were to be brought to another area. "The forgotten area," they called it, where men died unattended for lack of hope of recovery.

She couldn't think about it for long. Despite everything, sometimes she wondered if she made a good professional nurse.

She reached into her bag and removed a small white flag, staking it into the ground above the groaning soldier's head. The flag informed the stretcher bearers to remove him from active care.

"I never knew it could be this bad," whispered Allison, looking about at the hundreds and hundreds of injured soldiers. She wanted to simply sink into the dust and give up, but she knew she couldn't.

Emily's square jaw clamped. "I've seen worse."

"It's going to get worse," Marra clipped. "It always does. That's the way life is. There's no hope."

Emily turned on her. "Will you stop saying that all the time? There *is* hope. Haven't you been listening to a word Allison's been saying since she joined up with us?"

Marra looked shocked by Emily's emotional response. She started to say something, then turned and walked away.

When Allison was alone for a few minutes she splashed water on her face, her throat, and her arms, then leaned, exhausted, against the barrel.

In the distance the artillery exploded, and the barrels shuddered.

She lifted her head and stared off toward the horizon as another shell landed too close to the hospital field.

Couldn't the enemy see the hospital flag blowing in the breeze? Of course they did, and many had only contempt for the white flag and red cross. She shuddered to think what would happen to them all if the Turkish army broke through the British defenses. She recalled what Bret had said back at Basra about the genocide against the Armenian Christians.

She turned quickly and looked with dismay into the dusty horizon. The Sixth Division was withdrawing, and they were hoping to escape ahead of the Turkish army to Kut. She wouldn't consider the stark frightening thought that came to mind: How would they retreat with the wounded? How could they move out swiftly enough with the Turks pushing forward relentlessly? And if they didn't have enough wagons—

She turned and hurried toward the great open field and saw the endless line of soldiers spread out on the ground. The figures of Marra, Emily, and the other half dozen orderlies appeared pathetically inadequate to either handle the needs or manage the retreat.

She shaded her eyes and looked ahead across the wilderness. The British division was pulling back, marching back toward Kut. A company was moving forward across the field in open order. The men were bent double, haversacks on their backs, while wagons rolled by. There were soldiers on horseback, on foot, driving camel ambulances, and on trucks equipped with mounted machine guns.

A truck rumbled up scattering dust. Doc Murphy, Wade, and three medical orderlies poured out, sweating and dusty, looking thin and exhausted.

Allison ran toward Wade. He opened his arms and drew her close.

"You're all right?" she asked.

"Yes. We're evacuating."

"What about the wounded?"

"We'll take as many as we can. The trucks are coming now."

"But there can't be enough trucks!"

He didn't answer. He just left her, running after Doc Murphy who was shouting orders. A number of foot soldiers came up with stretchers and entered the main hospital where the critical were kept out of the sun. She heard Doc Murphy shout, "Check the tags! Only the red are evacuated!"

Many would be left.

Allison covered her ears. No. She wouldn't think about it. This wasn't happening, it couldn't turn out like this. Command wouldn't desert the wounded. No. Of course they wouldn't.

She turned in a daze and walked back to the men in the field. She went about her duties as though she didn't hear the rumble of guns or the sickening tramp, tramp of retreating soldiers going by. She simply kept working, as though she had all the time in the world.

She changed bandages on one soldier after another, giving morphine when it was essential, speaking words of bravery and comfort when she must refuse them help for lack of drugs. Her fingers grew clumsy, and she felt the sun beating into her back like a searing knife.

"There you go, soldier, that will make you feel better."

"Thanks, angel," he choked, looking at her through bleary eyes.

"God rest you, miss," said another.

One man stopped her as she moved to pass. "Nurse, when you get back to Abadan, will you see this letter is mailed to England? I wrote it a long while ago thinking it might come to this."

She took the letter. Others were asking the same thing of her, and the voices blurred into one petition. Her head throbbed; the glare of the sun and the sweat streaming down her face stung her eyes.

"It's going to be all right," she kept saying, and her voice speaking steadily surprised her. It sounded like the voice of a stranger.

"Nurse! They're not leaving us?" a young soldier cried in anguish. "Nurse!"

"No, no—we won't leave you," she answered. "Here, take this...." She put her last pill on his tongue and lifted his bandaged head, letting water from the canteen dribble into his mouth, careful to see that he swallowed before adding more.

"God!" a soldier cried out helplessly. "Don't leave us here!"

Tears blinded Allison's eyes. She stood, dropping the canteen, and looked around wildly, turning full circle. Soldiers, everywhere. Some unable to move. Some tried to get to their feet to crawl after the wagons. A thundering sound of voices beat at her, reverberating in her heart. She reached up to cover her ears.

Just then, she saw a motorcycle with a mounted sidecar come speeding up to the field hospital. She knew before she saw him who it was.

The cycle came to a stop and Bret jumped out, glancing hurriedly about. The vehicle was dusty, and one door was rippled with bullet holes. She saw machine guns mounted on the sidecar.

Bret must have been caught in several battles. His uniform and boots were dusty, and Allison noted several dark stains on his uniform that had to have been dried blood. The dry breeze blew the hem of her gray nurse's skirt, and she almost laughed at the thought of how she must look. Her white pinafore was filthy. She and the others had long given up hope of keeping them white or even clean. But the red cross was clear and bright and stood out like a badge of honor. Her hair, rolled up hastily upon arising, had long wisps undone and hung loosely from beneath her nurse's scarf.

Bret glanced about at the hundreds of men who lay side by side on the ground, but his face was in shadow beneath his hat. Although she couldn't see his face, she knew by instinct when his gaze found her's. The emotional impact that struck her as their gazes met awakened her from her daze.

She stood, waiting, watching, hearing the artillery.

Bret came to her, stepping his way over the long endless stretch of soldiers, many of them delirious and crying out in their fevered conditions. He carried a rifle slung over one shoulder and a shoulder holster with two pistols.

Her eyes held his, searching, but they barred her entry. Instead, when he reached her, he barked, "Orders were given yesterday to evacuate! What are you still doing here?"

Allison didn't answer. She just stood staring at him. His eyes narrowed, taking her in, and she saw a flicker of tender understanding. He reached out to take gentle hold of her arm. Something warm and vital surged through her, though she wasn't sure if it came because of his touch or because of the small but abrupt shake he gave her to stir her from shock.

She blinked and drew in a breath, forcing herself to match his emotional distance, though her heart would not go along with her ruse.

"Are you all right?" he demanded.

"Y-yes."

He didn't look as though he believed her and grimly glanced about. "Where's Wade? He was supposed to be looking out for you!"

When had he seen Wade? Or was the remark Bret's way of attacking her confidence in Wade? The accusation stiffened her backbone.

"He's with Doc Murphy, where he's been all along, serving honorably and at great sacrifice."

A brief smile lifted Bret's mouth. "Excuse me, madame, I forgot the Victoria Cross. But maybe I'll bring it next time, if you can spare the trumpets and drums on his behalf?"

Her praise of Wade had been a little too blatant, she agreed. She didn't know why she always felt as if she must rush to his defense around Bret. Wade certainly didn't need her good report. Then again, the man who stood before her in dusty uniform stained with blood was equally deserving of her praise.

Somehow, though, the words wouldn't come. The pain she felt choked them off, as though something deep within her refused to let her reflect upon the man before her.

"What are you doing here? Why didn't you go on to Cairo?" she half accused.

"I've been ducking Turks, blowing up a German railway, and keeping my options open, knowing I'd probably need to come back this way for you," he countered. "Otherwise," he added wryly, "I've not been doing much since we last went our separate ways. If you'd listened to me a few weeks ago—"

"Please, don't start that now. What about these wounded soldiers? Are you going to get them out or not?"

He pushed his hat back and regarded her.

"My dearest Allison, am *I* going to get them out?" He looked at her as though she'd sprouted a second head. "If I were in command of this unit, it wouldn't *be* in this situation. I don't need to be here at all. As you said, I could have gone back to Cairo and forgotten the lot of you."

He was right, of course. She owed him gratitude, not rebuke. "Then why didn't you? By now, Colonel, you might be enjoying roast duck at the Ezbekiah Gardens Hotel."

He caught her gaze and held it, searching for the meaning to her question, and she flushed.

"Maybe I wanted the chance to warn Crawford again, even though I knew he wouldn't accept it. Then again, perhaps it's as I suggested, to find you. After Jerablus and Aleppo, I couldn't let you fall prey to the Turks now, could I?" He smiled, looking disgustingly handsome, even under all the dust. "And maybe I don't like to eat roast duck at Ezbekiah Gardens alone."

She wanted to believe his assertion, but she knew it was concern for these men—not just for her—that made him risk his life. "You bought the general time," she said, "by dynamiting the railway. And where is David? What have you done with him?"

"Done with him?" Wry amusement danced in his blue eyes. "What interesting ways you have of saying things, my dear. He's safe. I sent him ahead."

Relief swept over her and she relaxed a little.

"Where are the other women?"

"I don't know where Emily is, but Marra is with Wade and Doc Murphy." She pointed. "Over there, evacuating the hospital."

"Now? Ruddy luck! They were to do that yesterday! Didn't orders arrive?"

If they did, Allison knew nothing of them. "We heard the guns and saw the army retreating toward Kut. It was the first we knew something was wrong."

"Something is wrong, all right! Very wrong. We've got about two hours to get out of here before the Turkish Thirty-Seventh overrun this place."

Two hours!

Having faced danger with him in the past, she knew he did not exaggerate. If anything, he underrated the moment with bare-bone facts that left no room for argument.

She looked about at the men lying helplessly on their mats, then back at Bret. Her alarm and horror must have been evident in her expression, for his eyes narrowed.

"There's no way to save these men, Allison. I don't have the trucks or wagons. A full-scale retreat is underway."

She read the restrained rage he felt. She shook her head, hopelessly, looking about her.

"We can't leave them here!"

"I'm sorry," he said, and she knew he truly was. "You have absolutely no choice in the matter. They can't be saved."

The thought stunned her. For a moment she could do nothing except look at him as though he were to blame for the catastrophe. She shook her head again and looked at the men. Douglas, Charles, Higgins—these were soldiers she knew, men she cared about, had fed, attended through the hot day and night...and he was telling her she must leave them lying helpless for the Turks while she fled?

"Allison," came his firm but low voice, jarring her out of her desperate thoughts.

She looked at him as the insects buzzed with sickening indifference, even anticipation. The sun beat upon her head, sapping her remaining strength, her will to believe, to fight.

Had it all been in vain? The long drudgery, the endless hours?

"Allison, this is the time for your greatest bravery. Are you up to it?"

She looked at the dismal field of wounded and dying. He was telling her she must walk away from them.

"My bravery..." she echoed, and she heard the waver in her voice. She blinked hard against the tears that threatened to overwhelm her. "I'm not brave at all, not when I see these men...and know—"

"You're wrong," he said with unexpected softness. "If my recollections are correct, you have the heart of a ministering angel and nerves of steel. I want you to pull yourself together and do as I say."

His response was unexpected, and she could do nothing to prepare her emotions. Silence encircled them.

Bret took hold of her arm, drawing her closer, yet keeping a small distance between them. Still, she didn't need to be touching him to feel the pull between them.

"You're too brave," he said gently, his blue eyes filled with admiration. "Do you know how lovely you are, standing here like this?"

She didn't, and couldn't imagine why he would say so now, except that danger and death did strange things to people, caused them to say and act differently than they normally would. Her throat ached and she refused to look at him. Instead, she occupied herself with tucking a strand of blowing hair under her scarf.

After a moment he said, "I'll get the others. I've managed to commandeer one truck. Let's hope it will be enough."

It wasn't, of course. He left, and she heard him barking orders. They were quick and brutal. They were to retreat. Allison thought she could not bear it.

She stood within the sea of wounded. A soldier caught the hem of her skirt staring up with dazed eyes. "Ma'am, don't let 'em leave us here,"

She pulled her skirt away gently and looked at him with pity. "God aid you, sir, for I cannot."

"Give us our weapons!" choked another, rising to his elbow. He fell back again in a coughing spell.

"If they leave us, they're worse then the Germans and Turks!" another cursed. "You bunch of blighty cowards! Go ahead, run!"

Dismayed, Allison began walking through the men. Their hands reached out to her, grasping; their eyes pled with her, haunted and fearful. She froze, covering her face with her palms.

"Allison."

Bret was standing beside her again.

"I can't leave them."

"I know." His voice was filled with understanding…and something more, something deep and oddly unsettling…something that made her tremble, though not from fear.

The next thing she knew, she was swept up in his arms, held secure, cradled against his chest. He started to walk, stepping over the wounded carefully.

"No—"

"There's nothing more you can do except get yourself killed or captured," he said, his voice hoarse. His arms tightened around her. "You're not to blame for this tragedy, Crawford is!"

Tears filled her eyes and ran down her cheeks. She looked back over Bret's shoulder.

Those who could walk, limped forward; the badly crippled crawled after the overloaded wagons, all beseeching them not to leave them in their need. And, on the road, there were others too, some lying down in the dust, exhausted. They called after the departing trucks. She turned her face against Bret's chest and wept.

Soldiers' prayers were intermingled with curses from others, and, far behind them, she could hear the artillery in the darkness.

For Allison the hour spoke the end of things, of betrayal. *Better to die with them than remember this!* she thought bitterly.

The thunderous explosion of shells filled the sky with sound and flashes. The Turkish army was progressing in its forward thrust to overtake Major General Crawford.

Bret reached the truck and he held her tightly for a moment. Allison grasped hold of him, clinging. He buried his face in her hair.

"Allison, sweet, sweet Allison."

Then he lifted her into the back of the truck where the wounded were packed together so tightly there was hardly room for her to breathe. He turned to go. Surprised, she reached her hand to catch him and touched air.

"Aren't you—you're not coming with us?"

His face was unreadable. "No, I'll catch up. Good-bye, Allison." And with that, he stepped back, giving a signal to the driver to pull away.

Her hand was still clutching emptiness as the truck drove away, and she watched him standing there, growing smaller in the distance.

With a cry she leaned her head against the side of the truck as it bounced along the ruts. Minutes passed. Allison's eyes blinked open with a start.

"O Father God!" She glanced about her in the bed of the truck and realized with utter dismay that Wade was not there. Nor were Marra or Emily.

CHAPTER

NINE

Put my tears into Your bottle.

PSALM 56:8

ARRIVING AT ABADAN DAYS LATER, Allison, fighting illness and worry, waited for Bret, still hoping he would arrive. She'd learned all she could from the military command post there on the island regarding the whereabouts of Wade, Marra, and Emily. The message remained the same: "No news we can report yet, ma'am. You'll need to wait until tomorrow." When tomorrow came, the answer remained uncertain. "We're doing all we can to account for the missing. As soon as General Paxton knows anything for certain, a public announcement will be made."

The announcement didn't come. Allison continued to visit the command post daily, along with scores of others trying to locate the missing or gather news for the wire service for the London newspapers. Allison was growing weaker, and with the medical facilities packed with those needing urgent care, she couldn't bring herself to complain of a simple fever and chills. Daily she hoped a message would arrive from Bret or that she'd find the others in the large tent facilities set up to accommodate those who were seeking the missing.

She knew no one would blame her for falling into despair, but surrendering to hopelessness would only add darkness to the fiery trial she endured.

"The Lord is my Light and salvation. The Lord is the strength of my life," she continually reminded herself, when the enemy attacked her mind with whispers of "It's no use. There's no reason to pray and hope."

The Father knows where they are, she told herself. *That's all that truly matters. He can do what I cannot. He asks me to pray, to trust, to rest in him. And if the gloom of trial has driven my friends and me apart, I will trust him with the thorn that pricks so painfully, for he is Love.*

Nearly four days had passed when, pressing her way through the throng to gain a copy of a military news release being handed out in the tent, a voice shouted: "Allison!"

Allison turned and saw Marra, her nurse's uniform torn and dirty, and her face thin and worn with care, trying to make her way toward her.

Allison's heart leapt with joy as she pushed her way toward her friend until they reached each other, embracing.

"I feared you were dead or captured," Allison said, glad tears streaming down her face. "I'm so relieved to see you. The others, are they with you?" She looked about.

Marra's brown eyes rimmed with tears. "Emily's dead."

Emily...

"A German aircraft got past the artillery as we were in the final stages of evacuating. Emily was in the hospital tent when a bomb hit. Everything was fire and smoke—and I tried but—"

Marra wept then, her body shaking, as Allison held her. The other woman's defenses at last had crumbled. Allison knew no one could come through the fires of loss and trial and not experience the dark depths. And she knew there was only one comfort, in the promises of the Father.

"The others—I don't know where they are," said Marra. "It all happened so fast, there was hardly time to think. The Turkish army was arriving as Colonel Holden got me onto a truck with some wounded. Even as we drove away, I could look back and see the Turks. There was terrible fighting going on."

Allison's heart turned as chill as the wind that came from the snowy peaks.

"You—you didn't see what happened to Wade...or to Colonel Holden after that?"

Marra shook her head. "I've been here for two days and haven't seen any of our friends from the hospital unit. Doc Murphy, Wade, the others—" she couldn't go on.

Allison stood, her heart empty.

A weary sergeant pushed his way toward them. "Excuse me, but are you two nurses from the medical corps at Baghdad?"

"Yes!" cried Allison. "Is there news of what happened to the others from Kut?"

"Yes, ma'am, there's a message here just come over the wire. Major General Crawford and his troops made it safely into Kut, but they're under siege."

"Siege?" said Marra dubiously. "You mean they're surrounded by the Turkish army?"

"Yes, ma'am," he stated gravely. "That's exactly it. There's about thirteen thousand soldiers held up inside Kut, that's our guess. But don't worry, we'll get 'em out some way."

Were Bret and Wade in the siege at Kut or dead like Emily?

"Have you—a casualty list?" asked Allison.

"Not yet, ma'am. We haven't been able to get in that area to remove the wounded and dead." He looked from one grim face to the other and grew suddenly embarrassed. "I'm sorry. Would—ah—you like a cup of tea? We've a little hut out back away from the crowd. You can rest there awhile if you like."

"Yes, Sergeant, that would be good of you," said Allison. "We don't have any place to go, and we've lost all our personal belongings."

Two hours later the same sergeant brought them a wire from Cairo. She was to be transferred on ship to Port Said. Allison believed Bret had contacted her father about her situation long before the battle. Now she was being called home to Cairo—on a six-month medical leave.

She looked over at Marra, who was seated in a rattan chair across the hut, her shoes off, her feet tucked up under her long soiled skirts. Anxiously their eyes met, then Marra smiled. "My new orders are the same. Looks like we're both going to serve in Egypt."

Allison stood, smiling. "At least we'll be together. You can spend weekends with us, and I'll invite David over, t—" Allison broke off, for the world about her was spinning crazily. She'd been having dizzy spells for weeks, but this was the worst one yet. She knew it was because she'd gone without food for two days, but she'd been too overwrought with concern for Bret and Wade to eat. Now that seemed a poor choice....

She felt herself going down and grabbed the edge of the table.

Marra was beside her, easing her back into the chair. "Why, you're burning up with fever and you didn't tell me!" She took Allison's pulse and checked her eyes, scowling. "How long have you been feeling sick?"

Allison shook her head weakly. "I'm all right, just tired."

"You're *not* all right. You're going to curl up on the settee here and rest. I'm going out to see what I can dig up from that sergeant in the way of a doctor and some hot, nourishing food. If you have cholera, we may not be allowed into Cairo."

When Allison awoke, the shadows on the wall told her it was late afternoon. Marra was in the hut with the sergeant and a doctor from Bombay, who sported a gray walrus mustache.

"So, you're awake," the doctor said. "Well, you haven't got cholera, you can be sure of that, or you'd not have made it this far.

138

But it is malaria, and that's bad enough. You've passed to a critical stage. I'm surprised you've gotten this far without collapsing." He replaced his instruments into his bag and scribbled something on a piece of paper. "Not much I can do here except give you some quinine. Bedrest back home in Cairo is the best thing that can happen to you, Nurse Wescott." He looked down at her. "After what you've been through, you can accept the prescribed rest as a deserved interlude. I've met Sir Marshall, and he'll want you sailing home on the next ship to Alexandria."

"You've met my father?" Allison looked up at him. "Is he still in Bombay? Were my mother and sister with him?"

"Lady Eleanor was with him, yes, and Beth, too. They'll be arriving in December. You should have a happier Christmas this year. You need to put all this out of your mind."

Could she ever do that? Did she even want to?

He snapped his satchel closed and prepared to leave, when he paused and cast her a somewhat curious look.

"Lady Eleanor's cousin, Sir Edgar Simonds, will be making the voyage from India with them in December."

Allison remembered the letter she'd gotten from Beth about her mother's widowed cousin, and especially his son, Gilbert. She knew little about either father or son, for her mother had never mentioned them. Allison had had little time until now to give the matter much thought. She wondered what her mother's cousin had done while living in India. Most everyone served in either the civil or military government.

"There, now," said the doctor. "That quinine will help you sleep."

"Do you know what Sir Edgar Simonds will do in Egypt?" murmured Allison, growing drowsy.

"Yes, he's been assigned the post of new inspector general of Cairo police." He looked thoughtful. "Rather a surprise, considering—" he stopped, as if catching himself thinking aloud, and his professional demeanor returned.

Considering what? she wanted to ask, but she was growing drowsier by the moment. She watched him walk to the door with Marra and the sergeant.

She wanted to pursue the matter. To ask why he'd thought it odd that Sir Edgar was to become inspector general. But it didn't matter now. Nothing seemed to matter but surrendering to the demands of her brain to sleep.

When Allison awoke the next morning, the sun was beating on the hut roof and the air was hot and stuffy. The voices of soldiers and the sounds coming from horses and mule-drawn wagons mingled with the rumble of military trucks.

How long had she slept? A day must have passed since she'd seen the doctor. By nightfall they would be boarding the steamer for Port Said. Marra must have gone out in search of a warm meal to bring back from the camp, but the thought of food made Allison nauseous. She picked up the quinine bottle and looked at it, wondering how much they'd given her. She was extraordinarily thirsty and went to the pitcher that sat on the table, smelling it. It was stale and warm, but they were lucky to have any water at all. How many of the soldiers left behind had none?

Left behind. She couldn't bear to think about them, what they were going through, what may have happened—

Where were Wade and Bret? No, she couldn't think of them, either. Not now, for it hurt too much. She drank thirstily, not thinking about how warm it tasted. Afterward she managed to use a little to wash her face and arms and brush her teeth. Still weak, she managed to braid her hair and pin it up off her neck. The day would be scorching, and the temperature in the hut already felt over 100 degrees. Voices outside the window cut through her misery. Her head turned swiftly as a rugged form passed by, speaking to someone walking beside him: "Find a doctor. Bring him here."

"Doc's already seen her, sir. Said it was malaria."

Bret!

Allison left the table and took several hurried steps toward the door when it opened and he stood there. A quick glance at his dusty, sweat-stained uniform assured her he was not seriously injured, though his right hand looked bruised and swollen, and a soiled bandage was wrapped hastily around it.

She couldn't move, though every pulsating beat of her heart demanded she run to him and hold him close. How easy, how right it seemed it would be to press her lips to his. But she knew she mustn't, knew to do so would be to betray herself and him. She had to hold firm, even now. For Bret, for herself, and for Wade.

She couldn't betray Wade now, not if she was to live with a clean conscience. Not while danger prowled like a lion.

And yet for all that she knew these things to be right, she wanted to break down and cry.

She stared at Bret. He held himself erect, watching her, studying. The barrier between them seemed intact. He was not inclined to let her close; she was not inclined to force her way in.

"You're all right?" he breathed quietly.

She swallowed and nodded wearily, still holding onto the wobbly rattan table, feeling as if her feet were slipping from beneath her.

He walked to her, took hold of her, and pulled out a chair for her to sit on. She looked up into his even gaze, waiting for news about Wade.

"When does your ship leave?" he asked.

"Five o'clock."

Why doesn't he tell me? Why doesn't he say something?

He walked to the window and looked out. Allison knew what he was seeing; she'd watched them often enough herself. Soldiers in retreat, exhausted and dragging their feet along, heads bent. A curious moody look came to Bret's face.

Wade's name came to her lips several times, but she was afraid to say anything. Maybe that was why he was delaying, too. He knew. Let the dreadful moment wait, hovering in the unknown. She plucked at her torn sleeve.

"Your parents couldn't possibly have known you were here, or the conditions you served under." He looked over at her.

She turned her head and looked down at the beat-up rattan table. Several flies buzzed about the unwashed coffee mugs. Ants crawled, searching for crumbs or grease. "No," she agreed.

"What did you tell them? That you served in Alexandria?"

"I'm of age," she reminded him quietly. "I didn't want them to worry, but I did tell Beth."

"They're going to be surprised when their daughter shows up as one of the injured in the war, struggling with malaria and depression and looking as if the wind will blow her away. You know, don't you, that you'll probably wake up in the night screaming, remembering the Zeppelin, remembering the evacuation. You'll need someone with you. Is Marra going?"

She placed both hands on her head. "I'll be all right."

"You're not all right."

She stood, resisting the dismay that wanted to turn her into a weeping child. She wouldn't cry, not in front of him.

"Am I any better than the others? Than Emily?" her voice broke. "She's dead, Bret, and she gave her life for her country as honorably as any soldier."

"I know that."

142

She turned away. "I'm not any different than Emily. Why should I be? Because I'm the daughter of a man who's to become the chief consul of Egypt? I should stay safe and sheltered, my soul protected from the tragedy of life, caring only for myself and my ease, my comforts." She turned toward him. "Is that it? Is that the kind of woman you would have me be?"

He turned his head and gave her one look, which wrapped around her, embracing her as completely as he had done so long ago in the deserts of Arabia.

"You *are* different," he gritted. "You know it and so do I. I've reminded myself of that a hundred times. Why do you think I've treated you—" he stopped.

Allison sank back into the chair and stared at her lap.

"And if Wade knows you as well as you think he does, he wouldn't have expected you to follow him into this ruddy mess. He would have insisted you stay on your aunt's medical boat and work out your God-given calling somewhere else."

"That isn't so," she denied wearily. "He didn't expect it, but he didn't fight it when I came to serve willingly, where I felt the need was greatest. It was selfish to sit on the *Mercy* enjoying the blue Nile."

"Is it selfish? I rather thought your aunt was a fine old saint, just as sacrificial and noble as Emily, who got blown to bits."

She covered her ears. He came to where she sat, caught her wrist, and pulled her to her feet as though she weighed nothing. She tried to draw away, but he wouldn't let her. He brought her even closer, until her senses spun with his nearness.

"Wade doesn't know you like I do."

"You're so sure of that? I don't think you know me at all."

"I know you well. I could have you in my arms now, if I didn't care about tainting the sweetness of your conscience. And if Wade were as wise as he is starry-eyed, he'd have known it as well and been wise enough to keep you away from me."

She flushed, feeling unmasked. Furiously she tried to jerk away.

"I know what you are," he went on in a quiet, intense voice. "Virtuous. And it so happens it becomes you. It makes me want you even more." His gaze wavered to her lips. "But to give in to those wants would be selfish—and foolish—and I won't do either. I'm going to be generous, Allison. I won't take advantage of your feelings. Because I know where that would eventually lead. And, regardless of how you or I may feel, I am not about to surrender to marriage. I told you that at Basra."

She tried to jerk her wrist free. "I think you're horrid! Where is Wade? What have you done with him? Let go of me! Let go, do you hear me?"

"And that's why I'm getting you out of here back to Cairo," he went on as if she hadn't even spoken. "Safe in the care of Saint Lydia. And I'm wiring your mother as soon as we get the wiring service running again. I'm warning her she'd better take the first boat from Bombay home, because her valiant little angel is so sacrificial she's going to get herself killed before Christmas if she doesn't."

He released her and stepped back.

She stumbled from the suddenness of his release, then sank into the chair, rubbing her wrist as though it hurt, even though he'd been gentle. She was certainly sober now. She glared at him.

He lifted the water pitcher and drank from it, not bothering with a cup.

She watched him, furious with herself, determined to hold on to the remaining shreds of her dignity. So he could have had her in his arms, could he? She'd make double certain from this moment on that it never happened. He was a rogue—no, worse, a rake! So he was being generous with her by not taking advantage of her feelings, was he?

"My fiancé," she stated in a deliberate voice. "Have you any information, Colonel?"

His gaze lifted to hers and held it until warmth tinged her face.

"Your 'fiancé,' Miss Wescott, is most likely alive, though a very sick man."

"You might have informed me sooner, instead of carrying on with such disgusting arrogance. You knew I was anxiously waiting to know if he was alive or dead, too afraid to ask!"

He lifted the pitcher again and emptied it. When he finished he set it roughly on the table. "Wade is just one more soldier among thirteen thousand others trapped inside Kut. Your anxiety, my dear, doesn't take precedence over the other men."

She pushed herself to her feet and stood stiffly. "You sound terribly defensive, Colonel," she challenged, hating the tremble in her voice.

"Do I?" His voice was softly dangerous. "About what?"

"As if you didn't know! Could it be your conscience troubles you because you abandoned Wade?" For one tense second she didn't know what his response would be. There was no polite distance in his eyes now. The barrier was discarded and there was anger—and something else she hadn't seen before. Pain? His lip curled down.

"Despite our carnal attraction to each other, I've underestimated you. You come quickly to your better senses. You'd exchange Wade's safety for mine in a flash if you could choose which man stood here."

His response shocked her into confusion.

"But if you can wait a few weeks, and he can survive where I hid him, I'll bring him back to your loving arms." He snatched up his hat. "I'll get through the Turks to get him out myself. I wouldn't think of denying either of you to save my neck."

He walked to the door and flung it open while Allison, startled, stood there. This was the last thing she'd expected, and sudden fear squeezed her heart. She didn't want him risking his life to save Wade, but he'd never believe her if she said so. Still—

"Bret, wait!"

He shut the door firmly behind him, and by the time she'd rushed to throw it open and step out onto the sand, he was gone.

She walked after him, so weak she feared she might faint before she could get back to the hut. But she kept going. The withdrawing soldiers walked along, heads bent, many wounded. She soon found herself lost among a thousand faces, so dulled by fatigue that they didn't notice her.

"Bret! Bret!"

Hundreds of footsteps crunching in the hot sand drowned out her weak voice and she stopped, unable to go on, knowing she'd never find him.

Allison struggled back to the hut and was sitting on the doorstep, head in her hands, when Marra returned carrying two tin plates of food.

"Allison?" She came toward her balancing the plates in one hand and reaching the other down to her. "I've brought some hot stew. You must be famished by now. Our ship leaves in three hours. Allison! What happened? What's wrong?"

She didn't look up. She just shook her head. "I'm all right," she murmured.

"You sure? It's time for your medicine. Can you get up and go inside? Let's get away from the flies."

Allison stood. "Yes," she repeated. "I'm all right now."

Marra looked at her. "You've been crying."

"No, no I wasn't. It's the heat. The sand."

"You can't fool me. I've cried too many times not to see heart-break in someone else. Come, try to eat. Look, I've even got coffee.

146

The soldier was so nice. Oh, Allison, things are going to be all right."

"Yes, Marra, yes. They've got to be."

That night aboard the steamer voyaging toward Egypt, Allison dreamed she was in the back end of the truck again, her hand reaching out to grasp Bret, but he slipped from her fingers and ebbed back into a night torn asunder by exploding artillery shells and spreading flames. She awoke with a start and stared into the darkness of the cramped little cabin she shared with Marra.

She got up from the bunk and walked silently across the bare floor to the window, looking out across the dark shining water toward Abadan, toward Kut.

The war continued. And with it, the bombing. The artillery. The death. Somewhere out there in the midst of danger, Bret was alone, on a mission to rescue Wade.

She leaned her forehead against her arm and felt the sea breeze softly touch her hair and cool the wetness of her face. *Please Lord, take care of him, of both of them.*

And then she closed her eyes, and let the tears fall.

PART TWO

CHAPTER

TEN

I went out full, and the LORD has brought me home again empty.

RUTH 1:21

Cairo

"TRUST GOD AND DO THE NEXT THING," Oswald Chambers liked to say, and Allison, remembering back to her year at his Bible Training College in London, decided to act upon that sage advice. In Arabia, her emotions had journeyed down a dark tunnel, and now she'd come to the one door that God seemed to have left standing open for her. It was November. Allison—ill, exhausted, and uncertain as to the whereabouts of Wade and Bret—had finally arrived with Marra at the family home in Port Said.

Allison glanced at her watch. It was five minutes after twelve noon. The steamer on which she and Marra were passengers, the *Meridian,* was finally waiting in Port Said, the northern gateway to the Suez Canal. The British flag snapped proudly in the Mediterranean breeze, and Allison looked at it with a new sense of pride, grateful to be home under its sway. She knew there were liberals among the British journalists and social voices who constantly raised questions of conscience that England should, and must, give independence to the young Egyptian activists. But that, she told herself, was a battle that did not concern her. Egypt was her home, her place of birth, and she didn't want to think of herself as part of an "occupying force."

More than ever now she considered this place, and these people, her home. And she looked to the coming of the Christmas season with great anticipation, for it heralded the celebration of the Child of Eternal Hope. With a weary but eager heart, she looked out at the dock, anxious to reach her home where she could await the glad arrival of her family from Bombay.

The voyage to Egypt had felt like being in another world after the war in Arabia. Despite knowing it was impossible, Allison kept thinking she might soon hear a Zeppelin flying over the ship or feel the ship suddenly shudder and tear with a great explosion, struck by a torpedo from a German U-boat lurking below the gray-blue Mediterranean waters. Instead, the two-week voyage proved restful and passed without incident. Allison sat on the sundeck basking in the mild November sunshine, with Marra for company. They'd become closer friends since surviving Kut and the loss of Emily. They helped each other deal with the possibility that the others might be dead as well. Marra had agreed to stay with Allison at the family residence until her two-month leave was up and she was restationed somewhere in a field hospital.

Allison frowned. Marra had continued to insist she would put in a request to be stationed again on the front lines, but Allison hoped to talk her out of it. She was sure Marra was trying to prove something by flirting with death, probably wishing deep inside to be reunited with her Robbie. Allison hoped to convince her that life must go on, that she should begin looking elsewhere for the man of her dreams...but even as she considered this counsel, she struggled with feeling a fraud. How could she encourage Marra to move forward in her life when her own traitorous heart so often brought her down the well-worn path that brought her face-to-face with Bret. When this happened, as it so often did, she, too, wanted to recoil into her shell.

With a sigh Allison closed her eyes against the sun and talked with her heavenly Father of all the broken dreams that scattered the path of life, both hers and Marra's. Allison knew that she might feel defeated or overcome, but he would not. He knew the way through the wilderness.

During the voyage, Marra had become somewhat of a private nurse to Allison, with Allison promising to pay her wages once at home in Port Said. The last few weeks since their departure from Arabia had been one of the few times Allison had ever been ill. She knew her condition was more serious than the physician back in Arabia and Marra dared tell her.

Marra...

Allison glanced to where her friend stood at the ship railing, looking out toward the harbor. Allison shifted slightly in her deck chair, breathing in the cool air. She'd put away her nurse's garb and was donned in a simple pale blue muslin dress, her straw sun hat fluttering in the November sea breeze. Marra still chose to wear her uniform, and studying her, Allison thought the laundered pinafore over her gray skirts suited her well.

"What does your Aunt Lydia look like?" Marra called over her shoulder, shading her eyes as she peered toward the throng on the wharf waiting for the docking of the steamer.

At the thought of her maiden aunt, Allison smiled. "You can't miss her. She always wears a hat, the biggest one you can find, and it's always adorned with white rose buds."

Marra peered carefully at the approaching wharf. "Oh! That must be her. There's a young man with her...do you suppose it's the cousin you told me about? What was his name? Neal, wasn't it?"

Neal? Allison looked at her, surprised. "It couldn't be. He's in England."

Marra looked again. "He's poshly dressed, wearing a hat, too, one of those fancy ones. Looks expensive."

Curious, Allison forced herself to rise from the deck chair and walk the short distance to the railing. She wasn't used to being so weak, and it was troubling; it made her feel helpless—something that, until recently, had been quite foreign to her.

She came up beside Marra, holding the railing for support, and felt her heart thumping from the exertion. Why, it was as though she'd been running! She could feel the color draining from her cheeks and the weakness stealing into her limbs, but she ignored it, getting ready to smile her greeting. She scanned the waving throng below until she spotted Aunt Lydia—and her smile widened.

Miss Lydia Bristow was standing on the dock near a horse-drawn calishe driven by an Egyptian. Allison recognized him as a man who had worked for her aunt at Luxor—a mule-faced cook and companion named Hassan.

Allison turned her gaze back to her aunt. At sixty-something years, one might expect Lydia to be a delicate and breathlessly sweet lady with silver hair, adorned in a lacy Victorian dress and holding a fan and smelling salts. Allison smiled again. Aunt Lydia was anything but the stereotypical aging British lady! She stood over five feet eight, with a middle as wide as her shoulders. Far from the expected Victorian dress, Aunt Lydia's favorite mode of clothing when on the missionary boat constituted a pair of faded canvas trousers with boots. Today, however, she wore a red-and-gold, loose-fitting kaftan, embroidered—from what Allison could see from this far away— with blue thread. And, of course, her usual reed sun hat was perched jauntily atop her head.

She saw Allison and removed the hat, waving it to and fro like a flag to draw her niece's attention. Her hair, fixed in a practical long gray braid, was looped and wrapped around her head, and her tanned face peered anxiously up at the rail. Her keen, crystal-clear eyes sparkled as she took everything in. She called out something, but Allison couldn't hear her over the steamer's whistle.

Allison smiled and waved and blew a kiss, noting with interest that Aunt Lydia still carried the cane she'd first been forced to use after a fall she'd taken years earlier when exploring the pyramids. Then a dark head leaned toward Lydia, drawing Allison's attention away from her aunt to the young man who stood beside her. Marra had been mistaken; he wasn't Neal. Allison had never seen him before, and she wondered who he was. He was lean and dark, with a melancholy face, yet even at this distance she could see he was handsome. He looked rather like an actor she'd seen play Hamlet. Marra had been right about one thing, though: his clothes were stylish and expensive—almost too stylish. The silk knot at his cravat, the loop of gold watch chain across his well-cut vest, the black derby on his head…all were fashionable and hinted of a young man full of himself.

"That's not Neal," she told Marra, curiosity in her voice. "I wonder who he is? He seems quite at home alongside Aunt Lydia."

Marra didn't reply. A glance told Allison her friend's quick eyes were studying her. "Better sit down again," Marra ordered. "I'll need to get some help getting you down the plank and into the carriage."

"No, I'm all right," insisted Allison, turning again to watch the man curiously. "I'll stand here and wait for the steward."

Marra looked below. "If he's not your cousin, maybe he's another student from Chambers's Bible College. If your aunt's a missionary, she'd likely find his company interesting. Maybe he's going to end up working on the *Mercy*. You'll soon find yourself with another admirer."

"No, thank you," said Allison flatly. If there was one thing she didn't need, it was an admirer. She'd had her fill of them. She was home again, and that was enough. All she wanted to do was enjoy being in Port Said without any complications.

In short order, she and Marra were making their way off the

steamer. Allison smiled, trying to ease her aunt's look of alarm when she saw her being wheeled down the gangplank by the ship's steward.

"Aunt Lydia!" she cried as she was engulfed in a fierce hug.

"Bless God, he brought you home safe," Lydia said, tears sparkling in her eyes. Allison felt answering tears in her own eyes as her aunt hugged her again and said, "Welcome home, girl!"

ELEVEN

❯❯❯━!━❮❯❯━●━❮❮❯━!━❮❮

He lies in wait secretly, as a lion in his den.
PSALM 10:9

"NOW AUNT LYDIA, I'M QUITE ALL RIGHT," Allison said in her firmest tone. "A few weeks rest in my own bedroom and I'll be my old self again, just in time for the holidays. It's only a mild case of malaria."

"Mild, nonsense!" she scoffed. "You can't trick an old nurse of forty years, m'dear. I know an ill person when I see one. How long have you been down with it?"

"Maybe two months. Please don't worry." She turned toward Marra, taking her arm and drawing her forward. "I've brought a friend and nursing comrade home. This is Marra Cohen. Marra, my Aunt Lydia."

As they smiled and exchanged greetings, Allison looked at the young man who lounged against the calishe. Up close he was even more handsome, with moody dark eyes and an artistic refinement to his features. And yet, for all his good looks, there was something about him that Allison didn't like. As he flashed a quick smile she suddenly knew what: she had the distinct impression he wasn't genuine. His stance, his expression, his entire carriage reeked with conceit and haughtiness.

"My dear cousin Allison," he said, his tone low and suave. "How positively grand to meet you. Home from the ghastly war, congratulations!"

Cousin? So this was the man Beth had written about in her letters.

Still, the only cousins Allison knew about were Neal and Leah, and Leah was buried in a lonely grave in the blowing sands of Aleppo.

The frank admiration in Gilbert's eyes was irritating, for unlike Bret who could scan her with masterful ease while showing nothing, this young man's thoughts were all too clear—and filled with a carnality that plainly was not Christian.

He swooped off his hat. "If you look this wonderful despite your illness, I daresay I can scarcely wait to see you in the full flush of health. I suppose you know you look nothing like Beth. Are you certain the two of you are sisters?"

The compliment was not for Beth, and Allison felt her irritation grow.

"A brunette and a redhead!" and he arched a black brow.

Aunt Lydia turned from Marra, seeming to sense the awkward moment as she glanced from Allison to the young man. "Dear, this is a relative of ours, Gilbert Simonds." She looked at the young man, something of sympathy in her eyes. "This is Allison, Beth's older sister. I told you about her...and her dedication to the Lord."

"Ah yes...how sweet."

"Hardly," said Allison.

"A rare moment, my meeting you like this fresh from the war. Beth's told me so much about you, and I am heartily overwhelmed."

Allison laughed at him. He was simply too obvious. From the look on his face, he didn't care for her reaction, but he merely smiled.

"So, we are cousins, are we?" repeated Allison, her tone clearly questioning the fact. If it were true, he was a very distant relative, one that her mother had never bothered to mention. "On my mother's side, I suppose? How odd she never mentioned your father. Sir Edgar, isn't it?"

"Ah yes, dear old Dad. Wait till you meet him." The flippant disrespect in his tone only displeased Allison even more. "He's at the house, flawed in manner and duty. He should have come. I told him so. He's quite uncouth at times. Everyone wonders how he could possibly have spawned me."

Allison struggled to contain her irritation. Instead of the guest relative, Gilbert was behaving the responsible host, welcoming her to her own home. She bit her tongue and hoped he would not remain long. She was well aware that Beth had a romantic crush on the man, and the idea worried her no small amount. Beth was easily impressed with the material, and Allison imagined Gilbert could put on quite a show when he wanted to.

He was rattling on. "Dear Daddy is always busy. I rarely saw him during the time he held his last position, but that sort of thing does have its advantages when one is in the university, doesn't it?"

"Does it?" asked Allison disagreeably.

He laughed and changed the subject much too smoothly. "Daddy's quite taken up with preparing for his new duties in Cairo." He looked at her, clearly expecting her to be impressed. When she said nothing, he explained as though she were a bit dense and hadn't caught the cue to raise her brows with admiring interest: "Daddy's the new inspector general of the police." He smiled somewhat smugly. "That, I suppose, could prove most beneficial. Let's hope Cairo is rather a bit more exciting than Port Said. I doubt I'll need Daddy's clout to bail me out of trouble, but it does help when you're dealing with people. It was a marvelous benefit in Constantinople."

The mention of Constantinople caught her interest, and she really looked at him for the first time. "Your father lived in Turkey before the war?"

"Indeed, in Constantinople. A marvelous city, Cousin. Have you been there? No? Ah, well, you don't know what you've missed. The night spots are incomparable." He smiled warmly, and she could see why Beth had written her, touting Gilbert's appeal. He did have a certain charm—oily, though it was.

"I promised Beth I'd take her there after the war. Unfortunately, that may be longer than we anticipated. They were sure it would all be over by Christmas. Of course, I could have 'joined up,' as they say, but I do have my studies. I've transferred them to Cairo University." He flicked an insect off his jacket with annoyance and disgust. "I study archaeology. You must tell me about the finds at the Charchemish digs some time. However, it's the Valley of the Kings I'm interested in. I expect one day to locate a burial treasure tomb."

Allison was only half listening—she wasn't thinking of tombs, but of Constantinople, remembering how professor Jemal, the Turkish agent who had worked with General Blaine, had come from there.

Gilbert turned from Allison then, giving only a careless nod to Marra, who evidently did nothing to stir his interest, as he hailed Hassan to load Allison's bag. "I gather your trunk will arrive at the house later," he said, his attention once again directed to Allison. He insisted on helping her into the calishe, then got in beside her, still chatting, clearly oblivious to the fact that he had assisted neither Aunt Lydia nor Marra. This task was left to Hassan, who showed a flicker of contempt in his black eyes as he scanned Gilbert.

Allison concealed an understanding smile. Apparently Gilbert Simonds had not won a warm welcome in the house. Allison wondered what his father, Sir Edgar, was like.

"Mum and Father have arrived?" Allison asked Aunt Lydia, who rode in front beside Hassan. He flapped the reins, and they started off along the seaward side of the street toward the house.

Her aunt looked back beneath her hat. "No, and more's the pity. They won't arrive until after the New Year."

Allison swallowed her disappointment. She had longed to spend the holidays with her parents. It would have been one of the first times in three years she'd been able to do so. "Did they explain the delay?"

Before Lydia could respond, Gilbert interrupted.

"Duty, my dear! That grand, patriotic word that justifies everything, even murder."

Startled, and not at all pleased at this comment, she turned to him. He smiled. "A figure of speech of course." His eyes were maliciously amused.

She kept a steady gaze on him, determined not to let him see how irritated she was. "Beth must have been disappointed not to sail out with you and Sir Edgar."

Pique filled his expression. "I did everything I could to convince your mother. I swore I'd take good care of her, but she wouldn't hear of it. The gossip, she said, would ruin Beth's reputation among her school friends. They have big plans for society in England, though the war's cut them short for now. Good heavens—" he laughed boldly—"One would think Beth a child."

"She *is* a child," said Lydia, her tone mildly rebuking. "And she's going to stay that way when she arrives in Cairo."

"Dear me, four women breathing down my neck and watching my every move. I daresay I shan't be able to frequent a nightclub without censure. Cairo shall turn into a nightmare."

Allison shifted uneasily. "In our family, we don't allow nightclubbing or entertainments without a chaperone."

Gilbert shrugged and smiled. "Your company, Cousin, would be quite appreciated, with or without chaperone. As for the trip from Bombay, Daddy was along, so Beth would have been perfectly safe. I *am* a gentleman, a graduate of gallantry. I know all the rules and intend to keep every one."

"Yes, I'm sure," Allison replied blandly. "I thought you were arriving from India with my parents. Why did you come on ahead?"

He flipped a hand with a bored air. "The urgency of the war. Like I said, Daddy is an extremely important man in the British government."

Allison glanced at Marra, who sat on the other side of Gilbert. She raised her eyes toward the sky, showing her utter boredom with Gilbert Simonds and his "extremely important father." Allison fought an amused grin.

Oblivious, yet again, Gilbert went on. "The authorities sent a wire asking Daddy to come here as soon as he could and take over the police investigations. It seems as though a few German and Turkish spies may be up to murder in Cairo."

"Murder?" asked Allison casually. "Another figure of speech?"

His smile was far from pleasant. "Maybe, maybe not."

Clearly Gilbert was hoping to frighten or unnerve the ladies in the carriage, but Allison had seen and experienced too much to treat the subject matter as a game. Aunt Lydia also knew something about what had happened—about General Blaine, Aleppo, and Leah's death—and she turned her head toward the front of the carriage and began talking to Hassan as if to end Gilbert's conversation.

Allison settled back against the seat. Strange that no one had ever mentioned Sir Edgar before. Did Bret know about the new inspector general coming from Constantinople?

It wasn't long before the irrepressible Gilbert began again. "Dad is a brilliant fellow. You haven't heard of him before?"

"No. A pity to be sure. Was he working for the British in Constantinople as a police inspector?"

"Hardly. The Veiled Protectorate doesn't look with favor on British inspectors nosing about Constantinople. But he was an inspector in Bombay before being transferred to the embassy in

Constantinople. When the war broke out, we had to leave. We had a house overlooking the Sea of Marmara, an old Byzantine mansion by the St. Barbara gate. Actually, it used to be a summer palace during the Crusades. It was marvelous. I hated to leave it."

A palace seemed a rather grand residence for an assistant to the ambassador, but Allison didn't pursue the matter. Her conversation with Gilbert had left her exhausted, and she drifted into silence. As though taking advantage of her fatigue, uneasiness fell upon her once more while the calishe moved down the street. She could almost imagine ghosts from Aleppo were loitering in the shadows of the buildings, watching her return home.

Would she never be free from the past?

Hassan turned the horses down a wide street that was lined with trees; Victorian-style houses rose above them on a slope overlooking the water. Ahead was the Wescott residence with its grilled verandahs and its tall roof thrust into the sky. Allison's second-floor bedroom faced the front, looking out over a crowded garden that was complete with a wrought-iron wall and gate.

Allison studied the house with a sense of relief. It was good to be home. It had been too long. This was the first time she'd been back in a year. She hoped this visit was less disturbing than the last. She frowned, recalling the night someone had broken into her bedroom when she'd returned from a ball. Later she'd discovered that Professor Jemal Pasha had been the culprit. He'd stolen a letter he'd written to her cousin Leah. Then another memory came to her, and Allison closed her eyes wearily as she relived Bret's arrival in the garden that night. He'd come just as Allison had escaped down the veranda steps. The memory brought a mixture of feelings: loss, longing, even a strange chill. Had Jemal ever been apprehended? There'd been no time to ask Bret in the camp at Basra, nor had her cousin Neal mentioned Jemal before he sailed months ago for England.

Put it out of your mind, she told herself. *Put* him *out of your mind.*

The surrounding streets were lined with buildings dating back to the previous century; the pillared porch facades hearkening back to the Vieux Carré, the French quarter of New Orleans. Allison's mother had preferred to live here rather than in Cairo. Allison knew that was because the British influence was strong here, as it was in the Suez Canal zone. She wondered what her mother would do when her father, because of his new position, went to Cairo to live and conduct the government's business. Her mother had wanted to take Beth to England, but with the increased influx of German U-boats, Allison was certain her father would not permit the voyage. That would mean more strain between them until the war ended.

And that could very well be a long time off.

The Mediterranean beaches facing the Victorian houses offered pleasant breezes and a view of the passing ships. The sight held a beauty all its own, and Allison could understand her mother's preference. Port Said, with a main street running along the beach, was very unlike the Moslem Egyptian atmosphere of Cairo.

The afternoon sun was high in the sky, and its brightness turned the waters to a glittering silvery-blue. Farther out to sea, the Mediterranean rolled with deep swells in the open waterway. Allison drank in the familiar sight of pomegranate and sycamore trees, which grew in abundance along the street near the house. The final days of autumn seemed long and forlorn this somewhat chilly day, with dried reddish yellow leaves still clinging tenaciously to the dry branches.

In a few minutes Hassan drove the calishe up past an entrance into a parkway bordered by a neatly trimmed hedge. The lush banana trees flourished in the front yard. The house stood before them now, pleasant and white and very Victorian, yet shrouded with the flavor of Egypt due to two engraved pillars standing guard at either end of the front porch. An old Egyptian panther that cousin Neal had given her mother as a birthday gift looked down at Allison with secretive eyes—eyes, she thought with a touch of awe, that had gazed upon an Egypt of a millennium ago.

Hassan pulled up the horse, and Gilbert climbed across Marra to get out of the calishe. Marra shook her head, a rueful smile on her face as she watched him come quickly around to Allison's door.

"You have an admirer," she said, grinning.

Allison grimaced. "You may have him, if you like."

Marra's grin broadened. "Oh, no, he's all yours."

The door opened, and Gilbert held out both lean hands to assist Allison down to the carriage block.

Struggling to hide her humor, Allison left the carriage and waited at the foot of the steps for Aunt Lydia and Marra. As she did so, she had the oddest feeling that someone was standing at her bedroom veranda gazing down at her. She glanced up quickly, but no one was there. Perhaps, accustomed as she was to the sounds of war, the stillness was feeling oddly oppressive.

On the heels of this thought came the realization that she was growing extremely tired. When she felt Marra's hand beneath her arm, she smiled weakly in gratitude.

The Persian lilacs, jacaranda, coral, and flame trees were no longer sending off a sweet fragrance. Strange, but thinking of jasmine brought Bret to mind, stirring images of the way Bret had tried to kiss her on her bedroom veranda the night of the intruder...the intoxicating fragrance of jasmine had surrounded them that night.

As Allison and Marra entered the front anteroom, Gilbert strode ahead, calling out pleasantly: "Father? We're back. We've brought Cousin Eleanor's daughter Allison."

Marra leaned toward her and whispered: "Isn't he odious? He's got nerve, acting as though *you're* the guest."

The warm mahogany tones of the hardwood floor sounded beneath Aunt Lydia's walking stick and were shaded by the drawn inner wooden shutters on the windows. Ahead of them was a set of French double doors leading into the large sitting room. Allison had always liked this room, for it faced the back garden, and sunlight streamed through the windows. She could almost make herself think her beloved mother would come walking in from the garden—her arms filled with roses, her face wreathed in smiles—as she had so many times in the past.

After the horrors of the war and the crowded tent quarters, the heat, the flies, the smell of sickness and death, Allison's senses were wooed by the old comforts. She looked upon the sofas, chairs, and ottomans upholstered in ivory brocade that was embroidered with small blue-gray leaves matching the thick drapes on the terrace windows. The drapes were drawn, and the doors stood open into the back garden. When Allison heard footsteps, she turned in their direction.

A man appeared, and though he was a stranger Allison knew this must be Gilbert's father. He was taller than his son and weighed, she was certain, over two hundred pounds. His square jawline was strong; his deep-set small black eyes keen and reptilian. His shoulders were wide and slightly hunched beneath a wrinkled ivory coat, and he wore a Panama hat. His white oxfords were scuffed and worn. He carried a heavy silver-handled cane and walked toward her, unsmiling.

Allison stared, not at Sir Edgar Simonds, but at his pipe. She loathed pipes—they were too reminiscent of Rex Blaine, who had collected them. As the sickeningly sweet aroma of tobacco drifted to her, her memory also drifted; back to Aleppo where she had hidden under a porch from a murderer, where the desert winds blew grains of sand across the floor above her head like a slithering snake. The boards had squeaked beneath his weight as he came down the steps.

She fancied she could hear his footsteps again, coming ever closer....

No, what she heard wasn't Blaine, but Sir Edgar's white shoes squeaking across the floor as he walked in her direction. She tore her fevered gaze from his pipe and looked into his eyes, and for a crazy moment she had the thought she was looking into the face of the deceased Rex Blaine.

Suddenly overwhelmed, she felt as though her mind were being pulled to some faraway place. Vaguely she saw Sir Edgar's bland expression turn to alarm, heard his voice warn: "She's fainting! Gilbert! My boy, quick, don't stand there!"

And then there was nothing.

"There now, my girl, you're going to be quite all right."

Aunt Lydia's soothing voice sounded from far away, and Allison's eyes fluttered open. Neither Sir Edgar nor Gilbert were there in the quiet bedroom. Lydia sat on the edge of the bed, her face full of mothering sympathy as she peered down at Allison. Her reassuring presence brought a wave of welcoming sanity, and for a moment, Allison could convince herself she'd imagined the whole unpleasant incident downstairs. She looked about her familiar bedroom, noting how the late afternoon shadows weaved against the walls from the tree branches outside her veranda. Hours must have passed since she entered the house.

"Why—I must have fainted!" She tried to raise herself to an elbow. "I'm sorry, that was quite silly of me!" She felt a red flush creeping up her face over the fuss she'd caused, but Lydia pressed her shoulders back against the pillow.

"Not silly at all. Our bodies sometimes demand what they need. You rest in bed until morning. Ah, here's Marra with the tea. Come in, girl, have a seat."

Marra came through the door of the adjoining bedroom, which she'd been given by Lydia. Close behind her came a middle-aged Egyptian maid carrying a tray with a pot of tea and three cups.

"Zalika, how nice to see you," Allison said, and the maid smiled her response.

"You're a much sicker girl than you're willing to admit," lectured Lydia in her no-nonsense tone. "And it's time you own up to it. I won't forgive myself for postponing the colonel's recommendations when he wired me from Abadan."

Allison glanced at her, keeping her response low key. "What colonel?"

Marra laughed as she poured tea, but Allison ignored her, and Aunt Lydia didn't appear to notice either response.

"Colonel Bret Holden from Cairo Intelligence. He wired me back in September that you were ill. He asked me to contact Sir Marshall in Bombay to have you sent home to Egypt since he couldn't get through." Lydia's brow puckered. "I'm sorry to say it was one time I allowed my love of nursing to override good sense. The day before the colonel's wire, I'd received a letter from you. In glowing terms you told me how well you were faring. Of the desperate need for more nurses for the soldiers. And, well, I'm afraid I took your suggestion more seriously than I did his. An error in my judgment."

Allison kept her expression blank, even under Marra's teasing gaze. But Marra wasn't fooled. "So Colonel Holden remains encased in bloodless armor does he?" she said. "He didn't send a wire recommending they send the rest of us noble nurses back to Egypt."

Allison accepted the cup of tea. "He has his ulterior motives for wanting me out of danger," she said casually. "And they have nothing to do with romance, I assure you." She ignored Marra's grin. "I do wonder, though, why he couldn't get through to Bombay?"

"The lines were cut, I think," said Aunt Lydia. "But let's not talk of that. You're here now and safe. I only wish I'd taken his warning more seriously."

"I'll be better in no time," insisted Allison, but even she heard how weak and listless her voice sounded.

"With Marra and me both watching you, you haven't a chance of getting up too soon."

"You heard your aunt," said Marra, handing her a cup of tea. "We've made a pact. You're not getting out of that bed for ten days."

"Ten days—!" Allison managed a groan. "Am I in prison?"

"You could say that," declared Marra unapologetically. "Your aunt's orders. You and I both agree she's a better nurse than either of us, so her orders must be followed."

"I'll agree she's a better nurse," said Allison as Marra helped her sit up and piled pillows behind her back. "But ten days! I've too much to do." She looked at her aunt. "I want to get in touch with David. He's in Cairo. By now the war office there will have further information on what happened at Kut."

Aunt Lydia grimaced. "Kut, a dreadful situation. It was in the papers. Don't worry about David Goldstein, though. He's been as pestering as a mosquito over when you'd arrive. I've invited him to Sunday dinner. By then you'll be feeling better. Here, girl, drink the tea while it's nice and hot. There's nothing like a cup of good British brew with a touch of bitters to make you sweat."

Allison grimaced her protest, but Zalika smiled at her and placed the tray on her lap. Beside the tea, a small gold-rimmed white plate held Allison's favorite cinnamon shortbread cookies.

Allison smiled at her warmly. "Zalika, how good to see you again."

"*I-wah, sah-ee-dah, Allison, shuk-run! Iz-zi-yik?*" she murmured, her dark eyes concerned.

"Yes, I'm feeling much better," insisted Allison, but she knew

Aunt Lydia was right about her condition. Rest was essential if she was to regain her strength anytime soon.

Allison smiled ruefully when she thought of her mother's cousin. "Sir Edgar must have wondered what was wrong with me when I stared at him and then fainted."

"Yes, well…he was concerned his presence may have upset you. And Gilbert's been hanging about the hall door, wanting to see you."

The last thing she wanted was Gilbert plopping himself down on the corner of her bed. "I'd rather not see him yet."

"Of course you wouldn't. I told him to run along."

"Odd, that Sir Edgar thought his presence would upset me," said Allison, looking at her aunt for confirmation of her curiosity. He couldn't have known that she compared him to Rex Blaine.

"It's always difficult to tell what another is thinking," she remarked with a slight smile. "And it must be a bit disconcerting to have someone faint dead away upon their first meeting with you."

"Yes, I suppose it must," Allison said, laying back against her pillows. Of course Lydia wouldn't realize Allison had found Sir Edgar's presence—and his resemblance to Rex Blaine—disconcerting. She'd never explained to her aunt that Sarah Blaine's husband was a German agent.

Bret had seen to it that Blaine's wife and friends at the polo club were all told the deceptively good-natured and bungling Rex Blaine had accidentally shot himself. For Allison, however, the secrecy shrouding the retired major's treachery would remain a horrible memory. Hadn't her reaction to Sir Edgar proven that?

Knowing the truth about Blaine had also made it quite uncomfortable to keep up a friendship with poor Sarah. If the war breaking out last August had done anything, it had allowed Allison time to be away from Egypt and from the need to keep company with her mother's close friend. Allison had written Sarah from Arabia, but that had been little hardship. Letters were always easier than facing someone across a luncheon table at fashionable Ezbekiah Gardens.

She supposed she would be seeing Sarah Blaine again, now that she was home. If Sarah learned of her illness, she would offer to take the train from Cairo and spend a few days here in Port Said. Allison wasn't ready for that. She wanted to ask Aunt Lydia not to contact her mother's friend, but the thought added a sense of guilt to her growing concerns.

"What do you think of Sir Edgar?" she asked, watching her aunt's response.

Lydia raised both brows. "Have you guessed already I find the fellow totally obnoxious? I thought I had managed to suppress my feelings better than that. Don't misunderstand me, he's a brilliant fellow when it comes to police work, or so I've heard. But he's decidedly callous when it comes to the Egyptians."

The news was far from comforting. She didn't need to wait long for Aunt Lydia to explain.

"It's in his jurisdiction to put a favorable word across the desk of the general to permit me to have the *Mercy* back, but I don't believe he will." She frowned to herself. "He knows I've medical work to do near Suez with the fellahin. I need the boat and permission to voyage down the Nile, but he's dismissed the cotton growers with indifference. Too dangerous, he says, for a woman 'my age.' Imagine! Sometimes I think he's more interested in the price of cotton than in the police matters he was appointed to oversee in Cairo."

Allison had heard that the price of cotton had jumped sky high since the war and was likely to climb still higher. The Egyptian farmers were making more money than they had in their entire lives of growing cotton for the British to export to England and her colonies. Still, European merchants and landowners were making even more. With the military in Egypt requiring the fellahin to loan their camels and donkeys for the war effort, and with the strongest Egyptian farmers commandeered to dig trenches, there wasn't nearly as much cotton being grown as there had been before the war. Those who had it to sell were likely to emerge very wealthy men after it was all over.

It seemed strange to Allison that Sir Edgar had come to fill his post in Cairo as inspector general with such an avid interest in the price of Egyptian cotton on his mind. Were he not a man of integrity, he could use his position to help control cotton prices—and thus gain a great deal of personal wealth.

"Regardless of whether or not he's obnoxious," said Allison changing the subject, "that's hardly reason enough for me to faint when he enters the parlor." She laughed at herself. "He's certainly not as frightening as a German Zeppelin dropping bombs on the hospital near Basra. I wish he wouldn't blame Gilbert, either, for what happened downstairs. Not that he isn't rather trying," she confessed. "He's so utterly vain and full of himself."

"Yes, isn't he," agreed Lydia thoughtfully. "He's forever bemoaning the dull prospects for his social life in Egypt. From what I gather, he was a man about town in Constantinople."

"He seems much older than his age," agreed Allison, and thought of her sister, Beth. No doubt Gilbert's flamboyant manner was part of the attraction.

"Don't worry about Sir Edgar," scoffed Lydia. "He well understands the reason for your collapse. He's looking forward to meeting you as soon as you're able to take supper downstairs with the rest of us. Of course, I've told him it will be some time before you can."

Trying to keep her concerns to herself, Allison inquired casually, "Will he and Gilbert be staying long?"

"So it appears. Eleanor has asked him and Gilbert to live with the family in Cairo since both he and Marshall will hold important posts for the London government, but I don't know how it will work out since the Residency is under repair."

"Cheer up, Auntie," she said trying to put a good face on things. "If the new police inspector general sits at the breakfast table each morning, you'll have even more opportunity to convince him to return the *Mercy* to you and allow the missionary work to continue. We'll both convince Sir Edgar before it's over."

Lydia smiled, though the action lacked confidence. "If anyone can thaw his heart, I'm counting on you, my girl, to do it. But between you and me, I don't think he has a heart to thaw."

TWELVE

>─┼─◄►─┼─◐─┼─◄►─┼─◄

Yea, though I walk through the valley of the shadow of death...
PSALM 23:4

EXCITED THOUGH SHE WAS AT BEING HOME and filled with curiosity about cousins her mother had never mentioned, any further information from Aunt Lydia had to wait. Allison soon grew weary and felt an overpowering need for rest. Whether the need came from the demands of her fevered body or from the medication she'd been given, she didn't know. She only knew she must sleep—and sleep some more.

With a gentle touch to her niece's forehead, Aunt Lydia stood and left the room. "Get your rest, my dear," she said as she pulled the door shut.

Allison did just that. In the following days she forgot all about Sir Edgar and Gilbert and the many questions that wanted answers. She saw no one except Aunt Lydia and Marra, who fussed over her diet, her hours of sleep, and her doses of quinine sulfate. Even the Sunday dinner with David was postponed.

The following Wednesday, Marra came up the stairs bringing a letter. "It's from David. He penned it last night when he couldn't see you."

"He was here in the house and no one told me?"

Marra looked helpless. "You were sound asleep, and you know your aunt. One might as well move a mountain as get her to change her mind about something she feels is important. There was nothing

I could do, but I did suggest the letter, and David jumped on the idea. Here."

Allison tore it open as Marra slipped toward the door that led off into her own room. Allison looked toward her with a sense of unease. "You needn't go."

Marra's expression was gloomy. "I think you'll prefer to be alone. The news isn't good. He told me last night. We had a walk along the harbor. If you need me later, just call."

Allison swallowed the sudden lump that formed in her throat. Her heart began to pound with fear, and she broke into a sweat. She held the letter with shaking fingers while Marra softly closed the door behind her.

Alone, fighting the fear that encircled her, Allison prayed before reading the letter, asking the Lord to prepare her. After a moment, she began reading.

Dear Allison,
You know me well enough to understand I nearly stormed the stairs tonight to get to your room to see you, but under the eagle eye of your family I had to be on my best behavior. I eventually settled on Marra's idea to write a letter.

There was more in the same vein but Allison skimmed the words until what she found leaped out at her:

A full report of the tragedy at Kut has reached the war secretary in London and the British viceroy in India, so I'm allowed to report the information. Most of it is already in the newspapers anyway.
    A week after the Sixth Division withdrew from an attack on Baghdad under strong Turkish resistance (as you must

well remember), Major General Crawford and his men were able to reach Kut with the Turks coming forcefully behind. With his troops sick and exhausted, Crawford took refuge in the town, which soon fell under siege. Unfortunately, they're without adequate food and water is scarce. Over thirteen thousand men are stuck there with no immediate hope of getting them out.

Kut will hold out as long as possible. I'm told London is doing everything it can to work with the Turkish government in Constantinople to see the thousands of men safely released, but the Turks are not known for generosity or mercy.

News arrived from Abadan of a massacre at the field hospital. As far as we know, since we haven't been able to get into the area, most of the medical corpsmen you served with are dead, along with the wounded patients. The field where the soldiers were laid was deliberately bombed by two raids from a German Zeppelin.

I hate to tell you this, but there's been no word from the colonel or Wade. There's a chance they are among the thirteen thousand in Kut, but the Intelligence Office has no way of knowing.

The letter fell from her hand onto the cover and she raised her eyes, staring blankly at the door. She relived the moment when Bret had walked out of the hut at Abadan...then saw again the image of Wade as he ran to join Doc Murphy....

Had she lost them both?

Tears filled her eyes and splotched the letter, causing the blue ink to run. She should have stayed with Bret! She might as well have died, also. Her throat ached as pain tore through her chest. *Please*

*Lord, not both of them, it can't be true. I don't think I could stand it...*and she dropped her face into her hands and wept. *Bret—*

The door opened softly, and Allison was dimly aware of footsteps, and then the bed dipping as someone sat down. It was Marra, and she reached out to draw Allison close. They cried together, and Marra said, "Oh, Allison, this is horrible. It's like losing Rob all over again. But you mustn't give up hope. David's still trying to dig up new information. Knowing him, he'll learn something soon."

"E-even if they're inside Kut, it won't do any—any good. The Turkish commander will have them killed!"

"You believe in God. You must trust him to hear your prayers."

"I do, but he may take them regardless of what I pray. I don't think I can bear it—"

"I don't know much about God, even though I was raised in the Jewish tradition, but what's important is that you believe him. He knows how much you can take, isn't that what you're always telling me? If he's as good and caring as the Bible says, then you can trust his decision, can't you? Whatever it may be?"

Allison wiped her face, her hands trembling, and she tried to smile through her tears. "I'm the one who's supposed to tell you these things."

Marra's eyes were filled with tenderness. "You're sick, don't be so hard on yourself."

Allison picked up the letter and looked at it. She sought the words again that hinted of hope. *There's a chance they are among the soldiers in Kut....*

Bret was strong. He had been in so many dangerous situations in the past and had always gotten out safely. Maybe he could get out of this one...but how? And what if he didn't? What if he was injured in the bombing raid? And Wade was sick—perhaps worse off than she was. How could he live for long without proper food, water, and medicine?

Marra spoke softly. "Last night when we walked along the harbor, David told me there was a possibility the colonel and Wade had been able to escape. Bret has Kurdish friends."

Allison looked at her, hope springing to life within her. She remembered the family of Bret's Kurdish assistant, who was killed by Rex Blaine that night in the hut at Aleppo. Wasn't the man's family located near Jerablus? Was David right? Was it possible that Bret and Wade might have slipped away in the confusion of the artillery bombardment?

Without realizing it, she was gripping the letter. She told Marra how she and Bret had escaped with David from Germans at Jerablus in the summer of 1914 and how they had made it across the wilderness to Jerusalem.

Marra seemed anxious to let her believe, to hope. "Yes, that's what happened, I feel sure of it. And as long as Kut can survive the siege, there's hope for all those soldiers trapped there too."

She leaned back against the pillows and closed her eyes. Yes, there was hope. Marra had to be right.

But were they merely deceiving themselves?

In the days that followed, the newspaper was filled with accounts of the war on the western front and in the Dardanelles near Constantinople. Allison read the headlines about Arabia: "Kut continues to hold out. Military says siege may last for months."

Other headlines held little hope: "London fears cholera outbreak inside Kut. Government warns of wholesale tragedy," "Prospects for 13,000 Brit soldiers grim. Kut fast running out of water," and

"Turkey refuses to bargain for release of trapped British soldiers. Accuses London of trying to buy soldiers' freedom."

She set the papers aside and closed her eyes, fighting against the sense of utter hopelessness that threatened to overwhelm her.

It was a warm afternoon two weeks later. The breezes coming from the harbor were reminiscent of Indian summer, and Allison, who was now out of bed, was beginning to recover her strength. She decided to cheer Aunt Lydia by taking afternoon tea with her and Marra out in the garden patio. Wearing a pretty pale yellow dress with long sleeves, she came down the private outer stairs from her terrace, surprised at how weak her legs were. I feel as feeble as a kitten, she thought, troubled. It seems as though I've been convalescing for a month instead of two weeks. She had a new appreciation for the frustration of the soldiers who'd been confined to their hospital beds for months at a time. Such a thing had to be even more difficult for a man bear, especially one who was used to independence and strength. She remembered what the Scriptures said about the apostle Paul and his thorn in the flesh. Though he'd prayed for healing, the Lord had not granted his request. "My grace is sufficient for thee," the Lord had said. And Paul submitted to the Lord's will with gladness. "Therefore I take pleasure in...weakness, knowing the power of Christ rests upon me."

Oh, what a hard lesson to learn! When I am weak in myself, then am I strong in Christ.

As she followed the stone pathway that circled the garden wall, she neared a smaller back gate that opened onto a narrow and seldom-used side street. She paused, surprised to see a horse-drawn carriage on the street, parked under the overhang of a coral tree. Both horse and carriage were unfamiliar, as was the young Egyptian driver.

Did Aunt Lydia expect a visitor for tea?

Cautious footsteps came from the other end of the garden near the drawing-room door. As they drew nearer, Allison paused, turning her head toward the shrubs to see who it was. A large, broad-shouldered man in a rumpled white jacket and Panama hat emerged from the privet hedge. Sir Edgar. He did not notice her standing in the shade as he unlatched the gate to the alleyway and went out.

The Egyptian driver climbed down from the calishe and threw open the side door. As he did, Allison caught a glimpse of a woman's hat with a veil. The woman drew back in the seat when Sir Edgar climbed inside. The driver shut the door behind him, and a moment later the calishe drove away with the brisk clop of the horse's hooves fading into the afternoon breeze.

Allison looked after them, wondering. She couldn't be certain since she had received a mere glimpse of the woman, but she could have sworn that woman was...she shook her head abruptly. No, that was impossible. It couldn't have been the Baroness Helga Kruger. Besides, why would a woman of such wealth and fashion wish to see Sir Edgar? And why in the world would she have concealed herself? *Of course,* thought Allison uneasily, *it could have been Sir Edgar who hadn't wanted to be seen.*

She was still musing over the puzzle a few minutes later when she joined Aunt Lydia and Marra at the wrought-iron patio table beneath a large canvas umbrella. Zalika had arranged a pretty tea service of white china decorated with pink rosebuds; a silver tea urn glinted in the pale sunlight. A plate of scones sat warm and tempting with bowls of honey and butter.

It was a wonderful afternoon, with blue sky and sea breezes, but there was a nip in the air, and Lydia wore a shawl as she poured the steaming brew. Allison took her seat, wondering if she should mention the carriage.

Aunt Lydia had been doing all she could to soothe Allison and get her mind off of Kut. It was clear she'd put her own concerns for her missionary work on the *Mercy* into the background and set about to work tirelessly at diverting her niece.

As Allison settled into her chair, Aunt Lydia smiled brightly. "I've some surprising good news."

The only news Allison could think of now that would be good was a hopeful message about Wade and Bret. She searched her aunt's face wondering if her prayers had been answered.

"About Kut?"

Lydia shifted position in her chair. "No—not that I'm afraid, but good news just the same." She pushed a piece of paper across the table. "Your father sent this wire from Bombay. Your parents have decided to return to Egypt in time for Christmas holidays after all. And Neal is coming home from England as well. We'll all be together. War or no war, it will be the best family Christmas we've had in years."

Joy flooded Allison's heart, and she smiled for the first time in days. Her soul ached to be enfolded in her mother's understanding, and to see her beloved father again. And cousin Neal! How she missed him and his protective, brotherly ways! It was almost too wonderful to be true. There would be only one thing missing from the holidays....

But she wouldn't think about that now.

The expectation in Lydia's eyes finally reached Allison. It was clear her aunt had hoped her happy news would at least cheer Allison a little. She smiled as brightly as she could. "That's wonderful! When will they arrive?"

"Marshall, Eleanor, and Beth will be here the first Saturday in December. And Neal's ship is due to dock at Alexandria soon, though the date is uncertain. We're all moving to the Residency—"

she frowned—"No, we can't. I keep forgetting."

"Forgetting what?"

"That the Residency is under repair. We'll need to find other accommodations. Oh, dear. And Cairo is frightfully crowded and all that, due to the thousands of soldiers arriving. The saddest part is that it's getting more difficult for families to follow, the paper says a ship arrived only a few days ago with wives and children—a dangerous voyage, I would think, with German U-boats firing torpedoes at everybody. And that means the hotels will all be filling up fast. Well, I shall let Marshall worry about lodging. Now, here, my girl, do eat a sandwich. You're losing weight."

Allison bit into the cucumber with its soggy bread, her thoughts roaming. The Residency was within walking distance of the Intelligence Office, and Allison knew she wouldn't be able to drive past it without the image of Bret coming to mind. At least she could see David.

"Why Cairo?" she asked, uneasy. "Mum always preferred Port Said, and the air is healthier from the sea. Shouldn't we stay here until after the holidays?"

"Yes, you're right about the air," agreed Lydia with a sigh, casting a longing glance toward the blue waterway. Allison was sure she was remembering the *Mercy* and her work on the Nile. "But we've no choice I'm afraid. Marshall will be taking up his new post earlier than expected. And Sir Edgar had a summons to go to Cairo at once."

Allison looked up. So that was it. The carriage and the woman. She must have been sent by the Cairo Department to meet him and arrange his travels. She relaxed. No mystery there. Thank goodness.

Lydia stirred her tea with a tiny silver spoon. "And since General Maxwell refuses the *Mercy* access to Suez and Ismalia, I shall offer my services to Oswald Chambers at Zeitoun." She looked up. "I wonder if the YMCA would think a woman in her sixties would only get in the way?"

Allison smiled. "They'll rejoice to see you, of that I'm sure. Especially Mr. Chambers. I didn't know he'd arrived yet."

"In October, I think, but Biddy and Kathleen are still in London. Military regulations are in a constant state of flux, so getting family members in is ever a trial. They'll be arriving soon, I think."

Allison nodded. The problem was not with civilians leaving England, but with being permitted to enter Egypt once they arrived. Allison had read that some unfortunates without entry permits were being detained at Port Said and forced to return to England on the next available ship.

Aunt Lydia fixed her with an assessing gaze. "About moving to Cairo...are you up to the train trip, Allison?"

"I'm feeling much stronger," she assured her.

"I've told Zalika to have the help arrange for our trunks to be packed."

"Well, at least Gilbert will be pleased about Cairo. There are more than enough government dinners to keep him amused there," said Allison, reaching for a lemon scone.

"Hmm, spoiled chap. He's positively heathen. I was reading the Bible the other morning in the sunroom and he asked me what it was! Imagine! The poor dear has gone to the ravages since his mother died. Doesn't even know what a Bible is. He's got no one to care for him properly. It's clear that Sir Edgar spoils him dreadfully, and he's paying the price of a lack of discipline." Lydia frowned thoughtfully. "I've got to do something about that boy. He's headed straight for disaster."

Allison nodded in agreement. "Did you say Sir Edgar went to Cairo?"

"He's leaving in the morning with Gilbert. They'll take a room at a friend's house until Marshall's situated in the Residency."

She frowned. "I saw him leave in a carriage. I suppose he was meeting with someone from the police. She must have come to speak with him about his new position. Inspector general is an important calling."

"And desperately needed. I understand corruption is rampant in this area and officers are taking bribes. Thank goodness we've a man like Sir Edgar to take over the police reins."

Marra had been quiet until now when her curious gaze caught Allison's. "You saw him leave in a carriage?"

Allison wondered why she looked so puzzled. "Yes, just now as a matter of fact, as I walked through the garden. I took the long way around to strengthen my legs. Why?" she asked pointedly.

Marra shrugged and lifted her cup. "No reason, except I happened to run into Gilbert this morning, and he said his father was a bit under the weather and did I have anything for the grippe? Oh, well, I suppose he felt better and went out."

Aunt Lydia refilled her cup. "Yes, that must have been it."

In the brief silence, Allison listened to the breeze stirring the dead leaves on the garden trees. She turned to her aunt. "Lydia, what do you know about mother's cousin?"

"Not much," she admitted casually. "He's a widower of course. Gilbert is his only child."

"When did his wife die?"

"Celeste? I'm ashamed to admit I don't exactly know."

Celeste. The name evoked the image of a woman much like her own mother. Allison couldn't imagine Sir Edgar married to such a woman. If Celeste was her mother's cousin, then they likely would have looked something alike. Certainly Gilbert didn't take after his father in appearance at all.

"I was busy on the *Mercy* for so many years, and Eleanor never wrote about her cousins, so I never met Celeste," confessed Lydia.

"Did Mother ever talk about Sir Edgar?"

"Oh, once or twice if I recall. You know how some families are about certain relatives," she said, as if trying to make excuses for Eleanor. "Some relatives can be quite a trial, and for one reason or another, they're relegated to the shadows. That can be either fortunate or unfortunate, depending on one's viewpoint."

"I gather the Wescotts weren't interested in the Simonds."

Lydia sighed. "It wasn't the Wescotts, but the Bristows. Eleanor's family didn't approve of Celeste's marriage to Sir Edgar, but don't ask me why, for I haven't a clue as to the reason."

"Yet mother has asked him and Gilbert to live with us in Cairo. Don't you find that curious?"

Lydia looked at her. "Perhaps, if I had thought about it."

Allison smiled. "You mean you hadn't?"

"I didn't say that—"

"No, you didn't. And I think you thought about it the same as I. I wonder who asked him to stay at the Residency? Mum or Father?"

"I wonder. You can ask them when they arrive. Don't forget things have altered considerably from the early days of disapproval. Sir Edgar Simonds is now the inspector general, dear girl."

"Yes, a lofty position, and one carrying a good deal of authority in the war." Allison thoughtfully leaned back in her chair. There were so many questions surrounding Sir Edgar....

"Maybe drawing him into the family circle is the result of a conscience reborn after Celeste's death," said Aunt Lydia. "The love of God certainly leaves no room for shutting people out, does it? We are, after all, the King's ambassadors."

Allison nodded. Knowing her mother, this rationale seemed a distinct possibility. "What was Celeste like? Was she anything like my mother?"

"She was a good deal younger than I, so much so that she related more favorably to Eleanor. I think she was brought up in Wales, then came out to Egypt as a young girl with her father. I wasn't here when she arrived. After Celeste married Edgar—who was a museum curator, I think—they lived for many years without contacting your mother. I recall one letter Celeste sent her, though. It was when Gilbert was born. After that, Edgar went to work for the government in the Civil and was transferred from post to post within the British Empire. Until he arrived ten days ago with Gilbert, they were both perfect strangers to me. I have heard, though, that his reputation in police work is exceptional."

"It must be, or he wouldn't have been assigned the Cairo post," agreed Allison.

"The past is over, my dear. I wish now I'd taken more initiative to contact Celeste and Edgar in Constantinople. But we cannot change the past, and so for the present, I am trying to be as helpful as I can to Sir Edgar, mostly for the boy Gilbert's sake."

The "boy" Gilbert didn't seem much of a boy to Allison. He was much more a young rogue than anything. "Mum won't like him paying too much attention to Beth this holiday season."

"No, and I can't say I blame her. Still, I do feel sorry for the boy."

"Did Sir Edgar say how long he'd been in Constantinople?"

Lydia pondered the question, drumming her fingers on the table. "You know, I don't believe he did. My guess is seven years, maybe eight. Celeste died there two years ago of a heart ailment, he told me. With the war, he had to leave and take his boy to Bombay. Once there, he contacted your parents to tell them of his new post in Cairo."

"Does Gilbert know we're all going to Cairo?"

"I'm sure Sir Edgar told him. As you say, he'll be pleased over the long list of festive entertainments sure to come. Oh, my, that

187

reminds me!" Lydia looked at her. "Your archaeology friend from Aleppo, Sarah Blaine, contacted me the week before you arrived from Abadan. Seemed quite anxious to speak with you. Asked that you contact her as soon as possible."

Allison kept her voice casual since she didn't want Lydia or Marra to sense any cause for concern. Which, of course, there wasn't. How could there be?

"Did she say what she wanted to see me about?"

"Holiday entertaining. We didn't have much time to discuss it since Sir Edgar came in from the garden—oh, did I tell you? He's a horticulturist by hobby. Positively has done wonders with Eleanor's lank rosebushes. You should take a look at them before returning to the house. Eleanor will be amazed when she returns and sees what he's accomplished. The poor roses nearly died under my care. I never had a green thumb—"

"Did she say where to meet her?"

Lydia wrinkled her brow. "Skies above! She left you a letter. Didn't I give it to you? Then I left it in the library with your stack of mail. You know how she always loves those grand dinner parties of Baroness Kruger. Sarah was saying when she was here how the baroness was sending out her invitations to her holiday festivities in Cairo a little early this year and wanted to know if you'd received yours."

It was true—Sarah Blaine adored fanfare, especially when it was touted by Helga. Was that what she wished to see her about? Maybe she thought she could gain her an invitation.

Marra wrinkled her brows. "Parties? With the war going badly? Won't people think it in poor taste?"

Lydia sighed her agreement. "They do in London, but evidently not in Cairo. It's frightful the way the Gezira Club goes on with life as though nothing exists outside their exclusive gatherings and polo games. I doubt they even know much about the war. Reminds me of the days of Noah—eating, drinking, carrying on unwisely, oblivious to impending judgment."

Marra shivered. "That story is in the Jewish Torah, isn't it? Noah building the ark. Ugh—I would have banged on that ark door just as soon as it began to pour!"

"It was too late then," said Lydia quietly. "You see, the Lord himself shut the door and sealed it, and not even Noah could open it again. It was too late for anyone to change his mind. It's like turning to Christ. That must be done in this life. There is no second chance after death. I know reincarnation is a popular philosophy, but I'm afraid it's absolutely heathen. The Bible is quite clear on this issue. 'It is appointed unto man once to die, and after that, the judgment.' So the Scriptures tell us in the Epistle of the Hebrews."

Marra looked at her surprised. "There's a book in the New Testament written to the Hebrews?"

"Oh, my, yes. I'll show you back at the house. It was written to Jewish Christians to show them how much better the sacrifice of Christ was then all the old rituals of animal sacrifice for our sins. Jesus fulfilled all the types of offerings that were required for cleansing and restoring us to God. He was the ultimate and final sacrifice. 'Behold the true Lamb of God who takes away the sin of the world.'"

Aunt Lydia's voice rang with conviction and reverence, and Allison smiled. Marra was certainly getting the gospel from all sides. And it wasn't even planned.

Her thoughts drifted again to Sarah Blaine and Helga's social gatherings. Allison recalled her surprise when she discovered that the baroness was involved in gathering information for the British government. Her role as a wealthy socialite put her in the perfect position to pick up facts from her guests that were useful to the British. In the past she had given data to Bret, but that was neither here nor there now. He wasn't anywhere around to work with the baroness... Allison frowned. Could that be the reason Helga wished to speak with her? Did she have news about Bret?

"I confess my surprise that, despite the war, Baroness Kruger decided to keep to her usual round of dinner parties and balls," Lydia was saying. "But she was adamant. With the headlines of the ghastly British defeats so liberally displayed, everyone needs something to make their spirits a little jollier, or so she says. I'm not sure I agree. A good prayer meeting would be more to the point. But the baroness is not one to be intimidated by popular opinion. Which is fortunate, since some may yet wonder if she, German that she is, might not be holding a bit of a celebration of the kaiser's victories on the western front."

Aunt Lydia paused, as though suddenly regretting her words, then reached over and patted Allison's hand. "Oh, dear, don't pay me any mind. I do hope you'll be up to the baroness's social affairs, my girl, because I positively shan't be. I've never been one to attend parties, but after what you've been through in the war, I think it would be cheerful medicine for you. A bit of frivolity is good for the doldrums once in a while." She looked at Marra who was enjoying a second scone drizzled with honey. "That goes for you as well, Marra. A few waltzes in a pretty dress will be good for you."

Marra's brows lifted. "Me? I haven't owned a party dress since before the war."

Allison looked at her friend and wondered if she truly meant to sound so disenchanted. No matter that she carried the torch of love for Rob, Marra was too young to bury herself with him. But she was a fine one to think so. What of her own feelings? She could not escape the fact that Wade and Bret could be prisoners of war or buried in the blowing Arabian sands like Cousin Leah. How could she don a ball dress and waltz with soldiers on leave?

"You can wear one of Allison's dresses," Aunt Lydia was telling Marra. "She's awash in the things. As is Beth."

"If the moths haven't eaten them by now," mused Allison. "It's been over a year since I wore anything except a uniform."

"They wouldn't fit me," argued Marra, running her long fingers through her short blonde hair. "I'm inches taller. I can see myself waltzing about government house with a ball dress six inches above my ankle."

The thought made Allison smile. "We'll do something. Take the hem down or add a ruffle."

"Even add a foot of lace if we must," agreed Aunt Lydia. "And now," she stated with a bop of her walking stick on the patio floor, "it's settled. I've never been a social butterfly, but I've enough proper upbringing to see the right responses are sent to Cairo acquaintances. I'll do it this afternoon, accepting every luncheon and ball we've been invited to in December. You can take my place, Marra my girl."

"What about escorts?" asked Marra uneasily, wrapping a strand of hair around her index finger.

"There are thousands of soldiers stationed in Egypt, m'dear. Eleanor can arrange something." Her eyes twinkled. "Actually, that young David would be perfect for you. You're both Jewish, aren't you? You should get along, as the saying goes, like two peas in a pod."

Marra gave a short laugh. "More like two kosher cockleburs."

Allison noted with interest the flush that rose in Marra's cheeks at Aunt Lydia's comments about David. With a smile she decided to speak to him about playing escort to Marra for the next six weeks. He'd do it if she asked him.

"Anyway," said Marra, her voice revealing her anxious desire to change the subject, "I should be getting my new orders soon so I

191

very much doubt I will be here."

"No, you won't. Not till after New Year's," said Allison cheerfully. "I won't let you wheedle out of this."

Lydia used her walking stick to push herself up from her chair. "And now I'm off to my writing desk. Join me later, Marra, if you wish to talk." She reached over and patted Allison's arm. "As for you, my dear, let's not think too much about Kut and Arabia," she said softly. "Nothing can leave its mark on our lives except those trials which first get past our Lord. And if he allows it, then we can rest in the knowledge that it's for our eternal good. Wade knows that as well. He's had three good years with Oswald Chambers before coming to Egypt. He knew what he was likely to be in for."

Yes, thought Allison, Wade had known, and he was strong spiritually. As for Bret...no, she wouldn't think of him. Doing so only brought renewed discomfort. Lydia was right. Leaving her cares and sorrows with the Lord was the best medicine Allison could take. Proverbs 17:22, the verse she'd meditated on earlier that morning in her devotions, came to mind: "A merry heart doeth good like a medicine: but a broken spirit drieth the bones."

Well, then, a merry heart she would have. It was time to gather her mail from the library and find out what Sara Blaine wanted of her.

THIRTEEN

He who is greedy for gain troubles his own house.
PROVERBS 15:27

DESPITE HER PLANS TO COLLECT HER MAIL, an hour had slipped by before Allison came down the stairs into the family library. The blinds were drawn on the western window to keep out the late afternoon sun, and the room was wrapped in silent shadow. The entire house was still. Aunt Lydia was napping, and Marra had gone shopping after they had finished afternoon tea in the garden. Gilbert had volunteered to accompany Marra, leaving Allison alone to collect and read her mail without being disturbed.

She walked toward the Queen-Anne-style cherry-wood desk, brushing against one of the armrests on the divan. She saw the woven-reed mail basket where Zalika always placed the day's mail.

Allison was still thinking about the calishe that had waited in the alleyway for Sir Edgar Simonds. She was almost sure the person he'd met was Helga. If that were the case, did Sir Edgar have any idea she was working for British Intelligence? She knew such agents rarely discussed their work even with those they should be able to trust—such as the new inspector general of the Cairo police, for example. But if their acquaintance didn't involve intrigue, then why the secretive meeting in the carriage? Why not come for Sir Edgar openly in front of the house? After all, it wasn't as if Helga didn't know her. She might have come in to say hello while waiting for Sir Edgar. Or why not have the meeting with him in Cairo since he would be there on the morrow?

Of one thing Allison was certain: Helga Kruger was no errand girl, nor did she represent the Cairo government. They would have sent an official aide from the department to meet Sir Edgar, not the baroness.

Allison frowned at her musings. Why did her mind find it necessary to persist in her thinking that the woman was Helga?

From behind her a leather chair squeaked.

Allison whirled, staring into the dusky end of the room. There was no reason for fear and yet her heart leaped to her throat when Sir Edgar stood slowly from the chair, his massive white-clad figure looking ghostly.

"I'm sorry I frightened you."

She didn't answer at first and covered her start by leaning against the desk. "Oh. Hullo. I thought you had—" she stopped. Maybe she shouldn't let him know she saw him leave an hour ago. The meeting had been short. "I thought I was alone," she finished quickly.

His beady eyes were amused. "We're off to a dreadful beginning, I fear. Both times we've met, I've frightened you."

He was right. This reaction of hers was absurd. Yet she couldn't still the rapid thumping of her heart.

"I realize I'm rather an unattractive mongrel compared to my son Gilbert," he began in an attempt at lightness, "but I've never evoked the reaction of causing a woman to faint twice."

The unexpected grin on his coarse features altered his demeanor considerably, changing what she'd judged to be a watchful, snake-like expression into one of actual good humor. He suddenly didn't seem so sinister after all as he stepped from the shadows and walked to the double windows to pull open the blinds.

He turned again to face her, and Allison had to admit there was nothing mysterious about her mother's cousin after all. She felt herself growing embarrassed over her actions. In the daylight he looked nothing like Rex Blaine.

She relaxed and smiled at him. The more she contemplated how foolish she was behaving, the sillier it all seemed, and she laughed.

He chuckled, too, his eyes twinkling in the fading sunlight coming through the glass pane.

"You had me worried for a moment," he said. "I thought I might need to ring the bell for Zalika and explain why you fainted on the floor again."

"I'm terrible sorry, Sir Edgar. It's not your fault, I assure you."

"Please," he gestured to a straight back leather chair near the desk. "I shall play host, if you don't mind, and ask you to sit down. With your health as it is, you mustn't stand too long."

She laughed. "I promise not to faint again."

"Shall I ring for coffee? You won't mind if I'm not a tea drinker? Thanks to my time in Constantinople, I was long ago won over to Arabic coffee."

She hesitated, not over coffee or tea, but whether or not she wished to stay. But it seemed rude to leave now, and so she sat down. "I could use a cup of coffee. The soldiers drank a good deal of it in Arabia, and I rather got adjusted to it myself."

He was anything but the uncouth boor she had judged him. Appearances were certainly deceiving—as was gossip. She'd allowed what she'd heard of this man to color her perceptions of him. Now, having seen him a bit more clearly, she found she rather liked Sir Edgar.

He groaned as he lowered himself into her father's big leather chair, settling back to look at her.

"I know how wicked malaria can be. I suffered from it for years when I lived in Burma serving the government. I've since recouped. No thanks to them. The government, that is. Quinine in warm lemon juice does marvels. You must try it next time. Not that cousin Lydia will take kindly to my novice diagnosis. She's quite the nurse, I understand." He moved his ponderous frame for more comfort and the brown leather of the chair squeaked again.

"I didn't know you served in Burma," Allison commented. "Lydia mentioned India, then the Ottoman Empire."

"I've served the Company in myriad loathsome little places through the years. I spent five years in Rangoon before I was noticed by the dense-minded governor general and 'promoted' to Bombay." He barked a laugh. "Not much of a promotion, as you can guess."

Allison paused, considering his words. What was it in his tone that reminded her of someone else—?

"Lydia doesn't mind out of the way places infected with flies and mosquitoes I gather," he went on. "She tells me she will most likely die in one of them serving the fellahin. Ah, the peasants! They are the backbone of Egypt. As long as they're content with British rule, we're likely to remain here for a good many more years, despite the cry in the Arab newspaper for our demise." He gestured to a paper he'd been reading before she entered. She recognized it as one that was written by Egyptians who were demanding independence from England.

"It will be my duty to silence these radicals," he stated. "Egypt must remain docile and cooperative during the war. The last thing we can afford is riots instigated by Turkish sympathizers."

She glanced up from the paper and realized he expected a response from her. "I'm not sure how I feel about Egyptian independence," she admitted honestly. "It is their country and we are their..." She hesitated.

His lips reflected a measure of contempt. "They say that we are their masters. We're hardly that. We've done marvels for the people, including overhauling their system of village laws. We've built schools, paved roads, taught them how to behave with civility. As along as the fellahin are content, the university-inspired rabble-rousers can be kept at bay. Perhaps it is good Lydia has offered her medical know-how to them along the Nile. How long has she worked with them, twenty years?"

Allison, still debating his conclusions about the university-educated Egyptians seeking independent rule, had to force her mind to focus on his question about Lydia.

"She's worked with them for more than twenty years. She's quite dedicated."

He didn't look impressed. "We're all dedicated to one thing or another."

"Yes," she mused. "Some things are worthy of our devotion, but others can become thieves and robbers of our hearts and souls."

He gave a half chuckle, watching her through lowered lids. "I see you're quite different from your sister, Beth. Like Gilbert, she's frivolous. You're insightful and serious."

The remark about her younger sister was troubling. Beth could be rash and as yet hadn't reconciled herself to things about her body she couldn't change. She was particularly displeased by her height, even to the point of feeling somehow cheated. As a result, she was always out to prove something to herself and others...but Allison was convinced Beth wasn't even sure most of the time what it was she wanted to prove. Perhaps just that she was worthy of being loved for herself.

"I'm afraid Beth and Gilbert have developed an infatuation," he continued. "Not that Gilbert hasn't ignited the sparks in every young girl he's met since he turned sixteen." He chuckled ruefully, and Allison had the impression this fact amused him as much as it displeased him.

Was this another sign of what concerned Lydia? Gilbert was the darling son who could do no wrong.

"He's left a string of wounded hearts wherever he's gone. Even older women find him attractive."

"Do they? I wonder why?" asked Allison. "I'm afraid I found him rather conceited and spoiled."

Now why had she said that?

Her eyes rushed to his, and she fully expected to see a flush of temper on his broad face. Instead, his smile remained as he reached under his jacket and removed a long, skinny cigarillo, then proceeded to strike a match, holding the flame to its tip.

"I'm so sorry. I didn't mean to offend you."

"You haven't. I'm under no illusions about Gilbert. Sadly, he's everything you've said and more. I can do nothing with him. I wish Beth were as insightful as you seem to be." He watched her over a small wisp of smoke. "I will speak to your father about the romance once he arrives."

Relief flooded her. "I'm glad you feel that way. Beth is young, but I don't think Gilbert will add her heart to his collection. My parents are quite strict about us dating at a young age. They're not likely to permit her to see him alone. And Gilbert doesn't appear the sort of young man to care for chaperones."

"Then I see I have nothing to worry about. He's a good boy at heart, you know. A trifle on the wild side. I have important plans for him, and I won't see them spoiled by immature romantic inclinations."

Allison felt a flash of embarrassment, as though it were Beth and not Gilbert who had caused the problem. She wondered about Sir Edgar's plans but didn't ask any further. It really was none of her concern.

Just then Zalika brought in the coffee, casting a glance toward Sir Edgar as she set it down on the table, then went out quietly.

He leaned forward for a cup of coffee, then fixed her with a musing glance. "I have grueling work awaiting me in Cairo, which means my schedule will rob me of time with Gilbert. Duty to country calls, you know. So I'm pleased to have this little chat with you before I leave for Cairo in the morning." He reached into his front pocket and drew out a slip of paper. "I have a question or two I must ask you."

Allison was overtaken by surprise in the shift of conversation. She smiled. "Questions by the inspector general already?" she asked with an attempt at lightness.

"I don't wish to appear rude, my dear. Naturally, if you'd rather wait?" he suggested.

She didn't know how to answer, surprised by the turn in their family chat.

His eyes settled on her with a fixed gravity.

"What kind of questions?" she asked casually.

He waved the paper in his hand. "Perhaps I should wait until you feel stronger. I can always call you to my office in Cairo."

Call her to his office!

"If you have questions, Sir Edgar, you may ask them now, but I don't see why you should think—"

"Yes, you are right," he apologized. "I should begin by explaining the task I've been called to Cairo to accomplish. Now that we're at war with the Central Powers, we can't be too careful about the civilians who are permitted to stay in Egypt. Spies are everywhere. Sometimes the least likely street merchant with a donkey cart might be working for the kaiser." He leaned forward to take the cup of coffee which Allison had poured him. "We must even be careful of friends and family. I'm afraid they've been known to be the worst of betrayers." He shook his head. "A nasty business, this."

He added too much cream to his cup and took a noisy sip, then leaned his head back against the chair and puffed on his cigarillo.

Allison watched him, fighting with confusion. Moments ago she had been convinced this man was harmless, even likable—that her earlier impressions were simply fancy born of a weary mind. Now she found his manner served only to reinforce her first thoughts about him. Such uncertainty only irritated her.

Who *was* this man, and what did he want with her?

He held up the piece of paper again. "I don't find it pleasant to interrogate individuals whom I may find it necessary to evict from Egypt," he stated, emotionless. Glancing at the soiled paper, she could see that it seemed to be a list of names. "This is the beginning. When I arrive in Cairo I shall have my inspectors searching every conceivable nook and cranny to ferret out whoever there may be with German and Turkish sympathies."

"I don't see how I can help you."

"I want you to tell me everything you know about certain individuals residing in Cairo. We'll begin with Baroness Helga Kruger."

Her heart lurched, and Allison had a sudden, sickening sense of the power this man now possessed. The bright, beady eyes that remained riveted upon her; the somewhat rueful smile; the deceptively relaxed posture...all now gave testimony to the fact that here was a ruthless man who would have no mercy when faced with obligation or perceived duty. That such a man was given so powerful a position spoke of the tyranny of the urgent when wartime positions desperately needed to be filled.

She held her silence a moment, studying him. Then she responded with a casual air, "Do you know, I almost get the idea, Sir Edgar, that you have come to form a German police squad."

He had the grace to wince. "Hardly, hardly, Allison. It is the German sympathizers I am obliged to ferret out from their nasty little rat holes. They are well entrenched in every facet of Cairo life, from business to society, and I must smoke them out and see them run for cover."

She set her cup down. "I'm not acquainted with any German sympathizers. Nor do I know of Turkish businessmen planning to assassinate British officials."

His quick smile surprised her. She'd expected anger.

"Ah, you do understand very well what this is about. I thought you might. Lydia is naive, and your little Jewish friend hasn't been to Cairo before. You, I think, can help me."

She didn't like the way he spoke of Marra, without using her name.

He stood and walked toward her, his shoes squeaking. She stared at them, noting their scuffed condition.

"You would do me a great favor, Allison, if you'd tell me everything you know about Baroness Helga Kruger."

Why did he want to know about Helga? Had she been wrong then about the woman in the carriage? She wasn't sure, but she did know this much: she must not give away the fact that the baroness was a friendly agent. She managed a blank expression under his stare.

"The baroness? Oh, yes, of course. The wealthy socialite. I met her in Aleppo one summer a year or so ago. She runs an archaeological club. In fact, she'll be giving a few parties I think, and we're all likely to be invited. You can ask her any questions you have then. I'm sure she won't mind."

"Her deceased husband built weapons for the kaiser's army and helped sponsor the Berlin Baghdad Railway."

She pretended not to notice the veiled accusation, though if he suspected Helga of secret allegiance to the kaiser, it would automatically eliminate suspicions of her working with the British.

Sir Edgar pressed on. "Was the baroness in Aleppo when Major Karl Reuter was murdered?"

So he knew about Reuter. Did he know he was a British agent? She lifted her cup. "Yes, we all were there."

"Your cousin Leah Bristow was murdered as well, I believe."

Caution. She looked at the coffee. Murdered *as well?*

"My cousin's death was believed to be accidental. I'm sure you know all the details."

"Yes, I sent for the full report from Aleppo."

The idea disturbed her. What was he looking for? And why was he telling her all this?

"I read it late into the night," he went on.

"I believe that case is closed," she commented, forcing a calm she was far from feeling into her tone. "The authorities are fully satisfied. I do wish you would not bring up Leah's death again, Sir Edgar. It's still a painful subject for me. Her death was a tragedy." She felt tears at her eyes, and they were not just for effect. She truly did miss Leah. "If you've read the report, then you already know what I said happened. I can't add anything else."

"Can't, or won't?"

She pretended as if his question confused her. "I beg your pardon?"

His eyes flickered and he smiled. "Where is Colonel Bret Holden?"

Her unease doubled. "I'm sure I don't know," she said evasively. "I haven't heard from or seen him since Kut. He went back for a friend of mine who served in the medical unit, Wade Findlay. As far as I know they are both prisoners." The catch in her voice was completely authentic. "Or worse."

"The colonel is an intelligence officer, you know. What was he doing with the ground soldiers?"

So he knew about Bret as well. She tensed. "I am not privy to Colonel Holden's thoughts and intentions. You'll need to ask him."

"Why would he risk his life in an unauthorized mission to save Wade Findlay?"

She stood abruptly. "I don't know," she repeated. "If you know Colonel Holden is an agent, then you would also know he would tell me nothing of his work. So I can't answer your inquiries. And now, if you'll excuse me, I'm beginning to tire." She turned to leave, more shaken than she wanted him to notice.

"Was Professor Jemal Pasha at that archaeological club meeting in Aleppo?"

His question stopped her. Jemal had been an enemy agent working with Major General Rex Blaine. As far as she knew, no one had seen him since that frightening night in the hut when Rex had intended to kill her. Did Sir Edgar know about Blaine, too? But how? Even Sarah Blaine didn't know her husband had been an enemy agent.

"Yes, Professor Jemal was there in Aleppo giving lectures," she managed casually. "He worked with Baroness Kruger at the Cairo Museum."

"He is no longer at the museum."

"Oh?" she asked in a tone that was the picture of disinterest. "Where is he?"

"I wish I knew." He fixed his gaze on her, as though gauging her reaction closely.

"And are you suggesting that I do?" She shook her head. "I confess, Sir Edgar, this conversation is as confusing as it is tiresome. I was never a close friend of Jemal's. Besides, I've been away for a year and have just returned. I assume you do recall that fact?"

"Ah yes, I am sorry if I sounded unsympathetic. However, Baroness Kruger knew Jemal very well?"

"Perhaps. You'll have to ask her." She added: "Or ask Jemal when you locate him. He must be around somewhere."

He smiled, but it didn't reach his eyes. He drew in on the cigarillo. "I wish I could ask him, but no one seems to have heard from Jemal since soon after the deaths of Major Reuter and Leah Bristow."

"Oh? Then perhaps he returned to Constantinople. He is of Turkish descent. Or the museum may be able to tell you. Perhaps he left a forwarding address."

He chuckled. "Berlin, perhaps?"

So. He either knew about or suspected Jemal's treachery.

"Was he a friend of Rex Blaine's?"

She sat down again, her knees weak. Did Sir Edgar know about Sarah writing to her?

"I don't know if they were friends or not."

"You know Sarah Blaine well. Did she ever mention any meetings between her husband and Jemal?"

So he did know about her connection to the Blaines. "Sarah is more interested in the social life at the Gezira Club than any of the tragic happenings in Aleppo. She wouldn't know anything that could help you."

"Is Sarah much into archaeology?"

"She has an interest, yes. She belongs to the Cairo Club."

"Is she a collector?"

"Perhaps. I don't recall seeing a particular collection. Why do you ask?"

"Curiosity. Did the major general have a collection?"

"I wouldn't know. He collected pipes, I think."

"Pipes. Interesting. Any Egyptian vases or dolls?"

"You'll need to ask Mrs. Blaine."

A nearly jovial smile tipped his lips, and he inclined his head. "I see I'm wearying you. We'd best break here, m'dear. Should any tidbit of information come to mind, though, do let me know. There's plenty of time to talk when you come to Cairo with the family. Take this list of names for your reference."

She took the wrinkled paper reluctantly.

"This is between you and me, of course. Naturally, police business is not to be discussed over tea and crumpets with Cousin Lydia."

She straightened with a haughty manner. "I've no desire to discuss such morbid matters with my aunt."

He continued to smile, but his eyes were determined. "I ask your help, m'dear, for the good of England."

She wondered. She folded the paper and stood. "I'll consider it," she responded curtly. "I doubt if I have any information to assist you in your work."

"Not *my* work, Allison, the joint effort of police and British Intelligence—as Colonel Holden could tell you if he were but here."

She had the distinct impression that he'd mentioned Bret to let her know he was aware of their acquaintance. It was clear he was hoping she would trust him and cooperate, but could she? He seemed more interested in Aleppo then he did over trying to ferret out German sympathizers to evict from Egypt. Why was he asking so many questions about Sarah and Jemal?

He bowed his head with deference, and Allison turned to leave when her eyes fell on the mail basket. Somewhere in that pile was the letter from Sarah! Should she risk drawing his attention to the mail or simply walk out? Sometimes the best cover was indifference. He knew she'd come in here for the mail—he must have seen her go to the desk and lift the basket when he sat in the shadows.

She turned to leaf casually through the stack of mail, quickly finding a packet wrapped with a ribbon. Her name stood out boldly on the envelope. Taking the bundle she walked toward the library door half expecting to hear him ask her to wait.

Sir Edgar Simonds remained silent as she walked out into the hall.

When she reached the flight of stairs she glanced back. He had come to the doorway and was watching her go up, that secretive look on his broad face.

Her mother's cousin or not, Allison did not care for the new inspector general.

Once back in her room, Allison tried to tell herself that Sir Edgar was simply doing his job. But somehow the espionage she'd experienced with the others—Bret, Leah, Neal, and Helga—seemed more honorable than Sir Edgar's work. Was she right in feeling there was something suspect about his quest? She didn't sense that his motivation was a desire to overcome evil...no, it had the feel of something self-serving, somehow, and odious. What was it? Did she even want to know?

And yet, her mind argued, why would the government appoint him to so important a position if he were not trustworthy? Who had recommended him? She would speak to her father about Sir Edgar as soon as he arrived home.

She fingered the folded paper with its list of names—people under suspicion—and could not bring herself to look at it. Why had he asked her to help him? What was it he expected to learn from her? Did he know she had worked with Bret and Neal? No, that wasn't possible. Bret would never have put her or any record of her involvement in his report to his superior. And Neal was on his way from London. He wouldn't have even met Sir Edgar yet.

She shuddered and looked toward the open terrace, aware that the November air turned chill when the sun set. She walked over and closed the double doors, paused, then swiftly bolted them. She thought of her mother's cousin Celeste, now dead. Suddenly she felt sorry for her. She couldn't imagine a woman of refinement being happily married to Sir Edgar Simonds.

She placed the list in the small drawer of her jewelry box. Locking the box, she put the key in her pocket. She ought to burn the list of names without looking at it. She had no intention of cooperating with Sir Edgar, even if he had dropped Bret's name as sugared bait. Rats were baited by sweets, and Edgar didn't seem to mind trapping them for his own use. Was he trying to trap her?

"Well," she murmured, "I shan't be baited."

Thank goodness he was leaving in the morning and she wouldn't need to deal with him again until after her parents arrived. She would speak to her father, maybe turn the list over to him. That was it. She'd roll the whole ugly affair onto the strong shoulders of her beloved father.

She hadn't liked the way Sir Edgar discussed Beth, either, as though her sister were some little fickle creature out to lure Gilbert. It was the other way around, of that she was certain. She had to admit, however, that she understood Gilbert a little better. Aunt Lydia was right. He was headed down a path that would end in destruction. Could anything be done to stop the ruin? Gilbert had received his instructions for living from his father. No matter that Edgar spoke of having "good plans" for his son, without a solid foundation of truth on which to build his life, Gilbert had little hope. The coming storm would shatter his house into a thousand broken sticks.

As if to bear witness to her thoughts, the wind came up suddenly, rattling the terrace doors as though trying to force them open.

Yes, she could even feel sympathy for Gilbert now.

Exhausted, she sank into a satin-covered chair beside the vanity table and leaned her head back to rest. Outside the wind stirred the vines. Her eyes moved to her door, which opened onto the hall, aware that it had no lock. If she was going to stay much longer in this house, she would have an inside lock installed. True safety was in the Lord, she knew, but precaution was sound wisdom. Trust didn't mean foolish presumption.

It was Satan who advised the Lord to jump from the pinnacle of the temple so angels might catch him, she reminded herself. How many times did Satan advise unwise behavior and pawn it off as faith or "trust" in God?

She looked at the stack of mail on her lap and realized she was gripping it. She let out a breath and relaxed. A moment later she untied the ribbon and leafed through the letters, tossing aside everything until coming to what she wanted: an envelope bearing the name of Sarah Blaine. She opened it and read:

Allison, as soon as Lydia informed me you were coming home I've been on edge, waiting. I must speak to you about something urgent that's troubling me. How soon can you come to Cairo? I'd love to have you stay any weekend. Don't bother about clearing dates with me, just come!
Sarah B.

Allison's fingers went cold. *It must be about Rex,* she thought. *Sarah must know, and now she wants to discuss the bitter pill she's discovered.*

The thought of facing Sarah and discussing the horrendous ordeal at the hut in Aleppo made her hands tremble. Sarah was harmless and giddy; even Rex hadn't wanted his dear wife to know he was a murderer and a German spy. How could she actually go to Sarah's house and sleep where the ghostly memory of the general filled the silent rooms?

"I can't do it."

She read the letter again and felt guilt stirring. Sarah depended upon her. She didn't want to go, but she must. Whatever it was that Sarah wanted to discuss, she needed to help her.

Her eyes lifted. She stared at the door. Downstairs in the shadowed library, perched in her father's leather chair, Sir Edgar Simonds sat deep in thought. He had asked many questions about Sarah.... Allison bit her lip in concern. Could Sarah have stumbled across something that put her at risk? She wouldn't know until she spoke with her at the Blaine home in Cairo. She must not wait too long, either.

Allison sighed. It was going to be a long week before her parents arrived. Anything might happen by then....

"Stop it!" she scolded herself fiercely. "Nothing is going to happen." But her fears would not calm, and so she turned to the one sure calming influence: prayer. She prayed urgently, pouring out her fears and anxieties, but the peace that usually settled over her heart was missing.

Could it be the Lord wanted her to go visit Sarah?

Allison made up her mind. She would take the first train to Cairo to spend the weekend with Sarah. If only she didn't have to go alone. Her history with trains was not the most encouraging. Images of her ride on the Hejaz Railway on that long trip back to Aleppo flitted through her mind. She recalled how she had felt herself being watched...only to discover that she *had* been followed. By Rex Blaine.

She heard Marra enter the adjoining bedroom, and a moment later a tap sounded on her door.

"May I come in, Allison?"

Marra! She'd ask her to go with her to see Sarah. "Yes, I'm up, Marra, come in!" she stood, still holding the letter.

Marra entered and paused. "Good grief, what happened to you?"

"What do you mean?" asked Allison, laying her mail on the table.

"You look as though you've had a relapse."

Allison gave a short laugh. "It's no wonder. I've just met the real Sir Edgar Simonds, inspector general of Cairo police."

Marra sauntered in and flopped in a chair, throwing her legs over the arm. "Sounds dreadful. What happened? I thought putting up with Gilbert's conceit all afternoon was bad, but this sounds worse."

Allison told her of the encounter, leaving out only his keen interest in the events at Aleppo. There was no reason to tell Marra about the past. Not yet, anyway. She finished with the assertion, "I think there's more to Sir Edgar than his work as a police inspector."

Marra glanced toward the closed door facing the outer hall and raised a hand for silence.

Allison's gaze swerved. Was someone out there listening? She should have been more cautious.

Marra got up and walked to the door, opening it. She looked out in both directions then turned, closing it again, looking for a bolt.

"They're not on the bedroom doors," said Allison. "Until recently I didn't feel I needed them."

Marra came back to her chair. "I must have imagined hearing someone." She smiled ruefully. "This is worse than a German Zeppelin raid. At least then everything's out in the open."

"Maybe I'm overreacting," hastened Allison. "After all, I've a fever that comes and goes, it's easy to imagine things, and I simply had an eerie feeling when I first met Sir Edgar. After all, he is...family."

Marra looked at her dubiously. "I can't say he gives me warm feelings, either. And you say that word *family* as though it's too big to swallow."

Allison sat down. "I did, didn't I? I guess it's just the surprise of discovering cousins I'd never heard of until Beth's letter."

Marra walked over and stood looking down at her. "Gilbert spoke of Beth tonight. He seems to think she's in love with him."

Allison was unable to hide her concern. "Beth met him first in Bombay at a ball. She wrote me a glowing report, trumpeting Gilbert's handsomeness and style."

"I don't blame you for worrying. He's a conceited boor, and spoiled rotten to boot. Which is rather odd, considering—" she stopped, and her eyes came quickly to Allison's—"I'm sorry. I shouldn't be speaking like this about your relatives."

Allison smiled. "Don't apologize. You're not saying anything that isn't obvious to anyone with eyes. Besides, I agree. Now, what's odd about Gilbert being spoiled?"

Marra shrugged. "I was thinking that Sir Edgar is not the sentimental sort who'd spoil his son. And yet, there it is. We both agree Gilbert gets exactly what he wants. And it now looks as though he may want your little sister. Or at least thinks he does."

Allison sighed. "Mum will never allow it. I fear there's going to be family difficulties in the future. And Gilbert's the type that will want Beth even more if he thinks he can't have her. But even Sir Edgar is against Gilbert's interest in Beth."

"Well, that's something. Perhaps Sir Edgar isn't as cold as we think he is. At any rate, we needn't worry, now that your parents will be arriving soon. Along with this cousin Neal you've told me so much about. He sounds almost as strong and dependable as the colonel."

Allison smiled, feeling a sense of relief. "He is. You'll like him, Marra. He's very interested in a Jewish homeland, too, like David. But I'll let him explain all that." She stood. "Look, something unexpected has come up. You've heard me mention Sarah Blaine? Well, she's written asking me to come spend the weekend. She has something to talk over with me, something she feels is rather urgent."

"Are you feeling strong enough for the train trip?"

"The quinine is helping. I'm feeling better each day. I'm going because I must. But I would like you to come with me."

Marra shrugged. "If your friend doesn't mind, I'll be glad to go."

From the tone of Sarah's letter, Allison was sure she wouldn't mind anything that enabled her to come to the Blaine house. "I'll let Aunt Lydia know tonight, then we'll take the afternoon train. I don't want to go in the morning. We'd end up bumping into Sir Edgar and Gilbert."

"Spare us that, please. Noon it is. Say—this Sarah friend of yours, is she the wife of that retired major general you mentioned who shot himself in the hut in Aleppo?"

Allison looked at her. "Yes."

Marra shook her head. "It's sad, you know. There seem to be too many people dying nowadays, don't you think?"

Allison nodded her agreement, fighting off the odd fear that Marra's words were somehow prophetic.

FOURTEEN

❯━❰❯━❮☉❯━❰❯━❮

As cold water to a thirsty soul, so is good news from a far country.
PROVERBS 25:25

THE NEXT DAY, ALLISON WAS SURPRISED to hear a horse-drawn calishe turning down the street and coming from the direction of the harbor. The driver turned into the parkway, and the excited sound of voices and footsteps on the front porch was heard. From below, a familiar, graceful voice floated up to the terrace.

"Bless you, dear Lydia, for caring for Allison. How is she?"

Mother! Allison's heart beat with joy as she hurried out her bedroom door and into the hallway. She quickened her steps to the stairway, a broad smile on her face.

The front door opened and Zalika stepped aside, allowing a graceful woman adorned in a sedate navy blue dress, which was the perfect setting for her reddish gold hair, to sweep inside the entranceway while removing her wrap.

Allison came down the stairs, and her mother hurried toward her, hands outstretched. They embraced. "Poor darling. I heard about the tragedy at Kut. Thank God you're safe."

"Oh, Mum! I'm glad you came home!"

Her father, Sir Marshall Wescott, stood in the open doorway blocking the gray morning light. Allison drank in the sight of him. Twenty years her mother's senior, short of stature, heavy of stock, immaculate in dress, and sporting a royal blue officer's coat with gold braid at cuffs and collar, he looked the quintessential diplomat.

His inch-wide mustache was impeccably groomed, and the silvery gray of his hair pleasantly contrasted with his perceptive brown eyes, which at that moment glittered with supreme pleasure as he came toward her.

"Well, my dear, you've a good deal to explain."

Allison left her mother to embrace him. "Father," she said with alarm, "you're limping."

"Gout," he grumbled, as though the reminder drew the shade on his buoyant mood. "A curse of the devil. Let me look at you…still a flowering beauty, I see. No wonder the rogue's taken it upon himself to wire your mother and urge me to come home. Does he have romantic ambitions, my dear?"

"Rogue?" What on earth did he mean? Could it be Bret? Her heart pounded. "What rogue?" she asked, leaning forward to kiss his cheek.

"I speak of Bret Holden, newly elevated colonel, a man due for further advancement in London if Kitchener has his way." He gave her a chiding look. "But a rogue nonetheless and a man to stay away from."

"Marshall, not now, please. We'll discuss Colonel Holden with Allison when she's feeling better," Eleanor admonished gently from the door. She stepped outside to call for Beth.

A sick feeling looped about Allison's heart and hung there like an iron weight. "There's no reason to discuss the colonel. He's either a prisoner of war in Kut or dead."

Strange, she could say the painful word *dead* and remain dry-eyed. Her father's presence put a ramrod in her spine.

Suddenly alert, Sir Marshall held her away from him, studying her with a scrutinizing eye that narrowed, making her feel guilty. "Lamenting, are you? You need not."

Her eyes eagerly sought an explanation. "You've heard from

Colonel Holden? and Wade?"

"So that's the story he passed on to you, is it? That he's in the cruel clutches of the Turks? A prisoner! Bah! Thank God he isn't. I need him for the Jerusalem campaign."

"He hasn't told me anything," she confessed. "I haven't seen him, except briefly near Baghdad just before the battle. And once, at Abadan . . ." her voice trailed off. "He got me out safely."

"Yes, a daring risk taker. I owe him for that. Well, you can cease your worries. A message was brought to me when we arrived. He reached Abadan with Wade Findlay over a week ago."

Swift joy swept over Allison. "They're alive!"

"It was a close call to be sure. The lad Wade was in a hospital in Alexandria, but the facilities there are so overcrowded with wounded from the Dardanelles that they've loaded the ill who can travel into ships to send them to Cairo. Wade is among that group. Cairo will soon become a depository for wounded. You know what that means, Daughter! There'll be no more excursions into enemy territory. If you go back to nursing, you can serve here in Egypt."

"How are they? Seriously injured?" she cried.

"Wade's ill—down to skin and bones with malaria—but the doctor thinks he'll pull through."

Allison blinked hard to hold back the tears and smiled, but her joy was short lived. "And Bret—Colonel Holden? He's all right?"

Sir Marshall cocked an eye at her. "Hard to say."

Her heart jumped to her throat. "What do you mean? He's not going to die?"

"No, I doubt it. Some men seem to thrive on danger and risk. They have an uncanny ability to get out of the worst situations without a scratch. He's a bit worse for having gone through the ordeal, and a whole lot more cynical, but otherwise he's as physically fit as ever."

Allison's smile faded. A stinging prick to her conscience convinced her she was to blame for his rise in cynicism. "Where is he? The same hospital ship as Wade?"

"No, he's already back in Cairo at Intelligence, but I believe he's taking the holiday leave for a few weeks. He's up for a Victoria Cross, but the scoundrel dares to say he doesn't want it! A rather hard-boiled agent at times."

A Victoria Cross—the highest award for bravery.

She noted something else: her father called Bret an agent.

"So you know?" she said quietly, glancing about and seeing no one near them. "About his being an agent?"

His brows lifted. "Daughter, it was I who brought him to the attention of Kitchener. I'm surprised, however, that *you* know what he is."

Which could only mean her father didn't know about Aleppo. "A good deal has happened since you went to India, Father. You know about Cousin Leah?"

"Your mother told me. Her death is indeed a tragedy."

"Yes, it is." She met his eyes. "Do you know about her work with Neal out at the Carchemish Digs?"

His keen eyes shot to her face, searching. "Yes. And I'm beginning to think my daughter is mixed up with much more than I ever guessed or approved. I'll need to speak with Bret about this."

"It wasn't his fault. Leah involved me—and even she had no choice."

"Some matters are best not spoken of openly, my dear."

"Yes, of course," she hastened. So Bret was in Cairo. Oh, joy! She didn't take the time to analyze that her father had just called Bret by his first name instead of his rank. She would think through all of this later. All that mattered right now was that Bret and Wade were alive. And safe.

Her father moved to a chair, settling himself in it uncomfortably and watching her expression. "Stay away from him, Daughter. He'll be the first to tell you you're not his caliber of young woman. He's not the marrying kind. He lives a dangerous life. One that makes him expendable."

She met his eyes. Expendable? The word rang in her mind, and she understood her father's grim expression immediately. Naturally he wouldn't want his daughter involved with a man whom he could send with a stroke of a pen on a mission that risked his life.

"You're meant for Wade," he was saying comfortably. "A fine young man, which Oswald Chambers will be the first to tell you, if you ask him."

Allison didn't reply. Her heart began to sing again. They were alive. Oh, how good God was! But Oswald Chambers would hasten to say that God was good all the time. He would have been good even if Bret and Wade had been killed, for God always planned the best. He never made a mistake. He was never caught off guard. He knew the end from the beginning, her thoughts before she spoke them. Her downsitting and uprising, and Bret and Wade's minutest actions as well. It was Satan who whispered questions about the goodness of God, even as he had to Eve in the Garden when he suggested God was keeping something beneficial from her.

"Yes, Father," she said brightly, "anything you say! I'm too happy to argue! Oh, Father, welcome home!" she leaned down and laughed and kissed his rugged cheek again.

"Do I take it that this appreciation is for your poor gout-suffering father, or for the one who brings the news that Wade is safe in Egypt?"

She laughed. "You know I'm delighted that both you and Mum are home. I've missed you tremendously."

"As much as you've missed your young chaplain? And your rogue?"

"Are we back to the rogue again?" she managed in an indifferent tone and smiled. "I didn't know rogues were awarded Victoria Crosses."

Sir Marshall cocked his head and cleared his throat. "Yes, well...I see what you mean about that. Most of the time they're not. Anyway—"

"Now, Daddy, you know I don't cavort with rogues."

"And we'll be keeping it that way, not that I'm blaming you, or him. But you're practically engaged to Wade. And I've heard from your mother that the colonel's equally occupied as well, to a rich young woman in Cairo."

Cynthia Walsh. Allison had all but forgotten about her. The resentment she'd been nursing before Bret's appearance at Baghdad resurfaced. "If you're speaking of Cynthia Walsh, she returned to London last August before the war broke. It was Lady Walsh who came to Egypt assuming a public engagement that the colonel had never promised. And Cynthia's been chasing Bret for months."

"Now, now, we won't discuss that. What the man does is his own business as long as it doesn't affect my daughter. They can chase him all they want; but you'll be known for walking like a lady. And as for young Cynthia, I've no interest in her schemes. It's the colonel's military talents I'm interested in. As soon as Holden is recouped, I'll ask General Maxwell to send him on a reconnaissance mission into Palestine. It's a dangerous job. Until then, of necessity we'll be seeing him in Cairo. So from now on, Daughter, you'll stay away from him and await the return of the godly young Wade."

It was painfully obvious that, in her father's mind, her engagement to Wade was a settled issue. Strange that he would think ill of Bret when he'd risked his life more than once as an agent for England.

218

"Besides, Cynthia must have turned around and come back to do some more chasing. Your mother received a letter in Bombay from Mrs. Walsh. She and her daughter are in Cairo. But enough! You heard your mother, it can wait." He groaned as he moved in the chair.

So Cynthia was in Cairo. By now, she already would have seen Bret since he'd been there a week or more.

"Not that it's any of my concern," he commented, watching her. "Or yours."

"Indeed, no, Daddy. It was you bringing it up, not I, remember? I'm sure I couldn't care less." She remembered what her father had said about sending Bret into Palestine and thought of Rose Lyman. "What will Colonel Holden do on the mission to Palestine?"

"Now, you know better than to ask questions about such matters."

She tried to lighten the moment. "A moment ago when you mentioned rogues, I thought you were speaking of Sir Edgar."

His brows shot up. "Ah, so you've met your mother's darling cousin. Never mind Edgar, as well. There are many other things to draw our attention at present. Such as General Crawford, blast his eyes! His stupid decision to seize Baghdad without adequate forces and supplies has cost thousands of soldiers their lives. And it's brought God only knows how many others into torture. He can rot in Kut as far as I care!"

"Daddy!"

He threw his hat onto a hall chair, his face flushed with sudden temper. "And to think I helped get him that command! If it weren't for all those men trapped with him, I'd forget the insane notion of sending in a division to try to save his skin—!" Sir Marshall broke off, looking at her quickly. He paused, then cleared his throat sheepishly. "Now, Daughter, I didn't mean it. I'll do what I can to rescue him." He clenched his teeth. "But this is a day of infamy for the British soldier."

She went to him and took hold of his arm. "I understand. I was there. I saw what happened. At least eight hundred soldiers were left behind in the retreat to Kut. And the enemy came in after us and bombed the field hospital, killing them all. If I think about it for long I—" She stopped, and he patted her hand.

"Don't think about it. I shouldn't have riled you about General Crawford. The man has his good points. It's a sin of mine, this exploding with frustration. I should know better. There's nothing we can do now but wait for that ruddy viceroy, and London, to give orders. It's bad enough that Egypt stands in danger of a German-Turkish assault, now I've got the fate of thousands of trapped soldiers weighing on my conscience." He slumped into the hall chair. "And my gout is killing me."

"Oh, Daddy, I'm sorry."

He looked at her, scowling. "Why don't you medical geniuses do something to cure gout? You and Lydia both! Where is she?" He looked about crossly as Allison stooped to raise his trouser and look at his swollen leg.

"Oh, dear, it does look painful, so red and swollen."

"Lydia!" he shouted. "Where are you? This is a fine welcome home."

Allison looked up at him startled by his tone, but he winked down at her. She hid a quick grin as Lydia came in from the front yard, and he scowled in her direction. Allison doubted he would have much affect, though—his eyes were too full of affection.

"Well, woman? You've been a nurse for forty years. What do you intend to do about my rancorous condition?"

Aunt Lydia thumped her walking stick on the polished hardwood floor and scanned him dubiously. "It's a just reward for your backslidden condition. Why should I relieve your just suffering? The Lord chastens those he loves."

"You will ease my languishing if you want the *Mercy* returned. The matter is in my good hands, you know. A stroke of my gilded pen can have the boat returned when we reach Cairo."

Allison smiled and looked across the hall at her aunt. Lydia's pretended scowl gave way to cheer. She came toward them. "Well, that's different, Marshall! Edgar is likely to disagree with that action, however. I rather thought him an unpalatable sort of fish to swallow. He arrived some weeks ago and has been snooping about unceasingly. He paused when Allison came home so dreadfully ill, but only for a short time. He left early this morning with Gilbert for Cairo. An odd fellow...rather reminds me of—" she stopped, frowning.

Allison glanced up. "A snake."

Marshall cocked an eye toward her. "A cobra, I suppose."

Allison smiled, and Lydia sniffed. "Now look here, Marshall, I daresay you're amused, but we are not, are we, Allison? There's just something odd about the man—"

"Now, Lydia," he interrupted waving a hand, "let's not go too deeply into discussing Eleanor's cousin. Where's your Christian charity?"

"Intact, I assure you, and I do care about his boy. Gilbert needs guidance, else I fear he's headed for ruin. And as for snakes, I am warned about them."

"I think you're overly prejudiced about the creatures because of the Garden of Eden. My memory of Edgar's response to things biblical is that he was aggressively opposed. Now, what do you have for gout? That ruddy doctor on the ship was an American and didn't know what he was doing. A typical colonial clod."

"*Now* who's showing prejudice and a lack of Christian charity? Oswald Chambers held meetings in America and adores those 'clods,' as you call them," said Lydia breezily.

Sir Marshall winced as Allison examined his leg. "Easy, Daughter. Your father is an old man, not one of the young soldiers you examine."

"Sorry, Daddy—" she lifted her head—"Lydia, he's right. It's a dreadful case of gout."

"Here, let me look. Allison, run get my bag will you?"

"And don't bleed me," growled Marshall to Lydia. "I need every drop I have."

"Bleed you? Dear fellow, that went out with the Dark Ages. Don't tell me the American put leeches on you?"

"No, but he might as well have for all the good he did me. The fellow had little left to try except throw me overboard for a German U-boat to run over me."

As Allison walked from the hall into the library for her aunt's medical bag, she heard Aunt Lydia saying to her father: "I suppose you're right about Sir Edgar. He does have a good deal of wit. He expects to become a rich man in cotton. Did you know he's fully invested in Eleanor's plantation?"

Surprised, Allison paused and looked back toward them. The plantation, as Lydia called it, was not extravagant, but was two hundred acres with a bungalow. It remained a bungalow because the family had never cared to live there. It was actually a Bristow enterprise, and so her father had never involved himself in the running of it until a year ago when cotton prices jumped. Great-grandfather Bristow had owned rich Nile Delta land since the building of the Suez Canal in the late 1800s. The property had been willed to Eleanor when her father died in the Turkish-Italian war of 1911. Eleanor rarely visited the place, though. Allison recalled little about it except the many acres of fluffy white cotton in rich dark delta soil, which was worked by the fellahin. Aunt Lydia went to the planta-

222

tion twice a year to offer medical services to the workers, and Allison had sometimes accompanied her. She had gone soon after returning from Oswald Chambers's BTC and before she went to Aleppo in the summer of 1914 with the archaeology club.

Curious that Sir Edgar was invested in her mother's land, Allison stood in the library door and looked at Aunt Lydia.

Her father did not sound surprised at the news, but her mother said as Allison came in from the porch: "Edgar, invested in family cotton? Who gave him the right?"

"I did," came her father's calm voice.

They all turned and looked at him. A moment of silence followed.

Eleanor removed her stylish hat, showing her reddish gold hair smoothly arranged in a Paris chignon. Her fair skin was only faintly lined, and her delicate brows arched with questioning grace above eyes a lighter green than Allison's.

"You gave Edgar the right to buy in?" she asked, walking over to where her husband slumped in the chair and laying a hand on his shoulder. "I realize you wanted Edgar in Cairo, but was that wise?"

Allison's father held her mother's gaze steadily. "Yes, I believe it was. Edgar will be able to contact German buyers in Switzerland, which can only be good for the plantation. And now, about Gilbert—" and he glowered—"Where's Beth? I expect to have a good talk with her about him before we move into the Residency."

"We're not moving there until February, dear, remember?"

"Don't change the subject." Marshall was looking toward the front porch, scowling. "Why can't the girl be more like Allison?"

The words were no sooner out of his mouth than Beth walked up to the porch. Allison glanced at her sister's face quickly, catching the way her mouth set into a hard line. "Allison, again," she moped. "It's so unfair, so positively mean, so beastly of everyone to forever compare me to my sister! Oh, Daddy!"

"Now, now, I meant nothing of it, my little one, so cease your cantankerous scowling. You know I'm proud of you, and your music has earned a letter of recommendation from Raja Sing in Bombay. Why Allison can't even find the middle C on the keyboard!"

"There, you've done it again, Marshall," said Eleanor impatiently. "How many times have I pleaded with you not to compare your daughters?"

As Beth flounced in, Allison thought she made a lovely picture. Her red dress showed off her sultry dark hair and eyes. If only she didn't have that pouting expression, she would be the image of loveliness. She stood there, arms folded, head held high, her eyes flashing. She'd grown much prettier in the year she'd been in Bombay, Allison noted with pleasure—but her sister's next words deflated her positive feelings.

"Gilbert doesn't compare me with Allison. He thinks I'm the prettiest girl he's ever met."

"Until he meets the next one," grumbled Sir Marshall.

"Daddy, you're being unfair!"

"Beth, please don't speak in that tone to your father," her mother admonished. "We'll have none of that."

Allison left the library doorway. "Hey! A fine welcome home you're giving me, Sis," she called to Beth, trying to ease things a bit. She moved in Beth's direction, arms held out, a welcoming smile on her face.

Beth snapped out of her pout immediately. "Allison!" She smiled and hurried to embrace her. "Allison!" She stepped back and looked at her, eyes wide with surprise. "Yikes, you look awful! You're as skinny as a beanpole. Oh, thank God the Turks didn't kill you! Malaria, how ghastly!"

Allison laughed as they hugged again.

"Would someone please get Lydia's medical bag?" moaned Sir Marshall. "If not, we won't need the Turks, for I swear gout will do me in!"

"I'll get her bag, dear," Eleanor told him. "Where do you keep it, Lydia?" But when she turned to look for her sister, she was not to be found.

"I've got it," Aunt Lydia's voice came from the doorway as she entered the room again, her black satchel in her hand. "If I've told Marshall once, I've told him a dozen times, it's his temper that brings the flare-up of gout. More illness is caused by emotions than germs any day."

"Never mind, Lydia," said Marshall, looking over at Allison. "And Beth isn't the only one who'll get a good talking to before Cairo. Well, my dear Allison, you've a lot to answer for. You implied in your letters you were nursing soldiers in Alexandria all these months. It was Colonel Holden who wisely alerted me you were in Mesopotamia!"

"Yes, dear, you should have told us," said Eleanor gravely. "To think you were in that dreadfully disgusting place since April and we didn't know it."

"I knew it," said Beth smugly. "She told me so. And I know why she went there. Because of Wade Findlay. He didn't go to Zeitoun as chaplain as he promised, he became a medical orderly in Arabia. And Allison, saint that she is, went dutifully to be by his side."

"Beth," warned her mother. "With Wade on the hospital ship, it's cruel to tease your sister."

Beth looked guilty. "I didn't mean anything by it."

Allison squeezed her arm. "It's all right. Anyway, I'm going to see him at the Cairo hospital as soon as he arrives next week. I'd like to go tomorrow, Mother. Is it all right?"

Eleanor was removing her wrap. "Of course it's all right, but I don't think you should go alone. And where will you stay?"

"I received an invitation to spend a few days with Sarah Blaine, so this will work out well. I'm sure she'll let me stay until Wade arrives."

Sir Marshall looked at her with a frown. "You'll be staying with Sarah Blaine?"

"Yes, she has a number of spare bedrooms."

"I don't like the idea."

Allison was about to ask him why when Beth spoke up: "She needn't go alone, Daddy. I'll go with her."

"Oh, no, you don't," said her father. "I'll not have you where you are free to see young Gilbert when you want without my overseeing the situation."

"I won't be going alone," Allison broke in, hoping to forestall yet another confrontation. "I've a friend staying with us until after the New Year. Marra was a nurse with me in Arabia. You'll like her."

"Good, because I don't think I should leave your father until his gout improves." Eleanor looked over at him as he scowled and scratched his chin. "It's all right if she goes dear, isn't it? It's understandable Allison wants to pay Wade a visit as soon as possible, and her visit will cheer him as well. And Sarah Blaine has always been a dear friend."

"When will you leave?" he asked, eyeing her dubiously.

Allison looked over at her mother, anxiously. "Marra and I intended to leave this afternoon, but tomorrow will do."

"Since Marra is a nurse, I don't see why you shouldn't be able to take the train trip. And I've been worried about Sarah. She wrote me in Bombay. Poor thing, she so misses Rex."

Allison glanced at her father—he must know that the general had turned out to be an enemy—but his ruddy face was blank.

"You'll be staying at the Blaine house then?" he repeated. "Did she invite you?"

"Yes, why? You don't sound pleased. Sarah could use a little holiday cheer."

"Very well, a few days isn't long."

Allison saw her mother smile at him, but the smile faded to a troubled expression as she walked toward the back of the house calling Zalika. She wondered if her parents had reached any conclusions about their troubled marriage while in Bombay. She knew her mother had gone there to inform him she could take no more of his work in Egypt and that she was leaving him. At least her mother hadn't insisted on returning to England with Beth, now that prowling German U-boats made voyaging unsafe. The longer her parents remained together, the more opportunity they would have to work out their differences. Perhaps the Lord was working even now in their lives, leading them to face the problems that had driven them apart.

As Aunt Lydia treated Sir Marshall and Beth chattered to Allison about all the balls she'd attended in Bombay, Allison sat quietly on the bottom stair happily drinking in her new circumstances. Today had been one of the happier times she had experienced in the months of ongoing worry. Bret was in Cairo, and Wade was safely on his way from Alexandria. David was free from Turkish imprisonment in Jerusalem, her mother and father were still together (at least for the time being), and the family would all be together for Christmas. Even Neal was coming home.

Oh, if only life would stay this way far beyond the New Year!

Later that evening, Allison was repacking her bags to add more belongings for the longer stay in Cairo and trying to decide which dresses to take along. She couldn't make up her mind whether to pack the dinner gown of apple-green satin or the lemon floral print.

She had packed several cotton skirts and blouses, and the cool cotton brought to mind the plantation and the ever-spiraling prices driven by Greek, French, and British speculators. She'd heard her father say a new tax was going to be levied against the European merchants to curb their expansion. She wondered again why her father would allow Sir Edgar to invest so deeply in the family enterprise.

As she opted for a bigger trunk—adding matching straw hats, shoes, and jewelry—she heard the doorbell below and Zalika hurrying to answer. Allison paused, listening, both dresses in her hands. She expected to hear the voices of visitors who came to welcome her parents home, but a moment later the door closed again. Zalika mounted the stairs. It must have been the mail. She went to her door and looked into the hall just in time to see Zalika walk to her parents' bedroom, where she tapped on the door.

"Mrs. Wescott?"

Allison knew Sir Marshall was in his office working, so she was not surprised to see her mother come to the door. "What is it, Zalika?"

"A letter for you, ma'am. The Arab boy's waiting to return with an answer, he says."

Allison came out into the hall and waited, curious, as her mother opened the envelope and read the message. Beth came to join her sister, too.

"Why—how kind of her."

Allison walked toward her. "What is it, Mum?"

Eleanor looked up. "An invitation from Baroness Helga Kruger. She's learned we can't move into the Residency and invited us all to be houseguests until after the New Year. I'll ask your father, but I think he'll be relieved. She's invited others for the holidays as well, but says she has more living space than she can possibly use. What a relief! Even if we could get a suite at the Shepheard's Hotel, it would be dreadfully crowded and noisy. And the baroness does such marvelous entertaining."

Beth clasped her hands together, excited at the news. "Of course it would be frightfully horrid to leave out Cousin Edgar and Gilbert," she told her mother. "They're part of the family and it is going to be Christmas."

Her mother walked to her desk and sat down to write a response. "This is heaven sent," she was saying. "Allison, you can stay with Sarah until your father and the rest of us arrive at Helga's, then join us there. Maybe I can arrange for Helga to invite Sarah as well. She won't be any problem, and it would do her good to be included in a few weeks of festivities."

"Sarah would be delighted, I'm sure," agreed Allison. "She's wanted to attend one of Helga's dinner dances for quite some time."

"I'm sure I can arrange it. Helga loves houseguests. I wonder how many she'll have staying there."

"The house is like a mansion," said Beth clapping her hands together. "And you should see the terrace—it's huge and encircles the entire house."

"How do you know?" asked Allison with a smile.

"Really, Allison, don't you know anything? Francis told me. She went there with her mother once. Oh, the holidays are going to be so much fun this year, war or no war."

"At least the house is large enough so we won't get on one another's nerves," said Eleanor. "Your father will appreciate that. You both know how he loathes balls. This way he can sneak into the drawing room to a comfortable chair to read and no one will even miss him."

Allison wondered who the other holiday guests would be, and how Helga had learned so quickly about the repairs going on at the Residency and their need for housing. Had she expected Eleanor and Sir Marshall to return, or had she found out from someone in Cairo? She thought of Bret. Her father had said he was back in Cairo. Bret knew Helga well, of course. Would he be at any of her dinner parties over Christmas?

It doesn't matter if he is, she scolded herself. *As Father said earlier, he's all but engaged to Cynthia. He's not interested in you, nor you in him, remember? He's a friend, and nothing more.*

But all of her admonishments couldn't keep her heart from beating more rapidly at the thought of seeing Bret again.

CHAPTER

FIFTEEN

➤┄┽◆❯┄⊖┄❮◆┾┄◄

Turn your eyes away from me, for they have overcome me.

SONG OF SOLOMON 6:5

AS THE CROWD OF PASSENGERS SPILLED OUT from the sun-baked dusty train coaches of the Egyptian State Railway, Allison and Marra stood on the platform, their baggage at their feet, glancing about the throng for a glimpse of Sarah Blaine.

"Allison!"

She turned toward the voice and saw Sarah emerging from the shadow of a black train blowing steam. Sarah waved and pressed forward, calling out, "Over here, I've a motorcar! Anwar will load your baggage! Oh, marvelous, you've brought a ton of stuff. That means you'll stay at least a week!"

Allison waved back at the familiar petite woman with big brown eyes and delicate gray at her temples. Sarah was her mother's friend, but she was looked upon as somewhat of a relative and considered Allison a niece. Their interest in archaeology had formed a bond between them; before the war had broken out the two of them had belonged to the Cairo Archaeology Club run by Baroness Kruger and several Egyptologists from the local university. As far as Allison knew, Sarah remained actively involved in the club, as did Helga and the others who had vacationed at the Aleppo huts in July of 1914.

A handsome young man who looked to be either Turkish or Egyptian moved forward to claim her and Marra's baggage. He glanced at Allison, then away. She studied him for a moment, frowning. Had she seen him somewhere before…? She didn't have time to ponder the thought, though. She and Marra left the platform, keeping Sarah in sight as she led the way, and edged their way through the throng of soldiers and diplomats of all nationalities.

Donkey carts, horse-drawn wagons, and even camels vied for space with British motor ambulances. Arab boys moved through the crowd undeterred, balancing stacks of thin, round loaves of bread atop their small, dark heads. Other boys peddled fresh fruit and water. Soldiers were coming and going on the trains, and on the street there were sheltered European ladies in fine dresses and veiled Egyptian women in black.

"Sarah, how good to see you again!" Allison said when she finally reached her friend.

"Not nearly as jolly as it is to see you home from the war. I feel positively guilty, chasing about Egypt with the archaeology club while you've been doing your patriotic duty and all that."

"Patriotism or not, I wouldn't wish the Mesopotamian experience on anyone. I'd gladly involve myself again in archaeology if I had time," said Allison. "So don't feel guilty about a thing. Is Helga still secretary?"

"The woman is marvelous. She was holding lectures and tours nearly every month until the dreadful war closed our doors to Arabia. Not that I'd want to go back to Aleppo." She looked as though a chill wind had blown across her heart. "And by now the Turks and Germans have been tramping all over the Charchemish Digs. Any word from your cousin Neal?"

"He returned to the British Museum last September, but he's due in for Christmas."

"That should please Eleanor. Come along, you look famished. I've arranged for luncheon at Shepheard's Hotel on the terrace. You deserve some spoiling, and today the best of society is lunching. It's luck that the new sultan is to show up. I wonder if he'll wear his ruby? I should think he'd be afraid he'd splash a dash of mustard sauce on it."

Allison laughed. That was one of the things she'd always enjoyed most about Sarah—and about Rex. Their sense of humor. She knew, if Rex were with them now, he would say, "Come along dear Sarah. Maybe it will be our luck to snitch the ruby from him when he's busy with his frog soup."

Sadness washed over her again at the loss of a friend—and at the difficult realization that the man she'd always trusted had not been at all what he'd pretended to be. Thank heavens Sarah, at least, was genuine.

Allison turned to introduce Marra to Sarah. "This is Marra, a good and dependable ally. We served together in Arabia and cried on each other's shoulder a lot."

"Welcome to the club, dear. But you'll need to bring your own hanky. Mine, I'm afraid, are all used up."

Sarah chatted amiably all the way to the motorcar where the young Egyptian opened the door for them to slide into the backseat. And yet, despite Sarah's seemingly cheery air, Allison could see the tension in her face and guessed that her sprightly behavior was merely an act.

Then the oddest thing happened. As the driver placed their bags in back, Allison was surprised into silence by the expression on Sarah's face. She was watching the man with an almost furtive look. As soon as his back was to them, her expression became one of distrust, even dislike. Allison frowned slightly in confusion. If Sarah didn't like the driver, why keep him in her employ? She could dismiss him easily enough and hire another.

The strange moment altered Allison's mood, and she was quiet and thoughtful as they drove along. Fortunately, Sarah and Marra had no trouble carrying the conversation.

It was a short drive into central Cairo, where the British elite met in the flowering square of Ezbekiah Gardens. This spot was reserved for fine hotels, eateries, and shops, and was frequented by a mostly European clientele. The area was considered an oasis, distinct from its arid surroundings. As the motorcar weaved in and out of foot traffic and British military medic vehicles, Sarah explained that there were at least sixty thousand soldiers now in Cairo.

"From every corner of the British Empire," she said, "and many from India."

There were military camps encircling the city, with Zeitoun about six miles away.

"There are so many overcrowded hospitals and convalescent centers, the government doesn't know what to do with all the wounded. In the first weeks after the invasion of Dardanelles in April, sixteen thousand sick and wounded were brought to Egypt."

"Are Alexandria's hospitals all full now?" asked Marra.

Allison knew she was trying to decide whether to seek a transfer to Alexandria or to remain in Cairo, just as Allison herself was. Neither of them had made up their minds, but Marra would need to decide soon. Allison's health would delay her from returning to service for several more months.

"Alexandria's so full I saw the ill and wounded soldiers in the open parks. Some were even lying in the streets near the harbor," said Sarah. "It's heartbreaking to see, but then I don't need to tell either of you about heartbreak, do I? Cairo has become the new hospital zone. Nearly every hotel is in use along with schools and outdoor parks, even Ezbekiah is up for more medical tents soon. And still Cairo is running out of space."

With so many camps, thousands of soldiers were all around,

some on leave, some merely in transit through the city. Across Kamal Pasha Street, toward Ezbekiah, was the Muski, the ancient bazaar that was crowded with Egyptian shops and vendors. Allison had heard that drugged liquor was served there to the soldiers and that it was a place where every vice known to the sinful nature of man could be bought and sold. Particularly opium and prostitution. Lonely soldiers were easy victims. Sarah told her that the YMCA had opened a Christian club for soldiers in Ezbekiah Gardens.

"They hold nightly meetings there to draw the young men, and I do think I heard somewhere that your fine friend Oswald Chambers is holding Bible studies and handing out tea and cakes."

Allison was delighted. She would have to look Mr. Chambers up just as soon as she was settled in Cairo. It would be especially wonderful if she were able to bring Wade there with her.

Thank God for the Christian work among the soldiers, she thought. She had already heard about the infamous "First and Second Battles of the Wozzer," the immoral district, where riots had broken out between the Australian and New Zealand soldiers. She knew that the military commanders looked to the YMCA and other Christian ministries serving in Egypt to provide wholesome activity centers and alternatives for men who were far from home and family. But Oswald Chambers had a deeper motive for serving with the soldiers in the YMCA hut. He had come to make Jesus Christ known to young men who would otherwise face death—and eternity—without him.

It was comforting to Allison that there was such a place as the Young Men's Christian Association. She knew they firmly held to a two-fold purpose: "To unite those young men who, regarding Jesus Christ as their God and Savior according to the Holy Scripture, desire to be His disciples in their doctrine and in their life, and to associate their efforts for the extension of His Kingdom among young men."

It was comforting to know that among dissolution, war, and death, the Lord had his ambassadors at work. They offered hope and forgiveness to the soldiers before they went off to fight and perhaps never return. She prayed, thanking God for bringing Oswald Chambers to Egypt for the war.

Use me, too, Father," she prayed. *I don't want to waste my time or my life on lesser things. Use me to somehow touch these multitudes of men with the news about your son, the Lord Jesus, our only hope.*

Cairo, as usual, assaulted Allison's senses. All around were side-street cafes and countless minarets, and the air about was the aroma of spicy foods and the sound of an eerie Muslim call to pray to Allah.

The famous Shepheard's Hotel was filled with the British and European elite, along with military officers and diplomats and their wives and daughters. The area's weekly newspaper, *The Sphinx*, usually focused on the prominent diplomatic and social figures who graced Cairo. At Christmas an annual gala was held in the hotel's grand ballroom, and so the paper devoted space to reporting on the holiday events in the hotel and garden square.

It was almost one o'clock by the time Anwar had parked the motorcar and came to help them from the vehicle. A white-clad Egyptian waiter escorted them into the spacious dining area, which opened onto an upper terrace. The tables were situated becomingly on the terrace, and Sarah asked for one between a row of arches along one side, which would offer a good view of the terrace and garden.

"Who knows who we'll see," whispered Sarah. "I'm sure the sultan is here."

Allison noticed the strain on Sarah's face even while she affected her customary good humor. What was she worried about?

They took their seats, and Allison, who was seated between Sarah and Marra, had an unobstructed view of the terrace and garden where the afternoon tree shadows formed a complicated mosaic patched with light. "What a stunning view..." she began in a low voice, but her words trailed off and were left hanging. Straight across from them, much to her shock, was Colonel Bret Holden, seated with his top military aide, David Goldstein. A sudden, overwhelming desire to jump up and run to him washed over her, but as her muscles coiled, ready for action, she noticed something that very effectively kept her in her chair. There, seated on either side of Bret, were Lady Walsh and her daughter, Cynthia.

As though sensing her presence, Bret glanced her way. Their gazes held, but neither smiled a greeting, and Allison looked away first, stunned by the hurt that now seemed to fill her. She wouldn't say anything. With any luck, Sarah and Marra wouldn't notice Bret and she wouldn't have to face him.

"It's the colonel and his friend," said Sarah, dashing Allison's hopes to the floor. Sarah gave a little wave in their direction, adding a low voice of warning: "Uh-oh, Lady Walsh is in attendance, touting her prized blue-ribbon chickadee."

"Dratted luck, Allison," murmured Marra as she lifted her teacup.

Allison managed a smile despite her feelings and sipped her lemon water, then picked up the luncheon menu and studied it. "Nothing is going to ruin my lunch, Sarah. What are you going to order, Marra?"

"How about the proverbial sour grapes," she said wryly, casting a glance toward David Goldstein.

Allison smiled and held the menu in front of her, ignoring Bret, not caring a whit how handsome he looked in his new uniform.

Instead, she concentrated on reading the menu: "How does this sound— 'Fresh sautéed Nile fish with parsley?'"

Marra grimaced.

Allison lifted her eyes above the menu to meet Bret's coolly observant gaze. She dropped her eyes again to read about stuffed snapper in wine sauce.

I won't allow his presence to control me, she promised herself angrily, turning her mind instead to wonder why Sarah had wanted her to visit. She couldn't rush Sarah into an explanation with Marra present, and so allowed her to chat about what had been transpiring in her life since the general's death. She had been busy attending social events, Sarah explained, and spending time with the archaeology club.

"We still meet monthly in Cairo, though the war has nearly put a stop to our expedition trips. In fact, the monthly meeting is going to be held soon at the Cairo Museum. We'll be discussing the possibility of a small expedition. Helga wants to revisit Luxor."

With uncertainty Allison recalled how she, Sarah, and Rex had taken a boat down the Nile to meet Aunt Lydia on the *Mercy.* A letter had been waiting for Allison there from Leah explaining where the book belonging to the murdered Major Reuter had been concealed at the huts....The idea of returning to Luxor brought feelings that were anything but pleasurable.

"The Nile trip isn't certain," said Sarah. "It will need clearance with General Maxwell—or is it Murray? I always get those two mixed up. Anyway, Helga will be able to tell us at the monthly meeting. Why not attend the meeting, Allison, for old times' sake? Everyone we know will be there except Neal Bristow and—and one other person."

At first Allison thought she was speaking of her husband, but Sarah's expression of disquiet made her change her mind. Well, if she wasn't speaking of Rex, then who among the past club members wouldn't be there? And why had Sarah appeared to stumble over the name as though she didn't want to mention it?

"Why does Helga want to return to Luxor?" asked Allison, frowning.

"Something about some new finds around Karnak. It would be wonderful if you could at least come to the lecture at the museum, almost like old club times. What of you, Marra? Are you into archaeology at all?"

"Who, me? I wouldn't know the difference between an Egyptian heirloom and a ten-cent replica peddled on the street."

Sarah smiled, reminiscing. "My husband was like that, too. He went along with my excursions to keep me company. He was such a dear that way. We did so many things together." She sighed. "I miss him dreadfully. Sometimes I can hardly stand it." She looked down at her cup and stirred her tea a bit clumsily.

Allison exchanged glances with Marra and they lapsed into silence. There was something curiously depressing about Sarah that seemed to go beyond the normal grief and loss for a husband.

Marra appeared to pick it up as well and was looking at the older woman with the scrutiny of a nurse.

"I'd like to attend the club reunion, Sarah, when did you say it was being held?" asked Allison.

"In a week, I think. The actual date isn't set yet. We'll meet at the Cairo Museum. The club members are to bring an item for the auction. Monies go to benefit the club." She frowned. "I'm trying to decide what to bring."

"Too bad it wasn't being held a week later. Neal would be back by then and able to attend," said Allison.

"Well, count me out," said Marra. "I'll choose that day to make some serious decisions about where I want to transfer in the medical corps." Marra went on to tell Sarah how she had read in the paper of a new general soon to come to replace Maxwell. "Maxwell is being sent to Ireland," she said. "The Germans were doing well in stirring the Irish to riot and keeping the British troops occupied."

"General Maxwell is leaving Egypt? Who is coming in his place?" asked Allison, surprised.

"Oh, I read about the military change, too," said Sarah. "Someone named Archibald, I think—a dreadful name don't you think? General Sir Archibald Murray of the Egyptian Expedition Force. The article said the military was busy reinforcing positions on the Suez, expecting Germany's General Kress von Kressenstein to attack Egypt again."

"I hope not," Allison said.

"As amazing as it may be, a Zeppelin actually reached Cairo," said Sarah. Her hands fidgeted nervously. "I was caught in the motorcar on the way home from shopping, and my driver was killed! There were bombing raids in Port Said, too." She looked at Allison. "A good thing your house wasn't blown up."

"Your driver was killed?"

"Yes, Anwar took his place. With all that's going on, I hope you both ask to be stationed in Cairo. The hospitals are crying for nurses again," and she went on to tell them about Maxwell's call for English ladies to do their part in volunteering to help out. "The Gezira Club has been criticized for continuing their luxurious social lifestyle while soldiers are dying. Everyone took the criticism to heart, and I'm told the ladies are on a waiting list to serve the BEF." She laughed. "General Maxwell is reported to have complained that he now has too many tea club members, and what he really needs is dispatchers to ride motor bicycles back and forth to the camps. The man has a dour sense of humor. He should do quite well in Ireland."

"Hullo, Sarah dear."

The women looked up to find Lady Thelma Walsh smiling down at them. She had paused on her way out, Cynthia at her side. "I hear the baroness intends to invite you to her Christmas celebration," Lady Walsh gushed. "How did *you* ever manage such a coup when the woman positively has neglected *Cynthia* and me?"

"Good afternoon, Mrs. Walsh, Cynthia," Sarah greeted them. "I believe you know Allison Wescott, don't you? This is her friend Marra. Oh, hullo Colonel Holden."

Polite greetings passed smoothly about. Bret spoke with military courtesy, greeting Marra, then Allison. Apparently Allison was the only one who noticed he had spoken to her last.

"Colonel," Sarah was saying enthusiastically, "we've all heard of the tragedy at Kut, but how brave of you to rescue our own Wade Findlay. We've heard you're up for a medal. I do trust you're recovering from your combat injury?"

Allison was careful to keep her appraisal of Bret casual. She saw no evidence of the injury that had caused his earlier stay in the hospital at Alexandria, but Bret would not flaunt such a thing. Unlike some who wore their bandages far longer than necessary, he would not want to attract attention to any weakness. He was in uniform and looking as handsomely suave as ever. He made all of the appropriate responses to Sarah and, as usual, offered little illumination.

Mrs. Walsh was lowering her gaze on Allison with an almost pitying look reserved for the doomed or dying and breathed in a soft sick-room tone of voice: "My dear, I've heard of your service on the Arabian front."

"Have you? I hardly think—" she began a trifle embarrassed, taking the woman's remark as a genuine compliment, but Mrs. Walsh headed her off.

"I must say, my dear, I was frightfully shocked. I mean, I simply can't get accustomed to women out on the war front with our brave soldiers. My Cynthia would never think of doing anything so...common. Too frightful. *Really,* it's a bit *much* isn't it? Not only do our dear boys have to take care of themselves, but they must watch over and take care of a host of helpless women, as well. It hardly seems cricket."

A brief uncomfortable silence followed, in which Allison felt her face grow warm. She should have expected a little dig from Lady Walsh, but she'd been caught wholly unprepared for the cut.

"The wounded soldiers don't share your opinion, Mrs. Walsh," said Marra. "They want to live. Allison and I and our fellow military nurses are helping to see they get back home—" she paused, casting a disdainful glance at the younger Walsh—"to women like *your* Cynthia." Marra fixed Mrs. Walsh with a glare, as if to say, "There, you old cat. You got what you deserved."

But Cynthia, who was the image of sophistication in white hat, gloves, and a matching linen column dress with lace collar that flattered her willowy figure into the picture of a Vogue model, only smiled. "Poor Allison. Mummy didn't mean to sound critical. She was merely overwhelmed thinking about the horrors. She can't imagine my being out there facing German Zeppelins and Turkish soldiers!"

Allison smiled humorlessly. "I'm certain you can put that fear aside, Mrs. Walsh. I can't imagine Cynthia out in the Arabian desert toiling in such circumstances either."

A flicker of a smile showed on Bret's mouth.

Cynthia's eyes turned chill, but warmed when they turned their blue depths on Bret. "Allison's right," she said, a note of regret in her low tones. "Her heroic war effort is so sacrificial that I almost feel guilty."

A teasing glint showed in his eyes. "Do you, my dear? Well, how fortuitous for you that a guilty conscience can be alleviated quickly. General Maxwell is asking for women volunteers to run motor bicycles out to the camps about Cairo. Perhaps you might prove as valuable running dispatches as you are charming?"

There was a moment of silence, and both Sarah and Marra ducked their heads as if to cover their smiles. But Cynthia, put in her place by the person Allison had thought least likely to do so, refused to show she accepted it as such.

"I should be glad to do anything to please a man up for a Victoria Cross, Bret darling. And now, we must run." She turned to Mrs. Walsh. "Ready, Mother? It's nearly three o'clock, and you did ask your dinner guests to begin arriving by half past five."

"Yes, we must be running," hastened Mrs. Walsh. "We'll see you again, Sarah. I hear the baroness has arranged to expand her holiday guest list, so perhaps we'll hear from her yet. I'm told the new consul and his family will be there, too—oh!" her hand went to her heart. "How frightfully stupid of me—that includes you, doesn't it, Allison darling?"

"Yes," said Allison, laughing. "The last I heard my parents still owned me as a daughter, but one never knows. They aren't exactly pleased to have learned I was stationed with the Sixth Division in Arabia, either."

Cynthia looked at Bret. "Don't forget tonight. No later than six o'clock. Coming, Mother?"

They left by way of the terrace stairway through the garden where their chauffeured Mercedes waited, and Allison fought feelings of irritation. What could Bret see in that woman other than a pretty face and figure?

David, who had stood back unobtrusively all this time, now came up, looking as though he had enjoyed the verbal exchange. With a wink at Allison, he turned to Marra.

"I don't believe it! It's the grumpy nurse from Kut. Hello, Marra, you're looking as dour as ever."

"Oh, no, not you again."

"Welcome to Cairo, Brown Eyes. What's for dessert? Mind if I share? Thanks." He grinned as Marra smirked, then seated himself beside her without waiting for an answer, thereby forcing Bret to seat himself in the empty chair beside Allison.

As Sarah, Marra, and David talked, the prolonged silence between Allison and Bret grew. She became too aware of his presence beside her.

At last he leaned toward her and said in a low voice: "What, no solacing words for a wounded soldier freshly released from Alexandria?"

"Thank you for bringing Wade back safely. I didn't expect you to, nor did I want you to risk—" she stopped under his riveting gaze and felt herself growing warm again. "You're all right?"

"And if I'm not?"

She looked away, both flustered and frustrated. "You look as though you're recovering quite satisfactorily. I'm certain you've received an abundance of solicitous words from Cynthia. You certainly don't need any from me."

"On the contrary, I languish in a depressed mental state."

She met his mocking gaze. "Do you, indeed?"

"I feel rejected and aggrieved. In Basra you convinced me it was your high calling to risk great odds to hold the bleeding soldier in your willing arms. Here I have bled, and where were you? At least you might have taken pity by visiting the battle-fatigued colonel. Instead, for all my pains, what did I receive? I was abandoned by the lovely and noble Nurse Wescott! Alone and forgotten in my gloomy recovery."

She lifted her teacup, looking straight ahead, avoiding what she knew would be flickering in those dark blue eyes.

"If I had known, I would have rushed to your side."

Bret's smile was brief. "To thank me for rescuing your darling from advancing Turks, or to soothe my aching brow?"

Her father was right. The man was a rogue! "I'm sorry, Colonel, but I just can't imagine you ever being abandoned and lonely."

"No," he said with a faint edge to his voice. "I suppose not. If I recall your parting words in Arabia, I'm 'nothing more than a colonel in a uniform. Absent of feelings.'"

So he remembered. Well, she would not be drawn into guilt. "With Cynthia to call on you, how could you ever feel abandoned?" She met his gaze again determined to let him see her indifference, but she wasn't prepared for the spark of blue fire in his eyes that melted her offensive as effectively as a raging forest fire.

"Maybe I prefer brave and noble nurses with tender hearts who offer a comforting arm for valorous soldiers."

Her mouth felt suddenly dry at the look in his eyes, but she forced herself to speak with a detached air. "I'm quite sure you could find willing arms to oblige you easily enough. I'm on extended leave, you see, so I'm afraid I wouldn't have had cause for serving in the hospital there."

"You pain my heart, Miss Wescott. What good is a Victoria Cross if the most dedicated member of the elite Nurses Corps is not impressed?"

Allison was trying to slow her pulse. "On the contrary, I am quite impressed. You have my sympathy and my gratitude."

"Now, what kind of a war hero would I be to have left your darling to face the Turks?"

It was the second time he had made a point of calling Wade her "darling." A denial flew to her lips, but she would not give it voice. She could not give so much away to this mocking man beside her, not when he so clearly saw her as little more than a chance to sharpen his wit. But she was saved from making any response when her attention was wrested away from Bret's smooth goads thanks to a glimpse of someone across the room.

Sir Edgar Simonds was there, alone, his broad back toward the wall. He sat with glass in hand, looking across the room—but he was not watching her or Bret. His drowsy gaze was turned toward the open terrace.

At that moment he pushed his heavy frame up from his chair and walked slowly toward the terrace. Once there, he stood with his back toward the dining room, resting both arms on the rail and looking below to the garden while he smoked.

A moment later he was joined by an unobtrusive looking gentleman of European nationality, a drink in one hand, who struck up a conversation. Something about the casual scene was disturbing, but what was it?

David, who had been talking with Marra, broke into her thoughts. "Allison, how long will you be staying with Sarah?"

She dragged her mind away from the terrace. "Until my parents arrive. We're spending the holidays at Helga's mansion, just outside Cairo."

"What's wrong with moving into the Residency?"

"It's under repair," spoke up Sarah. "I'd love to have all of you there, it's so close by. I loathe being alone, and the house is so quiet without Rex."

Allison glanced in the direction of the terrace. Sir Edgar had left, but the man was still there finishing his drink. A moment later he turned around to walk back from where he had come. She was sure the tension she felt went unnoticed and was relieved when Sarah glanced at the big clock on the back wall and said: "Oh, dear, I do hate to end this pleasant visit, but if I don't get back to the house

246

before 4:15, I'm likely to lose my Arab cook. She asked to get off early tonight. I promised she could have it since things will soon be too busy to spare her before Christmas. Come along, Allison, Marra!"

Bret and David stood, and Allison avoided Bret's gaze as he handed her wrap and handbag to her.

David bowed to Marra. "Maybe I'll come by to see you if I get time."

"Thanks," quipped Marra. "You make a girl feel really wanted."

"Of course you're wanted. You're Jewish aren't you? I'll need someone to help me celebrate Hanukkah." He grinned at her as she cast him a wry look and followed Allison and Sarah from the dining room.

SIXTEEN

➤━◆➤━◑━◅◆━◆━◄

Her house is the way to hell, descending to the chambers of death.
PROVERBS 7:27

THE SKY WAS A HARD GRANITE BLUE without a trace of cloud, and the afternoon sun was warm and strong for December as Sarah's Egyptian driver, Anwar, drove from the western section of the city and edged into the narrow, crowded streets of Old Cairo. It had always been a curiosity to Allison that the Blaines would have a house in this section rather than in the British sector, since neither Sarah nor the general had Egyptian friends.

On either side of the street were closely spaced houses of stucco with wrought-iron lattice work. But the Blaine house, located at the very end of the street, stood back from any other structures. A blue-roofed, tall house, it was flanked by rambling shrubs losing their leaves and set deep among a yard growing with stunted bushes, tangled briars, and an overgrown fig tree.

Sarah looked at them apologetically. "The garden is grotesque. Rex used to keep it up, and I'm afraid I've let it run wild. But I must confess it is too horrid to stand any longer, so I've recently hired a gardener."

Anwar drove up the shady, tree-lined driveway, stopping in front of the gravel path that lead to the door.

No sooner had they arrived than Allison's mood grew more somber. The ghostly memories of Rex hovered, depressing the atmosphere. Even Marra lapsed into silence. Sarah looked grim and preoccupied, a far different personage than she'd presented so far. The once-happy brown eyes that had been so full of love of life and laughter were furtive, as though she were uncertain…or hiding something.

They walked up the path and went inside. The house, comfortably but not expensively furnished, was roomy and silent—and too dark, thanks to overgrown bushes near the windows. Allison thought, in looking about her, that she understood Major General Rex Blaine a little better now. He would have deplored such average surroundings. His many years of service to the British government clearly had ended in a retirement of only moderate wages. Most likely he had soured on his own failed ambitions, which had led him to devote the later part of his life to gaining money and power by betraying his country and spying for Germany. She recalled his bitter explanations when he'd held the gun on her in the Aleppo hut. He had done it for Sarah, to give her more…and yet it had cost her everything. For Rex Blaine had been, in many ways, Sarah's life.

Allison shivered at her sad thoughts and turned her attention to Sarah, who was saying with feigned cheerfulness, "Well, here we are. I hope you'll be comfortable. You'll each have your own room, though I'm afraid, Marra, the only other bedroom is located on the other side of the house, so you'll be a bit away from us."

"I'm usually so exhausted I'm asleep as soon as my head hits the pillow anyway," said Marra, looking about. "I like your house, Sarah. It's got a personality all its own."

"It's Rex's personality," she replied, removing her gloves as she walked into the entrance hall. "I'll tell Neith, my Egyptian cook, to make tea. I feel a headache coming on. Neith?" she called.

Allison looked up the staircase that led from the wide hall to a narrow landing running around three sides of the stairwell. From her vantage point it looked as though the landing gave access to four rooms: two bedrooms with an office in between, and a large sewing room at the end of the hall. On the first floor, a large draw-ing room and a smaller dining room looked out on a surprisingly large garden at the back of the house.

Marra had declined tea and went to unpack in her small bed-room, leaving Allison and Sarah together. The lines of strain show-ing in Sarah's face were more pronounced now that they were alone, and Allison expected her to mention the urgent matter that had caused her to ask Allison to come and spend the weekend. But she didn't. Apparently the matter could wait. Either that, or Sarah now wanted to avoid talking about it.

She sat in a chair in the entryway, her hand at her temples. "This is dreadful, Allison. I fear I've a sick headache coming on. Would you mind too terribly if I rested in my room until dinner?"

"Not at all. You do look a bit under the weather, Sarah. You're sure it's just a headache?"

Sarah's gaze swerved to meet hers, startled.

"You're not coming down with the flu?" Allison expounded hastily.

"Oh," relief washed over Sarah's features, "No. No, I'm certain it's a headache. They've been troublesome recently."

"Shall I fix you some tea? Perhaps a light sandwich?" she asked, giving Sarah an encouraging smile. "I'm actually quite handy in the kitchen."

"I don't think I could possibly take anything right now," Sarah said, a slight moan in her voice.

"Then I'll even oblige you with a headache pill," said Allison amia-bly, digging into her bag and producing a pillbox. "Here, this should help." She smiled. "A nap will do us all good."

"How odious of me," apologized Sarah. "I've completely forgot-ten you're the malaria patient. Let me get you tea—"

"I'm doing well enough. Run along and don't worry about me.

I'll see to my unpacking before dinner. If I want someone to chat with, I'll bother Marra."

Allison followed Sarah to the stairs, then stood watching her go up to the landing, then turn left and enter her room. The door closed. Allison stared after her, musing, her concerns beginning to percolate. Something was quite wrong, of that she was certain. Sarah had changed, and not for the better. True, the loss of her husband would have left its mark, but the change in Sarah went beyond grief of a loved one to—what? Fear?

That idea made little sense and she pushed it away. *I'm letting this house get to me and stir up false imaginings. I was afraid coming here might do this to me.* She glanced about her. Sarah was right; the house did reflect Rex's personality. The old general could be seen everywhere, behind every piece of furniture and painting, in every creak and groan of the Blaine house.

I shouldn't have come here. I should have asked Sarah to come to Port Said and stay, instead. Why didn't I think of it then, when there was time? Now it's too late.

Too late? Too late for what? Why had she even thought that?

She shook her head abruptly and went to unpack her things. Perhaps being busy would keep her mind from going down such odd paths.

The rest of the day passed too quietly. The December afternoon turned gray and shadowy, and a wind came up. Allison tried not to pay any attention to the seemingly eerie atmosphere of the house, but she found it nearly impossible. With the old wooden lattice shutters and roof timbers of the Blaine house, the creaking sounds took on a life of their own. As Allison unpacked her bags and hung her dresses in the teakwood closet, she found herself turning several times to look behind her toward the hall. She could swear someone was there, watching her!

Of course, no one was, and she chided herself yet again for giving in to her imagination.

She placed her undergarments in the antique bureau of dark polished cherry wood, then straightened and looked around. It was a pleasant room, she told herself. She liked the clean white ruffled curtains and crisp blue draperies that matched the bedspread and woven rug. She reminded herself that she was far removed from frightening events of Aleppo. She must get it all out of her mind.

Even as she tried to convince herself of this, another creak came from behind the closed door on the other side of her room. "All right now," she muttered, "that's quite enough!" She marched toward the door, then reached out to throw it open, determined to take the bull—or ghost, if needs be!—by the horns.

She didn't know what she'd expected to see, but she was delighted to discover a private bathroom with a tub. The cause of the creaking was quickly apparent: the hook and eye latch had come undone and the window creaked with each gust of wind. She looked below and saw the front gravel drive. She tried to latch the hook but discovered the wood was rotting and the screw was loose.

"Oh, bother!" She peered out the window again. "Well, at least I'm too high up to worry about flies coming in."

She latched it as best she could and drew down the reed blind. There was no stairway or ledge she reminded herself a moment later as the nervy rattle continued. No one could get in unless they first climbed onto the roof, which they would do at the risk of a two-story fall onto the red flagstone courtyard below. *By then I'd hear someone on the roof and be yelling my head off.*

She ran her bathwater and turned her mind to her one true source of protection. *The Lord knows my downsitting and my uprising,* she told herself, thinking of Psalm 139. *He keeps my path before, and behind. Since that's true, nothing can befall me without his knowledge.*

And I can trust him with whatever befalls me in this life of uncertainty, and evil. The Lord is my light and my salvation, whom shall I fear?

She turned her attention to her bath. Let the window rattle! She would pay it no more mind. Her one concern was to find out what was troubling Sarah. She would have to have a talk with her before dinner.

By the time Allison had bathed and dressed in a blue topaz column dress that flattered her thick flame-colored hair, it was nearing five o'clock. She left her room to discover that no one else in the house had stirred, either. Sarah apparently was still in her room. Knowing how painful headaches could be, Allison hesitated to knock and awaken her.

Neith had not even bothered to turn on the lights, and in the gathering twilight the lower rooms stood chill and shadowy. Allison glanced across the landing to the closed office door. Rex's office. Feeling a small repulsion, she turned to look toward Sarah's bedroom to see if the light was on. The crack beneath the door was dark. Poor Sarah. She had been through a great deal in the past year. She was still asleep, probably feeling comfortable at last to know that Allison and Marra were in the house with her and that she was not alone.

Allison left the landing and came to the top stair. The sun had been moving swiftly down in the Cairo sky, and now as she stood in the silence looking toward the windows, the light dipped behind the distant trees and left the garden and the house to the twilight.

She came down the hardwood stairs, her heeled slippers making the only sound in the darkness. Then she paused, frowning, as thoughts of Bret drifted into her mind. His behavior at the Shepheard's Hotel at luncheon that afternoon had halted her from adequately showing gratitude for what he had done for Wade. His mood had set her on edge and reminded her again that the feelings between them must be held at bay.

If only it wasn't so difficult to do so!

She went down the stairs, determined not to think of him again. Neith brought in supper at six-thirty, but Sarah didn't come down.

"Don't you think we ought to awaken her?" asked Marra, who had just joined Allison a few minutes before. "She doesn't seem the sort to neglect propriety and have her guests eat alone."

"I gave her a headache pill. She's deep in slumber, I'm sure. Still, maybe you're right. I'll go check on her." Allison poured a cup of hot tea and carried it up with her, tapping on the door. "Sarah? Awake yet?"

A light switched on. "Come in, darling."

Allison didn't know why she was so relieved. What had she expected, for heaven's sake? She entered smiling and said with an attempt at lightness: "Nurse on duty, madam. Feeling any better? I've brought you a wake-up cup."

She handed Sarah the cup, and the older woman groaned and leaned forward as Allison arranged the pillows so she could sit.

Sarah's eyes glinted strangely, and the last vestige of color was gone out of her pale face. "This headache is dreadful. I don't think I can eat supper tonight."

Allison masked her concerns, not for the headache, but for the strange way Sarah was behaving. "I'll send Neith up with a bowl of soup. A good night's sleep will do you good."

Allison went back downstairs to the dining room where Marra waited at the table and told her Sarah wouldn't be coming down. Even though Marra didn't say anything, her pensive look told Allison she, too, found Sarah's behavior a bit odd.

Allison ladled the soup into a bowl, added a slice of white French bread, and when Neith appeared silently enough to make her start, gave it to her to take upstairs. When the woman went up to Sarah's room, Marra asked: "How long has Sarah's husband been dead?"

"Since July of 1914," said Allison without hesitation. The date would forever be lodged in her mind. She shuddered, but Marra didn't seem to notice.

"That's rather long enough. I'd expect her to be getting over the worst of the loss by now. From her actions today, I thought he might have died a few months ago."

"You noticed, too, then?" Allison considered uneasily.

Their voices had automatically lowered.

"Who wouldn't notice? She was nervous, almost afraid. I couldn't figure it out. She put on a good front at luncheon and was talkative and friendly, but several times when I looked at her, she seemed to be thinking about something else. Something unpleasant." Marra looked across the table at Allison.

Allison looked at the food before them but could work up little enthusiasm. Her appetite had waned. "Yes, and I can't help wondering if what's bothering her concerns her loss, or some other matter."

"What do you mean? What else could it be?"

Allison was aware of the quiet house, the shadows that seemed to lurk in the corners of the rooms next to the dining room. "I don't know. Except it must have to do with the letter she sent me at Port Said. There was something urgent she wished to talk to me about. And now it rather appears as though she wants to avoid talking at all."

Marra was alert. "You think the headache was an excuse not to come down tonight? It doesn't make any sense, though. Why would she do that? She was the one who asked you to come."

"I don't know," and Allison found herself looking about, almost as if she expected someone to be listening in the shadows. "Unless something happened since she sent the letter. Something to change her mind about discussing it."

"What are you going to do?"

"Nothing yet. I may be wrong. I'll wait until tomorrow and see what she does. She may be trying to decide how much she wants to share with me."

After supper, with the dishes cleared away and Marra in her room, Allison went in search of Neith. She found her in the kitchen, wiping down the counters carefully. Allison noted Sarah had an abundant supply of cooking utensils displayed on the wall. She smiled as she remembered cooking and baking with her mother and sister. They would have enjoyed having such an extensive collection of tools to use.

The thought of her family brought a pang of homesickness to Allison, and she turned to Neith before it could depress her too badly. "Do you stay here in the house?" she asked casually.

"I not sleep in," she replied brusquely. "I leave after I clean kitchen. Anwar will give me ride home. I am back again at five-thirty in morning."

Allison's interest perked up. If Anwar gave the older woman a ride home, then they must be on friendly terms. Perhaps a few discreet questions could help her discover why Sarah had watched the man so uneasily in the motorcar on the way from the train station.

"Anwar is a new driver for Mrs. Blaine, isn't he? Did he know the poor man who was killed in the raid from the German Zeppelin a few months ago?"

Neith began filling the kitchen sink with water and soap, her lined face as fixed as a carving.

"He knew the driver."

"Have you known Anwar long?" she ventured.

"Anwar my son."

Her son! "Then you must be the one who recommended him to Mrs. Blaine." Allison gave a friendly smile. "Coming to work together must make things easier."

Neith looked at her, her dark eyes remote. "Anwar is good driver. He takes care of Mrs. Blaine's Mercedes. Nothing is, as you say, easy. We work very hard. There are no gifts. No favors."

"I'm sure of that," hastened Allison, not wanting to offend her. "Anwar seems very bright."

"Anwar is student at Cairo University. He will not remain driver like his father."

Allison started. "Anwar's father—you mean, your husband is a driver, too?"

Neith didn't look at her as she answered, "He was Mrs. Blaine's driver. He was driver killed when Zeppelin came."

Allison's hesitation lasted a mere fraction of a second. "Oh, I see—I'm sorry. That must have been very difficult for you both."

Neith returned to scrubbing the dishes with too much energy. "Yes," she admitted briefly.

Allison stored the information away to muse over later when she was alone. "So Anwar goes to the university. What is his interest?"

"Archaeology. He has summer expedition coming next year for Cairo Museum. He will dig mummies."

Perhaps twenty minutes later Allison was in her bedroom, her door not quite shut, when she heard low voices below. She stepped out onto the landing and padded quietly to the stairs. The voices were coming from the kitchen area, and she recognized Neith's voice speaking to someone in Arabic. She heard a male voice respond, then heard a name. Anwar. Neith was talking with her son. Allison picked up a few familiar words....Anwar was upset with his mother about something, but Allison wasn't sure what, exactly.

Allison was still standing there a minute later when Neith appeared below in the hall. She looked up the stairs at Allison and held up a key. "Mrs. Blaine always locks kitchen door behind me. Anwar and I go now for the night. You will lock?"

Allison came down the stairs and followed her through the kitchen to a back pantry and out onto a porch.

Anwar waited outside below the steps where a walkway led off into the dark, shapeless garden. Allison could not see the young man's eyes, but her skin prickled and she had the distinct impression he was watching her closely. She glanced his direction and caught an unpleasant look on his face—one she'd seen often on the faces of those nationals who did not approve of the "British occupiers of Egypt."

She turned away quickly and bade Neith good night. She closed the door, turning the key in the lock, listening carefully as their footsteps faded into the night.

SEVENTEEN

>━┼━◆━━☯━━◆━┼━<

Hope deferred makes the heart sick.
PROVERBS 13:12

A MINUTE OR SO LATER THE MOTORCAR LIGHTS flashed on in the driveway, and Anwar backed out and drove his mother home.

Allison stood thoughtfully, listening to the enveloping silence settle over the house. Taking the key with her, she walked back through the kitchen into the dining room. The big clock chimed on the half hour.

She mounted the stairs and went to her room, laying the key on the vanity table. A glimpse of herself in the mirror startled her, as though her image belonged to someone else.

If I don't watch out, I'll talk myself into a fit of nerves like Sarah, she thought.

Allison wasn't sleepy, so she decided to lounge on her bed and catch up on some reading. She was just getting into the story when she caught the sound of a motorcar nearing the house. Surprised, she wondered why Anwar was returning. Was his mother with him? Uneasily, she got up and laid the book aside, going to the window that looked down on the drive and drawing aside the curtain.

A man was coming up the walk, taking the steps up to the front porch. She hardly recognized Bret out of uniform. His knock sounded below on the front door, quiet but insistent.

Her heart was pounding in an irritating manner, and she drew a deep breath to calm herself. What was he doing here? Why wasn't he having dinner with Cynthia?

Without asking herself why, she rushed to dab fresh color to her lips and smooth her hair, giving a critical glance and comparing herself with Cynthia Walsh. Allison was relieved that she had dressed up for dinner out of habit, even if Marra had been the only one present. Tonight, Allison told herself, in her topaz blue column dress with its satin collar and cuffs, she looked as sophisticated as Cynthia. Bret had rarely seen her in anything but her nurse's uniform, with its starched white pinafore and red cross....

Stop it! she scolded herself. *Bret Holden isn't here to admire your appearance. Something must be wrong.*

She left her room and hurried down the stairs, crossing the hall to the front door as his rap sounded more urgently. In another moment Marra would be roused.

She pushed back the bolt and pulled open the door, letting in a draft of December chill along with Colonel Bret Holden, who now looked anything but a colonel in the British army. He wore a white dinner jacket and tie. So he had come from the Walsh's exclusive dinner party. Or was he now on his way?

It didn't matter. *I refuse to be jealous,* Allison told herself, but the admonition lacked much conviction in the face of her raging emotions.

He entered, shutting the door behind him, casting a glance through the archway into the lighted drawing room. Allison had the impression he wanted to be sure they were alone. Apparently satisfied, he turned his full attention back to her, studying her carefully. His slight frown was not what she had expected, and she self-consciously reached a hand to touch the back of her neck, as if a strand of hair had come loose from her upward sweep.

"Are you going out?" he asked, his tone of voice revealing nothing.

262

He probably figured Wade was too ill to take her out, so there would have to be someone else escorting her. She was tempted to keep him guessing just to see his response, but quickly rejected that notion.

"No, actually, I was all settled in my room with a good book. I simply felt like a change from my nurse's uniform. Besides, I often dress up at home for family dinners. My mother raised me that way."

He looked toward the drawing room; the lights were glowing. "Anyone else here?"

"Not other than Marra and Sarah. The cook and driver left over an hour ago. Why? Would you mind telling me what this is all about, Colonel?"

"You can drop the 'colonel,' Allison. We know each other too well for formalities."

Do we? she wanted to ask but caught herself.

"Sarah had a headache and went to bed," she explained. "And Marra retired to read, but I can hardly believe the busy colonel drove by just to learn that. Is something wrong?"

Bret glanced about, taking in the layout of the house, then looked at the stairway with the dim night-light glowing at the top. "I need to talk to you. Alone. Drawing room all right?"

Allison nodded, then led the way. She sat down on the champagne brocade divan and clasped her hands about her knees, watching him, wondering.

Bret went to the large glass windows facing the back garden and looked casually out through the drawn curtains. "Is that a garden?"

Her nerves prickled. "Yes. Why do you ask?"

"Is there a back gate?"

"I don't know. I haven't been out there yet. I suppose there is. Why?"

"No reason. We need to talk, but I've changed my mind about doing it here." He looked her over, taking in her face and hair. "You look nice," he said. "Too good to sit here alone all evening. Would you like to go out?"

She stared at him, stunned. "I—you—" She cleared her throat and started again. "Isn't Cynthia expecting you at her dinner party?" That was better. She'd managed the same tone of indifference he had used.

He walked to the darkened alcove, where there was a flight of short wooden steps. "What's up there?"

"The guest room, where Marra's staying, and a storage closet, I think." *What was this about?* "Why?"

"Is there another door to the garden from that direction?"

She followed his gaze. "I think so. Near the laundry room."

He looked at her. "Keep the doors locked while you're here." He paused, and then, "I told Mrs. Walsh a situation came up and I couldn't make it tonight."

Allison assumed that she was the situation that had interfered. She couldn't resist: "Oh, please, I wouldn't want to take you away from Cynthia. Experiencing her cat claws this afternoon was quite enough. I do not care to earn another dose of that."

"You couldn't take me away from Cynthia," he said, and paused. "Unless I wanted you to." He smiled. "I'm faithful, you see, when I choose to be, and I didn't choose dinner at Cynthia's. She did." He looked out the window again, analyzing the layout she supposed. "I would like to take you out, Allison. We could talk."

The invitation was offered in such a casual way that she couldn't make anything of it had she wanted to. She suspected that was deliberate. She turned on the divan and looked over at him, curious.

"Strictly business, Nurse Wescott," he said, interpreting her look. "I promise not to abduct you on a slow boat to Constantinople. We do need to talk," he explained. "And I don't think this is the place to do it. Better get a wrap. It's cold out."

She stood, thoughtful. What was on his mind?

She felt Bret's gaze on her as she went up the stairs, and a quick glance back confirmed this...and caught a frown of concern on his face. Her racing pulse picked up speed.

A few minutes later, a white silk shawl about her shoulders and sparkling earrings and a whiff of perfume added to her ensemble, she was ready to go. She glanced toward Sarah's bedroom. All was dark and quiet. She wouldn't awaken her to tell her she was going out.

A few minutes later they were in the military motorcar, and Bret backed up and circled the half driveway, the headlights flicking over the bushes. Allison stiffened.

Bret picked up her mood and cast her a glance. "What is it?"

"Over there—I—thought I saw someone just now. He ducked behind those bushes when the headlights swept the drive."

Bret stepped on the brake, shifted in reverse, and backed up. "Lock the doors."

Before she could protest he snatched the keys and disappeared out the door, in the direction of the shrubs that sent swaying shadows across the moonlit drive. Allison sat tensely, looking after him, the familiar fear that came with danger turning her palms sweaty and cold. Had she imagined seeing someone?

Perhaps five minutes had slipped by before she heard footsteps on the gravel coming from the opposite direction. Bret must have circled the entire house. She leaned over and unlocked the door, and he got in behind the wheel, started the motor, and drove on.

"Well?" she asked in a dry whisper.

"No one there. But I did see a black-and-white cat. He spat at me," he said with dry humor and a slight grin. "He must belong to you."

She smiled in response and relief. "That's Sarah's cat. Pepper doesn't make friends easily." She looked through the rear window. The Blaine house faded from view as he turned a corner. "My nerves must be on edge. I suppose it's seeing Sarah again," she admitted. "General Blaine comes to mind far too often, and his shadow seems to be everywhere in the house." She drew her wrap around her, covering a shudder.

Bret made no reply, and she noticed he seemed most thoughtful as they drove toward downtown Cairo.

They soon arrived at Ezbekiah Gardens where he parked, then walked her toward a long, tree-lined lane which meandered through lawns and flower beds toward a square all lit up with Christmas decorations. Allison realized it was the perfect place to talk without worry of being overheard. She looked up at the star-splashed night that was conducive to sharing secrets—then heard someone walking behind them. She felt a tingle run up her back and started to turn but Bret's hand closed over hers, and he said in a low voice: "Don't turn around. If we're being watched, I want them to think this is a romantic rendezvous."

Drawing her arm through his and holding it firmly against him, he turned her to face him. Making no attempt to lower his voice, he said: "I haven't had a chance to be alone with you since I returned. I think we need to discuss Wade and come to some agreement. You're going to need to choose between us one day."

She stared at him, speechless.

"Smile," he whispered. "Look as if you're a bit infatuated with the daring colonel up for a Victoria Cross."

Gazing into those warm midnight blue eyes, she suddenly had little trouble following his direction.

Bret's eyes widened a fraction, and something flickered deep in his eyes. "That's much better," he commented, but for all his effort at being flip she noted an oddly thick sound in his voice. "In a moment you'll have the hard-boiled colonel in a boyish swoon."

She flushed. "Oh, really, Bret! This is going a bit far—"

He cut her off by circling her waist with one arm and holding her close against him as he walked her away down the lane. Once they were walking in the direction of the square, Allison whispered, "Are we being followed?"

"Don't keep your voice so low. If we are, we want whomever it is to conclude we're discussing a romantic triangle."

Seeing a hint of smile, she looked away. "Which triangle might that be?" she sparred, her eyes wide and innocent. At his quick look, she smiled guilelessly and went on, "About Wade, I don't feel I've thanked you enough for going back for him."

"You don't need to thank me."

She looked at him in the moonlight, quite sincere now. "Yes, I do. How did you manage? It must have been dreadful, since you're up for a medal for what you did."

"As much as I dislike unmasking myself as a hero, I must confess that Wade had already managed to escape the hospital tent and was driving with Doc Murphy and some orderlies toward Abadan when we met up with the truck. He would have made it without me, Allison." His tone, too, was serious.

And yet, she didn't quite believe him. She knew too well how Bret persisted in avoiding praise for his actions. "You wouldn't be up for a medal if it were as simple as you make it sound. What happened to Doctor Murphy?"

"I'm sorry. He's dead. Heart attack."

She walked on quietly, her heart paying tribute to a man who had given his best for the soldiers.

Bret squeezed her waist in wordless comfort.

In the distance a Christmas carol was being sung, and Allison glanced up at the starry sky, blinking back the tears. "How long do you think the war will last?"

"Until Hiddendorf realizes he can't take Paris."

"Will it come to that?"

He was quiet for a moment. "If it ever does, it will be because the best have decided that with or without victory, honor is worth dying for. They'll need to hold out when there's nothing left but courage. I was over there. I saw what was happening. Thousands are dying without pushing the Germans back an inch."

Her walk slowed as she thought of the long ordeal.

Bret looked at her, his arm moving away from her waist. "Enough war, let's talk about Allison Wescott. I want to know what is happening with you, beginning with why you were afraid this afternoon when you looked up and saw Sir Edgar Simonds at the restaurant."

Surprised, she returned his gaze, and he lowered his voice. "I noticed the change in you at once. What disturbed you?"

Allison's speculative gaze clung to his. Amazing. He always seemed to be able to read her so much better than anyone else. "Is that why you came tonight? Because you thought something was wrong?"

"I knew at the hotel that it was, but I couldn't very well ask you then. I didn't want to worsen matters and give you away in front of Sarah Blaine."

Mention of Sarah made her defensive. "What's Sarah got to do with it?"

"Maybe nothing at all. One thing at a time. Tell me about Sir Edgar. Why are you afraid of him?"

Was she actually afraid of him? "What makes you think I am?"

"Come, Allison, you needn't play games with me. If you don't know by now that you can trust me, you never will. I want to know why you behaved strangely when you saw him. Reason tells me you would normally relax and feel comfortable around a relative—even a distant one such as Sir Edgar. Instead, you looked tense, but you were smart enough to catch yourself before anyone at the table noticed."

"I wasn't smart enough. You noticed."

"I'm naturally the suspicious sort. It's my job to notice things. Besides, you stung my pride. One moment you were looking into my eyes enchantingly, and the next you looked as though I'd turned from the prince back to the frog."

"I didn't know I was so easy to read," she said wearily.

Bret laughed. "Don't look so disappointed. Your secrets are always safe with me—even in the moonlight. I'm dedicated to your safety, my dear, don't you realize that? Now, tell me what you know about the new police inspector and why he frightens you."

She hesitated...what if she were wrong? She would not only appear silly but possibly harm Sir Edgar's reputation. He was, after all, her mother's cousin.

"Maybe I was simply a bit jittery this afternoon—" she began, but Bret headed her off.

"No, none of that. Maybe tonight, but not at luncheon."

"Maybe it wasn't fear, but well...dislike," she confessed.

"You're not noted for disliking someone without giving them a fair chance. So why not confess all and tell me what it is about him that unnerves you?"

"Sir Edgar and I started off wrongly," she finally explained, keeping her voice low. "That has something to do with my feelings, I'm sure. I was ill when I arrived from Abadan. As you know fever can sometimes induce hallucinations."

"Is that what you had? A hallucination?"

"Not exactly, but the first time I saw him he was coming in from my mother's garden and for some reason he reminded me of Rex Blaine. For a moment I thought he wasn't, well, dead." She looked embarrassed. "I'm afraid I fainted."

Bret watched her, his steady, calm demeanor helping to calm her as well. "You can rest assured Blaine is dead. There will be no resurrection of the unjust yet. And when he does answer to the Lord for his sins, he won't be free to walk in anyone's garden smelling flowers. But go on, that can't be all that's bothering you. What else?"

His watchful gaze was disturbing. What was he trying to find out?

"The next time I met Sir Edgar, matters had improved. He was friendly, even likeable. I began to think I'd misjudged him. I wanted to like him since I knew he was to be received as part of the family. He's to move into the Residency with us when the repairs are finished."

"But your father will be home by then. You won't be alone with Sir Edgar. So then what? You met him the second time and he was friendly."

"He openly discussed the work that brought him here."

"Which is?" he asked when she lapsed into thoughtful silence.

She looked at him, seeing his chiseled profile in the starlight, aware that his gaze was alert. There was no reason to conceal anything from a British agent.

"He spoke of Cairo being a hotbed of German and Turkish spies. Normally I would have agreed, especially after working with you and Neal—"

"You didn't tell him that!" he said with sudden sharpness.

"Of course not. And betray your cover? And Neal's? Anyway, he already knew you were an agent."

"I wasn't thinking of myself, Allison, but of you. Don't tell him you met me in Aleppo. He doesn't know about my German alias, Holman."

So...Bret was leery of Edgar, too. "Normally I would have respected the kind of work he's been called to with the war and all, but I detected something about him that made me cautious, and I didn't want to help him."

"Ah, curious. He asked you to help him, then. What did he want?"

Allison only now realized that she'd been so concerned with Sarah she'd forgotten about that list and whose names might be on it. Reluctantly she told him about it and how she had forgotten about it until now.

Bret's eyes narrowed slightly. "I'd like to see it. Do you have it?"

After the successful work she had done in Aleppo in helping to recover the Constantinople papers, she felt foolish and avoided his direct gaze. "I...um...left it in Port Said."

Oddly, Bret didn't appear disappointed, but almost pleased. Perhaps because he didn't want her involved, or maybe he thought the list was more secure there.

"No matter," he said, "I can take you there to get it, or if you give me the house key, I'll go there myself."

"Sarah expects me to stay the weekend. My family is at the house, though. You can get in easily. Still, I'll give you the key since they may leave tomorrow for Helga's." She told him about the box in her dressing table and where to find it. "I've the little key with me. But perhaps you're expecting too much since it couldn't have been much of a secret list, Bret, because he wanted me to offer him any information I had on the individuals involved. He knows so little about me. What if I were a talkative female who would tell all her friends?"

There was a faint smile on his lips. "I think you're right and too smart for your own good. Maybe that's what he wanted you to do."

"You mean tell them?" she asked, surprised. "But why?"

"So he could watch their reactions. Anyone guilty might try to run."

"I hadn't thought of that. Anyway, he'll be disappointed. And I felt anything but clever when he questioned me. I began to wonder if I might not be on his black list, the way he pushed me. It was all I could do to behave as if I didn't see through him."

He frowned. "It was a mistake letting you meet him before your father arrived. I don't know why they allowed it," he said, half to himself. "They should have waited."

She assumed he spoke of her parents. "They hadn't arrived until yesterday. At first, Edgar was to voyage with them from Bombay, but then he and Gilbert came ahead."

Bret looked at her, frowning. "They arrived...?" Then understanding dawned in his expression. "Your parents. Yes, yes, I knew that."

So he hadn't been referring to them. Then who was it that "should have waited"?

"Anyway," she said, "whoever appointed Sir Edgar to the head of the Cairo police may have made a mistake."

"You think so? You're very insightful. I hope no one else picks up on that fact," he commented.

"It doesn't take much insight to see that Sir Edgar has unlimited authority to hound Cairo residents shamelessly," she said a little angrily. "He can, if he chooses, have individuals banned from Egypt until after the war."

"That's true," said Bret noncommittally.

Encouraged in her deduction, she went on: "Anyone considered a German or Turkish sympathizer is open to intimidation by Sir Edgar."

"Yes, if that's what he actually wants."

"What else could he want?" He didn't respond. She looked at him. "What if he's after Helga Kruger?" she whispered.

"Helga is no novice. She can handle him if it comes to that. It's you I'm worried about. I took too much for granted about your return. I should have kept you in Abadan until Sir Marshall arrived."

"What do you mean *you* took too much for granted? You seem to know all about Sir Edgar already, so why are you questioning me as if you know absolutely nothing?"

"I didn't know I was," he said and smiled.

She didn't believe him. "Now you're being evasive, Colonel."

"I asked you to stop calling me that. Do you call Wade 'Chaplain'?" She refused to answer, and he shrugged. "So you think Sir Edgar might use his position to harass Helga and other questionable Cairo merchants?"

"Isn't it obvious? Perhaps he has extortion on his mind."

He shot her a glance. "Why do you think that?"

"Because the war gives him an excuse to harass merchants who don't want their businesses closed down. I wouldn't put it past Sir Edgar to politely demand of them a payment to stay in Cairo. He could become a rich man by the time the war is over."

Bret said dryly, "Maddeningly perceptive, as ever, my dear."

"You didn't want me to be? Then you think Sir Edgar might be into extortion?"

"I don't know," said Bret abruptly as though disturbed by her discernment. "But you know too much for your own good. What else do you have bouncing around in that too-sharp brain of yours, my charming detective?"

"That's all, except—" she hesitated—"At Port Said after I was recovering and able to walk in the garden, I saw him meeting someone," she whispered.

He stopped and released her arm, turning to face her. "What's that?"

She told him about the luxurious calishe that had been waiting for Sir Edgar. "I assume he and whomever he was meeting didn't want to be seen together because the driver, an Egyptian, had parked in the alleyway—" she stopped in midsentence, her own words startling her.

Bret's fingers tightened about her arm. "Yes?"

She couldn't tell him who she'd suddenly realized the driver might be. It would cast Sarah in a suspicious light.

"What is it?" he demanded.

She said instead: "Edgar got into the calishe. I don't know why, but at the time I thought I saw Helga."

"You're not sure who it was?"

"No," she said firmly. It was true. She *wasn't* sure. She only suspected…"Anyway, Sir Edgar wasn't gone long. I came down to the library an hour later to get my mail and there he was. He startled me because he was sitting in the shadows."

"It was then he gave you the list of names?"

"Yes. And then I came to Cairo this morning, so I haven't spoken to him since."

"But you saw him at the hotel. Did he notice you?"

"I don't think so. He seemed…preoccupied."

"Does he know you're staying with Sarah Blaine?"

"No, I don't think so."

"He could find out easily enough." He turned to walk on. "We'd best not stand here."

She fell into step beside him, looking up at him in surprise when he commented, "It may surprise you to know I share your feelings about Sir Edgar."

"I wasn't aware you knew him. When did you two meet?"

"Recently. The Cairo police are involved in doing some work with Intelligence, but I was already aware of his work for the ambassador in Constantinople."

She remembered that Bret had done work in Constantinople before the war.

"I hope you didn't masquerade as the German colonel there?"

He looked thoughtful. "Strange you should bring that up. As a matter of fact, I did work in Constantinople, but I don't think Sir Edgar knows about it, unless—"

"Unless what?" she asked dubiously.

"Unless the ambassador for whom he worked told him about me. I don't think he did. It's against regulations."

Allison drew her wrap about her shoulders as a chill wind touched her throat and face. "But he is the new inspector of police," she said, arguing against her own uncertainties. "Even if he knew about you, it wouldn't matter. I mean," she said incredulously, "why would the authorities arrange for his appointment to the post if they thought they couldn't trust his allegiance to England?"

He turned his head and looked at her, and she caught her breath at the expression in his eyes. "So that's it—!"

But before she could say more, he propelled her forward. "Keep walking, Allison, if you please."

She had a sudden horrid premonition. And Bret wasn't doing anything to alleviate it. In fact, he was all but confirming it. "You don't trust Sir Edgar, either. And I doubt if Cairo Intelligence does. Which must mean that either you or someone higher up arranged for his appointment in the hopes of finding out something about him. But what?"

He considered her question for a moment. "You're right. Intelligence expects to find out information by using Edgar. He's bait for a trap. Your deductions about his interest in extortion may be right. I suppose there's no use asking whether or not you noted his seemingly casual rendezvous on the terrace?"

"Yes, I noticed. I've never seen the man he met before. Who is he?"

"It's not my responsibility to find out, but he's most likely some smuggler dealing in cotton and more glamorous items, like ancient Egyptian artifacts. It's a relief you don't know him. I was hoping you wouldn't be involved this time."

"You mean you came to the house tonight to find out how much I knew about all of this?"

"Yes. After what you've been through at Kut—and before that with Blaine—I didn't want you involved. The sooner you join your family at Helga's the better."

"Is this a new case for you? Like Aleppo?"

He didn't answer, but she sensed a definite change in his mood.

"Bret?"

"No, this isn't my case. I'm on medical leave until the middle of January. I'm leaving in a few days for the Mediterranean beaches."

Allison did her best to hide her dismay. Somehow the thought that he was involved had made her feel more secure. And that, she assured herself, was the only reason she was distressed he wouldn't be staying in Cairo. "I hope you enjoy your vacation," she said. "I, um, suppose David will go with you since he's on your staff?"

He caught her glance and held it until she dragged her eyes away. They walked for a moment in silence.

"Helga has a place she's offered me," he explained. "She'll be busy here in Cairo with holiday guests. I want to be alone—" he held up his hand when she looked at him, as though anticipating her query—"for reasons I'd rather not discuss right now."

"I wasn't planning to pry," she hastened, wondering that she felt such relief he was going alone to a Mediterranean villa. Had she expected Cynthia to accompany him? It was satisfying that Bret preferred his vacation alone, but she wondered what was troubling him. Perhaps nothing except war fatigue. She realized she had paid scant attention to his military risks and weariness, and that he had probably been as seriously wounded as Wade and received less care. Even though he appeared fit and formidable, perhaps he still belonged in the Alexandria hospital. She considered again how little she knew of his private life, his feelings, his dreams, his desires.

You don't need to know those things, an inner voice warned. Even wanting to know them means you're treading dangerous waters.

They came to a square in Ezbekiah Gardens that was decorated with Christmas greenery and ribbons. Allison saw that the first of many seasonal balls was underway.

Because the Egyptian weather was pleasant, the dance was held outdoors where blue-, amber-, and red-colored lanterns were arranged hanging from a circle of trees. Huge woven baskets of sweet-smelling flowers were gathered near a large lily-and-fish pond, where the waters shimmered over an arrangement of white rock. Egyptian waiters in white walked slowly about carrying gleaming trays filled with refreshments. An orchestra seated on an elevated bandstand was playing, and there must have been fifty couples waltzing while an equally large crowd sat at private tables, watching and chatting. Everyone was dressed to the hilt, the women in glittering ball gowns; the men in white dinner jackets.

Bret arranged for a quiet table away from the acacia trees bordering the lawn. It was apparent he didn't want their conversation to be overheard.

The air was laced with fragrance, and Allison took in a deep breath and sighed, glad to escape their ominous conversation for even a few minutes. She was with Bret, it was nearing Christmas, and for a short time all else was forgotten, carried away on the wings of the symphony.

"This is lovely," she said, chin in hand, looking toward the orchestra. "I can almost forget the lurking shadows of war."

"I wish we could do just that." He sat silent for a moment, then turned to smile at her ruefully. "Sadly, I'm afraid I must break our illusions by continuing our discussion. But first—" he gestured for the waiter, who was lingering near the trees—"What would you like? Are you hungry?"

"No, but something cool and sweet to drink sounds pleasant."

After ordering, he regarded her. "And now, tell me what you're doing in Cairo with Rex Blaine's widow? Somehow I suspect it's more than a friendly slumber party for old time's sake."

"Sarah sent a letter to Port Said asking me to come for the weekend. She said it was urgent."

"Urgent?" he repeated firmly, and Allison could detect the restrained concern in his words. "Why didn't you tell me sooner?"

She looked at him defensively. "Whyever should I have done so? There were so many things to discuss that I—"

"Do you still have the letter? I'd like to see it."

"I don't remember keeping it. Why is it important? I mean, Sarah didn't explain, just asked me to come."

"Sir Edgar was in the library when you went down to gather your mail. Did he see the letter?"

Allison hesitated…should she tell him what had just occurred to her? No, she would keep it to herself for now. She felt his intense gaze and hastily replied, "I don't think he saw it. As for Sarah, all I know is that she's afraid, but I haven't a clue as to why. Or of what. She actually went to bed early with a headache."

Bret's eyebrows raised. "She didn't come down for dinner, to be hostess to her guests?"

Allison shook her head, and Bret's frown deepened.

"I don't like the idea of your staying in Blaine's house."

She smiled. "Neither did my father."

"Now I'm doubly convinced it's a mistake. Sarah would never

neglect her duties as a hostess. Something is very wrong there."

Allison masked a shiver, not wanting to let Bret see how his words had affected her. She didn't want him any more concerned than he already seemed to be. Besides, she could take care of herself. Hadn't he seen that after all their...well, *experiences* together?

"You can't possibly think I've anything to fear from Sarah," she said in as calm a voice as possible.

"My poor innocent, the Sarahs of this world often surprise us when they take off their masks. We learned a painful lesson from her affable husband, did we not?"

Allison didn't want to admit that she had briefly entertained the same disturbing thought about her friend. "But the general was different," she protested. "Sarah never had any of his political ambitions."

"Political, no, but socially she longs to move in what is considered all the right circles."

"As do Lady Walsh and her daughter," quipped Allison.

"If that is meant as a blight upon the company I've been keeping, I can only say I agree. Cynthia can be an utter bore. I met her on leave in London several years ago. The effort to cultivate our acquaintance has come only from her."

Allison pushed away the little jolt of pleasure his words brought her and smiled ruefully. "You sound hounded and put upon, Colonel. You'll excuse me if I can't see you as a victim in this drama. Indeed, most men would find it...flattering, shall we say, to have a beautiful woman follow them all the way to Egypt, determined to get a solitaire on her finger."

"Flattering? Hardly. Distracting, definitely. And now—feminine aggression aside, let's discuss the more flighty Sarah, who may appear an innocent, content merely with social teas and chasing after the archaeology club, but could very well be hiding something far more behind that sweet, harmless facade."

Allison frowned. "I'm sure Sarah is exactly who she seems to be. I think I've said before that she was my mother's friend before I ever knew her in the club. It was our shared interest in archaeology that teamed us up. Now that it has, I'm convinced she's genuine."

Bret watched her speculatively. "You wouldn't be keeping anything back from me to protect her, would you, dear Allison? That could prove detrimental to us all in the end."

Thankfully, Allison was saved from answering when the waiter brought their lemonade. She sipped from the frosty glass and thought of Sarah and the odd way she had been behaving. "There's something on her mind, it's obvious."

"Unfortunately you're the only one who can find out what it is—" he studied her, his eyes glinting with unease—"but that fact isn't conducive to my being able to enjoy a peaceful vacation on the Mediterranean."

"Sarah is innocent," she said again firmly.

"I always thought so."

She looked at him. "And now you're not sure?"

He frowned at his glass, tracing the dripping frost. "I'm afraid right now I'm not certain of a whole lot of things."

She watched him, wondering what he meant. He couldn't be talking about Cynthia, could he? He seemed able to take or leave her without a qualm, which was both encouraging...and yet it made Allison a bit uncomfortable, too. After all, he appeared able to do the same with her as well. One moment their relationship quivered on the edge, like a volcano, ready to erupt—the next it seemed as dead and dormant as the grass in winter.

He looked up from his glass, his awareness of her clear in his eyes. A thrill of danger ran through her, making her feel as though she were about to step off a cliff into a bottomless void. Every nerve seemed suddenly sensitized, so that she felt as though her entire being was tingling. Dimly she was aware of her breathing quickening, her pulse leaping erratically.

She could get lost forever in that intense gaze....

Stop this! her mind screamed in desperation. *Stop it now before you do or say something you might regret.* She blinked, then pulled her eyes from his, grappling frantically for something to say, something to break the eloquent silence between them.

"If Sarah isn't innocent, she most likely suspected her husband a long time ago of being involved in espionage."

Silence. She looked up, was caught in his gaze again.

Please, she implored silently. *Please. Let's go back to the safety of talking about anyone—anything—but us....*

"My exact point," Bret said at last, wry humor in his expression. "Once Blaine retired from the service, they were the public picture of a close, happily married couple who did things together, something most women desire, or so I've been told. No marriage problems there, no disagreements over his preoccupation with matters that left her adrift in emotional solitude."

Allison wondered how he knew so much about what a woman wanted in a close relationship. Shared values, shared interests, a shared life. Somehow she had imagined that Bret would be an aloof husband. Now, she wondered if she might not be wrong.

"It was the general's dedication to Sarah," he was saying, "that prompted his accompanying her to Aleppo on the expedition to the Carchemish Digs. The Blaines were close, while others at the site were nursing unhappy relationships. Professor Blackstone, for instance. He was making a fool of himself with a younger woman."

"Yes," she agreed uneasily. "And Rex pretended boredom with archaeology but endured it with good humor."

"All for love of 'dear Sarah,' am I right?"

"Well, yes, but that doesn't prove—"

"No, but if they were so close, it would seem to suggest Sarah would be able see through to the real Rex Blaine much faster than anyone else."

Allison wanted to reject his reasoning, even when deep down in her heart she agreed. It didn't matter how things looked, Sarah simply couldn't have been involved in her husband's betrayal of England.

"That's not always true about knowing," she persisted. "Remember the old axiom about the poor wife always being the last to find out?"

"Granted, yet in those situations I'll wager the marriage already lacked intimacy. You can't convince me two people living together for thirty years can have many secrets, especially Sarah and the old major general."

Allison thought of how they'd always held hands, even in public. She had no reason to reject Bret's conclusion. Sarah might appear a gullible tea hopper, but she wasn't dense.

"All right," and she sighed her resignation. "I see your point. Even so, being close to Rex doesn't prove Sarah was involved with him in his murder and thievery."

"Of course not. If it did, I'd have called her in for questioning long ago. Then again, if she is somehow involved, allowing her to freely come and go could lead to future arrests in the German and Turkish spy ring in Egypt."

She sucked in her breath. "Is that why you agreed not to tell Sarah about Rex? Because you expected to gain more from watching her?"

Bret accepted her indignant appraisal calmly, raising his glass to drink. He watched her over the rim of his glass. "I couldn't cover up Blaine's suicide without explaining the reason to the department. I'd have been arrested for keeping back crucial information. The need to watch Sarah was the only reason they agreed to let her believe it was an accident."

"Then...they've been watching her even when you weren't?"

"Correct. And from the recent turn of events, it looks to have been a wise decision. Which makes me like it even less that you are involved in something our dear Sarah considers urgent."

Allison sat in silence, watching him, feeling a little betrayed that he hadn't told her what he was up to before now.

"So there quite probably was someone out in the shrubs tonight. Such as one of your own men," she accused. "Watching both me and Sarah."

He offered neither confirmation nor denial.

"You're not going to tell me?"

"I can't, because I don't know. I'm not involved in this case. I told you, I'm on leave, recovering from Kut, remember?" His eyes glinted. "I brought your true love home. As a matter of fact, the good chaplain should arrive in Cairo in a few days."

Allison ignored the reference to Wade and watched Bret thoughtfully, tracing the rim of her half empty glass with her finger.

Seeing she wasn't to be sidetracked, he went on. "Even if Sarah didn't know what Rex was up to at the time of his death, she might know something more by now. Something may have happened recently to alert her."

"Alert her to what? You mean the real cause of his death?"

"That. And more. Smuggling, for example."

She waited, fascinated. "Smuggling? Of what?" Then her eyes widened and her mouth opened in surprise. "Artifacts?" she whispered.

"That's my guess." He thought for a moment, then met her gaze. "About Sir Edgar, did he ask any questions about Sarah Blaine?"

"Yes, many."

"Such as?"

"What happened at Aleppo, whether or not she or Rex had an archaeology collection. And he asked about a connection with Jemal."

His eyes glinted. "Jemal," he repeated thoughtfully. "Yes, maybe..."

"Bret, what ever happened to Jemal?"

"He escaped to Constantinople."

She felt a small leap of her heart as she followed the trail he was forging. "And Sir Edgar has recently come from there...you don't suppose—?"

"That they know each other?"

She nodded.

"Yes, I think they do. I wasn't certain until now. I'll need to see what I can find out. In the meantime, try to learn from Sarah if Rex had cause to meet with Jemal here in Cairo before the club went to Aleppo."

Allison's concerns grew. "Sir Edgar asked that same question, if Jemal and the Blaines had met before Aleppo."

"Did he? Interesting."

"You don't think Sarah could be in danger?"

He looked at her sharply. "It's possible. And so might you be. How soon can you all go up to Helga's?"

"In a few days. Do you think Sarah discovered Rex was working as a German agent with Jemal?"

"Yes, but there may be something else that she's stumbled upon as well. If so, it may tie in with Sir Edgar. And Jemal. This urgent matter she wished to see you about could be what she's discovered. Maybe by accident. That she now appears to be afraid could be because of Edgar's recent arrival, or maybe—" he stopped.

Her blood ran cold. "Maybe Jemal's? Could he—be in Cairo?"

He didn't answer her hushed question, but said instead, "She may wish to share her troubles with a trusty friend who believes in forgiveness and grace. Confess regarding stolen items, perhaps. But if that's it, someone else intends to relieve her of her burden first."

She looked at him. "Which proves she wasn't involved in what Rex was doing! If she were, she certainly wouldn't have contacted me about it."

He was frowning at the lantern on the table, musing to himself while he watched a moth helplessly fluttering against the light. "Not necessarily. She may hope to find out how much *you* know. I wish I could be sure."

Allison shivered again. "I suppose you want me to use my friendship with her to benefit Cairo Intelligence," she said, feeling uneasy at the thought.

Bret leaned back lazily and tapped his tanned fingers on the arm of the chair. "That's certainly not what *I* want. I'm not even supposed to be involved in any of this. But it is an unfortunate fact that the department head thinks you're the person in whom Sarah is most likely to confide."

"So your department knew she asked me here?"

"They've been watching her more closely recently. They intercepted the letter she sent you before you received it in Port Said."

"They read my letter?!"

He inclined his head. "And they contacted me and asked me to meet with you tonight. To see what you knew before I departed Cairo on leave."

"They...*they* asked you to contact me." Allison didn't know whether to be relieved or angry. So much for his concern for her moving him to check on her and make sure she was safe. If his people hadn't told him to come tonight, he would be at Cynthia's dinner party. His interest in her was strictly, as he had said at the house, business.

As unpleasant as that thought was, it was utterly eclipsed by the next realization that came to her. She stiffened. "And just as Sarah is likely to confide in me, so they believe I'm likely to confide in you. Hence your orders to take me out tonight. I see."

"No, I don't think you do see," said Bret flatly. "I would have come anyway. I'd already made up my mind to check on you when they got in touch with me. I didn't know about Sarah's letter. I told you, I saw your reaction to Sir Edgar at the hotel and I was con- cerned."

She pushed the disclosure aside, refusing to dwell on it. She'd done it again—allowed herself to believe Bret truly cared about her and wanted to be with her, despite his behavior over the last year. *You're a fool,* she told herself. *A silly fool.* The thought only worsened the dull ache in her heart. She drew a deep breath, determined not to let him see her disappointment.

"Well, you've fulfilled your duty well, Colonel. And I think it's safe to say that I need fear no danger from Sarah, don't you?"

"It's not Sarah I'm necessarily thinking about, but being in the Blaine house. Nosing about the general's private world could pose a risk," he said quietly. "For you, as well as for Sarah."

"Yet that's precisely what *they* want me to do, isn't it?"

He frowned and set his empty glass down firmly. "I suppose it is." He stood. "Come along, Allison. We've spent too much time talking." His smile was more weary than mocking. "If someone is watching us, they've most likely started to grow suspicious. We want everyone to think we're agonizing over whether or not you'll choose me over Wade Findlay, remember?" He held out his hand. "Let's dance."

She hesitated, then resigned herself to doing as he asked. With as casual an air as she could manage, she placed her hand in his and let him draw her out to the dance floor.

Don't think about how this feels, she told herself as his arms encircled her. *It's all for appearances. Nothing more.*

The music complemented the canopy of stars, the moonlight, and the blossoms. If only the mood between them could be so full of magic and delight. They danced the waltzes on the edge of the lawn farther away from the crowd, and Allison didn't try to analyze the silence that held them—or the cautious, too-casual way in which he held her away from him.

He was watching her moodily, his eyes dark with some veiled emotion. When he spoke, his voice was deep and dour. "If I were wise, I'd have taken you home by now. And then I'd leave Cairo in the morning."

"I hope you enjoy your time in the Mediterranean," she said casually, feeling anything but that.

His mouth turned in a wry smile. "I doubt I will. You see, I didn't tell you why they're allowing me the time, or why I was accepting Helga's offer of a few weeks at her hideaway."

Her emotions tensed. What was he getting at? Their brief interlude together was taking a definite downward turn, and she didn't care for it at all. She wished she could simply get lost in the music and lanterns and the starry sky. But the look on his face made that impossible.

"You're in need of rest," she said. "What is there to explain? Every soldier must have a time of recuperation before the next battle. You deserve it."

"Only officers are allowed recuperation. The poor Tommy in the trench will be there until he's either blown to pieces or taken prisoner—" he broke off, then shook his head. "I'm sorry, we said we weren't going to talk about the war anymore, didn't we?"

"I don't suppose it will ever be possible not to talk about it," she said gravely. Her eyes searched his. "There is something more isn't

287

there, about you, I mean? It's not just a medical recuperation then?"

"No. I'm being transferred from Egypt to the BEF serving in France."

She nearly missed a step but caught herself from the blunder of giving away her emotions in time. The British Expedition Force was on the western front lines—and they were taking heavy casualties.

He was going away. Perhaps forever.

"But why? You're needed in Cairo," she managed.

Bret's face was unreadable now. "I requested it."

Requested it? She couldn't believe any man would request to be sent to the front lines of France!

Confused, she stared at him, and he said flatly: "I won't be fighting in the trenches, if that's what you think. I'll be doing undercover work. Dangerous, no question about it, but I'll be promoted again once the work is done."

"How many promotions do you need? What good will they do you if—if—" She bit her lip and looked away.

He did not answer. She chanced a glance at his face and saw that he was staring past her, a half scowling look on his face. Had he even heard what she said?

They danced in silence, but Allison found little joy in the action. The bright red-and-blue Christmas lanterns had lost their colorful glow; the music had lost its song.

"I'm sorry," she said a minute later. "I shouldn't have said that. You don't owe me any explanation, Colonel." The music came to an end, and she made to move away from him, but he didn't release her. "I think that's the last waltz," she said, meeting his gaze steadily. "Shall we go? It's getting late."

He looked down at her, frowning a little, but remaining silent. She wanted to scream at him, to make him tell her she misunderstood, that he had no desire to leave Cairo...to leave her.

But he can't say that, she thought, a sickening empty feeling in her stomach, *because it's not true. He wants to leave. He wants distance between us.*

Don't think about it now, she warned herself. If you do you may make a fool of yourself. You might cry or blurt out how you feel about him and drive him even further away....

But how much further away could he go? What had he said at the house about her not taking him away from Cynthia? He had said it in a light vein, nevertheless, it revealed a little of what he actually felt: "You couldn't take me away from Cynthia unless I wanted you to."

Trying to hold on to him when he wanted to back away would, perhaps, be the worst mistake she could make. It was clear that he wanted no bonds or ties, not with any woman.

At long last he let go of her, watching her with the same intense moodiness that had haunted his features all evening. "I'll get my wrap," she said, surprised her voice remained steady and calm—and that her legs supported her without giving way as she walked away from him.

By the time they arrived back at the house, the moon had set, leaving the yard in total darkness. One light burned on the porch, casting dancing shadows as their feet crunched over the gravel. She dug in her handbag, then removed the small key to her treasure box in Port Said.

"The list I mentioned earlier should be where I told you at our house in Port Said. Here's the key to the box. How you manage to retrieve it from my bedroom is another matter."

"I'll find a way. Now, do you have the key to this door, or do we need to awaken Sarah or Marra?"

289

"No, I have a key." She pulled it from her purse and handed it to him.

He took it and opened the door, then reached out to take her arm as she moved to pass him and go inside. She looked up at him and found herself caught by the intensity of his expression.

"Whatever you do, don't let on that you know anything about Blaine's ties with Germany, or his involvement in smuggling. They're equally dangerous at present."

"All right," she whispered.

"There are a few matters I need to take care of before I leave Cairo." He hesitated. "Maybe I'll come back in a few days to see if you've learned anything from Sarah. If you need help before then, call David. He'll be at the department."

She nodded, weary and depressed. She wouldn't allow herself to think of his departure.

"Is there a lock on your bedroom door?"

Her eyes widened and she frowned. "If you're trying to give me a case of nerves," she breathed, "you're succeeding."

"Good. You'll be more careful that way. You didn't answer my question."

"Yes, there's a lock, but—" she stopped, thinking of the bathroom window.

He cocked his head. "But what?"

"The bathroom window doesn't have one. The wood is rotting…but I'm two stories up and no one could get in even if they wanted to."

He stepped back and looked up to the second floor. "If I wanted to get in badly enough, I could; by way of the roof. Get someone out here first thing in the morning to fix the lock."

"It seems rather rude of me to ask Sarah to fix the window latch when I'm only a guest."

290

"Fine, then you needn't ask her. I'll send someone myself. Right now, I don't care what Sarah thinks. I want it fixed."

"Anything you say, *Colonel,*" she said, irritated by his overbearing tone. "I wouldn't want you to leave for France with any concerns on your mind."

His eyes narrowed, then dropped briefly to her lips. "I want to hear the door lock behind you. Is there an inside bolt?"

"Yes."

"I'll wait until the light's on in your bedroom before I leave."

"How do you know which one is mine?"

"There was only one light on when I came. You said you were up reading, so it must have been yours. And Allison, be careful, will you?"

She nodded, then moved to close the door and bolt it, feeling empty and drained. She wanted nothing more than to sink into the nearest chair or couch and not move, but she knew he was waiting outside to see her light come on, so she went to lower the lights in the drawing room, then went quietly up the stairs, pausing on the landing between her room and Sarah's. All was quiet.

Inside her room she flipped on the light, then locked the door, She moved to the window; Bret stood below. She could just barely make out his silhouette in the starlight. She lifted a hand to wave good night before she drew the blind closed.

She stood there, and it was several minutes before she heard the motorcar drive away. She assumed he had made a quick check around the yard and the garden before leaving. With a sigh, she moved to sit on her bed, but she knew sleep would not come soon. Too many troubling thoughts circled in her mind.

She'd been so relieved earlier when she'd thought Bret would be here to watch over things. But now...now she was on a road that could lead her to more espionage, even murder, just as she'd found in Aleppo. But this time there would be one terrible difference. This time, Bret wouldn't be here.

CHAPTER

EIGHTEEN

➤❡❦❖❦❡❤

There is one who makes himself rich, yet has nothing.

PROVERBS 13:7

OVER BREAKFAST THE NEXT MORNING, Sarah insisted she felt better, though her taut face did little to convince Allison.

"It must have been the sleeping pill you gave me. I slept like a brick," said Sarah with an attempt at cheerfulness.

"Well, I'm glad *someone* did," murmured Marra, glancing meaningfully toward Allison.

Allison smiled and took a bite of scrambled egg. She hadn't mentioned being out late with Bret, but Marra's remark told her she must have been awakened by Bret's motorcar last night in the driveway.

Sarah was preoccupied and paid no attention. "I need to visit the old shops today. The archaeology club will hold its auction on Thursday, and I need to bring an item to sell. What about it, you two? You haven't seen Old Cairo yet, have you, Marra? The shops should be interesting. They usually receive new shipments this time of the month. I'd like to get there early and browse before the collectors come in."

"Sounds exotic and fun," replied Marra. "We'll need to bring umbrellas though, it's beginning to rain."

"It's just a light morning drizzle. Nothing at all to be considered," Sarah said. She turned to Neith and told her to have Anwar make arrangements to drive them into Old Cairo for some sight-seeing.

293

Allison and Marra were ready to go before Sarah, and so they went to sit together in the drawing room to wait. Marra cast Allison a curious glance.

"May I ask you something?" she inquired, and Allison noticed her cheeks had grown a bit red.

"Of course," she replied, hoping it wasn't about last night.

"Do you—" Marra glanced around quickly—"Do you hear…well, *sounds* at night?"

Allison stared at her friend in surprise, then nodded. "Yes, as a matter of fact, I do! Creaking and squeaks—"

"As though someone's walking about?" Marra finished, and Allison nodded again. Relief washed over Marra's face.

"Whew! I thought perhaps it was just me imagining things," she said with a grin.

"Well, I'm not sure but that I wouldn't rather that were the case. Because if we're both hearing it, then it must be real."

Marra nodded slowly. "So it must." She met Allison's gaze. "Do you think Sarah is walking about at night?"

"No…the sounds haven't come from that direction. It's more like someone is, as you said, walking about in the hallways, or even in my bathroom."

"Your bathroom?" Marra said aghast. "But how…?"

Allison shook her head. "I haven't any idea. Besides, every time I check, there's no one there."

Marra was silent for a moment, then she shrugged. "So we've a haunt, then."

"A what?"

She grinned. "A haunt. Oh, not a real one, of course," she said soothingly at Allison's expression. "I've not gone soft in the head and started to believe in ghosts. That's simply what Em and I used to call anything that went bump in the night."

Allison found herself smiling. "Yes, that sounds like Emily. A haunt, eh?"

"The Haunt of Blaine House. Has kind of a ring to it, don't you think?"

Before Allison could answer, Sarah came into the room. "Oh, good. You're all ready. Come along, then, let's see what treasures we can find today."

The dim, alleyed streets were thronging with men wearing *galabiyas,* and Moslem women shrouded with black gowns and veils. The motorcar inched along and was soon in the midst of the turbulence of noise and confusion of the Khan el-Khalili, the fourteenth-century bazaar in the center of the district. The area bustled with wealthy merchants and beggars; camels, goats, and donkeys; shops offering fancy silk and plain cotton; open-air coffeehouses and bawling street vendors selling water from a bronze communal cup. In such surroundings, it was hard to believe that, beyond Cairo, the vast golden desert stretched toward an endless horizon now engaged in troop movements and war.

Allison remembered her last visit to Old Cairo—she'd come to collect Aunt Lydia's medical supplies, which had been shipped by mistake to a shop owned by Helga Kruger. At least, they'd been told it was a mistake. It hadn't taken long to discover they had been "hijacked" by Rex Blaine, who thought a book he wanted had been hidden in one of the crates by Cousin Leah.

Here's hoping this visit is less eventful than the last, Allison thought.

As they drove past the shop she'd visited, she looked across the narrow street and saw the familiar bronze pots and pans, bolts of cloth, and Turkish rugs. Vases, bowls, lamps, and dinnerware of every size, shape, and color, from pomegranate purple to Nile blue, were all painted with birds. What had Bret once told her? That the shopkeeper dealt in opium as well? He never had explained Helga Kruger's reason for keeping a shop in Old Cairo, and what it might have to do with her work for British Intelligence.

"Anwar! Pull over by Galli's," Sarah ordered. She looked at Allison. "I'd nearly forgotten. I promised Professor Blackstone I'd speak with the shopkeeper about an item he's looking for. You remember Blackstone, don't you? He was at the huts the night Major Reuter was—well, let's not get into that. Do you want to wait here or come along inside and look about?"

Allison had no wish to step back inside that dim, secretive shop—she could still smell the Eastern incense that filled the air and see the goods crowding the floor and walls...but Marra was already getting out of the motorcar.

"Come on, Allison, it looks interesting, and I want to buy a silk scarf."

Oh, it's interesting all right, thought Allison. *You've no idea how interesting....* She didn't want to budge, but since Sarah was watching her she smiled and stepped out to join them. "I'll come, but I can't spend a shilling. I'm broke."

"As if a Wescott would ever be broke," said Marra. "The consul general's daughter?"

Allison expected Sarah to make light of her own penury as the widow of a retired general from the Civil in India, but she remained in her preoccupied mood. Allison followed her friend's gaze toward the mysterious shop. An Egyptian shopkeeper in white had apparently heard the motorcar stop, and now appeared in the open doorway. The man bowed and smiled, and ceremoniously waved them inside, his eyes filled with an eagerness—he probably hoped for some good sales.

Allison reluctantly followed Sarah and Marra inside.

Another Egyptian man emerged from behind a dusty, heavily embroidered curtain and greeted them enthusiastically.

The wood shutters were pulled closed, and a heavy cloth draped the doorway, so that no light or fresh air could enter except what came through some high, narrow windows. Suddenly Allison felt a chill, as though someone were watching her—someone unfriendly. She looked up from the shadows of crates and bolts of cloth to the high windows. Something moved away from the windows—it looked like a silhouette. But the whole thing had happened so quickly she wondered if she had imagined it. Perhaps it had been the shadow of flying pigeons...but even as she tried to convince herself of this, she knew it wasn't true. The shadow had been too large for a bird. Still, she argued, the window was too high for anyone to be standing outside looking into the shop.

"Mrs. Blaine, I received your message yesterday," said the merchant. "I do not have the piece you speak of, but fortunately my son-in-law who runs a shop in Luxor has many friends throughout other shops in Egypt. So far, there is no good news, but who knows? Perhaps Allah will bring good fortune in a few days? If so, I will send a message at once to your home."

Allison listened with half an ear, her mind remaining on the silhouette she was certain she had seen watching through the window.

"That would be good of you, Mr. Galli. Do you think you could send word by December eighteenth? That's the night the club will be meeting at the Cairo Museum."

"I shall do my best. And now? You wish to look at our new shipments? They arrived yesterday. Some items are still in crates, but most are on display. This way, please," and he bowed, gesturing her past him.

He glanced at Allison, saying, "If you wish answers to questions, ring chime, please." Then he went toward the back of the shop where Sarah had already disappeared. Marra was on the other side of the room, her back toward Allison, sorting through the display of silk scarves from India.

Allison walked to the front window and looked out to the street. The rain had ceased, and the driver was leaning against the motorcar, smoking. As she looked at Anwar, she remembered the idea she hadn't wanted to tell Bret last night. Could she be right? Was Anwar the young Egyptian driver she had seen in Port Said, the one who had waited for Sir Edgar? If so, then wasn't it logical to think the veiled woman inside the calishe was Sarah?

That was quite impossible, thought Allison, uneasily. If Sarah had written asking her to come and stay with her, she would have no reason to keep the fact that she was in Port Said a secret, would she? Allison wasn't sure, but if it had been Sarah, then she hadn't told Allison all the truth, which would lend weight to some of the things Bret had warned her about.

Allison turned away from the window, suddenly aware that the small cluttered shop had grown oppressively quiet. She glanced around her, feeling—what? Frightened? Uneasy? Even threatened? Yes, all of those things. She could give no reason for her feelings, she only knew she wanted to find Marra and go wait in the motorcar.

Casually, so as to avoid bringing attention to herself, she turned away from the window, and as she did, the hem of the drape that divided the storefront from the back room where boxes were stored, moved as if by a draft. She had the unnerving sensation that someone stood watching her. Who was it? Mr. Galli? His assistant? Sarah? Someone else?

Allison stood motionless, holding her breath, fighting the terror that wanted to overtake her. She drew a deep, steadying breath and walked over to one of the display shelves, pretending interest in the vases, aware that her hand shook as she fingered one. She did not hear footsteps, so Sarah's voice startled her from behind: "It's so close in here. The rain makes everything humid. I always feel as if my breathing wants to choke up."

Allison looked into Sarah's pale face and anxious eyes.

"What's wrong, Allison?" Sarah asked, looking alarmed. "You're not getting ill?"

"No—I'm fine. Did you find anything for the auction?"

Sarah appeared to relax. "No, I'm disappointed with what's available this time. I would have expected more items of archaeological quality, wouldn't you?"

"Yes, I suppose you're right. I hadn't thought of it." She fingered the vase again, studying it absently, then covered a start. This vase! Where had she seen it before? and when?

Sarah was looking around the shop. "Now and then they have something wonderful—oh, hullo, what's this?" Her gaze came to rest on the vase in Allison's hands. She reached over and claimed the small gold-leaf vase. "This is quite perfect, dear. Would you mind terribly? You don't really want it do you?"

"No, go ahead, I didn't want to buy it. Anyway, there are several others here."

Sarah clasped the small vase and walked toward the counter. "Mr. Galli? I've changed my mind. I've found what I want after all for the auction. How much? Not dreadfully expensive is it?"

Allison looked up to catch a startled expression on his face, but it quickly turned bland. "I am sorry, Mrs. Blaine, but this item is already claimed. I do not know how it got placed on the shelf. Perhaps I can show you another?"

Allison walked up beside Sarah, who was removing her pocketbook from inside her larger handbag when she gave a gasp. A little crash sounded, and Sarah's hands flew to her mouth as she stared at the floor.

Allison was staring, too. Sarah had dropped the vase, and it lay shattered in pieces like a jigsaw puzzle.

Mr. Galli came rushing from behind the counter. Marra, too, came up holding a simple blue silk scarf, embroidered with gold thread.

"I'm dreadfully sorry! Oh, how positively clumsy of me!" Sarah stepped back, looking embarrassed as the shopkeeper quickly stooped to gather the broken pieces. "I don't know how it happened," she continued. "One moment I was holding it—the next it slipped from my fingers. I'll pay, of course! Not that it will make up for the loss of the vase! Oh, I feel dreadful."

"No need to apologize, Mrs. Blaine," came his stilted voice. "Accidents happen—" He jerked his hand back, and Allison saw that he'd cut himself.

"Do let me help," she said quickly, stooping beside him.

"No! Miss Wescott!" His dark eyes flashed, then he bowed his head. "I mean—thank you, but it is nothing. I will take care of it," and he reached into his pocket and removed a handkerchief, which he wrapped around his finger.

Allison was turning away when her eye fell on the broken pieces. Something was glittering in the fragments....Allison's eyes widened in amazement. It was a sacred scarab beetle of ancient Egypt, such as one might see in a burial tomb of a pharaoh. Even in the drab overhead light it sparkled brightly before the shopkeeper's hand neatly covered it. He began to talk rapidly to Sarah, clearly hoping Allison hadn't noticed.

"I insist on paying," said Sarah.

"No, no, Mrs. Blaine, you are friend of this shop. It is not necessary."

Allison's eyes locked briefly with his as they stood up together, and in that second, she felt a chill run along her spine. Did he know

300

she had seen the scarab? He turned away from her to face Sarah, forcing a smile.

"If you insist on paying, I will send the bill to your house, Mrs. Blaine."

Marra approached him then, the scarf in hand. "Thank goodness scarves don't break. I think it's safe to handle this. How much?"

The shopkeeper did his best to appear patient and interested in selling the small, inexpensive item. With a nod of his head he gestured for Marra to go toward the counter. Allison watched him place the broken pieces of the vase inside a drawer while Marra was digging for change from her handbag.

When they were in the motorcar and driving away, Sarah said breathlessly: "What a dreadful thing to happen. I was so embarrassed."

Allison noticed Sarah's hands were trembling.

"How much will it cost you?" grimaced Marra.

Sarah shook her head. "I'll ask Helga. She owns the shop. Drat! Now I've nothing to bring for the club auction!"

Allison considered mentioning the scarab, then thought better of it. Marra hadn't been close enough to see it, but had Sarah? Had she even dropped the vase on purpose?

The shop was not mentioned again, and the remainder of the morning passed pleasantly enough. They arrived back at the house a little before one o'clock, and Neith, her dark eyes animated, told Sarah she had company waiting.

It was Baroness Helga Kruger.

Helga was the widow of a rich German financier from Berlin. Baron Kruger had made his money in military contracts awarded him by Kaiser Wilhelm's government. It was said he had been killed in a train accident on the Berlin-Baghdad Railway crossing through the mountainous territory of Bulgaria, and that Helga had collected a massive fortune from his business.

The sophisticated German widow was in her late forties, and there was talk that she was keeping social company with the new German industrialist who had arrived before the war broke out in 1914. The man, so it was rumored, had helped her husband plan the railway which had taken his life. Allison wondered if Sir Edgar Simonds knew of the recently arrived industrialist who was living and doing private business in Egypt. For that matter, did Bret?

Helga seemed to pay little heed to the whispers of a secret romance and publicly remained the devoted secretary of the Cairo Archaeological Club, maintaining her reputation for holding lavish dinner parties in her homes, which were located both in Cairo and Alexandria, for foreign dignitaries and their wives.

Due to interests in both archaeology and Palestine, Helga had first gone to Constantinople after her husband's death. There she entered the social scene, but then moved to Cairo where she became known as the most socially powerful of Europeans. She had a grand house on the outskirts of Cairo; before the war, she had been deeply involved in buying Hittite sculptures and inscriptions for the museum.

Allison recalled how Cousin Neal had said she competed aggressively with the chief Arabian representative of the British Museum for important pieces. Even though Helga was an elegant socialite and generally dressed the part to the nines, Allison had seen her driving about the Arabian desert before the war in expedition trousers and boots and carrying a Luger.

Now, after Aleppo and the death of two British agents, Allison knew why the baroness had carried the pistol back then. She suspected she still did, even though she now wore Paris fashions and elaborate jewels. And yet, as Allison looked at the baroness, she was surprised to see the woman's normally serene face looking quite pale and tense. She wore a smile, but it didn't quite reach her eyes.

Helga came through the drawing-room archway, extending her hand to a surprised Sarah. "Oh, you've returned! This is most fortunate. I was afraid I'd need to leave an invitation with your maid. I came over to ask if you'd join Allison and her family as my house guest this holiday season. I've friends and dignitaries arriving next week to stay until after the new year. Now, don't refuse, Sarah dear, because I'm sure Allison and Eleanor will also both insist."

Sarah recovered from her surprise. "Why, thank you. I'd love to come."

"Good. Then I'll have a driver come by for the three of you on Wednesday. And do bring evening clothes. We'll be entertaining each night. Oh—something else—the club meeting and auction is delayed. It's most difficult to get everyone together so near the holidays. We may need to wait until January. Then again, perhaps I could have the meeting at my house. I'll invite Professor Blackstone and the others." She looked at Allison. "Eleanor sent a message asking I relay the news that she and Sir Marshall will be in Port Said a day longer. They're waiting for your cousin Neal to arrive in Alexandria. Unfortunately the ship is delayed, but they said not to worry."

Her invitation delivered and accepted, Helga gave them another smile and left. Sarah stood, watching her drive away, and laughed. "Imagine! I'm to be a houseguest for three weeks in the baroness's mansion! Whatever could have prompted her to invite me?"

Allison suspected it was the successful work of her mother. "Well, whatever her reasons, you've a reprieve from collecting a new piece for the auction."

"Oh, you're right! More's the good luck. I was so surprised to receive the invitation that the horrid incident at the shop slipped my mind."

Allison smiled and nodded, wondering as she did so why she was so certain Sarah was lying, that she hadn't forgotten anything at all.

NINETEEN

➤·❮◆❯·◉·❮◆❯·❮

Though I walk in the midst of trouble...
PSALM 138:7

"DID I TELL YOU THAT DAVID IS COMING BY TONIGHT to take me to the theater?" asked Marra, helping herself to the luncheon salad. "It seems he's had these tickets for so long they're about to mold. If he doesn't use them, they'll expire. So he's asked me. Want to come along, Allison? We can buy another ticket at the door."

Allison saw her opportunity to be alone with Sarah. "Thanks just the same, but I think I'll make an early night of it. I didn't sleep all that well last night."

Sarah said absently: "Then let's have hot soup with a cold supper, and let Neith have the afternoon and evening off. You can leave some cold cuts for us to fix for sandwiches, Neith," she told the woman who was going around the table pouring tea.

Neith looked surprised and pleased and returned a short time later with an unexpected dessert.

After the meal, Allison went to her room to relax and read for a while. She settled herself in a chair and was soon lost in her book. Vaguely she became aware of a sound coming from behind her...a creaking, as though someone were walking up to her chair with a soft tread, not wanting to be heard. She froze, every nerve alert, her pulse starting to race.

Drawing a calming breath and winging a prayer for protection toward heaven, she spun around. No one was there.

Frustrated, she stood and went to look around the room. Again, no one. She was alone. Then the creak came again, this time from behind her closed bathroom door.

"Stop it!" she said out loud. "Go find someone else to haunt!" When her outburst was met by silence, she felt as foolish as a child who is startled by the tree branches brushing the window in a storm.

Jutting her chin out in determination, she marched to the bathroom door and threw it open. She turned on the light, finding exactly what she'd expected: nothing. With a huff she went back to throw herself in her chair.

"Father," she prayed, "calm my heart. I know there are no such things as ghosts—" she glanced around the room—"but if ever a house were haunted, it's this one! So, please, I'd appreciate it if you'd make…" she paused, then remembered Marra's name for the noises. "If you'd make the haunt, *whatever* it is, go away."

Silence met her, and she reached to pick up her book again, determined to focus on the story rather than give another minute of her attention to the odd, troubling sounds.

David arrived a short time after four o'clock to pick up Marra. Neith had left before two-thirty, so when she heard the door close behind David and Marra as they departed, Allison knew she and Sarah were on their own.

When the clock in the drawing room below struck five, Allison laid aside the book she had been reading and stood from the chair, stretching. She wasn't hungry, but she supposed she had better go down and help Sarah with their supper. The house was quiet. She opened the door and glanced across the landing toward Sarah's room. The door was shut, but she heard a floorboard squeak downstairs in the dining room and supposed Sarah was arranging the table for their light supper.

Tonight, thought Allison, she would confront Sarah over the reason she had asked her to visit. She went to change into a comfortable dress to go downstairs. With them on their own, she thought, running a brush through her wavy hair, there was no reason why Sarah should need to be cautious.

She left her room, glancing at Sarah's room as she did so. The door was not quite shut and Allison noticed that the bedroom light had been left on. Since Sarah was most likely in the kitchen, Allison walked across the landing and pushed open the door to turn the light off, but stopped, startled. Sarah was sitting in front of her vanity table, brush in hand. Hearing Allison behind her, she whirled about, then her hand holding the hairbrush dropped to her lap in relief.

"Skies above! You frightened me!"

Sarah's jumpy mood only added to Allison's nervousness. "Oh dear, I'm dreadfully sorry to barge in like this. I thought you were in the kitchen. I saw your light on and meant to turn it off."

"Come in, dear. Close the door and—and lock it, will you?"

"Lock it?" Allison repeated, about to say there was no need since they were alone. But she held her tongue and simply did as she was asked, sliding the bolt into place—noticing as she did so that her fingers shook.

Sarah turned back to the mirror. "I want to talk to you anyway and I'd rather do it here with the door locked and my drapes drawn. I've always disliked the downstairs drawing-room windows, with those sheer curtains that anyone can see through. But Rex always liked them."

Allison was on the brink of telling her she was free to change them now but decided against it. Sarah was so sensitive to being reminded of the general's absence from her life.

"Has Marra left yet?"

"Yes, over an hour ago," Allison replied, walking up behind her friend. She glanced at Sarah's reflection and almost started: Sarah's eyes were wide and a look of fright showed in her face.

"Sarah, what is it? You asked me here because you said you had something urgent to tell me, but it seems you've been avoiding it since I arrived. It's time to come clean. I want to know what this is all about. You look frightened."

Sarah's hand touched her throat. "Because I *am* frightened!"

"Of what?"

"Of being murdered."

Allison sank into the rattan chair. The confession was completely unexpected. She had thought Sarah would tell her she suspected Rex of wrongdoing and was worried about what it meant for her...but murder?

Allison's knees trembled and she clasped her hands about them. "If I didn't know you better, I'd think you were making an odious jest."

"I quite understand why you'd think so, but do I look as though I'm joking? I tell you I know I'm in danger."

"How do you know? And why? Do you have any reason why anyone would wish to—to harm you?"

"Yes."

Allison noticed a curious inflection in Sarah's voice. She studied her friend's face and saw her frightened expression change. It became blank, and her brown eyes grew wary. She did not reply at first, only picked up her brush from the vanity table and ran it briskly through her hair.

The silence closed them in so profoundly that Allison sat listening tensely to every creaking sound in the walls and ceiling. She understood Sarah's recent dislike of the house. It was so empty and full of the memory of the general—particularly when one was alone in the house. She frowned. *Alone in the house....* She came alert remembering how she had been so sure Sarah was downstairs in the dining room setting the table. Footsteps. Wasn't that what had made the floorboards squeak?

She drew rein on her imagination, unwilling to allow her feelings to run rampant. She had to remain calm. Allison did not move, except for her fingers tightening around her knees. Were they being watched? And was Bret right? Did Sarah know much more than Allison had ever given her credit for?

The thought that Sarah Blaine might not be all Allison had always thought her to be did more to bring unreasoning terror to her heart than any unknown enemy who might be watching from the shadows. When someone seemingly incapable of wrong was unmasked as evil, terror reached its climax.

"Allison?"

She turned her head quickly to look at Sarah, who watched her with wide eyes.

"What is it?" whispered Sarah.

I'm being absurd, she thought sternly. "Nothing." She smiled reassuringly. "Now, tell me everything, or at the next squeak in the floorboard I shall jump to my feet and scream madly!"

"Maybe I am being a bit overly dramatic, but I'm frightened just the same. I've missed Rex frightfully. I trusted him implicitly, but I'm beginning to think he—he may have been involved in something dangerous."

Allison sat there, watching her. "Why do you think so?"

"At first I thought my edginess was because of his death and my being alone and missing him so, but I was wrong. I'm being watched."

"You're sure about all this? You've not imagined it? You did say you missed Rex tremendously, and we know grief and loss can do all sorts of things to our tattered emotions and minds."

"Even if I imagined someone or some thing—" she glanced about—"watching me, I couldn't be accused of imagining it when someone broke into the house." She stood up from the chair, meeting Allison's surprised eyes. "Yes. It happened while I was away in Alexandria, visiting a friend. I was gone for two weeks. When I came back all the rooms had been searched, especially Rex's old office."

Allison caught her breath. "You're certain someone searched the rooms?"

"Quite certain." Her tone was definite. "There were things out of place, things that I haven't used for months, even before Rex's death in Aleppo. For example, my old chinaware set that we got when first married in India. I had it put away in the high kitchen shelves. I haven't used the set for years. Yet, when I came home from Alexandria, it had been taken down and then replaced rather haphazardly."

"Maybe it was Neith? Perhaps she was simply in a hurry and you weren't home so she—"

"No, no, Allison, I'm not all that dumb, now am I?"

"No, of course not." She sighed. "I was hoping—"

"I tell you it's so. I thought you of all people would believe me. That's why I asked you to come. I know the house was searched because it—it happened again," said Sarah with a lowered voice.

This time Allison was out of her chair, whispering urgently: "Why didn't you tell me all of this at once? When did it happen?"

"Two days before I sent you the letter. I had gone out, then remembered I'd forgotten a letter I wanted to mail to Alexandria. When I came back home, perhaps fifteen minutes later, I unexpectedly caught whoever it was. That is, I knew someone was here—inside Rex's office." She looked toward the locked adjoining door.

310

"How do you know someone was in there? Did you see him?" pressed Allison.

"No. I heard someone moving about. Desk drawers opening and shutting hurriedly. I was too frightened to confront the intruder. So I bolted the door from the inside and also the hall door. I acted like a perfect coward. I hid in the closet until I was sure whoever it was had gone. I heard Anwar pull up in the driveway so I knew if anyone was still here they'd leave at once. When I got the nerve to go into Rex's office—" she stopped and moistened her lips—"the window was open. The curtain had a dirty mark on it, as though whoever it was had stepped on it in his haste to get in or out. And the entire room was in disarray."

Allison was staring at that office door now, wondering. "Was anything taken?" she asked softly.

"From his desk? No—that is, I don't know. I—I didn't look to see. I wouldn't really know anyway. I never went in there, even when Rex was alive. He had a fit whenever I'd clean and he always insisted I keep the maid out."

"Neith?"

"Yes. She never went in there. Nor in our bedroom. I cleaned it myself. After Rex's death at Aleppo, I just locked the office up." She threw up a hand in despair. "I couldn't bear going in there and seeing his things. You know how it is." She sank down on the edge of the bed. "Anyway, there was nothing of value stored there, I'm quite positive of that. Rex never kept money or valuables in the house, so whoever it was couldn't have found much."

"You mean you haven't looked to see if anything was taken?" said Allison.

Sarah fidgeted. "No. I told you dear, I can't bear going through his things yet. I'll start to cry all over again."

Allison stood and looked down at her incredulously. "You didn't call the police to report the intruder?"

"I didn't want to make a fuss," she said worriedly. "After Rex's death they asked so many dreadful questions. I didn't want them all back here again, tramping through my house and going through his office. They're so heartless and cold. I just couldn't bear it, especially at Christmas." Her eyes brightened. "I'll be so relieved to be out of here and to go to Helga Kruger's." She shook her head. "At any rate, I just couldn't stand for gossip to ruin things. You do understand, Allison?"

No, she didn't understand. What did Sarah fear from the police asking more questions and looking about the house? Weren't the police better to have about than the intruder? Then she remembered: Sir Edgar Simonds. Recalling Bret's warnings about him, she thought perhaps Sarah had more to fear from the big man than even she knew.

What could an intruder have been after? Could there be something else of importance besides the Constantinople papers that even Bret didn't know about? Perhaps the major general's German superior had arranged for another enemy agent to locate whatever they were seeking?

If that were so, then Sarah could be in danger, just as she had said, but not because either German or British agents wanted her eliminated. She might have accidentally stumbled upon a secret, as Bret had said at Ezbekiah Gardens. Perhaps that secret had nothing to do with espionage at all. Bret had seemed to imply it might be something different.

The image of that afternoon in the shop in Old Cairo drifted into her mind....

"I agree about one thing, Sarah, the sooner we move to Helga's, the better off we'll both be. If someone is searching for something, it must be important. And if they've come back, then they haven't found it yet. And—" she stopped, but Sarah had already figured it out on her own.

"And they're likely to try again. Whatever they expect to find could be anywhere."

"But what could it be? Have you *any* idea?"

Sarah turned away, facing the mirror. "No, how could I? Why should I? If Rex was involved with serving England on some secretive basis, he wouldn't have told me. And he didn't. I don't know anything."

"No, of course you don't," hastened Allison. "Maybe it has nothing to do with the government."

Sarah's gaze shot to hers in the mirror. "Why do you say that?"

Allison looked at her, surprised by her reaction. There was nothing of the flighty Sarah in that abrupt, demanding question.

"No reason," she said soothingly, "except that Rex was retired. Why would he be working on something important enough to cause enemy agents to come snooping about the house, not once, but twice?"

"Yes, I see what you mean. Anyway, Allison, I'm sorry now I asked you to come. I wish I hadn't involved you." She stood and smiled nervously. "Thank goodness we're leaving in another day for Helga's. Let's forget all about this and go down for supper. This is getting a bit much, like that dreadful time we spent at the Aleppo huts."

She walked to the door and slid back the bolt.

So Rex's office had been searched, thought Allison. Certainly not by Cairo Intelligence. They had already made their search after the general's death. If they had any reason to return, they would have come to Sarah openly. And Bret would have already known about it when she spoke with him last night.

That left...whom? Someone among either the German or

Turkish underground; Rex had worked for both. Perhaps they didn't know the Constantinople papers had been found at the Carchemish Digs. Perhaps they were watching Sarah to see if she knew anything or if she behaved suspiciously. But no—that made no sense. The war was already on. What good would those papers do anyone now that Turkey had already openly declared war on the Allies? There was no secret to hide. Then what were they looking for, and what could they learn from watching Sarah?

"Sarah, if someone thinks you know something, or have something they want, you could be right, your life may be in danger. Are you sure you've told me everything?"

Sarah shuddered. "I've been trying to think about what someone might be looking for but it escapes me. I'll keep trying, but I'd much rather do it at Helga Kruger's than here in this creaking house!"

"Yes, I quite agree," rushed Allison.

"Let's not think about it now, dear. I've told you everything I know. Let's have supper and play the Victrola to brighten the atmosphere."

"Yes, but I want to look inside Rex's office first, if you'll let me. Maybe I can think of something you haven't."

"Of course, I see no reason not to. I'll need to get the key."

Allison stared at her. "Wait—if the doors are locked, how did they get inside?"

Sarah's brows furrowed impatiently. "I told you, dear, the window was open when I looked inside. I've since had Anwar put a new lock on it. I suppose the intruder climbed up the wisteria vine growing up the wall. I've since had it trimmed."

Allison remembered her bathroom window. Hadn't Bret said he would send someone out to fix it? She should mention the window to Sarah now, but she didn't want to add to her anxious state.

"I couldn't be imagining all this," said Sarah. "Rex's office is just the way the intruder left it—with everything scattered. You can see for yourself." She went to her dresser, opened a drawer, and retrieved a key.

A moment later Sarah turned the key in the lock and swung open the door. Allison followed her inside, and Sarah switched on the lamps, bringing a glow into the darkened room. The drapes were tightly drawn, and Allison saw the scuff mark on the crisp white curtain.

The books had been removed from the shelves and were scattered on the floor, as though dumped there from the shelves. The paintings had been removed from the walls and were precariously propped against the walls.

Allison lifted one of the paintings and turned it to see if the backside had been tampered with, but there were no marks. Perhaps someone thought there might be a wall safe?

One thing stood out and arrested her attention: the desk. She walked over and looked at the neat stack of writing paper, pencils, and a pen still sitting in the now dried-up ink well. She opened the top drawer but the odds and ends were all in place. A cupboard had been left open, the larger items all removed and left sitting on the floor, as though someone had hoped to find something in the back.

Allison was aware that Sarah watched her closely, though she lingered by the door, anxious to leave.

The sound of a rising wind came from outside, along with that of tree branches shaking. Allison found herself concentrating so intently that she nearly gasped when Sarah dropped the keys with a little clatter.

"I'm sorry. I've been all thumbs recently." She looked over at Allison. "Rex was always friendly with you. I was wondering if he may have ever mentioned anything unusual to you, and, well, oh, I don't know what I mean." She sank onto the edge of the leather divan staring up at Allison intensely.

How odd that Sarah would ask such a thing. Then she remembered what Bret had asked her to do concerning Jemal, and said casually: "I don't recall anything, but do you think he would have said something? Perhaps to someone he trusted? What about his friends on the polo team...professor Jemal Pasha, for instance."

Sarah gave her a guarded look. "Jemal? He hasn't been working in the Cairo Museum since before the war. I don't know where he's got to, and anyway, Jemal was never a close friend of Rex's. In matter of fact, Rex didn't like Jemal, remember? He called him a mummy digger." Sara shuddered.

"Yes, I remember." Allison thought for a moment. "Then if he never came here to the house, I suppose we can leave him out—"

"No!" Allison looked at Sarah, startled, as her friend went on, "I mean, we shouldn't leave him out dear, because he did come here to see Rex once before the expedition in Aleppo."

Allison's heart raced, and Sarah frowned and continued: "The baroness sent him...I think that's what Rex told me later. Something about our reservations. It wasn't important."

Allison didn't reply. Not important? Then why had Jemal bothered to come? Couldn't a messenger deliver the change in reservations rather than a professor? Especially since Jemal wasn't friendly with Rex.

Sarah stood quickly. She wrung her hands as she walked about looking at the scattered items. "Nothing here is worth money. What else would they want, do you suppose?" she picked up the painting of Calcutta and rehung it on the wall.

If only Bret were here, thought Allison. *We'd be able to figure this out together, I'm sure of it. But by now he may have left Cairo for Helga's vacation house on the Mediterranean.* She sighed, then asked, "After Rex died, did the authorities come to look through his belongings?"

"They were all here," said Sarah with a grimace. "Men in street clothes, and the military brass, all searching, taking notes, asking silly questions—did we plan to go to Constantinople? Of all places! Of course not, I told them, with war soon to break? If Rex wanted to go anywhere it was Cape Town, not that I wanted to. I preferred returning to England, but Rex…well, it doesn't matter now."

While Sarah chatted nervously, Allison took another look in the desk drawers but found nothing of interest. She didn't think she would, since intelligence officials had already been through the house. A thought came to her. Why had someone thought it more important to search all the other rooms—including the dining-room cupboards and chinaware—than it was to search the office? Why had they searched it last?

Someone believed there was still something here, even though the Intelligence Office and police had done a thorough job. "One thing is clear to me," said Allison, watching Sarah's response. "Whoever came here to search must have known the authorities had already been through everything carefully. So why search again?"

Sarah didn't reply and appeared thoughtful.

"I'll tell you why," said Allison. "Someone obviously thinks Rex had something the rest of us know nothing about, not even the authorities."

"But why do you think so?"

"It's as plain as the two of us standing here. Look at this place. They don't think it's been found. So it couldn't be papers, maps, or letters or anything like that. Everything of governmental interest has already been taken."

"Yes, that's true. I hadn't thought of that."

"So whatever they want is still around. And they think it's hidden here in the house somewhere, or that you may know where it is. So they're watching you, hoping you'll lead them to it."

Sarah paled and sank to the divan again. If she was involved in all of this, she was playing the part of innocent victim with a nearly professional skill. "But I don't know what they want, so how could I lead them to it?"

"I'm guessing they don't know you're unaware of what they want. As far as they know, you were working with Rex—" She stopped abruptly.

How could she have made such a blunder!

Alert suspicion darkened Sarah's eye. "Working with him? Doing what? Rex was retired from the Civil. Everyone knew that."

"Yes, but perhaps they think you were privy to some other information, about archaeology, for instance."

A strange expression crossed Sarah's pale face. "It's no good, dear. Whatever someone may think Rex had—I'm sure I can't even imagine what it was. You're right about the police, though. As you say, whoever came in here to search must think they overlooked it or don't know about it." Sarah stood and moved toward the door, fingering the key she held. "Now I'll lie awake all night trying to think what it might be. Let's leave it alone for now, Allison. I can't take anymore."

She followed Sarah out the door, but before exiting the room she glanced at the leather chair and ottoman where Rex usually sat and read. A Barrister stood beside it with glass shelves, and Allison shuddered as she saw the pipe collection and ornately carved tins of tobacco. Snakes. How could Rex have found them so intriguing?

Back in the master bedroom, Sarah turned the key in the adjoining door's lock, her face bearing a look of strained wariness. "I could use a strong cup of tea, my dear. How about you?"

Allison nodded. "That would be nice."

"Come along, then. Let's forget all this—at least while we have supper." She smiled wanly. "Just for a little while, let's pretend life is normal and safe again."

TWENTY

>⊶⊷⊶⦿⊷⊶⊷⊰

In the twilight, in the evening, in the black and dark night.
PROVERBS 7:9

ALLISON NOTED THAT SARAH WAS DISINCLINED toward conversation as they sat down to their meal of cooling soup and cold sandwiches. The older woman was in deep thought as she dipped her spoon, her actions almost mechanical.

"I think," said Sarah a minute later, "that you're quite right about notifying Cairo police about the intruder. I'll do it on our way to Baroness Kruger's house. They could put a watch here for anyone who may decide to rummage for the third time while we're away. And at Helga's, with so many guests for the holidays, we'll be quite safe."

Allison pushed her soup away, her appetite gone, and looked toward the windows facing the backyard garden. The sheer white curtains had not yet been drawn closed, and the December breeze rustled the vines of the creeper that twisted about the patio pillars.

From somewhere in the house a door shut quietly. Allison looked across the table at Sarah, trying to ignore the leap of her heart. "A draft?"

Sarah turned her head toward the kitchen. "Neith has a key. She probably came by to take home whatever cooked foods are in the icebox. She knows we're going to Helga's. Speaking of locks—" and she looked back at Allison, puzzled—"I told Anwar last Monday to have that lock on the window in your bathroom fixed. I noticed it, too, when I was getting the room ready for your arrival."

"He must have forgotten. The wood is rotting, so maybe he needed to arrange for a carpenter to come."

Sarah pushed back her plate, rising. "Tell Neith not to leave yet with Anwar, would you, dear? I'm going up to have a look at that window now. Maybe there's something we can do about it tonight. I know it sounds silly, but I'll feel better with everything locked up."

Allison watched Sarah leave the dining room and pass through the hall, then go up the stairs. With a small sigh, Allison walked to the kitchen.

The light was burning, and Neith was emptying the icebox of the rest of the cold cuts and salad makings, including a chocolate iced cake.

"Hullo, Neith, could you ask Anwar to come in for a few minutes before you leave? Mrs. Blaine wants something done about the broken latch on the bathroom window upstairs."

"Anwar not come with me. I walk, pulling handwagon for shopping. Cannot send him back, either. He is out with friends."

"Oh, I see. I'll tell her."

"I go now, very well?"

"Yes, of course. Good night."

Allison walked back into the dining room and stood musing. Something about what had just happened disturbed her, but she couldn't think what it was. A few minutes later she heard Neith leave.

Absently, she went to collect the plates from the table to bring back to the kitchen sink. She rinsed and stacked them for washing later. While drying her hands she looked toward the back door. She went quickly and tried the knob. It was locked.

She knew what had disturbed her now. How had Neith been able to get in when Sarah said she had locked the door earlier?

Neith had given Allison her key last night! Allison had intended to return it to Sarah this morning, but it had slipped her mind.

Slow down, she cautioned herself, *before you think everyone is a conspirator against you. Neith must have found the key on the dresser where you left it.* Shaking her head at her fancifulness, she turned off the kitchen light and started toward the stairs to tell Sarah that Anwar would not be coming.

A board creaked behind her, from the back of the house. Sarah must have come down already. She turned, but there was no one there. Allison peered into the darkness. Beyond the shadowed open doorway of the anteroom she could see the short flight of steep steps leading to the back room where Marra slept. Marra couldn't have returned without them knowing it, could she?

It must have been the house cooling after sunset. Old wood had a dreadful way of creaking, snapping, and groaning—especially at night when everything was silent. Allison waited a moment or two and then turned back toward the stairs to go find Sarah when she thought she heard a soft footstep.

She froze. It couldn't be Neith; she'd left by way of the kitchen. And Sarah was upstairs. That door she'd heard close softly earlier, had it been Marra? She cast a glance toward the big gilded clock, ten till seven. Knowing Marra's temper, she could have had a small spat with David over something, which would explain Marra going straight to her room and not announcing her arrival.

With deliberation Allison walked through the dining room and open doorway into the shadowed alcove. She looked up a flight of short hardwood steps to the narrow upper passageway where a dim light glowed near Marra's room.

"Marra?" she called up to the top landing.

A door opened and closed—the bathroom door? A board creaked.

Allison let out a breath of relief. It was Marra.

Or the haunt...her mind suggested, and Allison fought a shiver. Either way, she was going to find out.

She went up the steps holding the banister and, reaching the landing, saw that Marra's door was open a crack and a welcoming light burned.

Marra's small guest room had no bath, she reminded herself, and she would need to walk the narrow hall past a closed door, until she came to the hall bathroom. But the other door between Marra's room and the bath, what lay behind it? It must be a large storage closet, she decided, since most of the houses had them installed when English occupants took over the houses. Sarah was a dreadful "pack rat," as she called herself, keeping everything for years. Sarah hadn't mentioned whether the big closet had been searched by the intruder, but it must have been. No one so intent as the intruder apparently was on locating something would overlook a storage closet!

Allison walked to Marra's room and pushed the door open wider.

The bed was empty. Marra's unpacked bags were on the floor; her clothes neatly hung in the closet. On the dressing table were jars of cleansing creams, a hairbrush, and other beauty aids. A towel was on the stool with an unopened bar of soap, a sponge, and a book. There was no evidence that Marra had undressed and gone to take her bath as Allison had thought. She turned, staring back out through the door into the hallway.

A troubling sensation of apprehension settled over the her. Allison left the room, looking down the passage that curved past the storage closet and the bath and ended at another flight of steps that led down to the laundry room.

As she stood there listening, she felt something, a faint, chilly draft coming from somewhere and wrapping about her ankles. Her heart beat faster. It must be coming from the steps..She walked to the edge and peered down, surprised that she could just make out the silhouette of a smaller side door that opened off from the laundry room into the backyard. It was open a crack, and a breeze sent the door inching backwards; the scent of flowers drifted up. Allison's hand closed tightly on the banister.

Sarah had never mentioned this door before, and Allison couldn't remember ever seeing it! Why would she make so much of an open window that could only be entered by the roof and overlook the laundry-room door? Why hadn't Neith locked it before she left? And if it hadn't been Marra that she heard earlier, then—?

No. It had to be Marra because her bedroom light was on, and the bathroom door had opened and shut a few minutes ago with no thought for being quiet—unless...unless someone wanted her to think it was Marra?

Someone had been up here! And it wasn't Marra.

A feeling that she was being observed from the shadows near the washroom prickled her skin. She peered down, transfixed with fear, afraid she would see something in the dark shadows. The question she now asked herself was had someone left the door open when they left...or when they came in?

Steady, she told herself. *You don't know if anyone was down there.* But if someone was, then she was alone and vulnerable—

Alone...she started. No, she was not alone. Sarah was here. Why hadn't she returned yet from checking the window in Allison's room? What was keeping her all this time?

Allison stared down at the floor below the steps, her eyes growing accustomed to the darkness. Was there something on the floor? No, not something...some*one.* Someone lay sprawled in the shadows.

Allison backed away, her heart pounding so hard she felt weakness in her knees. An inner compulsion prompted her to turn and run, but she couldn't move. Someone was on the floor.

Marra! She must have come home early as Allison thought, heard the same noises she herself had heard, went to investigate and—

Allison rushed down the steps, groping her way along the wall to where she expected to locate a light switch. Her hand brushed against the wood but she couldn't find it, and panic broke free when a shadow disengaged itself from the darkness of the laundry room and came toward her. At first she thought her eyes were only playing tricks on her until the sound of breathing and the creak of the floor reached out to grasp her.

Her scream ripped through the chilled silence. As it did, the shadow disappeared through the outside door into the night.

Allison froze, a prisoner in the darkness, unable to find the light, unable to respond except to stare down at Marra on the floor. Another minute must have passed before she moved, her trembling hand searching for the switch.

She heard the muffled sound of her name being called from the other side of the passageway, perhaps from the alcove near the dining room, then footsteps above.

"Sarah!" answered Allison, uncertain whether she could hear her. "Sarah! Hurry!"

It couldn't have been more than a minute before she heard Sarah above the steps, but to Allison the time was endless until a light flicked on, flooding the laundry room. She heard a sucking gasp come from Sarah's throat as she saw Marra's still form and halted her descent.

Allison moved from the wall where she had backed away, rushing to stoop beside Marra. Reaching a trembling hand, she turned her over. As she did, the scarf fell aside—

It wasn't Marra.

The woman, clothed in Moslem black, lay quite still. Relieved that it wasn't her friend, yet stricken with anguish, Allison kneeled beside the woman, touching her gently. "Neith!"

The Egyptian cook stared up with empty eyes; there was no life to the weight of her slack body.

Sarah had come down the steps. "Is she alive?"

The foolish question borne from trauma went unanswered as the chilly December wind caused the door to blow open wider and stir the hem of the black dress at Neith's ankles. Allison looked up at Sarah and saw that her friend's dazed face looked as though it had aged considerably. Sarah tried to speak, a gasp sounding in her throat as she stuttered, "S-she's been murdered."

The words lodged inside Allison's brain like a heavy dull weight. Yes, she thought almost stupidly, someone had killed Neith. She frowned, troubled by some niggling confusion. Someone had murdered Neith...but...but that was impossible because—

"Because she left over half an hour ago through the kitchen!"

"What?" whispered Sarah. "Oh heavens! The poor woman is dead—and in my house. Oh Allison, we've got to get a message to the Cairo police. Anwar! Oh, where is Anwar?"

"Out with friends. That's what Neith told me earlier. One of us will need to go for the police." Allison noticed for the first time that Sarah held the general's Luger in her hand. She gripped it until her knuckles turned white, but her hand was shaking so badly Allison feared she would drop it. She reached out to take the weapon from her, putting it in her pocket as she stood.

"Wait here, Sarah. I'll go."

"You don't expect me to wait here? Alone?" she said in a small voice. "What if he comes back?"

"Then you go. I'll wait."

Sarah shivered. "How—how did she die, do you think?"

Allison looked down at the woman, masking her own dread. "I don't know." She looked up to meet Sarah's horrified gaze.

"Please," she said gently, "the police."

Swallowing hard, Sarah nodded. "Yes, of course." She started back up the stairs, then paused, looked at Allison worriedly. "Will you be all right?"

Allison forced a confident look to her face. "I've got the gun," she said, patting her pocket. "I'll be fine."

Sarah turned and hurried away, and Allison leaned weakly against the wall, staring down at Neith's motionless body.

"What were you doing down here, Neith?" she whispered sadly. "Why did you come back. What were you after...?" Her voice choked and she fought back tears.

Whatever Neith had sought, Allison seriously doubted it could possibly have been worth the price the Egyptian woman had paid.

TWENTY-ONE

> ━ ┇ ━ ❬❭ ━ ◯ ━ ❬❭ ━ ┇ ━

Set a guard, O LORD, over my mouth.

PSALM 141:3

NEARLY THREE HOURS HAD PASSED, and Allison sat on the edge of the divan in the brightly lit drawing room fighting a pounding headache and a dazed sense of disaster. Sir Edgar had arrived with amazing speed. He had brought a doctor and several medical orderlies, and within an hour they had taken away the body on a stretcher. Police were searching the premises inside and out. Allison feared they would discover the general's office in disarray and confront Sarah about it. Another policeman was outside searching the yard, but Sir Edgar had commented that they would need to wait for morning to see anything.

He stepped outside and looked up at the dark sky. "A pity. By morning rain may have destroyed any footprints."

Allison had heard one of the officers say that Sir Edgar had two of his Egyptian aides searching for Anwar to tell him the dark news about his mother, but as yet, they'd been unable to locate him in any of the homes of his Egyptian friends in Old Cairo.

Since his arrival, Sir Edgar had pummeled Allison and Sarah mercilessly with questions. At times, Allison believed he was deliberately misunderstanding their answers in order to try to confuse and frighten Sarah.

Allison watched Sir Edgar standing before Sarah, gazing down at her. Why was he questioning her so vigorously? He couldn't possibly think *she* had committed the crime!

Sarah was sitting on the far side of the room in a winged-back chair near the double windows. Her haggard face was pale under the soft but persistent questioning of Sir Edgar Simonds.

"I already had the Luger in hand—and—and I ran in the direction of her scream."

"Where did you get a German pistol, Mrs. Blaine?"

"From—Rex. He collected pistols. He kept the Luger in the nightstand beside the bed. After I checked the window in Allison's bath I became unsettled. I went and got the pistol intending to keep it with us."

"Why should a window with a loose latch frighten you into getting a pistol, Mrs. Blaine?"

"I—I don't know. But it did."

Allison tensed. Sir Edgar could use that reply against her later when he learned about the intruder. Sarah should tell him the truth now. Allison wanted to speak up but feared her contradiction would put Sarah in a suspicious light.

Instead, she continued her urgent prayers for help. Her throat was dry and she was dreadfully thirsty, but she didn't want to get up and go alone into the darkened kitchen even though the police were everywhere.

"What else did the major general collect, Mrs. Blaine?"

Sarah plucked at her pearls. "Nothing."

"Nothing?" came the wheedling insult. "*Nothing,* Mrs. Blaine? You're certain of that?"

"*Mrs. Blaine!*" thought Allison tensely. If only he would stop calling her that over and over in that contemptuous tone—

"Mrs. Blaine, did the general collect vases?"

Vases! Allison's eyes shot toward Sarah, searching for a response. This time she hoped it wouldn't be there for Sir Edgar to see.

Sarah's eyes were wide. Her fingers twisted at the single strand of

328

pearls. "Vases?" The word ended in a shrill unnatural sound. "Why would he? Rex would loathe vases. Women collect vases."

"What would the general find stimulating, Mrs. Blaine? Egyptology?"

"Egyptology?"

"It is fascinating, isn't it, Mrs. Blaine? Mummies, coffins, ceremonial treasures from the burial tombs of kings. Did he know Professor Jemal Pasha of the Cairo Museum?"

"No."

"Did they ever travel together to Luxor?"

"No—"

"To Karnak?"

"Never!"

"Perhaps three years ago?"

Sarah stared up at him, her face a sickening white.

Sir Edgar smiled and remained silent, so that the ticking of the clock filled the room.

Allison's sweating hands tightened on the edge of the divan, and she leaned forward, feeling as though her nerves were like a spring ready to snap as the clock chimed nine. On the last chime the front door flew open. The three of them turned quickly to look.

Marra came in breathlessly, her blonde hair windblown and her cheeks flushed. Her anxious eyes darted about until they found Allison, then she hurried across the room to her.

"I'm sorry I wasn't here. Neith, murdered! What a ghastly happening!"

Allison's eyes clung to hers. "How did you know?"

Marra was about to speak when footsteps interrupted and David came in. As he passed behind the divan he leaned down to Allison. "Bret's here," he whispered, and then joined Marra.

A moment later Allison heard footsteps in the hall and she

looked up and saw Bret, solid and reassuring, in his uniform. She quickly arose from the divan. Relief came rushing into her heart. *Thank you, God,* she prayed earnestly. With effort, she held in check a reckless desire to rush toward him, to be encircled in those strong, protecting arms.

Bret must have informed Marra and David about the death of the Egyptian cook, but how had he found out? Sir Edgar must have sent word to Cairo Intelligence, but the look on Sir Edgar's face when he saw Bret enter the room convinced her that was not the case. Her relative's brief start of surprise changed swiftly into unmistakable resentment.

Bret must have noticed Sir Edgar's reaction as well, for he gave him a measured look before turning his gaze on Allison.

He walked over to the divan, his firm fingers closing about her arm. Something warm and vital surged through her. His eyes sought hers, searching.

"All right?" he asked briefly, and there was so much more left unasked in that question.

She managed a smile and nodded, making no effort to step away from him, even when it was apparent that Sir Edgar took keen notice of the way Bret was looking at her. Allison remembered Bret's deliberate attempt to make anyone watching them at Ezbekiah Gardens think he was romantically involved with her. Was he still playing a role, perhaps for the benefit of Sir Edgar? Certainly the warm, alert gaze he was affording her was quite improved from the distance he had last shown when telling her of his request for a transfer to France.

But whatever his motivation for comforting her, Allison didn't care. His arrival may have disturbed Sir Edgar, but it brought her a surge of relief and a sense of order to the confusion that had settled over her heart.

"Ah, Colonel!" said Edgar, walking to the center of the room. "I thought you had sailed for a much-deserved reprieve before taking up service in France."

Bret gave nothing away as he turned to look at him. "Hello Edgar. I leave in a few days. I'm waiting for the arrival of a friend, Allison's cousin, Neal Bristow. His ship is due soon. I hear there's been an accident here tonight."

"No, Colonel. No accident. A murder. Miss Wescott found the Egyptian cook in the laundry room a few hours ago."

Allison was sure Bret hadn't believed Neith had met with an accident. She met his dark blue eyes and saw his brow lift over the news that it was she who had found Neith. She saw restrained frustration in the depths of his gaze and received the clear sense that he was not pleased she was in any way involved in this danger.

His smooth voice washed over her. "Allison, darling, you've the unfortunate ability of being the first to discover the victims of mayhem. I do wish you'd be more careful. I leave for France with fear and trembling wondering who you may stumble over next."

Darling!?

That word of heart-thumping endearment took her off guard— though she was sure it was spoken for Sir Edgar's benefit. That being the case, she discovered she didn't want him saying it. She narrowed her eyes, displeased, and sat down again on the edge of the divan, staring at him.

Sir Edgar struck a match and held the flame to his cigar. "When did Allison find her first victim? You were there, Colonel?"

Allison sat quite still. She knew Bret hadn't meant to give Aleppo away, but he answered so indifferently that not even Edgar appeared to make anything of the revelation after all. "I believe it was when Leah Bristow was found dead, wasn't it?" he asked her, then shrugged. "No, I wasn't there, but you were, weren't you, Mrs. Blaine?"

The shift of attention in the room to Sarah caused a moment of silence. For her part, Sarah, seated in the shadows by the window, grimaced at finding herself the object of attention. "Yes…I was there, with Rex. It was a dreadful discovery. All of us in the club had ridden by camel to an old Roman ruin. Poor Leah was there, half buried in the sand. The doctor said she'd been bitten by a cobra. The same thing that happened to that German Major Reuter who met a gruesome death—oh, dear! And now Neith—!"

"Neith was murdered, Mrs. Blaine," said Sir Edgar calmly.

"And you think Miss Bristow and Major Karl Reuter were not?" asked David, speaking up for the first time.

Sir Edgar turned his dark gaze on David as if becoming suddenly aware of him. "I've read the report recently while staying with the Wescotts in Port Said. Accidental deaths, so it was concluded. You have reason to think otherwise?"

David shrugged. "Two people dying of a cobra bite within a few days of each other is a ruddy pot of lies as far as I'm concerned, Inspector."

Sir Edgar chomped the end of his cigar. "Perhaps, but in this case, I don't think you'll find a cobra slithering about in the laundry room. What I wager you will find, though, is a missing hammer. The poor woman was killed by a heavy whack to the back of her skull." He took the silver handle of his cane and illustrated the blow.

Sarah made a soft sound, her hand going to her throat. She leaned stiffly back against the chair, looking for all the world as though she might get sick.

Allison stood quickly. "Cousin Edgar! Please! May I suggest you refrain from needless gory details?"

"M'dear, I realize how upset you are. You were the poor unfortunate lamb who stumbled across her body. It must have been unsettling, to say the least. Nonetheless, your behavior is a little odd, considering."

Allison felt an uneasy shiver at the look in Sir Edgar's eyes, then heard Bret's cool voice say: "Considering what?"

Edgar set his cane down quietly. "No offense, Colonel. Considering that it's unlikely a nurse would cringe over a mere mention of a blow to the victim's head."

Edgar looked at Allison who was trying to hide her confusion. What was he getting at? "A nurse would inevitably see terrible wounds on the front lines. You must have seen your share of, shall we say, *severe* injuries on the Arabian battlefield near Kut."

Allison pinned him with a steady gaze. "You misunderstand me, sir. I was thinking of Sarah. You might take Mrs. Blaine's frail condition into consideration."

He barked a laugh, turned his large head, and gestured with his cigar to Sarah who sat there, fidgeting nervously. "The *frail* Mrs. Blaine, as you call her, once assisted during an operation on her father in a village of Burma. I watched her coolly help cut him open in temperatures of over one hundred degrees. The dear lady didn't blink an eye. Isn't that right, Mrs. Blaine?"

Allison looked at Sarah in surprise. She had once lived in Burma, working as a nurse? And Sir Edgar had known her there? Sarah's face was a study in restrained emotion, but her eyes flickered with anger. Apparently she did not care to have her secrets so exposed.

Astonished, Allison noted that the helpless look of fear that had been on Sarah's face all evening was unexpectedly gone. A resolved calm tightened her jaw as she watched Sir Edgar walk slowly to the window. Glancing at him, Allison caught a satisfied gleam in his eyes.

Sarah stood and paced, rubbing the back of her neck. "Yes, I used to be a nurse. After my father died of fever I married Rex. We left there when he was transferred to India with the Company." Her face set with impatience. "I do not see, however, what any of that has to do with what happened tonight."

Allison watched Sarah, bewildered by the change in her manner, until she became aware that she, too, was under scrutiny. She turned her head and saw Bret's cool, level gaze. There was no mistaking the look that warned her not to reveal her shock. She wondered if Bret had already known Sarah's past when they discussed her at Ezbekiah Gardens.

Bret picked up a magazine and began to fan Allison's face with a frown of concern. "Not feeling ill are you, my dear? Speaking of the brave sisterhood of nurses—what do you think, Marra? We don't want Allison to have a setback in her recovery, do we? Maybe she ought to be tucked in for the night."

Allison plucked the magazine away from him before Marra could reinforce his claim. "I am feeling *quite* well. As Cousin Edgar aptly suggested, if I can attend dying soldiers many hours a day, I can endure an evening of questioning. It's Sarah who is exhausted and really needs to rest."

Sir Edgar turned from the window and looked at them. "Perhaps we should let Mrs. Blaine take a brief respite with a spot of tea while I speak with you alone, Allison. After all, it was you who found Neith, not Sarah."

A flicker of irritation showed in Bret's eyes. Sarah, too, looked troubled.

"We both found her," Sarah said.

"Perhaps, but not together, Mrs. Blaine." Edgar was expressionless. "How long would you say it was between Allison's discovery of the body and your arrival on the steps above the laundry room?"

Sarah was silent, and Allison inserted, "Less than a minute."

"No, it was longer than that—" Sarah insisted, then broke off.

Edgar turned toward Allison, his eyes expectant. "Yes? Perhaps a full minute then?"

"Yes, a full minute."

A satisfied smirk on his face, Edgar turned back to Sarah. "A minute? Indeed. My dear Mrs. Blaine, isn't a minute a rather short space of time to overcome your fears and decide to respond to the scream, find your dead husband's Luger, come down the stairs, cross the hall into the dining room, go up the steps to check Marra's room where you said you thought the scream had come from, then go down the passage to the steps leading to the laundry room?"

Sarah paled but said nothing.

Allison glanced at Bret, only to be met by his penetrating gaze. Sir Edgar definitely had a point. How could Sarah have arrived so quickly?

"It was dark below the steps," explained Allison slowly. "And I couldn't find the light. So I didn't see Neith lying there at first. It must have been longer than a minute."

Edgar's eyes sparkled. "So it took you a minute before you actually saw the body."

"That's right. I couldn't see at first."

"Yes, but Sarah would not have been alerted to any calamity until after you saw the body and screamed, isn't that so? So any previous delay does not give Sarah more time to appear on the scene." Sir Edgar smiled broadly. "I suggest one of you is lying."

"I beg your pardon——!" Allison began in anger, but she stopped when she saw Bret watching Edgar, a cynical expression on his mouth, a dangerous glitter in his eyes.

"And is it Mrs. Blaine or Allison whom you're accusing of cracking the old Egyptian cook on the back of the head, Sir Edgar?" he asked, his voice low.

"Allison? Kill the cook?" Sir Edgar echoed. "Quite out of the question, Colonel. As for Mrs. Blaine—"

"Then," said Bret with a dangerously cool tone, "may I suggest this questioning has gone on enough for one night. Allison is just exhausted enough to contradict herself unintentionally, as you have seen. And I'm certain that's not your most-honorable intention."

For a moment Sir Edgar's eyes glimmered with wrath, then he bowed his head in deference to Allison. "Indeed, indeed. Apologies are due. The colonel is most insightful. I see you have friends in Cairo Intelligence as well as in the police department, meaning myself, of course. Now, my dear cousin, why don't you take a little rest? In fact—" and he pulled out his watch—"I think we all could use a strong cup of tea and sandwiches. That is, if there's anyone to attend us?" He looked about with arched brows.

Sarah, who looked relieved that the questioning had ceased, made a little gesture, but Allison moved away from the divan and started toward the kitchen. "I'll fetch it, Sarah."

She left the drawing room, heading through the dining room, where there was a light burning above the table. The windows facing the back garden gave her the usual feeling of discomfort, and she paused. The house was quiet except for the muffled voices coming from behind her in the drawing room. There were shadows in the hall and near the stairway leading up to the landing to her bedroom and Sarah's. She half expected to see a light on in the general's old office telling her the police were searching, but it seemed no one was up there. Then the police must have given up and returned to the office—except, of course, for Sir Edgar.

Allison walked past the table to the kitchen door. Setting her jaw, she pushed the door open and went through.

A light burned above the long wooden counter where the pots and pans were hung, and she gathered what she needed to make tea. Remembering that Bret preferred coffee, and took out the pot.

She went about filling the kettle with water and took down the box of matches to light the stove.

As she struck the match, her eyes noticed something missing from the utensil peg. Her throat tightened and she stared. She held the flaring match, staring, until the flame heated the tips of her fingers. "Ouch." She dropped it.

"Careful," a deep voice came from behind her.

She whirled to find Bret standing there. He picked up the box of matches and lit the stove, smiling at her. "Wade's in for trouble if you can't even light the stove."

When she didn't rise to the bait, he frowned and looked at her closely. With a muffled exclamation, he set the box down and reached out to draw her into his arms. "I didn't mean to frighten you, my dear. I thought you knew I'd follow you."

Allison clung to him, trying to let his strength and calm seep into her. She buried her face in his chest, closing out everything but the fact that she was, for the moment, safe.

"In an instant you'll have me forgetting why I came in here," his low voice whispered in her ear.

She smiled against his uniform, sniffing against tears that she didn't fully understand. "I'm not trying to do so, I promise. But between Neith's murder and Sarah's odd behavior and the haunt's antics—"

"The…what?" he broke in.

She looked up at him, feeling her cheeks flush. Oh, why had she brought *that* up? "The…um, the haunt." At the expression on his face, she shook her head. "Not a real one. It's just that, well, there have been the oddest sounds going on here. Creaks and such, for which there seem to be no reason."

He was struggling to hold back a smile, she could tell.

"It's true, Bret!"

"All right—" he began, but she cut him off.

"Marra has heard them, too," she insisted with a sniff. "Just ask her. And she's the one who named the noises the haunt, not I."

He cupped the back of her head gently and pressed her face against his chest, though whether to comfort her or to keep her from seeing him laughing at her, she wasn't sure. Well, whatever the reason, she wasn't going to argue. She was simply too tired.

How long they stood there, she wasn't certain. But after a time she forced herself to draw away. She leaned against the counter, breathing slowly, willing her nerves to calm. "I'm all right now."

He watched her carefully for a moment, then turned back to the matches. Allison's gaze swerved to the backboard above the counter where the utensils glinted in the light.

Bret struck the match, lit the burner, and placed the pot and kettle to heat. He glanced toward the door to make certain they were alone, then held her gaze. His frown deepened. "What is it?"

She pointed to the board. There was an empty spot. "If you find the meat tenderizer, I think you'll have your murder weapon," she said, surprised at the steady tone of her whisper.

He followed her gaze to the empty peg. "Do you know who was in here last?"

She swallowed. "I was. And Neith."

His brow lifted and he seemed to be fighting a smile. "We'll keep that bit of information a secret between us, all right? I'll look for the tenderizer in the morning, before the police come back." He turned his full attention to her again. "Now, tell me what happened. Have you any idea who it was you saw in that laundry room?"

She closed her eyes, shaking her head. "It was too dark. But there *was* someone in there when I went down the steps. I thought it was Marra."

"Why?"

She told him about the sounds she had heard in that area of the house, of the light in Marra's room, and the door opening and closing to the bath. "I thought she came home early and was taking a bath before going to bed." She glanced toward the door. "You don't think Sir Edgar had anything to do with it?"

"I don't know. That stunt with his cane was deliberate. He's trying to frighten Sarah."

"He's been horrid to her. And that matter about Burma was unfair. Did you already know about it?"

"Yes, and like I said, he's trying to frighten her, my guess is into giving away what she knows. If he can make her think she's under suspicion of killing her cook, she might let down her guard."

"She didn't have anything to do with it."

"Maybe not." His voice was not as confident as hers, and she looked at him, frowning. He shrugged. "Right now we don't eliminate anyone."

"There's so much to tell you. The way he questioned her before you arrived. I'm sure it means something. And then there was—"

"Wait!" he said with frustration. "We can't discuss it here, not now. I want Simonds out of the house first." He looked at his watch, his brow creasing. "He's likely to hang around until daylight. I'm sure he wants to search for footprints in the garden near the laundry room as badly as I do."

Allison's eyes widened. As badly as he did? Wasn't he leaving Cairo?

"Won't he take offense to your meddling?"

He grinned cheekily. "Not if he doesn't suspect I'm meddling. I'm on medical leave, remember?"

"But due to take flight on a sundeck for Helga's Mediterranean hideaway."

"I've changed my mind. I've decided Christmas in Cairo at the baroness's mansion is all the leave I'll need until my transfer to France."

Her heart skipped a beat at the news, and she met his eyes, which were dancing with laughter.

"After all, dear little Allison, if you're going to insist on colliding with murderers in laundry rooms in the dark, I think I should stay close." His grin broadened. "Maybe even sleep outside your door until we're all packed off to Helga's for mistletoe, eh?"

She caught her breath. He wasn't leaving! At least not until after New Years. Her heart sang with the news. Hesitant to let him see her pleased smile, she turned away to lower the flame under the coffeepot and open the upper shelf. "Can you reach that bag?"

He removed the bag of coffee beans that Neith had already ground and handed it to her. She handed it back to him with the scoop.

He looked at her, one brow raised.

This time she could not contain her smile. "I don't know how strong you like it."

His answering smile was purely self-satisfied. "Then you'd better get used to finding out, hadn't you, darling?"

TWENTY-TWO

➤➤﹣⟨◆⟩﹣⟨⊙⟩﹣⟨◆⟩﹣⟨◄◄

In You I take shelter.

PSALM 143:9

AFTER SANDWICHES AND TEA, Sir Edgar unexpectedly announced he was leaving, but that he would return early before breakfast. He had left a guard, he told them. Everyone was to stay out of the back garden until it could be searched at sunup. Allison would feel secure with or without a guard, since Bret and David were staying. David would park himself outside Marra's door, and Bret had turned to Sarah with a disarming smile and asked if she could part with an extra pillow.

Sarah appeared delighted to have them. *Surely that proves, in some small measure, that she's innocent?* Allison argued within herself.

"I feel so much better already," Sarah said brightly. "Two brave soldiers to care for us, what more could we ask, right girls?"

Marra caught Allison's eye and smiled behind David's back, but Bret was facing Allison so she struggled to look demure.

Sarah turned to Bret. "I wouldn't think of allowing you to sleep on the landing after your recent release from the hospital. You can sleep in Rex's old office. There's a divan there. Allison? Could you be a dear and get the colonel a blanket? I'll show Marra where the bedding is kept for David."

"Why, yes, of course," breathed Allison. She looked at Bret, careful to keep her face a blank. "This way. It's between my room and Sarah's."

She was surprised Sarah would actually ask Bret to stay in the office. But, she supposed, it was the most strategic spot for him if there was any trouble in the night. She obligingly led Bret upstairs, then paused. The door to the office was already ajar. She pushed it open, then switched on the light.

"I'm surprised she would have you sleep in here," she said in a low voice, although Sarah was downstairs with Marra and David.

He stopped, taking in the ransacked room. "I see what you mean."

"The house has been broken into twice," she told him hurriedly. "And Sarah has kept that information from Sir Edgar. I thought one of his men would surely see this room and report it, but I don't think they even came up here."

Bret quickly closed the door. "Ah, now we're getting somewhere. Did she say what she thought the intruders were looking for?"

"No, but it couldn't be anything official. Your department has already searched the whole house."

"Exactly, which tells me that my suspicions are correct."

"What suspicions? What are they looking for? Is Sir Edgar involved?"

"My guess is yes, but we haven't been able to prove it yet. He's certain Sarah knows something, and he's determined to frighten her into telling him."

"Do you think she does?"

"Yes. She's not as flighty as she likes to appear, you saw that for yourself tonight. Which probably means that if she's asked me to stay in Rex's office, there's nothing here that might incriminate him. Or her. One thing is certain, she's genuinely frightened."

He looked around the office, musing, and Allison folded her arms: "I've already searched. There's nothing here, as you said."

He looked at her, surprised. "You searched? When?"

She explained quickly. "I'm convinced the intruder is after something other than anything associated with espionage."

"You *have* been a busy little spy," he said wryly. "Besides finding the body, you've also searched this office. In the kitchen you told me you had much to explain. Well, let's have it. You have my full and undivided attention." He removed his military jacket and tie and hung them on the back of the desk chair, then sank onto the divan. He stretched out, placing his hands behind his head. "Draw up that chair. You'll need to keep your voice low. I assume that door across the office opens into the master bedroom. And—hand me that extra pillow will you, Nurse?"

She tried to ignore his smile as she followed his teasing bidding. She arranged the pillow behind his dark head, aware of his riveting gaze. When she drew away, he reached for her hand and guided her to the chair beside him.

Allison tried halfheartedly to pull her hand away, but he held it tight.

"This would be pleasant," he said, "under different circumstances." He looked about. "Somehow I keep expecting the major general's charming self to materialize like a genie. Rather dampens the enjoyment of your kind ministrations." He looked at her. "I keep thinking of Helga's cozy little villa on the Mediterranean."

Allison didn't want to think about it.

He watched her. "Aren't you going to tell me I still have time to catch the steamer?"

"You've made up your mind to spend Christmas in Cairo," she said lightly, avoiding his eyes. "There's no reason to try to convince you otherwise."

"Maybe I need a nurse to oversee my convalescence at the villa." He tugged at her hand, and her eyes reluctantly came to his. She expected to find a warm, teasing glint in their depths, but he watched her soberly, and the change embarrassed her.

She pulled her hand free and stood. "It's getting dreadfully late. And somehow we've forgotten all about Neith. I think this can wait until morning."

His mouth curved and he swung his feet down from the divan and stood, hands on hips. "There's nothing like a bludgeoned victim to wilt the budding thoughts of romance...never mind villas and warm beaches. But Allison, I don't think this can wait. Simonds will be poking about in the garden at the first crack of dawn. Sit down, please. You have something to tell me. Let's hear it."

He walked over to the desk and sat on its edge, arms folded, a moody look on his handsome face.

Allison nodded. "Does Helga still own the shop in Old Cairo?"

He looked at her. "Yes, why?"

"Something happened there this morning you should know about."

"Galli's shop? You went there?" Bret's voice had an edge to it.

"It was Sarah's idea. I wouldn't have gone otherwise, but something happened there that I'm sure is important."

"We've learned a few things more about Helga's smiling shop-keeper. He's not only into smuggling opium from India, but he's far too friendly with the Turkish pasha in Constantinople. What did Sarah want from him?"

She told him of the club meeting and Sarah's search for an item to auction off to support the museum. "I didn't think much about it while it was happening, but afterward a conversation between Sarah and the merchant over a certain item Professor Blackstone was looking to buy seemed curious."

"You don't recall what the item was?"

"No, but he didn't have it."

"Blackstone," he said thoughtfully.

"Do you remember him?"

"Yes. The dour-faced archaeologist from the museum. He and Jemal both looked like a couple of walking mummies."

She shivered at the apt description. "Professor Blackstone was a working colleague of Jemal's and Helga's. I wish I had paid closer attention to the item Sarah was asking about."

"Something happened that drew away your attention?"

She told him about the shadow in an upper window and how she at first thought it was the driver, Anwar, but when she had gone to the front of the store and looked out he was leaning against the Mercedes smoking. "Anyway, I must have imagined it. There was no way anyone could have been looking through one of those upper windows."

"On the contrary, there is. There's generally a ledge on the back of the building and back stairs leading up to it. I know, because I've used them."

Allison contemplated this information. "Then someone *was* looking in?" she asked incredulously. "Who, and why?"

"The why is obvious: someone is keeping a close watch on you. Or Sarah. Any visit to the shop connected with Blaine and German and Turkish sympathizers holds a good deal of interest for more than one person. You didn't get a look at this phantom, did you?"

"No, it happened too quickly, like tonight, when someone fled the laundry room. But that isn't all that happened." She knew it didn't sound good for Sarah, but she explained in detail about the vase. "At the time I knew I'd seen it somewhere before. Then, tonight, it came to me. When Edgar was asking Sarah if the general collected vases, she behaved as if the question were incredulous. It was then I remembered."

She looked at him, feeling cold, and glanced again toward the door into Sarah's room. Even if she stood there listening she couldn't hear, but Allison was uneasy.

Bret stood and moved toward her. He reached out, encircling her gently, and drew her against his chest. One hand came to cradle the back of her head, and the tenderness in that touch almost undid her. She relaxed against him, her hands resting against the smooth fabric of his shirtfront.

They stood that way for a few moments, then he spoke in soft tones. "I'm here, Allison. You're safe. Go on."

"I'm certain it was that vase—or one very much like it—that Rex intended to buy for Sarah's anniversary that day when we were all in the shop a year ago."

"A vase? Which one is that?"

"Remember when we all supposedly bumped into one another there last year, when I'd gone for Lydia's medical supplies?"

"Vaguely," he said wryly.

"Well, as I looked at the vase this morning, I remembered something that happened back then. Rex had arrived before I did on that day and was waiting for me, so he said, to play protective uncle to his godchild. When I arrived he came from behind the curtain with a vase in his hand. He implied he was looking to buy something for Sarah's anniversary present. It was the same vase Sarah wanted to buy this morning."

Bret came alert. "Ah."

"When Sarah saw it in my hand, she behaved as though it were the perfect piece to buy for the auction. I can't be sure, but I think she recognized it, but don't ask me why she would, because—" She broke off.

"Because what?"

"Because Rex didn't buy it, don't you remember?"

"No," he said flatly.

She leaned back and looked up at him. "You were there!"

"I'm sorry," he said wryly. "Enlighten me."

"We came out of the storage room. You were pretending to discuss a visit to Luxor—" she raised an eyebrow—"and you were saying you thought you'd bring Cynthia along. You were discussing the famous Rosetta Stone, and Rex spoke up and said it was in the British Museum. Then he held up an Egyptian doll and said, 'What do you think, Allison? Will Sarah like this instead of the vase?' I recall being surprised by his choice. The doll was some sort of an heirloom, from an early Egyptian dynasty. Choosing it showed discernment and knowledge, and Rex wasn't supposed to have either."

A curious glint burned in Bret's eyes as he leaned back on the desk. "An Egyptian doll...does Sarah still have it?"

She shrugged. "Probably. You know how she holds on to anything he gave her. I think she had it put away, though, since it isn't the sort of thing you'd display with modern furnishings—" she stopped, her eyes coming to his.

He looked at her sharply, and his hands tightened about hers so that she winced. With a quick motion he lifted her hands to his lips and kissed them—throwing her heart into total confusion.

"The doll," he breathed. "That's it! Allison, my dear Allison, *you* are a doll."

"They were looking for the doll," she breathed in wonder.

"That must be it."

They were looking for the Egyptian treasure doll! But who were "they"? "Do you think then that Neith was involved? Was that why she was murdered?"

"I don't know yet. I keep thinking of Anwar...there's something about him..."

"But he wouldn't harm his mother!"

"No, if she *was* his mother. Anyway, go on with what you were telling me about Sarah."

She continued, relating how Sarah had taken the vase up to the counter to pay for it. "The merchant was upset. He told her it belonged to someone else and he didn't know how it had gotten out on the floor. It was a mistake, he told her. And then—she dropped it. And watching, I couldn't help but wonder if she did it deliberately. He was very upset."

Bret's eyes gleamed. "There was something inside?"

Her mouth fell open in a surprised 'O'. "Yes, how did you know?"

"Smuggling. Go on," he urged.

"When the vase broke, there was an ancient Egyptian scarab beetle among the pieces."

"A scarab..." Bret was frowning.

"What's more, the shopkeeper behaved distinctly perturbed and tried to hide it with his hand."

"What interests me is Sarah dropping the vase."

"You think she did it on purpose?"

"Yes, but what was it about this vase that aroused her suspicions that something was hidden inside? It's obvious she wanted to learn something and suspected strongly enough to test it by breaking it. Artifacts, opium...we already know the shopowner is into smuggling. So this information isn't surprising. What I want to know is if the vase fits in with the Egyptian doll Blaine gave Sarah."

"What do you mean? How could it fit in?"

"I can only guess. But if there was a gold scarab in the vase, there could be something of even greater value in the Egyptian doll."

Allison's breath paused. "Of course!"

"Sarah may have suspected someone was trying to find the doll but couldn't figure out why."

"So when the opportunity came, she dropped the vase!"

"The question then arises, why hasn't she searched the doll?" His eyes widened. "Because she doesn't know what Rex did with it."

348

"But," she protested in a low voice, "Rex gave it to her as a gift."

"Can we be sure of that?"

She frowned. "I see what you mean. Then—what did he do with it?"

"That's what everyone would like to know. You saw the doll. As an item goes, it's not all that valuable, is it?"

"It was a fairly good piece, but nothing worthy of a museum or the black market. Could Sarah have known of the scarab being in the vase?"

"We can only guess. She may have had her suspicions of smuggling. When she recognized the vase maybe—well, who knows? I think we've gone as far as we can without more facts."

"She hasn't mentioned it to me. Anyway, there was no time to discuss it. Tonight she told me about the intruder—and *that* makes sense now, too. The house was searched before the office was. And the intruder looked through chinaware and closets, and not in the general's desk among papers, because that is where one would find a doll."

"Well, obviously, if Sarah interrupted the intruder, he hasn't found it yet. Sir Edgar may think she knows where it's hidden."

"But how would he know about it?"

"He may have worked with Professor Jemal in Constantinople."

Jemal! She shuddered.

"An Egyptian doll," he said thoughtfully. "Where do you suppose Rex hid it?"

"Why don't I simply ask Sarah if she has a clue?" she whispered. "If I confront her—"

He was shaking his head. "No, dear, because all this is bigger than Sarah. And the more you get entangled, the greater the risk you take. Others are involved. Sarah is being watched and will lead the enemy to the bait."

She shuddered. "Like I was the bait for Rex Blaine as he hunted for the book at Aleppo."

Bret squeezed her slightly. "Not quite that dreadful. And Sarah won't be alone. We'll all be at Helga's. And that will present an opportunity for the trap to spring."

Her eyes searched his. Then that was why he decided to stay until after the holidays? Her heart thudded in disappointment.

"Try to remember, Allison. What was it Sarah asked the shopkeeper about? A vase for Blackstone?"

"No, not a vase...something about an object he said he didn't have, but that his son-in-law in Luxor might be able to hunt down."

"Luxor?"

"Bret, what could it mean?"

"I don't know, but I'm going to find out." He loosed his protective hold on her and leaned back, looking down at her with a slight smile. "Well, it looks as if the Egyptian doll now has two more who are interested in locating it."

"But what about Neith? Why was she was murdered? What would she have to do with all this?"

"Maybe it was an accident."

"You mean—she was in the wrong place at the wrong time."

"Something like that." He frowned.

"Then, that would mean the intruder was waiting for someone else?"

His frown deepened. "Earlier you mentioned the Egyptian driver Anwar...what about him?"

She told him about Anwar being Neith's son. "He took his father's job when he was killed in the Zeppelin bombing."

Bret's eyes narrowed thoughtfully. "His father? That's odd."

"Why is it odd?"

"I remember that driver who worked for Blaine. He was on our list. The department watched him for over a year. I don't remember if he had a family. If I'm right, he wasn't that much older than Anwar. I'll ask them about the two. Maybe they know something about them."

"You mean Neith's husband helped Rex in his work for Germany? Then that could explain her death—at least it might have something to do with it. She might not be the innocent victim in the wrong place after all."

"I do know she was lying about her husband being killed in the Zeppelin raid. No one in Cairo was killed. The previous driver disappeared after Blaine's death."

Allison's expression must have given her away, for Bret gave her a careful look. "There's something else?"

"It—it was Sarah who first told me the driver was killed in the bombing, which means she didn't tell me the truth. Because she told me she was in the motorcar when the Zeppelin attacked. And Neith told me the same thing. She also said Anwar was a student at the university majoring in archaeology."

"Archaeology?" His eyes rested on her, sympathy in their blue depths. "Yes. It looks dreadfully bad for poor Sarah, doesn't it?"

"But Bret! She couldn't be involved in anything Rex was doing. There must be a reason why she didn't tell me the truth."

Bret watched her, one finger rubbing his chin. "I think I made it clear that I don't underestimate what Sarah might know or what she's into. Whatever it is, something happened to convince her to change her mind about confiding in you when you arrived. Things have changed since she wrote you. Telling you of the intruder was more likely just part of what she knows."

Allison remembered the calishe that had come to Port Said for Sir Edgar.

Bret tilted his head, his eyes narrowing. "You're telling me everything you know, Allison?"

The soft question brought her eyes back to his. Her gaze faltered, then she turned away with a sigh. "No. Do you remember how I told you I thought the woman in the calishe who came for Sir Edgar was Helga? I don't see how it could be. I'm now almost certain the driver was Anwar."

He turned her around. "Anwar?"

"When I first arrived at the train station there was something familiar about him, but he was dressed differently and I didn't see it then. It wasn't until later that I recognized him. And there was a time when I caught Sarah watching him when his back was toward her. I've never seen such a look of dislike on her face before."

Bret fell silent, seemingly lost in his own thoughts. After a moment Allison whispered, "What is it, Bret? What are you thinking?"

He smiled. "Don't you think you've enough to worry about for one night? As a matter of fact, we both have." He looked at his watch. "It's after two. I think it's time we both got some rest. Dear old Edgar will be in the garden at the first glimmer of dawn, and I've got a lot to do between now and then. Come, I'll walk you to your room."

"Wait—you're not staying after all?"

Somehow the idea set her nerves on edge again.

"I'll be back here before Edgar." He touched her face gently. "Don't worry. Everyone else thinks I'm staying. That's half the effectiveness of having a good watchdog: convincing the thief he's awake." He smiled and opened the door into the hall. "Besides, David will be here."

Bret walked her to her room. He turned on the light for her, then made a careful search. He came out of the bathroom frowning. "That window—why isn't it fixed? I sent someone this morning."

"You did? Odd, no one came, but then we were out and maybe

352

Neith and Anwar had their reasons not to respond."

He drew it closed. "It's simple to fix. I'd do it myself if I had a screwdriver."

"Bret, it doesn't matter now. We'll be leaving tomorrow and the night is half over. You just said half the secret is convincing the thief I have a watchdog. Whoever killed poor Neith thinks you're staying overnight."

"Perhaps, but why don't you sleep in the office instead? There are locks on both doors *and* the window. I checked."

She shuddered. "And have the memory of Rex Blaine filling the room? Thank you, no. I prefer right where I'm at."

"All right," he said reluctantly. "There's no one in the bath or under the bed. And David is just downstairs. I'll be back soon."

She followed him to the door and smiled sleepily. "Thank you, *Colonel,*" she teased. "Good night."

Instead of leaving, he leaned into the doorway. "Even a watchdog gets a treat, or a good night pat on his head. Don't I get anything for all *my* endeavors?"

Her heart skipped a beat when his gaze dropped to her lips.

"I did give you something," she whispered, glancing toward Sarah's closed door and seeing the light under the crack. "I gave you information. Lots of it. You should be impressed with my intellect."

"Oh, I am." He smiled languidly. "I'm impressed with a good many things about you."

She smiled ruefully. "Good night, watchdog. I'll buy you a biscuit in the morning, I promise. Besides, you're going far, far away to France, remember? So there's hardly call for a kiss between us."

She made to push the door closed, but he lifted his palm and kept it from shutting. "You should know me well enough by now, dear Allison, to realize nothing is certain. Maybe I've changed my mind. About France—" his gaze dwelled on her face—"about a lot of things. I can be difficult when necessary—" he pushed the door open again, and his strong fingers closed on her wrist—"and I think this is necessary."

Before she realized what was happening, he drew her into his arms. "This is how you say good night properly," he whispered against her cheek and pressed his lips gently to hers.

His lips were warm; his embrace, wonderful…and she melted into his arms.

When he lifted his head, she was in a daze. The kiss may have lasted a moment or days, she wasn't sure. With a smile he stepped back, pulled the door closed behind him, and left Allison staring at the wood panel.

CHAPTER
TWENTY-THREE

>━┃━◆>━◉━<◆━┃━<

When my spirit was overwhelmed within me...
PSALM 142:3

ALLISON HAD NOT PREPARED FOR BED until long after she knew Bret had left Rex Blaine's office. He was so quiet, though, that she couldn't tell when he left the house, or whether he had even returned to sleep on the divan. She had lain awake for over an hour listening to the silent house, wondering if he were in the back garden, or whether he had gone into Cairo.

And she kept replaying, over and over in her mind, the kiss they had shared and the emotions that brief contact had sent washing over her. She closed her eyes, struggling with tears. She could no longer deny it to herself: she was in love with Bret Holden. If only she could be sure of what he felt toward her....

You know Wade's feelings, her heart whispered, and she was overcome with regret—and guilt.

It was true. Wade loved her, and he was open and clear about that fact. She'd thought for a while that she returned those feelings, but now...now she knew, though she held a great fondness and respect for Wade, she was not in love with him. Could not be, for her heart belonged—completely and solely—to another.

He's not a safe man to love! her heart cautioned, and she turned her head to let the tears roll down her face. No. Bret Holden was anything but safe. And yet, she could not deny how she felt.

God, what am I to do? If these feelings aren't right in your sight,

355

please…please take them away from me. But if I am right to love Bret, please help me to tell Wade in a way that he will understand and accept. I don't want to hurt him, Lord.

She lay there, thoughts and images roiling through her mind. Just before she drifted into an exhausted and weary sleep, she remembered the Egyptian treasure doll. Tomorrow she would confront Sarah about it.

The next morning, Allison awakened to a murmur of voices below her window, where the oleander bushes grew high and thick. The horror of the night before came rushing back. Someone had killed the Egyptian cook, and her son, Anwar, was missing. She listened carefully to the voices, recognizing Sir Edgar and his policemen. *They must be combing the area for any evidence of who might have killed Neith.*

Allison was anxious to leave this oppressive house, with its ugly memories. She wished she were already on the drive with Marra and Sarah to Helga Kruger's. But the afternoon wasn't that far off.

Her head felt dull from lack of sleep. A quick glance at the clock on the white cane spiral stand announced that she had overslept. It was after nine o'clock—by now Bret would be back from his late-night excursion into the garden and who knew where else. Had he been able to find out anything?

She rose and went to run her bathwater, glancing with distaste at the window with its rotting latch. Thank God nothing had happened. She wouldn't need to worry about getting it fixed now since tonight she would sleep in one of Helga's luxurious guest bedrooms. She would see her mother and father, Beth and Aunt Lydia—along with Cousin Edgar and Gilbert.

When she came down the stairs a bit later, sunlight poured in through the wide dining-room windows, and the back garden shone with lively green shrubs and late-blooming azaleas that seemed to laugh at the ominous darkness of the night before. She could almost believe it had all been a nightmare, until she caught sight of Sir Edgar strolling by in his rumpled white jacket and wide Panama hat. Sarah walked beside him, and she looked to be protesting. Edgar's bland face, of course, kept the door shut against any revealing emotions.

Cousin Edgar is certainly determined to harass people with his questioning, thought Allison, troubled. Was it because he thought he could break Sarah emotionally into betraying the location of the Egyptian treasure doll? Or was it possible they were wrong about him? What if he was not an enemy? Then who was?

"He's worse with her than a cat ferreting out a mouse."

Allison turned to find Marra in the dining room. She was wearing an apron, and apparently had been clearing the dining room table of breakfast dishes. She nodded toward the window, and the view it offered of Sir Edgar and Sarah.

Allison recoiled at the illustration she'd just given. What was it Cousin Edgar said in the library at Port Said? *"It is the German sympathizers I am obliged to ferret out from their nasty little rat holes."* He couldn't think Sarah Blaine was a sympathizer, or that she had murdered Neith, could he?

"He's been here since the first crack of dawn, he and two Egyptian detectives. By now they've swarmed over every inch of front and backyard."

Allison didn't reply, for she was watching Sarah through the window.

"I've kept your breakfast warm and just made another pot of tea," called Marra, "or would you prefer coffee? I'm playing chef till we leave for Baroness Kruger's."

357

Sir Edgar was walking away, and Sarah had turned to come into the house.

When Allison did not reply, Marra left the table and walked into the hall looking up at her.

Allison quickly came down the remainder of the stairs. "Just some tea, thanks." She followed Marra into the dining room, remembering the kitchen utensil missing from the backboard rack. "Did the police find anything in the garden?"

"David says not so much as a footprint. Strange, but it's as though someone came back in the gloom of night and used a broom. Ugh! The sooner we can leave here the happier I'll be. Doesn't seem like holiday time at all does it? And they still haven't been able to locate Anwar. If he wasn't her son, I'd think he was guilty."

Anwar was missing. Where could he have gone? "Then David and the colonel are here?"

"David is our bodyguard for the day," Marra said lightly. "Bret was here around dawn, but then went out again. He's asked David to bring us to Helga's. Your parents are there and asking for you. They're quite upset about what happened last night, as well they should be. I'm already packed, how about you?"

It would only take Allison a short time to pack her bags, but she wasn't thinking of that now—rather she was wondering where Bret had gone and why.

Marra had gone into the kitchen and returned now with the warmed-over breakfast. She frowned at it. "The eggs are shriveled up, I'm afraid. I never was much of a cook. At least have some coffee before David drinks it all. He's been up all night and is trying to stay awake."

"Is he here now?"

"Would I leave two lovely females all alone in harm's way?" said

358

David, walking in from the kitchen and giving Allison a wink. Seeing the platter of toast in Marra's hand, he stole another slice and spread it thickly with butter and jam.

"Men always stay around where there's food," said Marra wryly, looking at him. "It draws them worse than bees."

Allison smiled and sat down at the table, taking the pot and filling her cup. David set his cup down beside hers for a refill.

"You see?" said Marra.

"Cynical beast," accused David with a smile.

Allison smiled too and poured, and David took the stack of dirty dishes away from Marra. "To prove you wrong about hanging around for selfish motives, I'm going to be unconventional and wash these for you."

Marra laughed. "I don't believe it," and she watched, amazed, as David returned to the kitchen carrying the load. Marra lifted a palm to her forehead and followed as though in a daze.

Allison's smile faded and she was looking into her untouched cup of tea when she heard the door open. She turned to see Sarah walk quickly across the hall and up the stairs. A moment later her bedroom door shut firmly. Allison stood, looking after her, prepared to go up to see what was wrong, when Sir Edgar appeared from the drawing room.

"Good morning, m'dear Allison. That you're looking none the worse for last night cheers me. I would loathe thinking I had caused your health a turn for the worse." He removed his hat, holding it against his round middle, and came forward across the room, the floor squeaking beneath his oxfords.

"What's wrong with Mrs. Blaine?" asked Allison. "She seemed upset."

He sighed and lowered himself into the Queen Anne armchair in one small corner of the dining room where Sarah kept a table that held her daily mail. "Ah, that tea looks very refreshing. Would you mind?"

She poured, troubled to find her hands trembling.

"If Sarah is upset, its for another reason besides the death of her Egyptian cook," he said taking the saucer. "I rather feel like a bully."

Allison's brow lifted. "Do you, Cousin Edgar?"

He didn't miss her intent and smiled unbecomingly. He lifted the cup and took a big swallow, sighing with satisfaction. "Nothing like steaming tea to brace a fellow's worn spirits."

"Have you discovered anything new regarding Neith's death?"

"No, it's becoming a dead end, and I must say it's maddening. Perhaps the colonel will come up with a tidbit or two."

She said carefully, "I thought he was on medical leave and due for a transfer to France?"

"So he implied. He does seem anxious to be out of Cairo, doesn't he?"

She ignored the curious look in his eyes. If he wanted to know about her and Bret, he could jolly well ask someone else. "Yes, so it looks as if he won't be much help to you in locating whoever killed Neith. Would you mind telling me why Sarah is so upset?"

"I'm afraid I've insisted she remain here rather than stay at Baroness Kruger's over Christmas."

The idea was unfair, thought Allison, knowing how Sarah was troubled by depression during the holidays. She wondered if he had the authority to force Sarah to comply. Perhaps more disturbing was the reason why he might want her isolated in the house.

"Isn't that going rather a bit too far? You've no more reason to suspect Sarah of murder than me! Why trust me?"

"Maybe I don't," he said quietly, and when she stared at him shocked, he handed her his empty cup and pushed himself up from the chair. "I must be on my way. We're still looking for Anwar." His eyes hardened. "If he thinks he can hide in the Turkish quarter, he's mistaken. I'll find him eventually." He placed his hat on his head and picked up his cane and left the room.

Allison looked after him, alarmed for Sarah, but confused as well. Why would Cousin Edgar think Anwar was deliberately hiding from the police? It was much more reasonable to believe the young man would be outraged over his mother's murder and therefore cooperate with the authorities to find her slayer. Hiding implied he might have a legitimate cause to run.

She stood pondering all of this as the front door closed behind him. Something else he had said was odd, too: why would Anwar hide among Turkish acquaintances in Cairo? If there were any reason to run, wouldn't he choose his Egyptian relatives and friends? Unless Neith and her son were not of Egyptian blood. If that were true, it might tie both Anwar and his mother with Professor Jemal Pasha—and hadn't Neith proudly told her that her son was an archaeology student? Would Anwar have had an opportunity in the past to associate with Professor Jemal at Cairo, either at the university or the museum? After Rex's death at the archaeology huts in Aleppo, Jemal had fled to Constantinople, but Bret had said there was reason to think he may have returned to Cairo.

Allison shivered and glanced toward the stairway. Was there any connection between Jemal and Neith and her son? This was just one more question she must ask Sarah, along with finding out what she knew about the Egyptian treasure doll.

Marra had told her that Bret expected David to bring them to Helga's soon. That left little time to discover any information Sarah knew and then have it ready to pass on to Bret that evening at the first of Helga's holiday dinner parties.

With that in mind, Allison went upstairs to Sarah's room and tapped on the door.

A moment later Sarah's tense voice demanded: "Who is it?"

"Allison," she responded calmly. "We're leaving soon for Helga's. I must talk to you first."

Footsteps hurried across the floor and a bolt slid back, and the door opened wide. "Has that repulsive man gone?"

Allison's sympathy was stirred to life by her worried face. "Sir Edgar?"

"He's the only creature I know who's both odious and belligerent." She closed the door with a jolt. She twisted her hands together and paced. "He insists that I stay in the house. If I leave, he says he could claim I was trying to run away and will arrest me. Allison! I'm afraid!" She turned abruptly, her eyes wide.

"Sarah—don't, dear! You can't stay here alone, not after what's happened."

"He thinks I killed Neith, imagine! Therefore he thinks I'm not in danger from the murderer."

"We both know that's nonsense. I won't let you stay the night alone. If necessary—" she hesitated—"I'll stay with you."

Sarah looked surprised, then shook her head. "That's generous of you, but you've done enough in coming here. Look what I've done, got you caught up in a ghastly murder. Besides, neither Eleanor nor Marshall will allow you to stay now. You're even expecting Neal to arrive in time for Christmas, not to mention that handsome colonel staying as Helga's houseguest. I simply won't have it, even if Sir Edgar is impossible."

"Forget the colonel," Allison said breezily. "He'll soon be on his way to France anyway. And I won't have you a prisoner alone in your own house."

"What could Sir Edgar have in mind, forcing me to stay?" she cried. "What if that intruder comes back? He's looking for something he hasn't found yet, and he'll come again."

"Pull yourself together, Sarah, it's not going to be that way. I'll send word to my parents through Marra that I'm staying here for a few more days to keep you company. By then, surely Sir Edgar will let you come with me for the rest of the Christmas holidays."

Sarah looked hopeful for a moment, then sank to the edge of the bed. "Will they let you stay? I wouldn't blame them if they didn't." She looked toward the window. "That's the motorcar coming for you now."

Allison sat down calmly in the chair opposite her friend. "I'll explain about Edgar's unreasonable demands to my father. I'm sure there's something he can do."

"Do you think so?" she asked hurriedly, her eyes anxious. "Another night here alone in the house would make me terribly unsettled. How could he think I killed Neith? And all because he insists I arrived in the laundry room too soon. He can't prove I did! No one can—not even you. Even you don't know for certain the exact moment I arrived, do you?"

Allison looked into the strained pale face and felt her spine tighten. Sarah watched her from the edge of the bed, her brown eyes alert.

Allison felt the closeness of the bedroom around her. There were footsteps out on the landing followed by Marra's voice: "Allison? Mrs. Blaine? The chauffeur is here for our bags, do you have them?"

Allison looked away from Sarah to the door, then went to open it.

Marra was across the landing ready to tap on Allison's door. She turned. "There you are. We're soon to leave, are you and Sarah ready?"

Sarah was beside Allison, her cool hand tightly on her arm. "'Don't forget, you promised, I won't be able to stand it if you leave me here alone," she said in a low voice.

"Wait here," said Allison, "I'll explain to Marra."

"Please—don't let her talk you out of it."

Allison came out into the hall, closing Sarah's door behind her and walked over to Marra, who was looking toward Sarah's room with an odd expression. "What's wrong with Mrs. Blaine?"

"She can't leave yet," said Allison in a low voice. "Sir Edgar's orders. If she does, he's warned he'll arrest her."

Marra frowned. "He can't do that, can he?"

"I'm afraid the inspector general of the Cairo police can do pretty much what he wants. And I can't leave her alone. You saw how distraught she is."

"You're not staying!"

"Yes, but I've my reasons. Sarah knows something, and I'm going to find out what it is."

"Then I'm staying too, and David—"

"No, if you do, she won't be nearly as upset as she is now. She's afraid and on the verge of talking. All I need do is be here and I think I'll get the information Bret wants."

"Now, look here! You're out of your wits if you think David and I will leave you unguarded for the night! What if—" she dropped her voice quickly and whispered—"if the killer *is* Sarah?"

"It isn't. If I thought so I'd run out of here without looking back. Everything will be all right, Marra, just tell David to explain to Bret."

Marra glanced suspiciously toward Sarah's closed door. "What if something goes wrong and we don't see Bret at Helga's?"

Bret had told her he would be there. "Everyone knows where I am, including my parents. But if things go as expected, I'll have the information I want before tonight."

"Okay, but David isn't going to like this. And I've a feeling Bret will be even more upset."

"Right now I'm more worried about Sarah. I don't want to walk out on her."

A few minutes later Allison went to her bedroom window and watched the motorcar drive away. There were soft footsteps behind her and she turned, jumpy. Sarah lingered in the doorway, a watchful expression on her face. "Are they gone?"

"Yes, and so is Cousin Edgar. You look dreadful, Sarah, have you even stopped long enough to have breakfast this morning?"

"Who can eat at a beastly time like this? If Rex were here I can imagine what he'd say."

"Yes...well, you're going to eat now. We both are. And then we're going to have a long chat. There's some questions I want to ask you and this time I won't be put off."

"Now, Allison, I'm sure I don't know what you mean—"

"We're alone, and there's no one here to eavesdrop. I've a notion we're going to spend the day doing some housecleaning."

Sarah was quiet through the morning meal, and Allison watched her, musing.

"Sarah, how long have you known my cousin?" she finally asked.

"What?" Sarah looked up, blinking.

"Sir Edgar implied last night that he had known you in Burma where you worked with your father."

Sarah stood up and walked to the windows, pushing aside the sheer curtains. "I really don't care to talk about the past. It's such a pleasant day, let's walk in the garden, dear." Without waiting for an answer, she unlocked the door and stepped out into the late morning sunshine. "I don't think I'll ever get over celebrating Christmas on what would be considered spring weather in the English countryside."

Allison stood by the table. Sarah was being evasive, no doubt about it. But she couldn't exactly force information from her. With a sigh, she followed her out onto the patio. "Sarah, we've got to talk about the past. Neith's death is involved somehow, and it all ties together."

Sarah looked at her sharply. "Don't tell me you're accusing me of murder along with Edgar."

Allison noted the familiar address she used for Sir Edgar. "Of course not. But you do know Sir Edgar Simonds a good deal better than you originally told me. He's not a stranger to you at all. I think you knew him well in Burma—and I think Rex must have known him, too."

Sarah left the patio and took the flagstone walkway that led toward the back garden. Allison walked beside her.

"Yes I knew him," Sarah finally said. "That is, I was acquainted with Celeste, but it was Rex who was friendly with Edgar. He and Celeste would come over to the house and visit. We had one thing in common: we were discontented with our government positions. Neither Rex nor Edgar liked working in Burma, and Celeste became ill while there. I was rather used to the weather because I'd worked with my father and I didn't mind it as much. Eventually things were arranged and both Rex and Edgar were transferred to Bombay."

"Arranged?" Allison looked at her curiously. "By whom?"

"I don't know, actually. Friends in India. Later, Edgar and Celeste were transferred to Constantinople and we lost contact, or at least Celeste and I did."

"You mean Rex and Edgar did not? They stayed in touch?"

Sarah didn't answer immediately and paused to examine her flowerbed. "Roses in December...beautiful, aren't they?"

"Usually it's the women who stay in touch," said Allison, watching as Sarah removed a pair of snippers from her pocket and clipped a red rose.

"I didn't know Rex was communicating with Edgar," she admitted. "I didn't know until the summer of '14 when we went to the Aleppo huts with the Archaeology Club." Something about her admission seemed to make Sarah uneasy. She looked up from the rosebush and gave a glance ahead, down the garden path, as if she might have heard something.

"Why Aleppo?" asked Allison softly.

Sarah looked at her briefly and snipped another rose. "It was something someone said in passing. For a time I couldn't even recall who mentioned Edgar. The remark wasn't meant to be anything worth noting. I'm sure of that because the entire incident slipped my mind until recently. Then something happened to help me remember—but—but I don't think I ought to talk about it now."

"Not talk about it! You simply must, Sarah! You can trust me. I'm on your side. You must also think so or you wouldn't have asked me to come here. I think you wanted to tell me something more than about the intruder searching the house. What is it? Neith is dead, and we may well be in danger of our lives! You can't keep it to yourself."

Sarah dropped the garden shears on the Egyptian sundial and stooped to pick them up. She stopped, staring. Then straightened, saying, "Don't be silly, Allison. What's Neith got to do with this? She was struck by a burglar. It must have been an accident."

"That's not what Sir Edgar and the Cairo police think, and I don't think you really believe that, either. What was Neith doing in the laundry room after she told me she was going home? I even locked the kitchen door after her. Something happened between the time when she was leaving and when I heard someone up in Marra's room. She came back, not to the kitchen, but to the back-porch door. It was unlocked. Why? And what made her go in? Was the laundry room light on or off? It was off when I found her dead—but would Neith have gone inside if it was dark?"

"Maybe—maybe the light was on."

"Then who turned it on? And why?"

"It must have been the same intruder who's searched twice before. I told you—"

"An intruder turning the light on when he crept in the back door?"

"I admit it doesn't make much sense."

"It doesn't make *any* sense, Sarah. He would have left the light off, intending to creep up that flight of steps to the upper passage."

"Then—that's what happened. And poor Neith caught him in the act."

"That doesn't make any sense, either, because she wouldn't have come through that back door in the darkness. It took every ounce of courage I had to go down the steps last night. I wouldn't have gone at all except I thought that sprawling figure lying there was Marra."

Sarah's eyes came directly to hers. "What are you saying?"

Allison lowered her voice, though they were alone. A breath of wind stirred the leaves on the oleander bushes. "I'm saying something had to convince Neith it was safe to go inside the back porch in the dark."

Sarah lapsed into silence. There was a stone bench facing the goldfish pond and sundial and she went there and sat down suddenly, as though her legs had gone weak. The two red roses lay on her lap, and she clutched the garden shears so tightly her knuckles were white.

"Yes, I think you're right," she admitted. "And I've been too afraid to admit it to myself." Her voice tightened and Allison went to her quickly, sitting beside her. Leaning over, she searched her face.

"You heard someone mention Sir Edgar to Rex at Aleppo. Who was it and what did he say?"

Sarah stared at the garden shears glinting in the sunlight. "It was

Professor Jemal. He was talking with Rex. He said something like, 'Edgar Simonds knows we have it. He's arriving from Constantinople. He'll need to be included.'"

Allison stared at her. "Included in what?"

"I don't know. Maybe—maybe in what everyone seems to be looking for in the house. Anyway, Jemal and Rex were talking alone near the dining hall. They realized I'd walked up and stopped talking. Rex made some light remark and changed the subject. And well, I forgot all about it because it was soon afterward that Leah was found dead out at the Roman ruins. And now Edgar thinks I've got what he wants—and he thinks I killed Neith to keep it."

"He doesn't really think you murdered Neith, and neither does anyone else."

"I'm not at all sure of that. You saw how he forbade me to leave the premises and threatened to arrest me if I dare. He didn't order *you* to stay, or Marra. Why me? Because he thinks I'm guilty."

"Does he? Or is he merely trying to frighten you for some purpose of his own?"

Sarah's head turned sharply. "Why do you say that?"

"I don't now. I just have that impression," said Allison vaguely. She couldn't explain what Bret had told her at Ezbekiah Gardens. "Come, Sarah, the longer you hold back the complete truth from me, the more risk we both may face. Do you trust me or don't you?"

Sarah looked at her, studying her face carefully—until her own face suddenly crumbled into anguish and her eyes filled with tears. "Yes, I trust you, probably more than anyone else I've ever known except—except Rex...." and her hand went to her mouth to try to silence a sob.

"Oh, Sarah!" whispered Allison, taking the other hand into both of hers and squeezing gently. "I know a little how you feel about— Rex...." she bit her lip as Sarah's brown eyes rushed to hers again.

"How could you?" she whispered. "You don't even know what I'm so afraid of."

"I do know because—" Dare she tell her?

The wind came up and the weather changed quickly, bringing a December chill to what had been a sunny morning. Some dead leaves below the oleander bushes were blown away by the wind and scattered down the flagstone path until they formed a little mound near the scallop bricks that edged the ivy ground cover. The silence lengthened while Allison debated with herself.

Finally Sarah turned her head away and said quietly, "How could I live with a man so many years and not know he was into smuggling?"

This confession was the last thing Allison had expected from Sarah, and she looked at her blankly.

Sarah's weary gaze met hers, filled with the struggle of hiding the shame she felt. "That's the ugly little sin I wanted to talk to you about. Greed. I had always known Rex hated his work for the government, but I never realized how much he hated being a worker...how much he wanted to be a ruler. Now, as I look back, I can see the times when he turned the wrong corner and began his quest for money. At the time it happened I was too close to understand that it was eating away at him. Sounds odd, I know, but I could take a simple life so much easier than he. While he blamed the wealthy for everything wrong in the world, he did it in such a way as to sound humorously cynical most of the time. I never saw the venom that was beneath his demeanor. I think now he actually hated Helga. And as much as he liked you, I think he despised your father, too—and anyone else who gained power and wealth. That's why he liked Edgar. They would sit and feed each other with hateful words about the powerful who kept them down. And always it was the same—those who had money or position got it by cheating, lying, or stealing. He and

Rex could therefore justify taking advantage of them."

She lapsed into silence, and, looking down at the roses, lifted up their crimson heads. They were wilting, their heads drooping.

"How did you find out about the smuggling, Sarah?"

She thought for a moment before speaking. "It all began three weeks ago. I received a letter from Mr. Galli at the shop in Old Cairo telling me he had a wealthy buyer from Berlin. The man, I don't know his name, had come to visit before the war and was a private collector of ancient Egyptian treasures, though he was working for the kaiser. He was still here in Cairo, caught in the war, and while the British authorities knew he was here, they preferred to look the other way as long as they were assured he was staying out of politics."

Allison wondered if the buyer from Berlin might not be the industrialist who had worked with Helga's husband before he was killed in the train accident. There was some talk that the Berlin industrialist had been seeing Helga in private.

"Mr. Galli asked me to bring two items to him at the shop for the buyer to look at. One was a vase that Rex had bought, and the other was a replica of an Egyptian doll. I was surprised, of course, since the vase wasn't a museum piece. I didn't want to sell it since it was the last gift Rex had given me, but I've been having difficulty meeting my expenses and I do like to travel with the club. So I thought I would bring the vase to Mr. Galli, even if it didn't seem worthy of the interest of the Berlin buyer. The shop wrote me a receipt and I agreed to sell the vase because he offered me a surprisingly large amount. Now," she said uneasily, "I know why. While the vase itself wasn't valuable, its contents were."

So Sarah did know about the golden scarab. "But Sarah—that vase—Rex never bought it. I know, because I was there that day. True, he looked at it, but then changed his mind and bought the Egyptian treasure doll instead."

Sarah frowned. "Then Rex must have changed his mind again, because he gave me that vase before we went to Luxor to visit Lydia. I thought he was a dear to do it, and I put it away with the rest of my collection of Egyptian artifacts, though it wasn't rare, or even expensive."

"But the doll," Allison persisted. "I know he bought it for you because he asked me if you'd like it. I saw him pay for it at the counter."

"Odd...because what you're saying backs up Mr. Galli's insistence that I have the doll. And I tell you, I don't have it."

"You don't have it, Sarah? Are you certain?"

"Of course, dear! I'd know, wouldn't I, if Rex had given me a doll with the vase?"

"Yes, I suppose you would. But then, where is it?"

Sarah swallowed and paled. "That is what I think the intruder would also like to know. Allison, I think the search of the rooms in the house and Rex's office has to do with that doll. Someone thinks I have it, and I do not."

Allison felt her skin tingle from more than the chilling wind. The oleander bushes rustled.

"Sarah, you dropped that vase deliberately at the shop didn't you?"

"Yes. I had begun to suspect Rex had been involved in smuggling. Then, after the house was searched twice like that, I began to think there might be something suspicious about the doll the shopkeeper insisted Rex had bought. He was so adamant that I had it. He told me the buyer would pay a great deal for it. I told him I'd keep searching, but I was sure he was wrong. I knew if my suspicions of smuggling were right, that there could be something hidden in the vase. When you arrived and we went to the shop, I intended to tell Galli I had changed my mind about selling it."

"I remember. He insisted it was too late, that the buyer was coming to pick it up."

"Yes, and it was a great temptation to me to take the money and forget the matter. But I had to know the truth about Rex. So—I did the only thing I could think of—I dropped it. And when I saw the scarab, I knew the truth about Rex and his partners."

"Partners? More than one? Sarah...one of them could be the murderer." Allison stood, looking down at her friend anxiously.

Sarah glanced toward the oleander bushes. "Yes. Remember in Rex's office yesterday when you asked me if he'd been friendly with Professor Jemal? I'm afraid I didn't tell you everything. Jemal came here to the house on at least two occasions. They also met at the huts in Aleppo and at the Gezira Club, where Rex played polo. I saw them together a number of times, but I didn't think much of it. Why would I? Rex always made little insulting remarks about Jemal, and Helga, too. There was no reason to think they were involved in anything together."

Allison nodded. While Rex's insults about Jemal had been pretense, his remarks about Helga most likely were not. Rex had learned that Helga was working for the British and he despised her. Did Sarah know the general's crimes went far beyond smuggling for personal gain...to espionage? Somehow she didn't think so.

"Then Jemal was his partner," said Allison in a low whisper.

"I think so, and Sir Edgar, too. But Jemal hasn't been seen working at the Cairo Museum since Aleppo. No one has seen him."

"Bret told me last night that Jemal is known to have left Constantinople a few weeks ago. He may be in Egypt. And if he is, then he's come for whatever is concealed in the treasure doll."

"I—I thought of that. It was what I was afraid of when you arrived, and I didn't want you involved. But if he is here," she said quietly, "then why didn't Jemal pick up the vase at the shop for the buyer as planned?"

Yes, thought Allison. *Why hadn't he?*

Sarah frowned. "I'm convinced that neither the shopkeeper nor Jemal intended to have the vase sitting about the shop."

"I see what you mean," said Allison, troubled. "If Jemal didn't show up—then where is he?"

Sarah glanced about warily. "Did you hear anything?"

Allison turned her head toward the oleander bushes. "It's the wind. Maybe we should go back inside. It's getting colder."

Sarah stood quickly, as if suddenly afraid. The two limp roses fell to the ground. "Who besides Jemal would search the house?" she said more to herself than to Allison. "Who else might know about the Egyptian doll?"

At first Allison thought Sarah was thinking of Sir Edgar—he had known Rex in Burma and kept in contact with him after his transfer to Constantinople. Was that why Intelligence had arranged for Edgar to be appointed as the inspector general? Bret had said Sir Edgar was bait to lure someone out of cover, but other than Jemal or Edgar, who was there?

Allison didn't know, but she sincerely hoped they found out before it was too late.

TWENTY-FOUR

Treasures of wickedness profit nothing.
PROVERBS 10:2

ALLISON AND SARAH WALKED BACK from the garden and entered the house through the dining-room doors. Sarah turned and bolted the doors shut.

The entire house seemed to Allison to be too silent, as though inanimate objects were taking on a personality of their own and watching them.

"Shall I make some tea?" asked Sarah.

Allison glanced through the archway into the hall and toward the stairway leading up to Rex's office. Silence permeated the atmosphere like a fog. If only Bret were here!

God, help us, she prayed. *Please protect us. And help me not be so afraid.*

"Do not fear, for I am with you. Do not anxiously look about, for I am your God. I will strengthen you, surely I will help you. Surely I will uphold you with my righteous right hand."

The verse, one of her favorites from Isaiah, rang in her mind, washing over her, bringing her a sense of peace and confidence. Of course, she did not need to fear. "The angel of the Lord encamps round about those who fear Him and delivers them." If the worst should happen and she met with a violent death, her soul would be safe. Nothing could separate her from the love of God in Christ Jesus.

"Neither death, nor life, nor things present, nor things to come," she whispered. Even Satan stirring up the evil nature of his followers could not ultimately harm her. *I will not be separated from my redeemer. He is the Lord of the Resurrection. Then—what have I to fear?* she told herself, and her spirit lifted, encouraged as if by a refreshing wind.

"Allison?" repeated Sarah.

Allison looked at her, struggling to remember what Sarah had asked her. "Tea? Yes, lets! And then we've got to search for the treasure doll, Sarah. I've a feeling it will answer much. Including who killed Neith."

"It's no good," said Sarah wearily. "It's not here. I've looked everywhere. And so has someone else. If Rex hid it in the house, one of us would have found it by now. You saw his office. And I told you how every room has been gone through. They even searched my chinaware set." She looked toward the glassed hardwood cabinet, which was built into the wall.

Allison turned to study it but saw nothing unusual. Sarah's set of china was all in place, and the two bottom cupboards concealed nothing more interesting than some silver pieces in need of polishing and a couple of cookbooks, one from India, the other from England. Allison went to leaf through them—after Woolly's book and the secret unearthed by code at the Carchemish Digs, she couldn't resist searching books for clues—but there was nothing more interesting than Indian curry recipes and Dickens's English bread pudding. She laid the book down.

"Think, Sarah! You knew Rex as no one else did. If he concealed the treasure doll in the house, where might he have put it?"

"I've *been* thinking, I tell you. I don't have any notion where he would have put it. We've no cellar, and I can't imagine a loose floorboard somewhere or a secret cubbyhole in the wall." She shook her head. "I'll go make the tea." She started for the kitchen, then paused.

"Did you say Marra would return with the colonel and David?"

"Yes, before nightfall. We've got to find the doll by then, which I think we will now that we know what we're looking for."

"*Do* we know what we're looking for?" asked Sarah with a frustrated scowl.

"Why of course we do—" Allison stopped. Maybe Sarah was partly right. Although she had seen the doll replica at the shop, Sarah had not. At least, she said she hadn't, and Allison had no cause to disbelieve her.

Allison remembered what she had been curious about the night before and walked over and stood in the doorway of the anteroom. She stared up the flight of steps to the passageway. Had it been Neith who turned the light on in Marra's room, then opened and shut the bathroom door, making her think it was her? Or had it been the killer? Had he been trying to lure her upstairs with evil intent? Perhaps Neith's unexpected arrival had actually protected her by distracting the intruder's attention. But why would anyone wish to harm her?

"My times are in thy hand," she quoted from Psalm 31:15. It was the same verse she had claimed before going to Kut.

If I wasn't afraid then, why should I be now?

"Sarah, that door…the one between Marra's room and the bath. Is that a storage closet?"

Sarah came up beside her. "Yes, a walk-in closet. Rex had it put in for me soon after we bought this house. It was one of the first places I looked. There's nothing there. Just some linens that belonged to my mother. Some photographs, a few other odds and ends, and a trunk."

"A trunk?"

"It used to hold the things we brought from Bombay when Rex retired. He kept his sword in it. And a brevet he won for bravery once." She sighed, remembering. "He was so proud of that medal. He used to keep it on the wall in the office when we lived in India." Her face shadowed. "He really did change, Allison. He grew so sarcastic about the British government. He used to say they didn't really care about his service for the country, that awarding a medal was a cheap way to pay a soldier off while they kept the booty."

Allison remembered his anger that night in the hut. "Medals are never cheap," she commented gravely. "Any soldier awarded one deserves the respect and care of those he fought for."

"That's what I told him, but my wit was never a match for his in a debate. He'd win every time with cynical humor." Sarah looked at her thoughtfully. "You know, you ought to show more pride about Colonel Holden being up for the Victoria Cross."

Allison felt her face flush and looked away. She *was* proud. She just wasn't comfortable showing it. "Bret doesn't belong to me in the way Rex belonged to you, Sarah. I've no right to show pride."

"Well, he certainly doesn't belong to Cynthia Walsh."

"He doesn't belong to anyone," Allison said, her tone flat. "Now, that trunk you mentioned, did you look inside it?"

"At once, but nothing was missing, even though my collection had been gone through."

"What collection?!"

"Oh, not exactly a collection, but a glass menagerie. Just some Egyptian pieces I've gathered since belonging to the Archaeological Club. None of them are valuable. I hadn't thought about it until now, but I suppose I could bring something to the club auction. Though if any buyer placed a bid, it's likely to be done more out of charity than professional interest."

"Was the trunk broken into?"

"No, it was already open. I lost the key years ago. Like I said, dear, if Jemal is the culprit, he must have been disappointed.

Anyway, he didn't take a thing."

Allison was far from satisfied. "Let's have another look anyway. Would you mind?"

"Of course not. It's why I asked you here. You're so clever."

Allison gave a contradictory laugh, but she was pleased Sarah had faith in her.

They climbed the steps, Sarah in the lead, and when they came to the middle of the landing, she held back. Allison looked at her and saw her mouth tighten with strain. "I never liked this part of the house, but I can't explain why. There's no logic to my dislike."

"Well, there is now," Allison replied, thinking of Neith's body.

Sarah grimaced, then shook her head sadly and went on.

Despite the sunny morning and the daylight pouring in through the windows in the dining room, here on the upper level the doors were all closed and the narrow passageway was dim. Allison glanced toward the opposite end where the flight of steps led down to the laundry room and back porch. Had it only been last night when she heard something and found Neith's body? It seemed like days...weeks!

Sarah opened the door of the storage closet. Darkness and the smell of moth balls came to meet them.

"I always keep a lantern here," said Sarah, taking the box of matches from a shelf and lighting the wick. A moment later a glow filled the closet, and Allison saw a small, ornate black trunk of Far-Eastern design, carved with birds in flight and cherry trees in blossom. Sarah pulled it out and, stooping, lifted the lid.

"Everything's here," she said a moment later. "The entire menagerie is worth less than five hundred pounds. Hardly anything worth smuggling. Certainly nothing worth poor Neith's life."

Allison carefully examined each item. There were ceramic replicas of mummy dolls and some small animal idols: a scarab, a frog, a leopard, and a brass cobra head with onyx eyes.

"Rex always had an interest in cobras," apologized Sarah, seeing Allison grimace.

"Yes, I remember...."

Sarah paused, looking in the trunk, and her brow puckered. "That's odd. Here's another cobra head, but it's broken. This isn't part of the menagerie. I wonder why he put—" she stopped, frowning.

"What's odd about it?" Allison dropped her voice to a low whisper for no reason except that the room made the back of her neck prickle. She glanced behind them toward the passageway. When she looked back at Sarah, she was removing her hand from her pocket.

"It's nothing. It just doesn't belong with the collection," Sarah was saying, her tone bland. "Here, I want to show you this—" and she drew out a short sword and a medal. "From his service in India," she said proudly.

Allison was silent, her interest not on the major general's old days in India but the broken cobra head that Sarah had slipped into her pocket. A slithering sensation of foreboding fed her imagination. Sarah's secrecy was unnerving. Should she confront her here and now, or wait and see what she did?

Wait...

The sensation was strong and convincing. She would wait. Afraid Sarah might guess that she now looked on her with suspicion, Allison stood as if disinterested.

"Well, you were right, Sarah. There's nothing here that even resembles an Egyptian treasure doll. I suppose we should look through the closet again anyway, just to be sure."

As Sarah closed the lid, Allison made a pretense of continuing the search. After a few silent minutes, Sarah groaned, placing her hands against the small of her back. "We're wasting time, dear. It's getting close to luncheon. Why don't you look through Marra's room while I go down and make some sandwiches. There's still some chicken left."

Allison watched her leave, going down the steps to the dining room. She stood a moment longer debating, then followed to the landing and looked below where the anteroom, which connected to the dining room, was masked with uncertain shadows. Sarah's footsteps died away.

She had no reason to search Marra's room now, since she was sure the cobra knob was a key to what they were looking for. Removing her shoes, she came down the steps cautiously. With all her heart she hoped she was wrong about Sarah.

Once below in the anteroom, she could look into the dining room and straight through to the swinging doors that opened into the kitchen. She listened, uncertain which way Sarah had gone.

A board creaked overhead. Then Sarah *had* gone up to her room, but Allison thought her ears must have played a trick on her for just then she heard sounds coming from the kitchen. If Sarah knew something about the cobra knob, she appeared in no hurry to disclose it. Had she mistaken Sarah's interest? It was possible she had kept it simply because, as she had stated, it didn't belong with her Egyptian menagerie. Then where did it belong? If only she could have gotten a closer inspection before Sarah put it in her pocket.

Feeling a little ashamed about her suspicions, Allison walked into the drawing room, looking about at the knobs on the furniture, but nearly certain she wouldn't find a hideous cobra. Sarah had better taste than that!

If Professor Jemal and Sir Edgar had been partners in smuggling and espionage with Rex Blaine, it was strange how neither of them had gone to the merchant shop to retrieve the vase with the gold scarab hidden inside. Wouldn't they have been anxious to have it in their clutches? From what she'd seen of it, the scarab was worth a

tremendous amount of money on the black market. And thinking
back to when she was there with Sarah and Marra, hadn't the shopkeeper seemed apprehensive that no one had come for the vase, as
though the so-called "buyer" were overdue?

Allison shook her head. There were so many questions still
unanswered…who was the intruder? What was he looking for? Was
Sarah innocent? Where was Anwar? Was Jemal in Cairo? Even
worse, was he the murderer…?

She went to the Queen Anne armchair in the corner and sank
down, musing. She remembered how Cousin Edgar had sat here
earlier that morning and also pondered and gazed out the window
into the garden. Bret, too, had asked about the garden the night he
came and took her out to the dance at Ezbekiah Gardens. Allison
frowned. What was it about the garden that aroused such interest?

Soon Marra would return with David and Bret. She would stay
calm and wait. It was daylight, she reminded herself, and she and
Sarah were safe. And as Bret said last night in Rex's study, no one
was likely to harm Sarah, not as long as whoever murdered Neith
believed she knew where the general had hidden the doll.

She became aware that a cloud had overshadowed the sun and the
garden was no longer sunny and inviting. Was it going to rain again?

Allison sat musing so deeply that it was several minutes before
she became aware of the dense silence.

She stood and walked through the swinging door into the
kitchen, expecting to see Sarah standing at the sidebar preparing
sandwiches or adding tea to the pot. But she was not there. The
water was boiling, the bread was sliced, and there was a white
porcelain platter of carved chicken breast, but no Sarah Blaine.

Allison went back through the dining room arch into the front
hall and called up the stairway: "Sarah?"

There was no answer. Her already-tense nerves grew tighter, and her heart began to race. She went back to the kitchen and looked around. Her eyes widened. The back door was ajar. Could Sarah have stepped outside for a moment? But why?

Allison turned off the flame under the kettle and went out through the door.

A thick overgrown wisteria sprawled overhead along an arbor. A wooden walkway led to the side of the house where Anwar usually parked the motorcar. Allison followed the walkway until she came to where it branched left into the garden, hearing the wind in the vine. What had prompted Sarah to come outdoors?

Hurrying across the yard, she headed toward the untrimmed oleander bushes that encircled the flagstone court where Sarah's rosebushes grew. The white stone bench where she and Sarah had sat an hour ago was empty, and the wind scattered pink-and-white flowers across the stone. If Sarah had come this way, she had left again.

"Sarah?"

She listened for her footsteps and heard the bushes moving instead. Then something gleamed on the flagstone near the stone birdbath. Allison picked up the pair of gardening shears that Sarah had used earlier to clip roses. The roses, too, were still lying there, wilting, the petals looking like bright red stains on stone.

Footsteps. Sarah must be coming, she thought and turned toward the oleander bushes moving in the breeze.

"Allison?"

Allison was startled by the voice, for it didn't come from the direction where she'd first heard the footsteps. She must have been mistaken, because the footsteps came again, this time sounding confidently along the walkway from the back kitchen door. Only the voice wasn't Sarah's.

Allison turned her head and saw a woman standing there, perhaps twenty feet away, a tall willowy figure fit for a model, her short blonde hair ruffling in the wind. Marra was alone.

Relief flooded Allison's heart at the sight of her friend.

"What are you doing, Allison?"

Allison snatched up the roses from the walk and hurried toward her. "Is David with you?"

"No, he went on to find Bret. They'll both be here for dinner."

"You shouldn't have come back."

"It seemed wise. I don't trust your friends," she said wryly, "including Mrs. Blaine." She looked at the wilted roses and wrinkled her nose. "Not thinking of dressing up our dinner table with those? They're beastly! Let's go back and pick some fresh ones—"

"Let's not," and Allison tossed aside the two roses, aware how Marra watched her. "You're allergic to flowers, remember? I didn't think you'd be here."

Marra shrugged. "Where's Sarah?"

Yes, where *was* Sarah?

"She must be in the house," said Allison, hiding her concern. How had Sarah gotten past her in the dining room?

"Not unless she's in her room. I called out when I arrived and no one answered."

Allison made no comment. As they walked toward the house she had a vague sensation that they were being observed, but she didn't want to look up at the windows and give away that she was aware of anything. It was only Sarah, she was sure. Somehow she had gone up to her room without Allison hearing her. But that didn't satisfy... why had the kitchen door been ajar?

"You look on edge," commented Marra. "Well, I can certainly understand why after last night. Please tell me nothing else happened while I was gone."

"Not really, I just can't find Sarah," she said casually, not wanting to cause a stir if she had gone up to her room—or Rex Blaine's office. If she had, by now Sarah would have discovered something about the cobra knob! *I let her slip away from me,* she thought, irritated with herself. What would she tell Bret?

"Can't find her? You mean she left the house?" asked Marra curiously.

"No, I don't think so. She'd be afraid of a confrontation with Sir Edgar. He meant it when he ordered her to stay within the confines of the house."

"He's an odd one, isn't he? I can't figure him out. It doesn't seem to me he's done much to find out who killed Neith. He's wasting time cornering Mrs. Blaine, but she's behaving strangely, too. Can't say I blame her, though. Not with Sir Edgar accusing the poor woman of murder."

Allison followed her into the kitchen and came to a halt. Sarah was arranging sandwiches on the platter, and the teapot was draped with a cozy. She turned, her eyes bright. "There you are, Allison. I was wondering where you'd gotten to. I thought you might have picked some roses for the dinner table tonight. We've guests coming—a number of them. You'll never guess! Oh—thanks for bringing my shears in. I wondered where I'd left them."

Sarah picked up the platter and carried it through the swinging door into the dining room. Marra reached for the teapot and cups, giving Allison an arched brow as she went out.

Allison stood there, surprised, then followed.

They walked through the kitchen into the dining room, and Marra set the platter on the table, pulling out a chair next to Sarah and sitting down.

Allison started to pull out a chair as well, then froze. There were footsteps approaching. Her eyes flew to Marra. "Was anyone else with you a moment ago?"

"No," she breathed, clearly startled.

Allison tensed, and just then, Gilbert walked in from the drawing room, immaculately and modishly dressed. He smiled when he
saw Allison.

"Oh, it's you," she said, but her relief soon turned to impatience
when his eyes danced with ironic humor.

"Don't tell me I frightened you?" he taunted, looking from her to
Marra, then Sarah. Allison glanced at the others. Marra looked surprised and bothered by Gilbert's appearance, but Sarah looked relieved.

She turned back to see Gilbert's sleek black brows shoot up.
"Why is everyone tiptoeing about the house? Expecting the murderer
of the old Egyptian cook to come popping out of the woodwork?"

"What are you doing here?" asked Allison, perturbed by his glib
manner. She'd been through too much to put up with his prankish
nature.

He gestured into the drawing room. "Dear Cousin, we've been
waiting for you."

We?

"Why aren't you at Helga's with the rest of the family?"

Gilbert sighed, his boredom evident as he deliberately looked
about. "Fortune's smile is often filled with the unexpected. There's
been a change in plans, thanks to you—" he gestured toward the
drawing room again—"and someone is ghastly disappointed."

Beth came into the room to stand beside him, her young face in
a scowl. "You've simply ruined the holidays, Allison."

Allison, caught utterly off guard, frowned. "I have? But why?"

"Because! We're not going to Helga Kruger's, after all." Beth's
voice was stiff with disappointment. Then she seemed to become
aware of Sarah, and her gaze faltered. She turned and went back
into the drawing room.

Allison followed, Gilbert just behind. "Don't let her make you
feel badly," he whispered, but Allison paid him no heed. He closed

the door for privacy, and she faced her sister, who sank moodily onto the champagne-colored divan.

"Mum's ordered us all *here* of all places," whispered Beth, glancing toward the closed double doors.

Allison stared at her, certain she could not have heard correctly. "Here? There's not enough bedrooms."

"That's what I told Mum, but it didn't matter. She said she was going to stand by Mrs. Blaine until Daddy comes to her rescue." Beth looked accusingly at Gilbert. "Shame on your father for keeping Mrs. Blaine here. Why, she's practically *quarantined!*"

"For murder, dear Beth. Hardly a light ailment," he lectured.

"So we spend Christmas with a murder suspect? Hideous!"

"Don't be silly, Beth!" Allison scolded impatiently. "And don't let Sarah hear you speaking so rudely."

"I won't, but it's awful. And it's *your* fault. If you'd come to the baroness's house as you were supposed to, Mum wouldn't feel it necessary to come here and keep a watch on you."

"Ah, guardian angels," said Gilbert. "You've more than enough now, Allison. But Beth is right." he looked about. "This place is about as stylish as a Turkish peasant house. Here I was looking forward to staying in the mansion of the Berlin baroness. Ah, dear old Dad," he commented dryly. "What a spoilsport he is. I wonder if I can get him to leave poor Mrs. Blaine alone. Anyone with any sense knows she wouldn't have whacked the old maid on the back of the noggin like that."

"Mum will be here soon," said Beth. "I can't guess where we're all supposed to sleep."

"On the floor, from the looks of it," Gilbert said. "We'll camp out. Dad used to camp in Thebes when he was a museum curator. He was a grave robber. Him and Jemal Pasha."

"What a boring Christmas this will be." Beth looked about dismally, and Allison thought her sister actually fit in very well with the depressing atmosphere of the Blaine house. "There's not even a sprig of pine or a red bow."

Gilbert struck a match and lit a sleek cigarillo. "And naturally, my precious, a sprig of pine and a tart red bow is what Christmas is all about." He gave a laugh. "And your old Aunt Lydia thinks *I'm* the materialistic hottentot, Tot."

Beth folded her arms, grimacing. "Do put that out, Gilly, it smells horrid."

"Get used to all my odious ways, darling. You want to marry me, remember?"

Beth's cheeks turned pink and she shot a glance at Allison to see her reaction.

Allison looked at her evenly. So she'd been bold enough to already let Gilbert think she was in love with him!

"We'll camp wherever we can find a spot to curl up," said Gilbert, and turned himself about. "Be sporting, Beth darling, it will be jolly fun. I've an idea hatching already to frighten the wits out of everyone. Dear old Santa is coming early down the chimney wearing the murderer's mask and carrying a weapon!"

Beth leaped to her feet. "Oh, Gilly, do stop! I don't think this is a *bit* amusing. Murder certainly isn't. I'm miserably disappointed. I wanted to spend the holidays in the mansion."

Gilbert slid both arms around her waist. "As did I, my sweet, but just think—if we can solve the murder, then Mrs. Blaine can leave the house and we'll join the baroness for the merry ball after all. Now smile prettily...that's it—" and he bent his head and planted a kiss on her lips.

Disgusted by this display, Allison cleared her throat meaningfully. Beth seemed oblivious to Allison's presence and gazed up at Gilbert, adoration written on her face.

Allison scanned Gilbert dubiously. "If my mother is coming, you'd best learn to watch your words of endearment—" she fixed him with a glare—"*and* your stolen kisses. She'll box your ears for kissing Beth like that."

Gilbert turned his head and smiled, and his gaze wandered over her. "Did you call that a kiss?"

The boyishness had fled his face, replaced by an expression that made Allison's skin crawl. She met his bold gaze coolly. The brat! She looked at Beth, but her sister hadn't seemed to notice any change in him. Clearly, she was utterly taken up with his dashing charms. *Infatuation is blind,* thought Allison.

"Anything you say, Cousin. Come along, Beth," Gilbert said cheerfully, "I'm famished." On his way out he stopped in front of the large windows and peered out. "After luncheon we'll see what we can do about picking some greenery for Christmas decorations. Looks like Mrs. Blaine has a big garden anyway."

After lunch Gilbert commented on the changing weather. "Looks like rain. Anyone for a stroll before it's too wet? If you don't mind, Mrs. Blaine, Beth wants to gather some greenery and flowers to brighten the rooms up for a holiday mood."

"I think that's a fine idea. I've some baskets on the back porch you can use, and some extra shears."

"Want to come with us?"

"I don't think so dear boy. You two young people run along."

"Coming Beth?" he asked.

Beth glanced at Allison, and she smiled and nodded. "Go ahead. I think Gilbert's right; it will rain soon. Better hurry if you want to decorate tonight."

Gilbert winked at Beth and, taking her hand, led her out into the hall where he took her hat from the hall tree and put it on her head. "You see? We'll make Christmas a jolly affair after all."

Allison watched him leave, aware that her sister looked happy and in love. Gilbert, too, at times, appeared tender and protective. Maybe he would grow into the family after all, she thought, then remembered Sir Edgar and was troubled. Bret was certain Edgar was involved in smuggling. Aunt Lydia was right: Gilbert was a young man in much need of prayer and help. From now on, she would try to be more tolerant and helpful. Perhaps she could even help Gilbert find the right and good path.

They heard Beth's laughter and then the kitchen door shut behind them. In the silence that followed, Sarah said: "That's the first laughter this house has heard in a year."

The sky grew more overcast, and Allison went over to the lamps and lit them one by one, pausing to look out the window into the back garden. Beth and Gilbert were walking hand in hand toward the red blooming roses. Afternoon shadows were falling over the oleander bushes and the sundial was darkened. A pigeon flew away from the birdbath as Gilbert approached with Beth, and he sat down on the bench while she clipped the roses and he held the pale wicker basket.

She swallowed, her throat tight, thinking of Bret and how he would soon willingly be transferred to France. Perhaps she would never see him again after that. As Beth and Gilbert laughed and talked, Allison's thoughts turned to Wade. It would be good to see him again. She needed a friend....

She turned from the window, forcing what she hoped would be an optimistic smile. "If my mother is to arrive soon, and Bret and David, I think I'll light the rest of the lamps."

"You're right," said Marra, but she wasn't smiling. "I'll light the lamps near my room and on the back porch. And I'll make sure the door is locked this time."

Sarah, too, disappeared, murmuring something about finding Gilbert in the garden and asking him and Beth if they would go into Cairo to shop for the things they would need for supper and the extra guests.

Allison walked into the front hall and lit the lamp by the stairs, then looked up to the landing. She paused, thinking. Where had Sarah gone when Allison thought she was in the garden? If she had remained in the house, why hadn't she answered when she called up the stairway? Had Sarah deliberately wanted her to think she was outside?

Allison slowly climbed the stairs, then paused midway. What could the cobra-head knob have meant? Why had Sarah hidden it from her? Had it simply reminded her of something more unpleasant and vaguely familiar? Allison wracked her brain for some clue, some idea that would help explain things...when she remembered something.

In Aleppo, after it was believed that Major Karl Reuter had been killed by a cobra bite, the general had lapsed into a discourse at the dining-hall table about the reptiles. Sarah had shuddered...and what had she said to him? Allison couldn't remember the exact words, of course, it had been too long, but she was sure it had been something along the lines of "Don't you ever bring one of those things home for your odd collection of creatures."

Allison stared at the closed door of Rex Blaine's office. If the general had owned a live collection of reptiles, Sarah would have gotten rid of them by now, but she didn't think that was what Sarah had meant about his "odd collection of creatures." Then what *had* she meant?

Perhaps nothing. Still, Allison couldn't help but wonder. She moved toward Sarah's room. Sarah was downstairs....

She slipped inside, turning on a lamp. A quick glance about

proved futile in coming up with brass cobras. She looked at the closed door into Rex's office and consider entering, but refrained with a shudder. She switched off the lamp and went back to the landing. Her own room waited, and the door was open a few inches. Odd, hadn't she left her door shut?

She tensed. Earlier, before Marra, Gilbert, and Beth had arrived, when she thought Sarah was in the kitchen making lunch, she had heard a floorboard creak upstairs. Sarah couldn't have been in both places at once! Was someone in her room?

She crossed the landing and pushed her door open but did not go inside. The room was dimly lit and she saw the outline of her bed, the vanity table, and the door leading into the bath.

The wind rattled the unlocked window with its rotting latch. She stood without moving, alert, then heard the same floorboard creak beneath someone's shoe. A cry died in her throat when a handsome colonel in uniform, his jacket slung over his shoulder, turned to look at her.

For a moment their gazes held. Allison feared her knees would buckle, but something in his expression strengthened her resolve, and she drew in a breath instead and walked in, closing the door behind her and slipping the bolt shut. She stepped forward, clutching the wooden newel on the bedpost with both hands.

He smiled. "You still haven't gotten the window fixed. Of course, I shouldn't complain. How else could I come and go with such ease?"

Allison stared at him in confusion. "Come and go?" she echoed, frowning slightly. Then understanding dawned, and her frown grew fiercer. "It's been you! All those creaks and squeaks and bumps in the night that have kept me on edge." She crossed her arms, schooling her features to be as scolding as possible. "You're the Haunt of Blaine House."

His smile was broad and lazy. "I confess it, you are right." He waggled his eyebrows. "And may I just say, what an utter delight it has been to haunt you, my dearest Allison."

CHAPTER

TWENTY-FIVE

>—!—‹♦›—☉—‹♦›—!—≺

The desire of the righteous will be granted.
PROVERBS 10:24

ALLISON SMOTHERED THE GRIN that threatened to break out over her face. The relief at finally knowing the source of her fears was intense—but not nearly so intense as the pleasure she felt from the realization that Bret had been here all along, watching over her.

Even if he had scared her silly in the process.

"Well, sir," she began, hoping she sounded sufficiently reproachful, "I hope your haunting days are over. I've had my fill of creaking floorboards." She fixed him with a mock glare. "After what I've been through, you should be quite happy I don't carry Sarah's Luger about with me."

"You're definitely right about that," he said wryly.

Allison sank to the ruffled chair beside the dressing table. "I've learned a number of interesting things, if you're going to be around long enough to hear them, Colonel."

"If that's a gentle rebuke, *dear,* you can sheathe your claws. I've been busy uncovering a number of interesting facts myself. I think we have our reason for Mrs. Blaine's dislike of Anwar." Allison sat up with interest, and he smiled. "He's Jemal's son, not Neith's. They both worked for him keeping an eye on Sarah."

"Jemal's son! But then, why would he kill Neith if she worked for him as a spy in Sarah's house?"

"Good question. Maybe he didn't. And now David tells me Sir

395

Edgar is refusing to let Sarah leave for Helga's, and you've decided to stay with her. That was a good idea, so I've built on it. Helga and the others will join you in Sarah's happy little house, including yours truly."

"So you're the one who arranged for the spoiling of Christmas plans at the Kruger mansion." She shook her head. "You have Beth quite upset with me, you know."

"Your father agreed with my idea, though, and whispered in your mother's ear. But cheer up, if things go well, we'll soon all be out of here. I hope."

Allison managed a smile, leaning back in the chair. She hadn't realized how utterly exhausted she was until she was alone and resting. But all was well. Bret was here; there was nothing to fear now. "Things should go well, as long as you're here to keep an eye on Sir Edgar. Are you coming downstairs to dinner?"

"I wouldn't miss it. Helga is coming. We have something planned to help entice greedy appetites."

"Helga?" she said surprised. "Does your plan have anything to do with the shop?"

"Yes, but I want you to wear a poker face tonight. Don't say a word." He wagged a finger at her. "I expect you to be on your best behavior, my dear."

"I always am," she retorted smartly.

He cast her a wry look. "That's debatable. I wouldn't call discovering bodies and getting mixed up in mayhem behaving oneself, would you? When you left the German Zeppelins for Cairo, I didn't think you'd walk into a murder." He regarded her carefully, and she felt a shiver go through her at the expression in his eyes. "What is it about you, dear Allison, that invites calamity?"

She gave a not very ladylike snort. "You're a fine one to talk. As though the dangers you've already faced and survived, by God's grace, weren't enough, you're all set to go to France. And you'll probably end up buried there."

He smiled slowly. "We'll talk about France later. Now, tell me what you learned from Sarah. Do you mind if I stretch out?"

"By all means, make yourself comfortable, Colonel!"

"Always a nurse at heart. Ah..." he piled the pillows behind his head, then sniffed the pillow case. "Nice. Midnight in Arabia?" he jested.

Allison stood abruptly. "No." She walked to the lamp and switched it on, then folded her arms and looked down at him. "Do you want to hear what I know or not?"

"But of course."

"You don't seem very insistent. I could almost think you already know everything."

"Would I keep anything back from my lovely and brilliant partner in espionage?"

"Yes," she said wryly, "you would. Nevertheless, *I* shall be faithful and tell all."

"Pull up a chair. You have my devoted attention. The only thing missing from this delightful encounter is a hot cup of coffee."

Indeed, that would be nice—to dump on your too-smug head, Allison thought tartly as she drew a chair beside him and began to talk. Minutes later, she drew her tale to a close with recounting the discovery of the cobra knob among Sarah's Egyptian menagerie.

"A cobra," he said tapping his chin, his eyes half closed.

"Yes. She pretended it wasn't important, but I'm sure it must have had something to do with the Egyptian doll. She slipped it in her pocket just before we left the closet. I was going to follow her, to see what she did with the knob, but she went into the kitchen to make tea—at least, I thought she did."

"She didn't, then?"

"I'm not certain. It was all rather confusing."

"Deliberately so, is my guess."

"I heard her in the kitchen, but I also heard someone walking quietly upstairs where we are now."

He showed alertness for the first time. "What time was that?"

"Around eleven o'clock."

He got up, a slight frown on his face and walked to the window, hands in his pockets.

Allison looked at him uneasily. "Then it wasn't you."

"No, I arrived after your sister and cousin."

"They weren't here then, either."

He looked over at her gravely. "Go on. Then what?"

"I called upstairs but she didn't answer, and when I went to the kitchen, the back door was ajar and she was gone. She wasn't outside. I went to look for her, and while I was out there, Marra arrived."

His expression grew even more sober. "Tell me about that cobra head. You say it was a knob of some sort? What did it look like exactly?"

"I'm afraid I can't say. I should have gotten a better look at it, but it all happened so quickly. I guess I should have been more aggressive."

A smile tugged at his lips. "Somehow I can't picture you being the aggressive sort...at least, I hope not."

"Be serious, please."

"I am always serious. Did the cobra look like a treasure...say from a pharaoh's tomb?"

"A pharaoh's tomb!" She laughed. "An antiquity? No! It didn't look valuable at all."

"Yet you said it was interesting. Why?"

She told him about the major general's remarks at Aleppo and what Sarah had said. Bret considered this but said nothing.

"You've been all over this house," he said after a moment. "Have you seen anything remotely resembling a cobra collection. We'll settle for either live or dead."

"No, nothing."

"As for Sarah, she'd be in danger if the people who want that doll find out she's discovered something that will help her locate it. But it might be that Sarah is much smarter than we think."

The sound of a motorcar interrupted them. Bret moved the curtain and looked below. "We've quite a party for tonight. Everyone is here, including Helga. She's arrived with your mother."

Allison went to stand beside him at the window and saw her mother and the baroness walking toward the front door. "Not everyone. You've left out Sir Edgar."

"I would never leave Edgar out of the party. That's our man arriving now. Good. I'll show up near dinner with David, as a surprise." He let the curtain fall back in place, turned, and looked at her evenly. "Are you all right?"

She nodded, but felt tense and cold. He must have realized it for he reached over and took her chin gently, turning her face toward his. They looked at each other for a long moment.

"Right now," he said, his voice low and warm, "there's something quite different I want to talk about. Before whatever will take place tonight happens."

Allison's heart beat a rapid pace when she was confronted by the blue spark in his eyes.

"This isn't the right time for romance," he said softly. "But I've always been a bit unconventional." His hand caressed her cheek, and his eyes held hers. "What would you say if I told you that despite everything I've said—or rather, left unsaid at Basra, and the other night at Ezbekiah Gardens—I've fallen in love with you."

She looked at him. What *would* she say?

She wouldn't say anything because she couldn't. Her throat went dry and she stared at him.

"Reluctantly fallen in love," he admitted. "I confess I didn't plan to, didn't want to—" he cupped her face in both his hands—"oh, but I have, despite my best efforts to the contrary."

She stared at him, dazed. Was this really happening? Or was she imagining it all…was he really saying those words to her, meaning them with all his heart…?

"What about your request to leave for France?" she whispered, surprised at the roughness of her voice.

He smiled again. "I was going to leave for France. I thought it might help me forget you." His eyes shone with tenderness. "But it's too late for that."

Ah…This was one of the few times the words *too late* were sweet and full of expectation.

"My sweet Allison—" he pressed a gentle kiss to her cheek— "your virtue and charm have made you unforgettable—" he kissed her forehead—"And so I've changed my mind. I'm staying."

"Can you do that?" she whispered.

"It was remarkably easy, thanks to your father. He has plans of his own, you see. He wants me to go ahead of Major General Murray to verify the information Rose Lyman sent through David. There's a move underway to take Palestine from the Turks. We didn't take Baghdad—but we're going to take Jerusalem."

"Jerusalem," she breathed, and her happiness over his declaration reached out to embrace the beloved city, David, Rose, and Ben Gurion.

"Murray plans to take El-Arish first. We'll use it as a base, and hospital, then begin the long march to Jerusalem. I wouldn't miss it for all the promotions in France! And you're here, right where I want you."

She continued to stare at him, her heart thumping loudly in her ears, not wanting the tears to come to her eyes, trying to understand the implications of his words. "What does a cynical colonel do when he's reluctantly fallen in love?" she whispered. "I've no experience with such matters. What does he expect, or even want?"

He smiled ruefully. "I want to marry you before I go."

She felt her knees grow weak. Marry her. He wanted to marry her.

He drew her closer, his arms slipping about her shoulders and waist. "I'm sorry, my love. I can't let you marry Wade. If you do, you'll break my heart...you wouldn't do that, would you?"

"You're serious!" she whispered.

Laughter sparkled in his blue eyes. "Do you think I'd waste your time or mine saying this if I wasn't? By now you should know I don't go around telling women I'm madly in love with them."

"What about Cynthia?"

He frowned as though confused. "Cynthia? I don't remember any Cynthia." His eyes met hers, and she saw he was suddenly serious. "There is only one woman in my mind, my heart. Only a noble young nurse with sea-green eyes and flame-colored hair, whose heart is devoted to the Lord. He's given you to me.... You're the best thing that's ever come into my life, Allison." The teasing tone came back into his voice. "If you refuse me, you might send me off to Palestine to my death."

"Don't even say that!" She gripped his arms fiercely.

He leaned toward her, his mouth only a breath away from hers. "You'd best say yes now. When will you marry me?"

"Bret, please—" she stammered, trying to think clearly in the midst of the emotions sweeping over her. "This is so shocking—I—I can't decide now—"

His embrace tightened. "I won't give up until you say yes."

"But—"

"You do love me, don't you?"

Did she love him! As if he needed to ask.

Her eyes pled with him to understand. "We need time—I hardly know anything about you. Who is your mother, your father? Your—?"

His lips met hers with wild, sweet passion.

"You do love me," he said a moment later, and his voice rang with triumph.

Of course I love you! she wanted to cry. *More than life itself!* And yet something within her would not let her speak those words...something held her back.

What is it, Lord? What's wrong?

There was no answer. Only the strong knowledge that she could not answer him...not in the way he desired.

He kissed her again. When he lifted his head, she was breathless. "Bret—wait! I don't understand...how can you—?"

"It's easy. Once I make up my mind about something, there's no more reason to wait. This is what you wanted me to say, isn't it? At Basra? At the Garden? Why are you holding me off?"

She feared she would lose him if she didn't yield at once, and her heart beat painfully in her chest. *What do I say, Lord? I don't want to lose him!*

"My soul, wait silently for God alone, for my expectation is from Him."

The psalm rang in her heart and mind, and she felt a calm settle over her. If that was what God wanted, then she would not turn away. She must wait. In silence. No matter how her heart cried out in fear....

She took his hands in hers and stepped back. "Bret, I can't answer you now. I need time—"

He frowned. "Time? For what?"

Her hands gripped his tightly. *Help me, God. Help me make him understand.* "To pray first, to seek the Lord's mind..."

His mouth turned. "Are you afraid we're not well matched, Miss Wescott? Am I not as well suited to you as, perhaps, Wade Findlay? After all, there's not much of a spiritual contest between the two of us, is there?"

She stepped back, stung. "Don't be absurd. I'm not expecting you to become a chaplain. It's following God's purpose that matters, regardless of whether you're a colonel in the British military or working with Oswald Chambers. It's just that—" she paused, at a loss for words to explain something she didn't fully understand herself. How did one explain a deep conviction that stemmed not out of solid fact, but out of an inner certainty?

His lashes narrowed and a cynical look of self-reproach came to his handsome face. "Be that as it may, you must admit few men can measure up to a man such as Oswald Chambers, or a willing martyr like Wade Findlay. Certainly not Bret Holden."

"That isn't true," she said fiercely. "It was *you* who went after Wade. You risked your life to save him."

His gaze met and held hers. "Allison, you can't waver in this decision. I told you the other night you were going to need to choose between us. I was more right than even I knew at the time. The time has come for you to decide where your heart belongs. With Wade, or with me. I'll abide by your decision. If you choose Wade, I'll leave quietly and not bother you again—"

With a muffled cry, she reached out to draw his head down and kiss him. His arms came around her, holding her as though he would never let her go. For one wild moment they were lost in the cascade of emotions pouring over them—and then she pulled away. Her heart felt as though it would shatter into a million pieces, as though it would never be whole again....

"My soul, wait silently for God alone..."

I know, Father, I know. I am waiting, but it's so hard!

Holding back a sob, she hurried to the door, slid back the bolt, and pulled it open.

Bret caught her arm, holding her back. His eyes refused to let her go. "Run away if you must," he whispered. "You can even run to Wade, but you've shown me your heart, Allison, and I have my answer. You belong to me. Wade may be a friend, but I will not give you up to him. You're going to marry me."

She looked at him, thrilled and dismayed at the same time. "How can you be so sure?"

He smiled at her whispered question. "Simple. I always get what I want."

They stared at each other in silence until she dragged her eyes from his, and he gently released her. She stepped out into the hall, and he closed the door.

Allison stood there, hands clenching at her sides, trying to still her pounding heart and bring a measure of composure to her face.

A proposal! He wanted to marry her. Joy washed over her. *He loves me!* Everything within her had clamored to say yes, to give in to him...and yet God had held her back. Why?

She shook her head, unable to think. She stood there in the shadows hearing voices below in the hall. Her mother, Helga, Beth—and Sir Edgar.

Allison walked to the stairway and gazed down upon them. Her mother looked up at her, a question in her eyes, and Allison forced a smile to her face.

"Mother," she said, and came down the stairs. "I'm so glad to see you."

TWENTY-SIX

>—!—‹♦›—☉—‹♦›—!—‹

I will be with him in trouble.

PSALM 91:15

"HULLO, BARONESS, THIS IS A PLEASANT SURPRISE," said Allison. On anyone else, the baroness's white fur and diamond earrings would have seemed out of place. But for Helga Kruger, such attire was to be expected.

"Allison, this is most fortunate. I did not think I would see you in Cairo. Now, my dear, since we are comrades from Aleppo, you must call me Helga."

If Helga meant anything by that casual greeting, her face concealed it. She went on to refer to the war in Arabia and Wade's injury but didn't mention Colonel Bret Holden, perhaps deliberately. Finally she commended Allison's service as a nurse with the Sixth Division. "I have heard the hospitals in Alexandria and here in Cairo are equally in need of nurses, so you will be requested to stay and serve here, I am most sure."

Allison told her she hadn't made up her mind yet what she would do, though it seemed her parents were equally determined to keep her home in Cairo for the remainder of the war.

Helga smiled at Lady Eleanor. "You must be quite proud of your daughter for her noble service."

"Indeed, though Marshall and I had no idea she was doing service in such a dangerous zone." Eleanor looked at Allison, her determination evident. "Your father learned the hospital ship with Wade aboard has arrived. You will be anxious to see him."

Allison felt the unsettling tug-of-war within her heart at the thought of seeing Wade and telling him of her feelings for Bret, and for once was almost pleased to hear Sir Edgar's voice from behind them as he came in through the front door and joined them in the hall.

"Ah, a pleasant evening to you, ladies. So we all meet at Mrs. Blaine's instead of your house, Baroness Kruger." He removed his Panama hat and held it against his broad chest, a wide smile on his creased face. The strands of hair stayed glued to his forehead with sweat, and his small eyes had a mocking gleam in them despite the deferential bow of his head.

"Hello, Edgar," said Eleanor, her tone uncertain. "I suppose Gilbert is already here?"

"Yes, he arrived with little Beth."

Something in that simple statement made Allison glance uneasily toward her mother, but Eleanor's face retained its practiced dignity. She merely said quietly, "Then I'll need to speak with Beth about that. You've met Baroness Helga Kruger?"

His scuffed shoes came together in a polished click of his heels, followed by a second bow of his head, and his hand reached out to take the baroness's and lift it to his lips. The movement was surprisingly graceful for such a big man, Allison thought, and she bit her lip, thinking. That night in the laundry room, when someone had fled so swiftly, she'd told herself it couldn't have been Sir Edgar. Had she presumed too much?

Helga's face was as expressionless as that of a porcelain doll. "Sir Edgar, we meet again. I have been anticipating this night. I have some most interesting information for you, thanks to Cairo Intelligence."

Her unexpected words clearly surprised Edgar—and Allison, whose heart leaped. She watched Sir Edgar carefully to see what his response would be to Helga's apparent trust of him.

"Ah!" he said, his brows lifted. "I presume this information has something to do with the murder that has taken place here. Unfortunate event, I must say. And how interesting that British Intelligence would give information to you, my dear, rather than directly to me."

He continued to hold her hand, and the diamond rings on her long fingers sparkled in contrast to the shabby lamp on the wall, with its faded rose paper.

Eleanor's voice rushed into the moment to try to rescue it from the tension: "Yes, the poor Egyptian cook. Who would have thought my Allison would come to visit an old friend like dear Sarah and end up enmeshed in a woman's death?"

"A woman's *murder*, Cousin Eleanor," interjected Sir Edgar, a note of apology to his voice.

"Yes, most astounding," agreed Helga, though she didn't look the least bit astounded. "Our dear Sarah has filled us all in on what has taken place to this point. I cannot conceive of all she has suffered in the midst of such thievery and mayhem. And what are your notions of motive behind such a senseless killing, Sir Edgar?"

"Baroness, if I knew that, I would know all. Until then, I shall plod along. Still, since the days of Cain slaying his Abel, the motives for such an act usually come out the same: jealousy, pride, greed!"

"Yes, so it would seem, Inspector, but with an individual twist here and there."

"Perhaps it was a thief breaking into Mrs. Blaine's house," Eleanor suggested, then she glanced about at the unimpressive surroundings, and Allison knew what she was thinking: there wasn't much here to entice a petty thief. "But who could possibly gain from what appears a senseless death of a mere serving woman?" continued Eleanor. "That a common thief from off the streets would sneak through the back door in the hopes of running off with any item to sell and accidentally come face-to-face with a startled serving woman, seems, well—"

"A thief? Edgar doesn't think that," interrupted Sarah Blaine's flat voice from the drawing-room doorway. "Isn't it clear he thinks I did it? Why else would he order me confined to my home during Christmas?"

They turned in her direction, and Allison felt a pang of pity. Sarah had grown more agitated since she had last seen her. The tension—or was it fear?—was visible in the tight lines about her mouth.

Sir Edgar responded first by walking toward her with a gesture of apology. "Now, now, my dear Sarah, I've merely taken precautions to have you kept under watchful care for your own protection. And look how your friends have come flocking to uphold you in this trying time. You are not alone in this."

"Oh, really, Sir Edgar," said Sarah, not bothering to hide her resentment. "You don't mean a word of your offered sympathy. I have been under house detention!"

"She's right, Cousin Edgar," said Eleanor, sweeping to her side like a graceful butterfly. "I've known Sarah since we were both girls in India. She wouldn't use a swatter on a fly, let alone a hammer on her cook."

"A meat tenderizer."

"Edgar!" Eleanor's eyes flashed. "The weapon is of little consequence. Your suspicion of Sarah is quite absurd."

He appeared to accept the rebuke in meek silence, lowering his head, but Allison saw the hard glint of mockery in his eyes, even if her mother had not noticed.

Sarah turned to Eleanor. "I can't tell you what your coming means to me. And Baroness, I'm both honored and embarrassed. Do come into the drawing room," and Sarah rushed toward the elegant woman with the excited energy of a dainty hummingbird.

Beth, Gilbert, and Marra were already waiting in the drawing room and stood up from the champagne-colored divan as they entered.

"Helga, you've met my other daughter, Beth? She was so looking forward to spending the holidays at your residence. As was Gilbert—" and Eleanor turned to the handsome young man, who was a startling contrast to his father. "This is the son of my cousin Celeste—and, of course, Edgar."

"Hello, Beth, Gilbert. Well, Edgar! You didn't tell me your son looked so very much like Celeste."

A silly smile showed on Edgar's plain face as he looked devotedly at Gilbert, who stood, lithe and darkly handsome, near Beth.

"Yes," Edgar said, "who'd believe this charming boy has my blood as well? He looks so much like my beloved Celeste, especially in the eyes. Pure and clean like fresh pools. I've wonderful plans for him after the war. Gilbert's going to England to Oxford. He'll be a barrister, maybe enter Parliament."

"Poetry, dear old dad?" Gilbert's mocking tones were a slap to his father. "Do stop, you make me feel like a baby angel with a bee-stung mouth and big blue eyes. Next thing I'll sprout wings and circle about the room to the tune of a violin."

Watching Edgar's reaction to his son's harsh words, Allison was moved with compassion. Here was the first crack of vulnerability she had seen in Edgar. He reminded her of the cast-off runt of an abandoned litter of alley cats wiggling up to a scurrilous mother, despite being refused nourishment. Only in this case, it was the father who so clearly desired love from his arrogantly superior son.

Beth giggled. "Oh, Gilly! Don't you know angels aren't the way artists draw them? Aunt Lydia says there isn't a single verse in the

Bible that says there are baby cherubs."

He looked at her with pained endurance.

"I was sorry to hear of your mother's death, Gilbert," said Helga Kruger quietly. "She informed me she was incurably ill, but I had no idea it would come so soon after I left her. If I had realized, I would have arranged to stay a month longer in Constantinople. It is one of my deepest regrets that I was not able to be with her when she so needed her friends about her."

Allison turned a surprised glance away from the baroness to Gilbert, hoping he wouldn't give a glib remark. She was satisfied to see that he had dropped the debonair smile he adopted in the belief that it made him irresistible to women, young or old. A flair of sincere surprise reflected in his dark eyes.

"I didn't know you knew my mother, Baroness."

Neither had Allison, who listened, alert. Did Bret know about this?

"I met Celeste in Constantinople, at the German ambassador's residence. I was there on a visit before the war. Celeste was interested in the archaeological exchange between the Cairo and Constantinople Museums. She came to programs that I helped conduct with Allison's cousin Neal Bristow." Helga looked across the drawing room to where Sir Edgar stood looking on, hands folded patiently behind his ponderous frame. "A pity you weren't there, Edgar. Celeste told me you understood ancient artifacts better than she."

"My wife was a generous soul. Gilbert is more talented in the subject of Egyptology than I."

"Not so," protested Gilbert. "Tell them how you were a museum curator before entering government service in Burma and India."

Edgar was unruffled. "I was a mere assistant."

"Dad wouldn't make a good robber of temples," jested Gilbert.

"The curse would reach out and grab him before he made his dash through the secret passage." He looked at Helga and snapped his fingers. "That's it! I remember now. Mother *did* mention you. And a glum-faced Turkish professor who came with you for the museum showings—what was his name?"

Helga's eyes flickered. "Professor Jemal Pasha. He is a brilliant Egyptologist."

"Didn't he disappear before the war?"

"I'm surprised you'd know of it."

"Oh, the papers were full of it. That and the suicide of Mrs. Blaine's husband. Poor old major general. He must have grown despondent over losing in polo," he jested.

"Gilbert!" said Eleanor sharply.

He looked at Sarah as though he'd forgotten she was there. "Sorry," he murmured, and Sarah sank into a chair.

"Jemal disappeared a month before the war," said Helga, ending the silence. "Strange, do you not think, Edgar? The Turkish authorities in Aleppo thought he may have wandered off into the Arabian desert and expired before help could arrive. Yet he knew the desert so well. I wonder if the war hasn't held him prisoner in Constantinople. The policies of governments decide our private destinies as well, do they not? Have you made any arrests here in Cairo of certain Europeans?"

"We are in the ongoing process, Baroness."

Anyone listening to Helga's unemotional discourse would be stunned to discover that her past with Jemal had included them being on opposite sides in the deadly game of espionage, thought Allison. Bret would have been proud of the baroness's acting abilities.

At the thought of Bret, she glanced around with a small frown. Why hadn't he or David appeared for dinner as earlier intimated. Was Bret still in the house?

Before long they had all moved to the dining room, where they took their seats. The dining table gleamed with the clear flames emanating from white candles, while red roses and sprigs of greenery added a festive touch. Allison commented on the roses that Beth and Gilbert had gathered from the garden earlier. The dinner that Marra had offered to prepare was going well, and at Sarah's request, the topic of death and tragedy did not resurface.

Not, that is, until Helga brought it up. Looking across the candle flames at Sir Edgar, she commented, "I cannot help thinking that the intruder who killed Sarah's cook must have been looking for something rather specific. When he heard the serving woman enter, he must have stepped inside the laundry room hoping she would leave again, but she did not. She must have started up the steps to the passage where Marra's room is located, then—the murderer stepped out and struck her. The question is, why?"

"What do you mean?" asked Allison.

Helga raised her white cup. "Had he wanted to avoid harming the woman, he could have allowed her to proceed on her way while he slipped silently out the door and disappeared through the garden."

Allison hadn't thought of that before, and the idea brought a moment of tension. She had always hoped the death was unplanned, an act of desperation.

"I don't see your reasoning," said Gilbert. "It seems to me it was more of an accident."

"The way she was lying on the floor contradicts that theory," said Helga. "Isn't that so, Edgar?"

"I quite agree, Baroness," he replied. "I long ago gave up the theory of a petty street thief caught in the act of burglary. I believe, too, that his act of murder was intentional."

"You're assuming the murderer was a he," observed Gilbert. "Women make better murderers, you know." Beth looked at him, mildly outraged, and Gilbert smiled. "But never anyone as sweet as you, Beth."

Eleanor glanced at him, displeasure in her eyes; Marra looked at him, bored.

"It was a man," said Marra, leaning back in her chair. Her blonde hair gleamed in the candlelight. "Most murders are committed by men. For money, or a woman."

"I could prove you wrong with statistics if I cared to, but I'm too much a gentleman," Gilbert answered.

"In the end the facts will prove you wrong," said Marra, and looked over at Allison. "What was that verse in Proverbs you mentioned to me the other day? I keep thinking about it."

"'Be sure your sin will find you out.'"

"In the end," said Marra, "the sundial will grow dark, and the wind will scatter the autumn leaves."

"Good grief," cried Gilbert, "listen to her!"

Sarah's knife clattered noisily on her plate. When Allison glanced at her in concern, she saw Sarah had hardly touched her dinner.

"As for *facts*, Marra," said Gilbert. "There aren't any. Not in this particular case. As my dear old dad will tell you."

"There are plenty of facts," Allison stated, goaded by Gilbert's superior attitude.

He turned his dark head to look at her. "Are there? Please, do share them with us. I'm particularly interested in anything that will stick in court. Dad hasn't a morsel of evidence, and we all know it." He sent a smile to Sarah. "So you see, you're perfectly safe, Mrs. Blaine."

"Why, thank you, Gilbert, dear," said Sarah tartly.

Gilbert smiled at Allison. "For that matter, there are as many facts pointing to Allison as to Mrs. Blaine."

"That's absurd, Gilly!" said Beth. "Next thing you'll be saying *I* did it."

"Maybe you did. Maybe I did."

"Such rubbish!" commented Eleanor. "Whoever killed the woman was a petty thief."

"I don't think so," Sarah replied tensely. "My house has been searched quite thoroughly. Twice. And both times nothing was taken."

The baroness lifted one finely shaped brow. "Nothing? That is unusual, my dear."

"It would be, unless the thief was looking for something specific, as you yourself said."

"Yes," the baroness's brow creased with thought, "but what?"

Sarah was silent for a moment, and Allison wondered what she would say.

"I think they were looking for something Rex brought home from one of his trips. Something that is hidden in this house some-place."

This time both of the baroness's eyebrows raised. "Oh, Sarah, I'm sorry, but that seems awfully improbable."

Sarah looked at her. "I wish you were right, Baroness, but Rex *did* hide something. An Egyptian treasure, I think."

Allison's head turned sharply. What was Sarah saying that for?

"But I've no idea what it is or where Rex put it."

Every eye was riveted on Sarah, who was concentrating on buttering her bread.

Helga's diamonds glittered and her smooth blue-black hair shone with pomade as she leaned back in her chair. "I have something of great archaeological interest to show you all after dinner in the drawing room if the colonel arrives. It may help to unmask what the general may have concealed."

Allison sat very still as a draft flickered the candle flame, her eyes glancing about the others seated around the table. Surprise, concern, and foreboding showed on their faces. The baroness knew something important. The uncertainty of what this revelation might mean prolonged the silence.

Allison looked over at Sir Edgar, but he was intent upon enjoying his cut of tenderloin. He had been silent for some time and now drenched his meat with a mixture of wine and mushroom sauce. "You are a marvelous cook, Marra." And he cut the meat sharply with his knife, then looked up again. "Now, what is your theory, Baroness?"

"Since Sarah's house was searched twice with nothing taken, someone is certain about what they are looking for. I've already mentioned that fact. Neith—was that her name?—must have known more than what you give her credit for, Edgar. Perhaps her son Anwar did, as well. Perhaps they both knew the murderer."

In the silence that followed her suggestion, Eleanor asked Edgar, "Have you found Anwar yet?"

"He's lost himself in the Arab sector of Cairo. I have a clever Egyptian assistant on the street asking questions, and there's a reward out. I'll find him."

The mood in the room had turned wary. Soon Sarah announced coffee and tea in the drawing room. She disappeared with Marra into the kitchen, refusing Allison's offer of help. Allison, who was taking mental notes to report later to Bret, followed the others into the drawing room to see Helga's display of Egyptian pieces.

Allison heard the front door open, and then footsteps. A tall brown-skinned white-robed Egyptian entered carrying a small black box. The box had a cobra-head knob! Allison covered her recognition, aware of Gilbert's gaze.

"Looks as though he carries the Sultan's jewels," he remarked, an odd note in his voice. "With the house having been broken into twice and an unsolved murder having taken place here, I wonder how wise it is to bring them here."

"It is quite all right, Gilbert," said Helga. "With the inspector general of the police here, and a colonel in British intelligence, the treasure will be quite safe, I'm certain. You can be sure both men are carrying revolvers—for their protection and ours." She stood from the chair, looking toward the hall. "Ah, Colonel Holden, you have arrived. That is good. Any news yet of Professor Blackstone's colleague from Athens?"

Bret came in from the hall looking official and formidable in his uniform. He removed his hat as though he had indeed just arrived from downtown Cairo. Allison watched him, as did Sir Edgar.

"No ship yet for your medical leave, Colonel?" asked Edgar, pushing himself up from a chair beside the window.

"It was torpedoed," Bret remarked blandly.

"Yes, I read about the U-boat sighting in the paper," said Eleanor. "Marshall tells me the *Mediterranean* is totally unsafe to travel now. Thank God you hadn't boarded, Colonel."

Bret's gaze locked with Allison's, and she looked away to the box still held by the Egyptian.

"This is Omar, an assistant to the baroness in her work at the museum," Bret told them. He turned toward the dining room. "Mrs. Blaine? Marra?"

"Here," Marra said as they entered the room.

Bret turned to Helga. "This is your area of expertise, Baroness. Would you be so kind as to explain?"

"Yes, Colonel, of course. Omar?"

Omar set the box down on the table and proceeded to open it. Bret leaned into the doorjamb, his expression giving nothing away while Helga proceeded to gaze about at those in the room, her eyes coming to settle on Sarah. "An archaeologist of renown will be arriving tomorrow to look at a certain piece the Colonel and my assistant

416

have brought tonight," she told her. "His arrival will bear witness to its authenticity. He is so enthralled at the prospect of the great find that he risked the U-boats to come to see it."

What piece? wondered Allison. *What archaeologist?* She began to feel the pounding of her heart, certain it had something important to do with the Egyptian treasure doll. Perhaps the murderer was seated in this very room now, drinking Christmas tea. It was mind-boggling, odious, and frightening. Yet she sat there as though such thoughts were far from her mind. She heard the tinkle of rain on the windowpane. Sir Edgar was toying with an unlit cigar, watching first Bret, then Helga, with an empty stare that explained none of the thoughts that must be rampaging through his mind.

"What is it? The treasure of Amenophis II?" joked Gilbert.

"Oh, Gilly," said Beth breathlessly.

The leather chair squeaked under Edgar's frame. He struck a match. The rain beat more loudly on the pane. Marra went and drew the heavier drapes across.

"You have your key?" the baroness asked Omar.

He fumbled, lifting a chain from beneath his collared robe, and unlocked the polished black box. Helga removed the items one by one until they all were displayed on the table. The lamplight spilled onto an anthropoid coffin of a pharaoh that stood on its miniature stand. The shadows evoked a shiver in Allison. Her gaze riveted upon the royal *nemes* headdress and its two goddesses: Wadjit, a cobra, and Nekhbet, a vulture, rested on his brow, watching with dead eyes.

The cobra! Allison held her breath. Wadjit, the cobra…her mind was working frantically, trying to recall where she had seen this symbol before. On that broken cobra head that Sarah had found in the trunk earlier, yes…but she'd seen it somewhere else, too.

If only she could remember where!

417

Suddenly the hairs at the back of her neck raised, and she realized she could feel that someone was watching her intently, but she couldn't bring herself to turn her head and look to see who it was. Instead, she set her teacup down, trying not to spill it.

"This is it," Helga was saying in a thrilled voice. "The gold scarab we think may have come from the burial room of Tutankhamen's tomb!"

A small gasp sounded in the room as everyone stirred. Sarah leaned forward, staring at the solid gold beetle. "Is that—is that the one that was in the vase?"

"Yes," said Bret.

"And this is the find that has brought our archaeologist coming tomorrow," said Helga. "I believe it's from the treasury of King Tut."

Allison heard her own breath drawn in, then realized most everyone in the room had been equally startled. If Helga was right, then the treasure in the Egyptian doll would be an item of rare antiquity as well. But it would also mean something far greater: that those who found it had discovered a new burial chamber where untold treasure abounded—and was, as yet, untouched.

"It's possible Major General Rex Blaine knew the whereabouts of tremendous untapped treasure," announced Helga.

Sir Edgar stood and walked forward. "Yes, that's quite what we think. I'm surprised you know, Baroness."

Helga shrugged her elegant shoulders. "My dear inspector, I do not see how you can expect me *not* to know. A find of such historic significance as this scarab can hardly remain a secret for long. You have not forgotten that I own an antiquities shop in Old Cairo?" She frowned slightly. "The colonel informs me some most unfortunate smuggling has been going on there of late. British Intelligence has questioned me fervently—" she looked toward Bret—"as naturally they must." She looked over at a white-faced Sarah Blaine. "This is the item you uncovered in the vase, Sarah?"

"Yes...I think so."

"Intelligence called me in to look at it. Professor Blackstone and others of the museum have also looked at it. Names of renown in the world of archaeology are already clamoring for more information. But we have none."

"It may be the item comes from the burial tomb of one of the ancient pharaohs," said Bret. "If that proves true, someone has stumbled upon a remarkable discovery: A burial tomb filled with treasures untold."

Allison, dazed, could only look about her at the others. Sarah's wide eyes stared.

"A burial tomb of a pharaoh," whispered Beth, and she turned to Gilbert.

He gave a low whistle. "No wonder someone thinks it's worth murder."

Allison looked at him, started to say nothing was worth murder, then became aware of Bret's gaze. She held her silence, but her mind churned with questions. Had Bret known all along that the two items belonged to such a phenomenal discovery?

"Why—whoever knows where the burial tomb is located would be a millionaire!" whispered Beth.

"Yes, all you'd need is a few items to sell on the black market," said Bret smoothly.

Beth looked at him. "Oh, I see. The scarab—and—and the Egyptian doll everyone is looking for."

Allison glanced at Sarah. Would she speak up now about the cobra head she found in the trunk? It was the logical thing to do. If not—

Helga looked calm. "Naturally so great an archaeological find would go to the museums of the world," she corrected.

Bret was looking at Sarah. "Unless someone in the team that dis-covered the tomb decided to keep it a secret."

Sarah's blank stare was riveted on the scarab.

"Professor Jemal and Rex Blaine," stated Sir Edgar. "They may have made a pact between themselves. Then the war broke out."

Sarah leaned forward in her chair, her brown eyes glittering in her white face. "That's absurd."

"I'm sorry, Mrs. Blaine, but the truth must come out," said Sir Edgar. "Did Rex leave you any information about such a find?"

"Absolutely not. Rex would never do anything like that. And where would he get access to such a discovery?"

"You know where Rex got his information. From Jemal. He's somewhere in Cairo. We know that. Don't we, Colonel?" said Edgar.

Bret looked away from Sarah to Edgar. "Yes, if he's still alive."

Still alive? What did he mean by that? Allison recalled that Anwar was not Neith's son, but Jemal's. Could it be that he was hid-ing somewhere in Cairo as Edgar said? Or was he with Jemal?

"I'm certain Rex learned about King Tut's burial tomb from Jemal," said Sir Edgar. "They were together several years ago near Luxor—Valley of the Kings. Even then Rex was involved in smug-gling with Jemal."

Sarah stood, wringing her hands. "Smuggling, yes, but Rex is dead. He couldn't have murdered Neith. So who does that leave? Jemal—or someone else. Someone who knew about the treasure."

Sir Edgar walked toward her. Allison looked at his oxfords, hear-ing their awful squeaking.

"But I don't have the doll," said Sarah tensely. "Rex must have done something else with it."

"And you don't know where he put it?"

"Of course not. I didn't even know he had it. I only knew about the vase. And I'd never have guessed he was into smuggling if my house hadn't been searched by whomever killed Neith. If Rex was, as you so confidently assert, involved with Professor Jemal in Luxor, I knew nothing about it until you mentioned it last night."

"Oh, I didn't say Rex was out with digging utensils," said Sir Edgar. "Only that he may have known of Jemal's discovery, made with an archaeological group some years before the war."

"If that's true," argued Sarah, "are you suggesting Rex and Jemal eliminated the other members of that archaeological team to keep the matter quiet? Everyone on that team would have known they discovered a new burial tomb! They can't all be dead!"

Allison looked from Sarah's triumphant face to Edgar. It was Helga who spoke.

"There was a French team out here five years ago. It consisted of two Frenchmen. General Blaine was never a member of any of our teams, but Jemal was. He helped them in some way. Colonel?" She turned to Bret with a questioning voice.

"The two men never returned to France. One was rumored to have died of blood poison. The other was never heard from again."

Gilbert snapped his fingers. "That leaves Jemal. He murdered them, then kept the information on the tomb's discovery to himself. Later he shared it with Rex Blaine. Since Blaine is dead and we don't know where Jemal is, the matter is pretty much closed."

Sarah stood abruptly. "I won't hear any more of this nonsense! I'm going up to my room. If you will excuse me Baroness, Eleanor, I've a dreadful headache coming on," and she hurried from the drawing room, brushing past Bret in the doorway.

Eleanor stood as well. "I think we've all had enough speculation for one night, Cousin Edgar. You were positively brutish to the poor woman. You can tell by looking at her she's quite beside herself."

Gilbert walked over to the window to look out. The dark splashes of rain beat against the window. "Dreadful mess," he murmured.

"Maybe there's a pharaoh's curse on the item everyone seeks. I once heard a fine tale about six people who died for disturbing the old pharaoh's resting place and carting off his collateral. Can't say I'd blame him. So far several deaths have occurred. How many more?"

Bret looked over at Gilbert, and Allison stood.

Sir Edgar's eyes were cold and black. "Superstitious nonsense," he muttered. "There is a logical reason behind these events, and I will not rest until I find out who killed Neith."

Gilbert turned and came back toward the others, inclining his head toward the small coffin that Helga had looked at earlier. He walked over to the black box. "May I?" he asked, and when Omar nodded and drew closer, Gilbert gently lifted the coffin and touched it with his thumb. "Maybe the pharaoh is sore at us all and has some naughty plans for Mrs. Blaine's holiday guests."

"Oh, Gilly!" cried Beth.

Helga considered his words carefully. "A curse is a theory of amateurs, one totally separated from true archaeology. Although—" and she looked off, musing—"the pharaohs did carry magic among their treasures. I'll show you a certain vase I have one of these evenings. It is...interesting."

Gilbert smiled and cocked his head at the coffin. "What's a thing like that worth?"

"It is priceless," Helga replied simply.

Gilbert shrugged. "Well, I've my own theories, but I loathe spoiling a party."

"Don't even say it. Where do we all intend to sleep tonight, Mum?" asked Beth dourly.

"You can double up with Allison."

"No, I—um—will sleep with Marra. I've already looked and she has two single beds. But that side of the house isn't my choice," grimaced Beth. "That's where they found—" she stopped.

"The body," said Gilbert, leaning toward her.

"Cheer up, I've an inside bolt," said Marra. "And once I lock it and cover my head with a pillow, I'm out till the chickens wake. Not even Gilbert's foolish chatter about a curse will keep me awake. You're all on your own. I've had enough of theories. Good night everyone, pleasant dreams. Coming, Beth?"

Beth glanced at Gilbert, then followed after Marra. She retrieved her overnight bag from the foyer, then called back, "Good night, Mum."

Eleanor turned to Sir Edgar. "I believe we will retire, too, if you don't mind. Sarah has made the upstairs sewing room into a makeshift bedroom for us."

"No, my dear Eleanor, I don't mind, and I apologize for this wretched business. I'm sorry it's come to this. I had hoped our first meeting after all these years might be a more pleasant one."

"Yes," she said tonelessly. "So had I."

"I assure you there will be two policemen on duty tonight. One in back, the other near the front door. I hope that will ensure you lovely ladies a night of beauty rest. And you, Colonel? You will be here as well?"

Bret glanced at his watch. "No. I've got to meet David. Something has come up."

Allison took this news in, wondering what was happening.

"Then, if you'll excuse me, I intend to have another look about the yard and garden while the rain's let up," said Sir Edgar.

"It will be a slushy mess," warned Eleanor. "Do be careful, Edgar," and she looked after him as he walked out of the drawing room to the dining-room door. After a moment, she turned back to the others. "Good night, everyone. Coming, Allison? Helga?"

Allison held back, glancing at Bret, hoping to talk to him before he left....*Or is he really leaving?* The thought ran through her mind, and she rose slowly from her seat. "Yes, I'll be up in a moment, Mum."

The Egyptian assistant came forward and deftly began to gather the items to replace in the box. Allison looked at the shiny brass cobra head with its onyx eyes—willing her mind to give her the answer she so desperately needed. But it still eluded her. She turned away and caught Bret's lazy stare upon her. "Good night, Colonel Holden."

"Miss Wescott."

A short time later, Allison walked up the stairs with Helga. "Was all this tonight meant to bait the appetite of whoever killed Neith?" she whispered.

Helga stared straight ahead and kept her voice barely audible. "Yes, it was Bret's idea." She smiled. "And it worked like a charm."

"Maybe too well," murmured Allison, glancing behind her.

Sir Edgar stood beside the open dining-room door, lighting his cigar before going out. Bret appeared in the drawing room, a silhouette against the backdrop of the lamps.

On the landing, Allison paused. Bret's eyes met hers, and they stood thus for a brief moment, and then she turned and walked to her room.

CHAPTER
TWENTY-SEVEN

>–:–‹›–•–‹›–:–‹

The snare of the fowler...
PSALM 91:3

ONCE IN HER ROOM, Allison unlocked the latticed window and it swung outward against the side of the house. The rain had ceased, and the cool air smelled of washed greenery. A breath of wind rippled the tops of the flame trees edging the drive.

The silhouette of a night bird flitted past, its wings whispering in the still night. Allison's nerves tightened, and she stepped back as it cried harshly, its wings blending with the darkness over the treetops.

She had heard Sir Edgar leave the house, but had he gone back into Cairo, or was he still walking somewhere in the garden? Looking for what, for whom? And where was Bret? Was he watching Sir Edgar?

Bret! If only he would return by way of the bathroom window! She longed to talk with him, to know all was well.

She slipped off her shoes and tiptoed to the bath again, pushed the door ajar and looked at the window with its rotting latch. She waited; listening. Silence alone responded to her longing.

She returned to the bedroom window, where an enormous white Egyptian moon turned the yard silvery. Croaking frogs bellowed from the distance. Then she saw it: a flash of light from a hand torch was moving through the shadows. Hope told her it was Bret, but despair knew better. He would never be foolish enough to give himself away by using a torch. Someone was in the yard below her window.

A second sound came, this one from inside the house on the

landing. She turned, listening, wondering if she'd imagined that whispering sound of something silky and soft floating by. A woman's dressing gown?

She glanced back out the window. Whoever was below had come along the path from the other side of the house...from the garden, perhaps? The moonlight fell upon the form, and Allison could make out a woman. Was it Sarah? She couldn't tell.

Then the woman looked up toward the windows of Sarah's room. Allison stepped back, enough to be out of sight, but not so much so that she could no longer see. The woman turned her head to study the windows to Rex's office, and finally toward Allison's room. The torch flashed off, and the woman stepped back out of sight, but not before Allison had seen a face in the moonlight.

Beth!

Just then another figure emerged from the trees, walking to meet Beth. Allison didn't need to guess who it was that came to keep a secret rendezvous with her sister. If their mother learned that Beth was meeting Gilbert at midnight alone in the yard, there would certainly be trouble.

Allison leaned out the window trying to keep her voice low, yet determined to gain Beth's attention: "Beth! Beth—!"

But her sister didn't hear and kept walking, flashing her torch back on—Allison clenched her jaw, aware her sister was unwittingly making herself vulnerable to anyone else who might be lurking in the darkness. Beth didn't know about the dangers that Allison did. She wondered frantically if she shouldn't have been more vigilant in speaking with her sister and mother when they first arrived.

Allison turned from the window to snatch up her shoes but stopped in the act of slipping them on when she heard another sound, not coming from the yard, but from inside the house. Someone had cried out.

All interest in halting Gilbert and Beth fled, and her pulse leaped in panic. She rushed toward the door, unbolting it with shaking fingers. She heard voices below and saw that someone had turned on the hall lamps.

She rushed to the landing and peered down. As she glanced across the wide receiving hall toward the drawing room, a dim light glowed in the open doorway. A woman's robe was just visible, and Allison saw that a body lay on the floor. Sarah. She must have fallen. But even as Allison made this explanation to herself, she knew it wasn't true.

Some of the others were gathering about the prone woman, and Allison hurried down the stairs and across the floor, making no sound. She came to the doorway as Marra arrived from the other side of the house. Marra stooped, lifting the woman's hand and taking her pulse.

"What happened?" gasped Allison, and then her eyes fell on the familiar wedding ring on the limp hand that Marra held.

"Mother!" Allison pushed forward, falling to her knees beside her mother, where she lay so frighteningly still on the hard polished floor.

Helga arrived, and seeing Eleanor, stopped and stood motionless. A look of guilt twisted her features, and she clasped her hands together and lifted her knuckles to her mouth. The words were barely audible: "She's wearing my robe. Someone thought it was me."

A brighter light clicked on and dispersed the shadows, throwing silhouettes across the wall and onto Eleanor Wescott, draped in Helga's champagne-colored dressing gown, lying face downward on the floor.

"Oh, Father God," Allison prayed in an agonized whisper. She hardly heard Marra's tight voice warning everyone: "Don't touch anything."

"Gilbert?" Marra called out, turning her head and looking about the drawing room. "We need a doctor! Gilbert!" She got up and rushed back into the entrance hall.

Allison's eyes were wide and frightened as she took hold of her mother's slack shoulders, desperately trying to turn her over.

"Mother?" she whispered. How could this have happened? *She tripped. Yes, that was it. An accident...the wind's knocked out of her, is all...she must have been coming after Beth...no...it can't be that...because why did she come in this room when Beth is outside?* "Mother?" she whispered again with more desperation.

The hall was suddenly full of footsteps and a murmur of voices. Other lights came on, other voices called out. Dimly Allison was aware of words circling around her. Omar the Egyptian was saying something to Helga, who answered not in German but Arabic. Then came Beth's voice, asking a question, then becoming hysterical: "No, Mum! No! Oh, Mum! It's my fault!"

There was a sharp sound: a palm against Beth's cheek, and then: "Beth! Pull yourself together. She's not dead. Helga, can Omar go for a doctor?"

"I've sent him," the baroness replied.

Allison glanced up and saw it was so. Omar was scurrying away into the shadows and out the front door.

Marra came back and knelt beside Allison and Mrs. Wescott. "She must have fallen—" began Marra, but Allison, her throat dry, whispered dully, "No, there's a gash on the back of her head. Someone struck her from behind with—with—something—"

Gilbert walked quickly across the room toward a drape.

Marra turned on him, her eyes suspicious. "Where have you been? I called for you two minutes ago to go for a doctor."

His handsome face was ashen. "Of what, exactly, are you accusing me?"

"I'm not accusing you of anything. I asked you where you've been!"

"I don't need to answer to you. Are you the new Cairo inspector general?"

Marra's eyes narrowed. "It might be well if I was."

"Marra, Gilbert, please," ordered Helga. "This is no time to be bickering and accusing."

Gilbert strode across the room and gestured. "The window is open. Your intruder must have decided to come back. Oh, hello, what's this?" he stooped to pick something up.

"Don't touch anything—" ordered Helga sharply, but Gilbert turned with a heavy bookend in one hand.

Marra's face hardened. "You've ruined the fingerprints, genius. Nice blunder." She fixed him with a hard glare. "Or did you do it on purpose?"

Gilbert flushed, looked at the bookend, and set it down quickly, wiping his hands on his trousers. "I didn't think."

"I could say something, but I won't."

He smirked. "What of you, Marra, darling? One cannot help but wonder if your outrage and concern are genuine?"

"What are you saying?"

"What were you doing snooping around earlier? Before Mrs. Wescott cried out?"

"You're absurd. What reason would I have to sneak about? And how did that window get open with you sleeping right here on the divan?"

"Simple. I didn't sleep on the divan. I slept on the back porch. Just in case someone tried to get in that way again. If you don't believe me, ask Omar when he returns with the doctor. He slept in the laundry room. I've a witness. That's more than you've got."

"I've got Beth—" she stopped.

He smirked again. "Do you, Nurse Cohen?"

Marra's mouth turned into a wry smile, but she said nothing and flopped on the divan, folding her arms. "And just where is David Goldstein when a woman needs a man?"

"I'm going to notify my father," announced Gilbert sullenly. "And don't try to stop me."

"Who would want to? We can hardly wait for the brilliant inspector. So far he's done wonders to solve this case, hasn't he? Neith is dead, and Mrs. Wescott is hurt. I doubt if you need to look very far for Sir Edgar. He's probably out in the back garden still prowling about—maybe you and he both have been doing a lot of prowling around together."

Gilbert took a step toward her as though to backhand her, but a cold voice spoke from behind them: "Better behave yourself, junior, unless you want to spend the night crawling around the floor looking for your front teeth."

"David—" Marra was on her feet, and David walked toward her, throwing his arms around her, looking evenly at Gilbert.

Gilbert strode out of the drawing room. A moment later the front door shut loudly.

Allison's cold, trembling hand was stroking her mother's face; Beth sat mutely on the other side of the floor stricken with guilt, holding her mother's limp hand.

"I believe it's a concussion, but she'll live," Allison told her sister quietly, then glanced toward Helga who was pacing. Allison was sure they were both thinking the same thing: that someone had meant the violence for Helga, not Eleanor, and whoever it was had wanted to do more than just leave her unconscious.

Allison continued her silent vigil of prayer. She heard Beth whispering in prayer, too, and thought—albeit a bit hysterically—that it was the first hopeful change in her sister that she'd seen recently.

The medical orderlies finally arrived with Dr. Hurley, who, upon completing his examination, arranged for Mrs. Wescott to be transported to one of the military hospitals.

"You're a nurse," he told Allison in a low businesslike voice, "so there's no need to color things brighter than they are. It's an atrocious concussion. I think she'll recover with proper care and rest. We'll need to wait and see."

Allison looked to where her mother's still form had lain, where Beth continued to sit, and gave thanks to the Lord for sparing her mother's life. Marra had accompanied the orderlies who were transporting Mrs. Wescott to the hospital. She had come up to Allison and whispered that she had better go to make certain her mother was properly cared for since the overworked military nurses had recently received a new shipload of wounded from the Gallipoli front. Beth, too, had wanted to go with Marra. It had been difficult to get her away from her mother, but Dr. Hurley had insisted. Dying soldiers, he said, were everywhere, and the recovering wounded needed attention. The hospital was so crowded that men were being transported to sleep in tents in Ezbekiah Gardens. Clearly, Beth would be better off staying with Allison at the house until Sir Marshall Wescott arrived.

"He'll be here first thing in the morning. Baroness Kruger has left to send a wire to Port Said," Allison told her sister.

Helga had already informed Allison what she was planning to do before she left. David had slipped away to alert Cairo Intelligence. "We're worried about the colonel. He should have been here tonight."

The added concern exhausted Allison.

When they had all left, she walked wearily into the kitchen

where Beth waited like a frightened kitten, sitting in a chair. She had bolted the lock and lowered the rattan shade on the window on the back door. The lamps were turned up brightly, chasing away the shadows in the nooks and crannies of the large kitchen. Either Marra or Helga had been considerate enough to have made hot tea, and Allison went to the sideboard to take down cups for herself and Beth.

Beth's eyes were red rimmed, her long, dark hair framed her pale face, making her look even more pathetic. Allison vacillated between sympathy and irritation.

"Don't keep crying, Beth, you'll make yourself ill. Mum will be fine." She glanced at the clock on the wall above the stove. "In a few hours it will be light, and Father will be on the first train from Port Said. It's going to be all right. And Marra is with Mum at the hospital. When I go to the hospital to see Wade, I'll take you with me. We'll see Mum, too."

Beth covered her face with her hands. "Yes, but it's still all my fault what happened to her. If I hadn't disobeyed her and sneaked out, she wouldn't have come down looking for me and—and run into the thief. She suspected what I intended. Before I left the drawing room to go up to Marra's, Mum told me to stay away from Gilly tonight. I promised her I would. I looked her straight in the eye and promised her, and then I didn't do it. I knew I was going to meet him even when I told her I wouldn't. I lied! If she's seriously hurt, I'll never be able to forgive myself—"

She broke into fresh tears, and Allison took hold of her shoulder, leaning down. "The Lord is taking care of her at this very moment. If you lied, you need to straighten it out with God, but getting yourself sick isn't going to help, is it?"

"No, but all the same, I'm ashamed of myself."

Allison pulled up a chair and sat down, so tired her knees trembled. "I'm not going to make excuses for your behavior. You know you shouldn't have told Gilbert you'd meet him like that."

"I know, but—it seemed harmless."

"Did he hear Mother tell you not to leave the house tonight?"

"Yes."

"That's what I thought. I don't like to say this, but I've got to. Beth, if Gilbert cared about you, he wouldn't have asked you to meet him alone. Not when he knows the family disapproves of such behavior. He'd respect Mother's wishes, and you. By trying to get you to disobey, he's really treating you cheaply. Handsome or not, I wouldn't want a man like that. I want a man who thinks highly of my reputation."

"He isn't like that. How can you say it? We care too deeply to stay away from each other."

"I say it because it's true. Think, Beth. Gilbert knows you must deceive Mum and Father to meet him. That means he's selfish enough to let you compromise yourself. If his love were true and mature, he would put your well-being before his desires. He'd wait and prove to the family he's not a young philanderer."

"I think you're unfair to him, but I do feel frightfully guilty."

"When Mum is better, she'll ask you about being outside."

"I'd much rather face her than Father," and Beth looked as if she would cry again. "You must stand by me so he doesn't fuss at me. You know he doesn't like Gilbert. And it was the first time we were to meet like that."

Allison nodded her head, though she knew it wouldn't do much good to try to soothe her father, especially with how it had all turned out. "I'll stand by you, yes, but you'll need to explain how you disobeyed family rules. I won't lie for you."

Beth moved uncomfortably on the chair. "You said he'd be here in the morning?"

"Yes. I've an idea. Maybe we'd best meet Father at the station and take him to luncheon first."

Beth looked up, hopeful. "You mean explain everything in the Ezbekiah Gardens Hotel in public first? Yes!" she jumped to her feet. "That way he'll keep his voice lowered and have time to mull it over before getting me alone here in the house. You're brilliant, Allison!"

Allison smiled ruefully. "That wasn't my reason, but it will help that, too."

"Anyway Gilbert was late, and the longer I waited, the more afraid I became, because I heard someone else coming."

Allison remembered seeing a form coming from the trees. "You mean it wasn't Gilbert? But I saw him coming from the other side of the house, from the back garden."

Beth shook her head. "Then he must have turned back, because I saw Mrs. Blaine in the rose garden, by the stone bench and sundial."

"Sarah!" It wasn't until this very moment, now that the taut-paced confusion over what had happened to her mother had come to an end, that she realized what everyone had apparently over-looked in the crisis: Where was Sarah? If she'd been anywhere near, she would have heard the commotion. Then where was she?

"And she kept looking behind her as if she were in a hurry or afraid. Her behavior frightened me, too. So when I heard someone out there, I hid until I could get back to the house."

Allison leaned across the table. "Someone else came to meet her? You mean someone she wasn't afraid of?"

"I don't know…at the moment that's what I thought."

"Why?" pressed Allison.

Beth frowned and ran her fingers through her long hair. "It was just my impression. It seemed as if there might be two people— someone coming toward her, and someone following. And she was nervous about who followed her because she seemed to hurry toward whoever was coming ahead. Oh, I don't know! It was all happening so fast. I was waiting for Gilly and growing more afraid with each passing moment."

"She kept looking behind her, you said. And this person ahead of her—where was he?"

"I can't be sure of that, either. I think—somewhere around the oleander bushes. I turned and ran toward the front of the house again. I don't think they heard me since I had my shoes off."

Allison grew silent. So Beth had been outside for a while before she saw her meet Gilbert..."How long did you wait before coming inside?"

"Oh, Allison, I don't know. In a situation like that, who remembers? Two minutes, three, five maybe. The lights blinked on. I heard voices. I came back."

"Which way?"

"Across the drive. Through the front door."

Allison stood. "Then if you're telling me the truth—"

"Naturally I'm telling you the truth!"

"Then Gilbert should have seen Sarah, too, and whoever else was waiting near those oleander bushes."

Beth flushed. "He didn't say anything in the drawing room?"

"No. He and Marra got into a disagreement. Then he left to notify his father. He—they—should be here soon."

Their eyes met, then Beth, as though too afraid to admit what was on her mind, looked away toward the swinging doors into the dining room. "Maybe he's trying to protect someone."

There was another possibility—one Allison wouldn't tell Beth: Perhaps Gilbert was too afraid to admit to anyone who he saw?

Now Allison wished Bret were here more than ever! He would help her sort through all of the confusion she was feeling. But the question that pressed her most was that of Sarah's whereabouts.

Except for Beth seeing her in the garden over an hour ago, when was the last time anyone had seen her? Thinking back, Allison recalled Sarah being the first one to leave the drawing room after Helga produced the Egyptian antiquity. Obviously, if Beth were right about seeing Sarah, she had either left her room after everyone retired for the evening...or she never went up there at all. If not, why not? Why had she risked going alone to the rose garden?

Allison shivered uncontrollably as she walked out of the kitchen into the dining room and through the arch to the hall. She looked up the stairs to the darkened landing.

She was startled by a hand on her arm, and she turned to look into Beth's nervous face. "We shouldn't have stayed here," Beth said, looking around her, drawing closer.

"It's all right. David will be back any minute."

"Shouldn't Gilbert have been back by now, too? And Cousin Edgar? And where's Colonel Holden?"

Allison wondered about that herself. "They'll all be here soon."

Beth's fingers wrapped tightly about her arm, and her dark eyes peered toward the stairs. "I—I don't think Sarah's up there."

Allison felt a chill inch its way up her back. "There's only one way to know for sure. I'll check."

Allison hurried up to Sarah's room, while Beth lingered midway on the stairway.

The door was unlocked, and Allison quietly opened it and fumbled to switch on the lamp. Her heart sank. The bed was empty. The satin coverlet was smooth. Sarah had not been here at all. Leaving the lamp burning, she turned and came back down the stairs. Beth followed her into the kitchen, protesting as Allison slid back the bolt.

"Wait here," Allison told her. "Go to my room and bolt the door—no! Not my room—" she thought of the open window. "Go

436

to Marra's room. Lock yourself in until I get back. Sarah may be in trouble. I've got to try to find her."

"Allison!"

But she didn't stop. She couldn't.

She would not allow Sarah to become the next victim.

TWENTY-EIGHT

➤━┆━◀▸━┄━⊙━┄━◀▸━┆━◀

The terror by night...
PSALM 91:5

THE FLAGSTONE COURT, WITH ITS STONE BENCH and birdbath, reflected a silvery hue under the oval white moon that was edging toward the rim of dark treetops. The tree branches, like black lacy silhouettes with the moonlight peeking through, made a rushing sound, much like nervous wings rising in flight. Allison's heart fluttered as well, but she gritted her teeth and walked forward.

She stopped near the goldfish pond, her eyes becoming accustomed to the night. Her vision traced the rosebushes that were Sarah's delight, then the bench that faced the Egyptian sundial where she often sat in meditation of the shimmering water that rippled on the surface of the pool. The fish glimmered and glided. A tiny splash broke the silence.

If Beth was right and Sarah had walked here to meet someone she apparently trusted, who had followed her, causing her uncertainty—even fear?

The bench was wet with rain and the roses glistened. Allison stood still, wondering. Her eyes strayed to the oleander bushes. The mound of crisp dead leaves beneath the base had been tossed by the wind and were scattered...unearthing something that shouldn't have been there.

As she stared, her blood going cold, the verse from Proverbs came to mind again: "Be sure your sin will find you out."

The body lying there was still, only partially covered now by the blowing leaves. Allison bit her lip to keep from crying out. It took a battle with her nerves before she could move closer to the bushes. She stooped, turning on her torch, flashing it along the half-covered body, expecting to see Sarah Blaine's still features.

Instead, it was the empty eyes of Jemal that stared up at her. She froze, fear and confusion warring within her. A chill raced up the back of her neck; a scream clawed at her throat.

Allison forced herself to steady her nerves. She had seen many dead bodies before and she knew they were mere shells that were vacated by spirit and soul in death. There was nothing spooky or frightening about a body. *No, what's truly frightening,* she told herself, *is the living sinner in rebellion against God.* Her eyes drifted back to Jemal's body. *The person who could do this.*

She shivered and struggled to calm herself. *Sort it out, Allison. Think.* Could it have been Jemal who killed Neith? She tried to remember what the silhouette had looked like on that night, but it had happened too quickly. Could Cousin Edgar move so swiftly? He carried a cane with a heavy silver handle, but she had never seen him limp. In fact, she'd seen him move quite effortlessly several times.

A wandering gust of wind ruffled her hair and made her skin rise with goose bumps, but it wasn't clear if the chilling sensation came from the breeze or from the dreaded conclusions that were taking shape in her heart.

Where was Sarah?

Her mind raced with possibilities. Who had killed Jemal? Sir Edgar? Sarah Blaine? The shopkeeper, Mr. Galli? No, it wouldn't be him—it had to be Cousin Edgar because it just couldn't be Sarah.

Please God, don't let it be Sarah. The idea that her friend had done these terrible things was simply too much for Allison to accept. She blinked hard, closing her eyes, trying to get control of her emotions and thudding heart.

Think it through, she told herself. *Calmly, without emotion. Consider all the possibilities....*

Could Sarah have deliberately asked her to come and stay with here just to see how much she knew? Had she perhaps wondered if Allison knew where Rex had hidden the doll? After all, as far as Sarah knew, Allison and Rex were close enough to exchange such information.

Quickly, repressing a shudder, Allison pushed the leaves over the body and straightened. She looked toward the side of the house, toward Marra's room and bath. Beth would be there now, locking herself in.

She rethought how Sarah at first had treated the discovery of the broken cobra head as though it weren't important, but then she must have recognized it, wondering how it had gotten mixed in with her Egyptian menagerie. As she did, she must have understood why her husband had put it there for her to find. Perhaps, because Rex, loving Sarah, wanted her to have the treasure should anything happen to him when he went to Aleppo. Rex had been a German agent, he had killed Leah, yet even a murderer was capable of loving.

And Sarah knew enough about Rex to associate the broken cobra head in her menagerie with why he put it there. Surely she must have known then where to locate the second treasure piece, the piece that was more valuable than the gold scarab from Tutankhamen's burial tomb. After Helga's display tonight, Sarah must have decided she had to find it at once, before it was too late.

The realization dawned on her then: Rex wouldn't have kept the doll to hide away. It would have been too clumsy, too obvious, too easy to find. No, Rex would have removed the prize first, then hidden it. There was no Egyptian doll to find!

Allison walked toward the house, thinking hard. Sarah had looked at that knob and guessed where it belonged. She had seen it, too, for a moment, and it had struck a chord…but why? She closed her eyes again, struggling to recall. Where had she seen it bef—

Of course! How blind of me!

Her heart raced. She turned and looked toward the empty windows on the second floor. She remembered. She remembered where she had seen a cobra head. Several of them, in fact.

"Rex always had a fascination for cobras," Sarah had said.

Yes. She remembered now.

Her heart pounding, she hurried across the flagstone courtyard, back toward the kitchen door.

TWENTY-NINE

>━!━◆﹥━❂━﹤◆﹥━!━≪

*You shall tread upon the lion and the cobra, the young lion and
the serpent you shall trample underfoot.*

PSALM 91:13

ALLISON CAME IN THROUGH THE KITCHEN and passed swiftly through
the dining room, the arch, and into the hall. The house was silent,
but it was as though an eerie tension filled the waiting rooms. The
solitary lamp glowed above the stairway, its golden light spilling
down over the landing. Allison started up the stairs when footsteps
sounded behind her. She turned.

Beth sped across the hall, her eyes wide. "Did you find anything?"

Allison couldn't tell her yet about Jemal. "I'm going to search Rex
Blaine's office."

"I'm coming with you."

Allison went up with Beth holding to her arm, peering over her
shoulder toward the back of the house.

Has Sarah already been here and found what she wanted? wondered
Allison. *Did she go to meet Jemal? Did she*—No! She would not allow
herself even to think it. Beth at her side, she hurried across the landing once more and came to Sarah's bedroom. The door was shut; the
light, out.

"Sarah?" she called in a low voice. "Are you in there?"

There was no answer in the stillness.

"Don't go in," whispered Beth.

"Come on." Pulling her sister behind her, Allison went to open the door to Rex's office. They entered, shutting the door noiselessly behind them.

"Ugh," whispered Beth. "This room is creepy."

"Don't be silly. Turn the lamp on. Hurry, Beth."

The drapes were drawn, the air stale and close, the corners heavy with shadows. Heart thumping, Allison stood without moving, her gaze shifting to the far end of the room…to the large black leather chair and ottoman where the general used to sit and scheme on behalf of Berlin and his own gain. Beside the chair stood a tall solid-wood Barrister bookcase. The shelves were covered with glass and the top two shelves held leather-bound books, but it wasn't these that interested Allison.

"What are you looking for?" whispered Beth. "The treasure?"

"Yes."

Beth's eyes widened in surprise. Clearly this was not the answer she'd expected. "But why would it be here?"

"You'll see."

Allison glanced behind her toward the door and went to shove the bolt in place. Locked safely within, she rushed to the bookcase and opened the glass doors.

Below the books, the shelf was stacked with pipes and tobacco. The general had collected pipes throughout his years of exotic travels; pipes that Allison and his acquaintances had seen him use on many occasions during his life. With a choking sense of foreboding, she recalled how he had been smoking a pipe on that windy night over a year before in the archaeological hut in Aleppo. On that awful night, she'd gone to the hut alone…it was when she caught a whiff of a fragrant tobacco that she'd realized someone had been there before she arrived.

Stop, she told herself. *Rex is dead. Don't think of him now.* Instead, she would think of the item he had hidden here among his trea-

444

sured collection of pipes and tobacco tins from all over the East.

Allison drew up the ottoman and sat down. Beth came to sit beside her as she scanned the shelf. What she was looking for was still here, just as she remembered it from the day when she arrived and spoke with Sarah about the office having been searched. Either Sarah had not guessed, as Allison had thought, or she had been too afraid to come here and was hiding somewhere in the house. Maybe she had nothing to do with Jemal's death....

There were odd-sized jars of tobacco and a collection of carved black embossed tins, each of which was topped by a brass knob shaped into a cobra head. The onyx eyes glared back at her.

Then she frowned. Something was wrong—none of the knobs was missing as she would have thought. Nor were any broken! But this *must* be the hiding place, she thought, bewildered, her conclusions arguing with her disappointment.

Her fingers brushed against one of the canisters, and her heart gave a leap of expectation. Quickly she lifted the first tin from its place but realized it was not heavy enough to hide a treasure. She removed the others but none of them were heavy enough, either. Nevertheless, she lifted each cobra-head knob. The whiff of aromatic tobacco leaves hung on the air. She shoved her hand into the dried tobacco, searching, but there was nothing hard and cold concealed within. Then she was too late. Sarah had come, found it, and fled.

"There's nothing in them," whispered Beth, disappointed as well.

Allison sank back on the ottoman, resting her head on the arm of the leather chair. "We're too late," she said dismally.

"Who was here do you think? Mrs. Blaine?"

Allison didn't answer at first. She was staring at the cobra knobs. If the broken head that Sarah found wasn't one of these, then where did it belong? A floorboard squeaked behind them.

Beth sucked in her breath and stiffened, her fingers latching hold of Allison's wrist, biting hard with fear. Allison sat very still, her free hand clasping the tobacco tin.

The footsteps sounded again, this time right in the doorway connecting the office to Sarah's room.

Beth jerked her head around, the color draining from her stricken face. She gasped: "Oh, no—!"

"So you figured it out too," he whispered, his dark eyes flashing. "Blaine outsmarted Jemal and my father. Dear old Dad was looking for the Egyptian doll and all the time beautiful Nefertari was buried in a filthy grave of tobacco!" Gilbert held out his slim hand expectantly. "Hand it over, ladies. It's mine. Blaine stole it from Jemal. He expected to leave with it for Berlin when he returned from Aleppo, but then met his end in the hut. You were there then, too, weren't you, Allison? You and Colonel Holden."

"But *you,*" protested Beth feebly, her face twisted with pain. "Oh, Gilbert, how could you kill that poor old cook?"

Gilbert looked scornful. "I didn't. Anwar did. But I did kill Jemal tonight. He got in the way. He insisted he wouldn't partner with me and my father after all. Said we had blundered."

"Why did Anwar kill Neith? I thought they were working together," asked Allison.

"Neith saw him that night in the yard when she was leaving and thought she could trust him. She went after him wondering what he was up to going in the back porch. She must have thought she was safe. But she was wrong." His dark eyes grew pensive. "You found him didn't you, Allison? I saw you. I came back here, waiting, knowing you'd guessed, too, about the cobra head."

"Why didn't you come get it yourself?"

He smiled coldly. "Too many eyes were fixed on me, my dear. I needed to wait until we were all alone. Just us...and Nefertari. I

446

shall return with it to Constantinople and live a life of wealth after the war. Too bad you didn't mind your business, Beth. I was going to take you with me."

"I'd *never* go with you!" she gasped. "You're—you're horrible—"

"You wound me, my dear," he said mockingly. "We've been so close. And now, hand over Nefertari."

Allison met his gaze defiantly. "I don't have it. It's not in any of the tins. We were both wrong."

Gilbert looked from her to the jars, then an ugly look twisted his handsome face into fury. "It *has* to be there! Sarah met Jemal and gave him the broken cobra head—" and he held out his trembling hand.

Allison recognized the head he held as the one Sarah had found in the trunk earlier. "You killed Jemal for it?"

"Yes! The treasure *must* be in one of those tins—"

"Sorry, but wrong again," said a deep voice from behind them. "And now that I have your confession, you can lift your hands over your head."

Gilbert spun around and Allison looked up, startled, only to feel joy leaping through her. Bret stood in the doorway between Sarah's room and the office, a Luger in one hand. "Don't do anything stupid, Gilbert. You've already made a fool of yourself. Don't make yourself dead to boot. Put both hands behind your head."

Bret gestured with the Luger, and, his face twisted with fury, Gilbert complied.

"Allison," Bret said, his voice almost conversational, "would you be so kind as to move Beth back against the wall? That's it. Quickly."

Allison leaned there, holding Beth as she cried quietly. Her own legs felt weak and shaky as she watched Bret gesture for Gilbert to turn around.

For a moment it seemed he would resist, then he did as he was told, submitting without a struggle, his young face drawn and haggard. A moment later he was handcuffed and led toward the door without a parting glance.

Allison remained where she was, weak and dazed, closing her eyes to shut everything out, while she held Beth.

From downstairs she heard other voices. "Stay right here," she told Beth and went to stand in the doorway, listening. Gilbert's voice whined: "You can't arrest me! My father is an important man. He's the inspector general of the Cairo police!"

"Not anymore," came Bret's dry voice. "We've found Anwar and he's confessed. Sir Edgar was arrested after he left the house tonight."

"Father didn't kill anyone."

"We're well aware of that, but Edgar did smuggle cotton into Switzerland to sell to Germany. And he extorted money from Turkish merchants. They were paying him to let them stay in Cairo."

"You can't arrest *me* for smuggling."

"No, indeed." Allison heard the hard humor in Bret's tone. "All we have you for is killing Jemal and Sarah Blaine. We found both of them in the garden."

Allison's eyes shut tightly. So Sarah was dead....It was all over for her now.

David's voice sounded from the hall, followed by Helga's voice asking if Allison and Beth were all right.

"Yes," Bret answered. "They're in Rex's office. But take Beth to another room, would you? Stay with her until Sir Marshall arrives in a few hours."

Helga came and led Beth away, and Allison was still leaning against the doorway, thinking of Sarah, when Bret returned.

He walked over to her and pulled her into his arms, holding her so tightly her breath was cut off.

"I'm sorry," he whispered into her hair. "It was the one way I could trap him. And I didn't think you'd find Jemal like that. I thought you'd come here, that you'd remember the tobacco tins. There was only one thing that worried me; I was afraid you'd slip the inside bolt shut on Sarah's door. I couldn't have let you do that of course, since you'd be locking yourself in with Gilbert. I would have had to make my presence known to you. I knew Gilbert was in the house, watching you, but I had to get a confession out of him. Besides," he smiled down at her, "being the bright girl you are, you didn't bolt the second door."

"I didn't even think about it," she admitted, then her eyes met his, and she was acutely aware that they held each other tightly. She swallowed with difficulty. "I'm glad you were there all along, but it would have made it more bearable if I'd known."

"I told you I'd never be far away didn't I? I'm a hard man to get rid of once I know what I want."

"Are you?" she whispered.

"Just wait and see."

They stood a moment in silence. He looked at her, his eyes warm with promise. The rain had started again and was tinkling against the windowpane.

Allison thought of the garden and shuddered. "I wouldn't have found Jemal if Beth hadn't been outside earlier tonight hoping to meet Gilbert. She told me she saw Sarah. I went looking for her thinking something may have happened to her, but I didn't think I would end up finding Jemal instead. And now Sarah, too—"

"We did our best to protect her, but she knows this house and grounds better than any of us. She was able to give us the slip." His expression was grim. "I wish it had ended differently, but I wasn't willing to leave you alone while we searched for Sarah. Her danger was a possibility; yours was a certainty."

"You were here all along," she breathed, taking it in.

"You were always safe, my love. David and I had you and Beth under watch all evening. I never left tonight. And David arrived soon after they arrested Sir Edgar. We caught Anwar this afternoon, and he told us everything, but I wanted Gilbert. He was a novice at crime, yet dangerous because he was. He had one thing on his mind: getting hold of the gold statue of Queen Nefertari."

"So that's what the treasure is."

"Anwar told us his father had taken it from the tomb several years ago, along with the gold scarab. Gilbert killed Jemal and Sarah for the broken cobra head, but he was wrong about its connection with the tobacco tins."

"As was I. I thought Sarah was upstairs searching. I had no idea it was Gilbert. Why did Sarah go to meet Jemal?"

"We'll never know. My guess is she didn't."

"What? But Beth saw her."

Bret's eyes, full of tender warning, met hers. "Are you sure you want to know all of this?" he asked.

She loved him all the more for wanting to protect her, but she needed to know. "Yes."

He nodded. "Beth saw Sarah walking confidently along into the garden, but I doubt if she knew Jemal was there until he revealed himself. He wanted that cobra head. He was the only one, other than Rex and Sarah, who knew what it meant. But Gilbert confronted them before they unearthed the secret. He assumed he didn't need them. He killed Jemal in a struggle, then struck Sarah unconscious and threw her in the fish pond."

Allison covered her face, and his arms tightened around her.

"Sarah never knew what happened, Allison. She was unconscious when he threw her in."

"It's absolutely horrible. Poor Sarah—"

He was silent, and she knew it was out of respect for her feelings. He still believed Sarah knew more than she'd ever let on. After a moment, Allison stepped back, reaching out to open his hand, which held the broken cobra head. She studied it silently.

"Odd, I thought it was a knob to one of the tins. Now I see it couldn't be. It's old looking."

"Yes," he mused, fingering it. "It's corroded. As though it's seen years of outdoor weather."

"I suppose we'll never know what it means. Or where to find Nefertari—" she broke off when she saw the look on Bret's face.

"Corrosion..." he repeated, and she saw his eyes were snapping with understanding. "And Sarah went to the garden." He dropped the cobra head into his pocket, reaching out to hug her close.

"What is it?" she asked, struggling to breathe.

"Maybe nothing," he replied, barely contained excitement in his voice. "But when the sun comes up, we need to have another look out there."

THIRTY

>━┥━<┤>━━╾◯╼━<┤╾━┝━<

Because you have made the LORD, who is my refuge, even
the Most High, your habitation.

PSALM 91:9

THE NEXT MORNING, ALLISON DISCOVERED that Helga had slipped away unnoticed, back to her masquerade as the fashionable and wealthy Baroness Kruger, who had to prepare for her holiday guests.

As for Sir Marshall, he arrived at dawn. After receiving a full report of what had happened from Bret, he turned his attention to Beth, who was so depressed over Gilbert that she refused any consolation. It was decided that the best thing for Beth was to leave the Blaine house with her father and visit her mother at the Cairo military hospital. Marra had sent a message telling them that Eleanor was awake from her concussion and, while she remained in critical condition, she had recognized Marra and even spoke a few words asking about Allison, Beth, and Marshall. The prognosis for her recovery appeared good.

David decided to escort Sir Marshall in the military motorcar to the hospital, and Allison stayed behind with Bret, lingering over a light breakfast of toast and tea.

The rain had ceased and the day dawned bright, but with a pall of gloom over the garden.

An hour later, Allison went out to the garden to find Bret standing in the flagstone courtyard, pondering as he gazed in the fish pond. She quietly walked up beside him, slipping her hand into his as they stood there. Birds sang in the flame trees, and the white-and-gold fish swam and darted about in the first rays of sunlight that hit the pond. Except for dark memories, there was no evidence of death remaining in the garden. The red roses were open and smelling sweet, wet with rain. And the sunlight shone on the sundial as it had done each day for unnumbered years.

Bret let go of Allison's hand and walked over to the sundial. "Time moves on, changing things and people. Only truth is unchanged and dependable. Friends slip from time into eternity, treasures fade away, a thousand yesterdays are gone…how many tomorrows are left? Only God knows."

Allison watched him, surprised. She hadn't heard Bret talk of such things often. As though reading her thoughts, he smiled. "I may not speak of it much, Allison, but my faith is as real as yours. I know who God is, and I serve him as best I can."

"I believe you," she said simply, and it was true. She knew with sudden clarity that this was why God had held her back. Deep inside, she had doubted Bret's faith, doubted his stand with God. Not because he'd given her any real reason, but simply because he hadn't demonstrated his faith as she'd expected.

Now she knew, it wasn't Bret's faith that had stood between them, but her image of what a man of faith should be. Bret had accused her of expecting him to be like Wade, and she'd denied it. But she knew now he was right. She'd been looking at him, comparing him to Wade, and finding him lacking.

Forgive me, Father, she prayed, grieved. *Forgive me for my judgmental heart, for my pride.*

"Allison?"

She looked up to find Bret watching her closely.

"You're crying," he said, clearly distressed. "I shouldn't have let you come here—"

"No, it's all right," she said, smiling through her tears. She walked to him, slipping her arms about his waist and laying her cheek against his chest.

He stilled, as though unsure what to think, and then his arms came around her to cradle her close.

"I love you, Bret." Amazing how easily the words came now. Her heart swelled with love for him and with wonder that God had given him to her to love. He was a man to be treated with respect, a man to be proud of, not just for what he did, but for who he was. She could see that now.

He lifted her chin with a finger, urging her to look at him. His eyes studied her face silently, his jaw clenched as though he were afraid to believe her.

"I love you," she repeated firmly, "now and forever. You were right, God meant for us to be together. And I know he'll be with us as we face the future, pointing us toward the right path. Together."

A triumphant smile broke over his face. Slowly, as though savoring each second, he lowered his head, and his lips covered hers. The kiss was sweet and wild and full of promise.

The future was theirs, together, with God beside them.

Suddenly he broke off the kiss and let go of her. Allison stumbled backward, looking at him in surprise.

"Of course!" he said, pulling the cobra head from his pocket. He held it, studying it, then looked in front of him. "Pointing us to the right path...it's not a handle, it's a pointer!"

Allison followed his gaze...and caught her breath.

"The pointer on the sundial—it's broken off," she whispered.

Bret went to the sundial and stooped, examining the missing pointer.

Allison knelt beside him, her heart racing. She noticed the corrosion on sections of the dial, and how it matched the markings on the cobra head in his palm.

"A pointer?" she breathed.

He placed the broken cobra head on the sundial. It fit perfectly. He looked at her and smiled.

Quickly he searched the rim of the sundial.

"It comes up," she whispered and watched, amazed, as after a moment's unsuccessful try, he finally got it loose and lifted it aside.

"A safe!" she gasped. "It's cemented in!"

"The scheming genius of Rex Blaine. Ah—there's something here."

Allison leaned over with excitement and watched as he removed an object carefully wrapped in a soft cloth. He unwrapped the cloth and lifted out a small statue of Egyptian antiquity, a ten-inch solid-gold statue of Queen Nefertari, a treasure from the reign of Ramses II. Nefertari gazed back at them coldly, the jeweled eyes glittering amid smooth and shiny gold.

"Wait," Bret said, "there's something else." He reached into the safe and brought out a small box. Opening it, he removed a letter and a drawing...no, a map. Jemal's signature was on both. Allison saw the date: June 8, 1912. And the name of the place: the Valley of the Kings.

"What is it?" she found herself whispering, afraid to accept what she was starting to believe. "A letter? To whom?"

For a long moment Bret said nothing. The silence was so profound that she began to feel uncomfortable. She glanced at the side of his handsome face, saw eyes widen as he read and studied the notes and small drawing.

"Bret?"

"It's a map. And directions." His eyes came to meet hers. "To a royal burial tomb."

Her mouth opened in a silent "O," and she stared at him, stunned.

Bret stood, pulling her to her feet. A half smile touched his mouth, and in the sunlight which grew brighter and hotter, she took in his chiseled features, his dark hair blowing in the breeze, the warmth in his eyes that made her heart leap at his touch.

"Ah, temptation," he whispered. "You beside me and the Egyptian treasure."

She gave a nervous laugh. "You are teasing me, aren't you? You wouldn't—"

A dark brow lifted.

Her lashes narrowed. "You *wouldn't*," she repeated.

His smile was mysterious. "Are you sure?" He released her gently, then as she looked at him, wondering, he stooped, replaced the sundial, placed the gold statue back in the cloth, and picked up the small box. His midnight blue eyes came to hers and the color brought an ache to her heart.

"Do you realize the only people who knew where this tomb was located are all dead? Rex Blaine, Professor Jemal Pasha, Sarah Blaine—and the two unfortunate Frenchmen who are probably buried there, or nearby in the sand."

"Anwar knows, and Gilbert, and—and Helga, too."

He smiled faintly, and she flushed as she read his thoughts. Her gaze dropped to the solid-gold image.

"No, they don't know," he said. "They know there was an archaeological discovery of some sort, but no one knows where it's located. They have the scarab. It's authentic, but that's all the information they have. Gilbert is likely to go to the gallows, and Anwar will spend his life in prison."

She reached a hand to her cheek, pushing away a strand of hair, aware that his burning gaze held hers.

"Just two people know where a fabulous fortune is hidden. You and I."

Allison tried to tear her gaze away but could not.

Bret folded the paper and placed it inside his jacket.

"Nefertari goes to Helga," he said simply.

Her eyes searched his face. "And—the paper? The directions to the royal burial tomb? Where does that paper go?"

"What safer place for such a treasure than with a colonel in the Cairo Intelligence Department?"

Allison paused. Two people knew where the tomb was located; actually only one, since she had not seen the directions or read what Jemal had written. The only one who now knew the truth was Colonel Bret Holden.

What does he intend, Lord?

And the answer came back, but not what she'd expected.

Do you trust the man you love?

Before she had a chance to ponder that question, Bret swept her into his arms. "I meant what I said about wanting to marry you, sweet Allison. What about a Christmas wedding?" He grinned then, his face lit with excitement. "I don't know what kind of future you were expecting, my love," he told her, "but I'd say it looks as though our real adventure is just about to begin."

"Our real adventure?" she asked, and his laughing eyes met hers.

"Marriage, my dear. What did you think I meant?"

She shook her head and pressed her face against his chest. "Nothing," she said, "Nothing at all."

Allison knew, deep in her heart, that God was there, watching over them, setting their feet on the path he had chosen for them. And yet...

She could not help but wonder where that path was going to take them.

Dear Beloved Reader,

Thank you for taking time from your busy schedule to write me and share your encouraging responses about *Arabian Winds*. I hope you enjoyed reading the sequel, *Lions of the Desert*, as much as I enjoyed researching and writing it.

Keep your messages coming! I appreciate learning who you are and what's going on in your hearts. I like to feel connected to my readers. Those of you who have sent me snapshots are smiling at me from the wall above my computer.

May I also say that if any blessing has come to you through my various books, the praise goes to Him. It's a joy to use each writing opportunity to say, "The Lord is ever true, ever faithful."

I've done a good deal of research on the Great War in and around Egypt and Arabia, and I'm looking forward to writing the final book in this trilogy about General Allenby capturing the beloved city of Jerusalem from the Turks. And, of course, the fun part is making sure Allison and Bret are there, too. Oh, by the way, *you* are invited to come with them, but I can't guarantee a completely safe journey, because Allison will first be stopping off at an Egyptian mummy tomb! And those kinds of stops are always unpredictable.

So watch for Allison and Bret—they will meet you again this spring in your favorite bookstore!

In His Love,

THE PALISADES LINE

Look for these new releases at your local bookstore. If the title you seek is not in stock, the store may order you a copy using the ISBN listed.

Surrender, Lynn Bulock
ISBN 1-57673-104-9

As a single mom, Cassie Neel works hard to give her children the best she can. This year, young Sarah and Zach want to show their appreciation for what she does by giving her a date with handsome police officer Lee Winter as a birthday present! Surprised and flattered, Cassie accepts. But little does she know where that one date will lead....

Wise Man's House, Melody Carlson
ISBN 1-57673-070-0

Kestra McKenzie, a young widow trying to make a new life for herself, thinks she has found the solidity she longs for when she purchases her childhood dream house—a stone mansion on the Oregon Coast. Just as renovations begin, a mysterious stranger moves into her caretaker's cottage—and into her heart.

Moonglow, Peggy Darty
ISBN 1-57673-112-X

During the Summer Olympics set in Atlanta, Tracy Kosell comes back to her hometown of Moonglow, Georgia, to investigate the disappearance of a wealthy socialite. She meets up with former schoolmate Jay Calloway, who's one of the detectives assigned to the case. As their attraction grows and the mercury rises, they unwrap a case that isn't as simple as it seemed.

Promises, Peggy Darty
ISBN 1-57673-149-9

Elizabeth Calloway, a Christian psychologist, finds herself in over her head when a client tells her about a dangerous twin sister. Elizabeth turns to her detective husband, Michael, asking him to find the woman. Unexpected events plunge the couple into danger, where they rediscover the joy of falling in love.

Texas Tender, Sharon Gillenwater
ISBN 1-57673-111-1
When Shelby Nolan inherits a watermelon farm, she moves from Houston to a small west Texas town. Spotting two elderly men digging holes in her field each night, she turns to neighbor Deputy Sheriff Logan Slade to figure out what's going on. Together they uncover a long-buried robbery and discover the fulfillment of their own dreams.

Clouds, Robin Jones Gunn
ISBN 1-57673-113-8
On a trip to Germany, flight attendant Shelly Graham unexpectedly runs into her old boyfriend, Jonathan Renfield. Since she still cares for him, it's hard for Shelly to hide her hurt when she learns he's engaged. It isn't until she goes to meet friends in Glenbrooke, Oregon, that they meet again—and this time, they're both ready to be honest.

Sunsets, Robin Jones Gunn
ISBN 1-57673-103-0
Alissa Benson loves her job as a travel agent. But when the agency has computer problems, they call in expert Brad Phillips. Alissa can't wait for Brad to fix the computers and leave—he's too blunt for her comfort. So she's more than a little upset when she moves into a duplex and finds out he's her neighbor!

Snow Swan, Barbara Jean Hicks
ISBN 1-57673-107-3
Life hasn't been easy for Toni Ferrier. As an unwed mother and a recovering alcoholic, she doesn't feel worthy of anyone's love. Then she meets Clark McConaughey, who helps her launch her business aboard the sternwheeler Snow Swan. Sparks fly between them, but if Clark finds out the truth about Toni's past, will he still love her?

Irish Eyes, Annie Jones
ISBN 1-57673-108-1
When Julia Reed finds a young boy, who claims to be a leprechaun, camped out under a billboard, she gets drawn into a century-old crime involving a real pot of gold. Interpol agent Cameron O'Dea is trying to solve the crime. In the process, he takes over the homeless shelter that Julia runs, camps out in her neighbor's RV, and generally turns her life upside down!

***Father by Faith,* Annie Jones**
ISBN 1-57673-117-0
Nina Jackson may not know much about ranching, but she knows business. So when she buys a dude ranch and hires recuperating cowboy Clint Cooper as her foreman, she figures she's set. But her son, Alex, doesn't think so. He's been praying for a father, and the moment he sees Clint, he tells everyone that God has answered his prayers and sent him a daddy!

***Stardust,* Shari MacDonald**
ISBN 1-57673-109-X
As a teenager, Gillian Spencer fell in love with astronomy...and with Max Bishop. But after he leaves her heartbroken, she learns to keep her feelings guarded. Now that she's a graduate student studying astronomy, she thinks she has left the past far behind. So when she gets an exciting assignment, she's shocked to learn she's been paired with the now-famous Dr. Maxwell Bishop.

***Kingdom Come,* Amanda MacLean**
ISBN 1-57673-120-0
In 1902, feisty Ivy Rose Clayborne, M.D., returns to her hometown of Kingdom Come to fight the coal mining company that is ravaging the land. She meets an unexpected ally, a man who claims to be a drifter but in reality is Harrison MacKenzie, grandson of the coal mining baron. Together they face the aftermath of betrayal, the fight for justice...and the price of love.

***Dear Silver,* Lorena McCourtney**
ISBN 1-57673-110-3
When Silver Sinclair receives a polite but cold letter from Chris Bentley ending their relationship, she's shocked, since she's never met the man! She confronts Chris about his insensitive attitude toward this other Silver Sinclair, and finds herself becoming friends with a man who's unlike anyone she's ever met.

***Enough!* Gayle Roper**
ISBN 1-57673-185-5
When Molly Gregory gets fed up with her three teenaged children, she announces that she's going on strike. She and her husband Pete stand back and watch as chaos results in their household, in a hilarious experiment that teaches their children how to honor their parents.

***A Mother's Love,* Bergren, Colson, MacLean**
ISBN 1-57673-106-5
By Lisa Tawn Bergren: A widower and his young daughter go to Southern California

for vacation, and return with much more than they expected.

By Constance Colson: Cassie Jenson wants her old sweetheart to stay in her memories. But Bruce Foster has other plans.

By Amanda MacLean: A couple is expecting their first baby, and each plans a surprise for the other that doesn't quite turn out as it should.

Silver Bells, Bergren, Krause, MacDonald (October, 1997)
ISBN 1-57673-119-7

By Lisa Tawn Bergren: Noel Stevens has to work up the ranks in her new job, but being assigned to Santa's workshop is too much. Until she gets to know Santa....

By Linda Krause: Writer Bridget Deans goes home for a restful Christmas vacation and finds her ex-fiancé there.

By Shari MacDonald: Madison Pierce feels lonely at the thought of her best friend's wedding...until she meets the best man.

ALABASTER BOOKS
Romance, mystery, comedy...Real life.

Homeward, Melody Carlson
ISBN 1-57673-029-8

When Meg Lancaster learns that her grandmother is dying, she returns to the small town on the Oregon coast where she spent vacations as a child. After being away for twenty years, the town hasn't changed...but her family has. Meg struggles with her memories of the past and what is now reality, until tragedy strikes the family and she must learn to face the future.

Arabian Winds, Linda Chaikin
ISBN 1-57673-105-7

World War I is breaking upon the deserts of Arabia in 1914. Young nurse Allison Wescott is on holiday with an archaeological club, but a murder interrupts her plans, and a mysterious officer keeps turning up wherever she goes!

Lions of the Desert, Linda Chaikin
ISBN 1-57673-114-6

In 1915, Allison Wescott arrives in Cairo to serve the British military and once again encounters the mysterious Bret Holden. And to mix things up even further, the chaplain she is thinking of marrying comes to Cairo as well.

Watch for the final book in the trilogy, coming in spring 1998!

***Chase the Dream,* Constance Colson**
ISBN 0-88070-928-6
After years apart, four friends are reunited through the competitive world of professional rodeo, where they seek fame, fortune, faith...and love.

***Song of the Highlands,* Sharon Gillenwater**
ISBN 1-57673-946-4
Kiernan returns from the Napoleonic wars to find out he's inherited a title. At his run-down estate, he meets the beautiful Mariah, and finds himself swept up in the romance and deception of a London Season.
Watch for more books in Sharon Gillenwater's Scottish series!

***Promise Me the Dawn,* Amanda MacLean**
ISBN 0-88070-955-3
Molly Quinn and Zach MacAlister come from very different backgrounds, but both seek to overcome the past. Enduring hardship and prosperity, the promise of a meeting at dawn brings them through it all.

***Redeeming Love,* Francine Rivers**
ISBN 1-57673-186-3
The only men Angel has ever known have betrayed her. When she meets Michael Hosea in the gold country of California, she has no reason to believe he's any different. But Michael is different. And through him Angel learns what love really means—the kind of love that can wipe away the shame of her past.